A Fall for Grace

BY: G.M. PARRILLO

Printed in the United States of America

First Printing, April 2025
Second Printing, July 2025
Third Printing, January 2026

ISBN 979-8-9928609-0-0

Edited by: J. Ann Beach

www.gmparrillo.net

G.M. Parrillo Publishing, a subsidiary of The Inkbound Publishing
Roselle Park, NJ

Reviews are the key to an Independent Authors success. Please feel free to post your review on both Amazon and Goodreads. Thank you for your consideration.

Dedication

To my Patsy, thank you "sweetie darling" for believing in my writing!

To the "Sisco Kids" thank you for always being there and supporting me.

*To my favorite poker player in the whole world, thank you for choosing me to be your "**Lady Luck**".*

For Palma!

PROLOGUE

September 1996

The ringing in her ears was much stronger than the sound of the rain, as it hit her windshield and the car. It was a stinging pain that had started just moments before, as her heart had been ripped out of her chest. As Grace sat in her car she tried to breathe, tried to focus on the rain, anything but the unbearable stabbing feeling of her heart breaking.

Jimmy and Grace were heading off to college, and they had decided to be sensible about their relationship. They both knew that with him living on campus, it could undoubtably leave him tempted. Reluctantly agreeing to keep things open, Grace sat there still baffled at what he had just said. *How could he have done this just a week after leaving*, she thought to herself.

Having made the drive up to get him for the party Nicole was throwing, she still couldn't imagine how quickly this had happened. This was supposed to be her first great college weekend party and instead her world was falling apart.

Grace would describe herself as average at best, her petite plus sized form was not without its charm, her beautiful face hidden by unruly brown curly hair, and her almond-shaped brown eyes were stuck behind glasses, but she hid her luscious curves under large t-shirts and jeans most days. Her armor - glasses, t-shirts, sweatshirts, jeans, and sneakers.

James Wooley, on the other hand was the polar opposite in appearance, tall, handsome, sandy blonde hair with stunning grayish blue eyes and a chiseled jaw was something to behold. Ever astute, Grace was not oblivious to the questioning looks they would get whenever they were out together, their unspoken question of why he was with someone like her.

It had been theater that had brought them together. They were in all the plays together and they were good at it, but as much as she knew that he loved acting, he loved cars more. Always there encouraging him to go after his dream, he had taken her words to heart and made the decision to go study automative engineering so that he could one day design cars, and Grace being Grace was constantly reassuring him that anything was possible.

Lightning flashed and five seconds later a clap of thunder broke the peace, but the inside of the car was silent. "5 miles". Grace said; she was doing the thing she always did when her world was crashing, disassociating.

"What?" he turned to her. "What's 5 miles?"

"The storm. It is 5 miles away." Her grandfather had taught her to count the time between the lightning to the clap of thunder and that was how many miles away the storm was.

𝄢

Jimmy leaned over, wiping her soft, tear-stained cheek, "I'm pretty sure the storm is right here. I'm so sorry."

He was, he should never have made her agree to this. It wasn't fair to her. Jimmy had known that she had chosen to go to a local university for English literature and business management and staying home instead of living in a dorm so she could help her mom with her new career. Wanting his cake and to eat it too, he realized now the one person he promised he would never hurt was hurting. And it was entirely his fault.

He had been honest at least; he could have been a dick about it, his roommate had told him not to say anything, but he needed to be honest with Grace, he owed her that. The truth was, what he really owed her was to break it off and let her move on and at least try and go back to being her friend. But he didn't see that happening right now and it broke his heart.

Jimmy stared into her tortured eyes, reddened from crying, he could see she was struggling to put on a brave face as she slightly smiled at him. "I should get you home before it gets really bad out there."

Always the strong one, he thought. "Yeah I guess so." Clearing his throat, because swallowing was too hard right now, as was looking at her. He was a villain, he thought, as he looked out the window knowing she deserved better.

They were both young, but he had learned that Grace was an old soul and deserved to find someone who would give her the same love that her mom wrote about. Great loves who found each other through the storms of life and could work through everything no matter how hard things were. He understood the concept; but honestly he was too young and too stupid to even know how to go about something like that.

The amazingly tender creature that sat next to him deserved to be needed, she deserved someone older, mature, set, and to be honest probably someone who already had their shit together, not some dumb college kid who wanted to build cars. She deserved the world, and he didn't deserve her. Someone to fall for Grace, truly fall for her, and treat her the way she needed.

As she started her car, it was as if the radio knew how to make things worse as a love song came on. His saddened grayish-blue eyes bugged out of his head as the knife in his heart just wrenched, listening to the words of the song he turned slowly over to her, watching her focusing on the road. Thankfully, his parents' house was only a 3-minute drive away. Her eyes never leaving the road as the rain came down harder, white knuckles on the steering wheel just as the lightning cracked again and now 3 seconds later thunder clapped.

Jimmy thought how fortunate he was that they were only 2 blocks away from his parents' home. He wasn't sure how much more of this torture he could endure.

He sat there praying that she was more focused on the road than the song and that it was not killing her as well.

As she pulled up to his parents' brick faced home, Jimmy felt completely lost, practically stumbling over his large feet scurrying to get out of the car as quickly as he possibly could. Yet as he closed the car door behind him, he couldn't pull away either, allowing the rain to wash away the tears he knew were starting.

The slamming sound coming from the car startled him as he turned to see Grace standing in front of him with his baseball cap in hand. The sky erupted around them; lightning illuminated the sky behind her. He was sure that it was almost as if her emotions controlled the weather. A second later the thunder roared, and the rain picked up. Deaf to the wind howling around them or the driving rain hitting the black pavement, all he heard with the elevated pounding of his heart as he stared at Grace. Her tiny form soaked, her clothes now clinging to her skin showing the curvaceous figure that she hid beneath those layers, glasses dripping and her drenched hair blowing as the storm raged around them.

Watching her chest heaving, trying to breathe, he knew that Grace had something she needed to say but it seemed liked the words were caught deep in her throat. Drawing closer to her, there seemed to be some kind of gravity that kept pulling him in, towards her. Standing there with her arm held out, she waved his Toselle Park Farmers cap unable to say a thing. Grace swallowed hard, and he was sure that not all the water falling down her face was from the rain.

"I can't keep this. It's yours, it's not mine."

But she wasn't just talking about the hat. His heart sank because what she needed him to do was to go, and he knew she couldn't do this.

"Please you need to take this and go and do amazing things. I can't keep this" - he looked down at the cap - "or you."

Instead of reaching for the hat he grabbed her wrist. Lightning flashed, a clap of thunder and the skies seemed to want to drown them. Her cinnamon-colored eyes were two black holes bearing into his soul and he knew that the storm around them was nothing compared to what was brewing within her. Pulling her in, he could not tell where he began, and she ended. Gently caressing her soft cheek, he lifted her face up to his and crushed his lips to hers. If this was going to be the end, he needed one last kiss. Greedily, he deepened their kiss as he teased his tongue along the seam of her lips until she opened to him and unleashed her hunger. With her free hand she tugged on his wet hair at the nape of his neck which produced a moan into her mouth.

To let her go was going to be unbearable, to forget the feeling of her, to erase the sound of her laughs from his memory, her wit, her brilliance, her desire; he realized this would be the punishment he deserved for breaking this creature's heart. The agony. But for now, he would take what he could.

9:

Finally dropping the hat as he released her wrist and wrapping his arms around her waist hoisting her up, making kissing so much easier. Grace wrapped her other arm around his neck holding on for dear life, deepening her kiss, wanting nothing more than to be held by him forever. But if this was goodbye, then she would make him remember, remember what he had chosen to give up. She would sear herself and her kisses into the recesses of his mind and heart never to forget. Let him live with the pain of losing her for good because she couldn't do this again. She would never hurt this much ever again.

The lightning cracked, thunder roared, the wind whipped, and in between the kisses her body finally broke, as she sobbed between kisses. She wanted to stay in these arms forever, to kiss these unbearably plump lips day after day, but she couldn't, and it was breaking her heart. Feeling the start of the warm tears on their cheeks, she prayed he would be brave enough to be the one to pull away first, because she couldn't. Thankfully, it was as if he had heard her silent prayer, he put her down, turned and ran, and she stood there watching him barrel through the front door.

Grace always made sure he got into the house, and despite everything tonight was no different. Drenched and feeling numb she got back behind the wheel of the car, drove down the street only to go just 2 blocks before pulling over to park the car and cry for the next half hour.

"Are you planning on getting out of bed? We got a party tonight and we need to hit the store. Also, Pauly said he will get us the booze but we gotta pick it up, so move your mopey ass." The spicy petite blonde was not going to take no for an answer. Thankful that she had Nicole to push her when she just wanted to do nothing.

Nicole was the blonde skinnier version of Grace and always up for a party. Yin and Yang. Two tiny firecrackers, Grace was the rule follower, where Nicole loved to break all of them. Going right to Nicole's after she had stopped crying had felt like the right decision last night, not just because she lived closest to Jimmy but because going home wasn't an option. Walking into her house looking like she had would have been torturous. Lord knows she couldn't handle hearing her younger brother or her mother. Kevin, although two years younger, would have gone on about how he had told her not to do this, how it was a bad idea and it had been. Although she loved Kevin dearly, having to hear him go off on a rant was not what she would need at that moment.

Yanking a clean shirt and jeans out of Grace's bag, Nicole asked, "Where are your undies in this bag?"

Laying on the cold hardwood floor like a sack of potatoes, Grace just watched as Nicole kept rummaging through, finally finding her undergarments. "Alright, enough of this, get your swampy ass in the shower now. I love you, I will do anything for you, so just let me know - do I need to slash tires or not?" Grace rolled her eyes and sighed; she meant well.

Turning over, Grace attempted to act like a human and grabbed her stuff out of Nicole's hands before heading into the shower. She already felt like a drowned rat after last night, and she hoped the hot water would help, but all Grace felt was nothing but cold, pain, and anguish. She may have been a teenager but never felt like one; losing count of how many times her own parents had said that she should be dating someone older and mature. That no one her own age would understand her, too mature for her own good.

But Jimmy did. Maybe it was all her own immaturity that she had hoped he could be on the same level as her, that he could feel the way she did.

As the hot water cascaded over her body, it awoke a different sensation. It felt like all the places Jimmy had touched the night before were on fire and he wasn't even in the room. The roughness of his hand on her wrist, the strength in his arms around her and those tempting lips. If she could ignite and smolder in water, she would. Would anyone ever set her aflame the way he did? The hot water was not helping the way she had hoped, so she finally turned it off. As she toweled off, she heard the phone ring.

"Hey Mrs. C, yeah I got her in the shower, I've got her coffee going so, yeah, do you want us to stop by or…"

Inside Grace prayed her mom said no, if the gods loved her then her mother would say no. She knew that her mom and dad would make a big deal about this whole situation. Jimmy's parents and her own had become rather good friends since they had started doing plays together and with them dating had grown even closer. His parents were lovely and really did care about her even when the two of them would be off and on again through the year, but her parents had explained why to them. Grace was complicated, everything about Grace was complicated and probably always would be.

"Yeah, we are just gonna have the girls over before a bunch of them head back tomorrow for the beginning of the semester. Nooooo. Come on Mrs. C, we are very responsible."

Grace rolled her eyes on that one. Nicole a.k.a Nikki was one of the least responsible people she knew.

"Yeah, okay, cool, I think she might be coming out of the shower, do you want to talk to her?" Grace emerged from the bathroom. "Yeah, here she is, hang on."

Nicole held the phone out giving her the look of *Speak or your mother will think you are dead.* Grabbing the phone, Grace placed it to her ear and sighed.

"Hi baby, how are you doing this afternoon? If you want to come home and just rest, you can."

Her mother's sing-song tone was her go-to for trying to brighten Grace's mood, which never worked, it usually made everything worse because all she heard was the pity.

"No Mom, I'm okay. I am just gonna hang with the girls. It's gonna be fine."

Listening to her mother's sigh on the other end of the phone made Grace realize that she hadn't been convincing, but Janie just said, "Grace just be careful." Grace smirked because she knew her mother knew Nikki better than she would let on.

"Thanks, I will. Love you."

Nikki had been making her coffee knowing that she would need it the second she hung up. The two girls looked at each other and embraced. She just let Grace cry until they collapsed to the floor and sat there for what seemed like an eternity. As the tears just flowed and her breath came in gasps, she made herself a promise she would never feel this way again. She would lock her heart up and throw away the key.

CHAPTER ONE

June 2023

W hy does Pappi and Grammy write books?" Grace glanced up to the rearview mirror in the direction of the tiny inquisitive voice coming from the back seat. Her youngest, Colin, was looking at the new horror book that was clearly too mature for him to be trying to read. Her oldest, Calvin, yanked it out of his hand, flinging it into the passenger seat next to Grace.

"You're too young for that. Mom, he was trying to read Pappi's new book." The fourteen-year-old clearly was either trying to be a good big brother or just starting a fight either way she was not in the mood for the constant bickering. Glaring into the rear-view mirror, she shot her oldest son a look.

"Can I have one moment where you two are not getting to each other?", looking squarely at both in the mirror. It had been an entire day at her parents' house of her needing to play referee, all the while she had been working with her dad getting things ready for the book tour. Taking a deep breath in and then finally letting it out she took another second to compose herself.

"Pappi and Grammy write because it is their escape."

It was an escape, she thought. Her parents had become authors, her mother Jane (Janie) Cartino was a romance novelist whose first publication was back in 1995, and she had successfully published thirteen more after that. Kenneth

Cartino, her dad, had published horror/suspense novels on and off for about 20 years. His first suspense book was written at the end of 1996 but never published until sometime later.

Grace was the one who had gotten the books published; running "their" business, which gave her time. Time she needed to be away, away from the truth of her awful marriage. But it also allowed her time with the three men that loved her unconditionally. Her dad and her two boys.

Calvin and Colin were both named from two of her favorite literary characters and matched their name sakes for sure. Despite the difference in their personalities, both were the most loving and caring individuals that anyone could want to meet, a reflection on how they had been raised by Grace.

The boys always had to snuggle with her and loved hearing her stories about what it was like growing up in the 80s and 90s, and whenever they stepped out of line or abused their electronic time, she would threaten to make them live their day like she had, feral, free, and outside – a very scary thought for her children who lived their lives in the digital era.

She had wanted to get home a bit earlier hoping that Hank would be home in time to say goodnight to the boys before they went off to bed, but her mother's insistence on baking cookies with Colin had forced a slightly later departure.

Hank had been her husband for twenty years now and, like most couples after twenty years things were a bit strained. Factor in her weight gain, work, the kids, and life, things just had been off for some time. Grace had hoped that going on a health journey and losing 100 pounds and doing hours of therapy, she would be able to get their marriage back on track. It had been far too long since she and Hank had been intimate, and she thought perhaps with her new body and fresh frame of mind she would see if she could get that fire rekindled tonight.

Pulling into the empty driveway, she realized that Hank hadn't made it home yet and her heart fell for a second. It was probably another late night, and he would be pulling in any second as she looked down the street to see if his car was coming, but there was nothing. Running into the house and up the stairs the boys got ready for bed. Grace went to her bag and grabbed her phone, seeing she had a text from Hank.

Gonna be late, client needed a late meeting. Sorry.

Right. If it had been March or April during tax season she could believe it, but it was June. As an accountant, he did work long hours in February, March, and April, it had been that way since they started their relationship, but at least twice a month he had been having these late-night "meetings with clients." It had been like this for the past four years. Right when she had put on all that weight and the depression had kicked back in. She had assumed that he didn't know how to handle her depression, or perhaps it was that she wasn't pretty to him anymore. But she had been working on herself for a while and had even changed her look and attempted to dress a bit better, but it hadn't made any bit of difference. All it did was make that gut feeling of hers kick up.

The boys settled in their rooms and Grace went to tuck them in. Colin was simple, she would lay across his bed and just hold his hand. His ADHD by the end of the day kept him moving before he officially passed out, his "last dance" as she called it. Tossing and turning, rambling on about his game or whatever he had made with Grammy, tonight was all about the cookies. Smiling at Colin, she kissed his hand and got up. "Love you, peanut butter cup."

"Love you mommy." Colin blew her a kiss from his bed as she shut off the lights, closing his door but leaving it ajar. Checking on Calvin was next. Grace walked to the next door and knocked. Peeking her head in, he nodded for her to come in as he tossed his dirty clothes into the hamper. Grace was thankful that he hadn't left them on his computer chair as she sat down in it.

"So, what are you going to do with your summer, sir? I have enough time to register you for camp. It's your last year before you can work there next summer," she started and raised her eyebrow as he settled himself in his bed with phone in hand.

"I don't know. It's late, I don't want to think about it now." Waving her off as he kept playing his game, Grace walked up to him and took the phone away with him huffing in the process.

"Bruh, come on."

"First off, I'm not 'Bruh', I'm your 'Mom' and I'm trying to have a conversation with you." Even her kid was blowing her off. "So, for that, it's time to unplug and get to sleep, we will talk about this in the morning." Her voice a bit firmer so she could make her point. Huffing at her request, Calvin plugged in his phone and pulled the blanket up. "Thank you." Grace said, before kissing his head goodnight. As she closed it behind her, she leaned back against the cold door. She hated having to do that, to always be the mean one, but she was getting tired of being ignored. She understood he was a teenager and dealing with raging hormones, but being ignored was not something she was going to tolerate anymore.

Her phone in her back pocket buzzed. She pulled it out and saw a text. Nikki had sent her a pic and a quick text.

Holy shit, did he get hotter, gonna need a change of underwear, don't tell Mike! Are we still pissed at him?

The picture was not what she was expecting. There in front of her was a picture of a stage with a tall man who had clearly aged beyond well with a bit of gray coming in at the temples holding a mic in his hand. Jimmy Wooley. The one that got away. No, the one who walked away. The phone buzzed again with another text from Nikki.

PS Divorced and single!!!!!! GUUUUURRRRLLLL!

Grace had known about the divorce. Her parents had remained friends with his for years and her mother made it her mission the past four years to mention him any time Grace would complain about Hank. It wasn't that she hadn't wanted to share this with Nikki, it was just that Nikki had been incredibly fortunate to have found a man that practically worshipped her. Mike McCarren was amazing and had become like a second brother to her and then there were their kids. Cristina and John were exactly like Mike - calm, cool, and even tempered; but Amanda, or rather Mandy as she loved being called, was exactly like Nikki. Grace and her boys loved them, but sharing any kind of news with any of the McCarrens would have opened her up to being pressured to leave Hank.

Her phone buzzed yet again and this time it was Denise. Denise Gagnon, was one of her mom friends from school; her daughter Jodi was an absolute riot and the same age as Cristina and Calvin.

YOOOOOO! Hotty McHotterson is your ex???? Gurl he needs to be your right now!

Buzz - Denise

Does he taste as good as he looks? I need to know!

Grace didn't want to answer that because she already knew - he was yummy. *Pull yourself together girl, you are married.* She couldn't look at any more of these texts. Taking a deep breath, she was about to put the phone away.

Buzz - Denise

Tell me again why you are not here?

These two really needed to stop. She was a married woman, maybe not happily, but she could be tonight if her husband ever made his appearance. Her eyes found themselves glancing back at her phone, to the picture of him singing and he did look very good. But she had seen pictures of him, they had friended each other years ago but had stayed just acquaintances. The occasional happy birthday, well wishes and likes on posts and to her dismay and due to her awful scrolling habit in the mornings, she would stalk his pictures. Grace couldn't seem to help herself, but she had kept herself distant by never actually reaching out or engaging in a conversation. The further Hank pushed her away, the more Jimmy's posts seemed to come up in her feed. That awful temptation, James Wooley, was nothing but a bad habit, and like all her other bad habits she had quit, she let him go.

Walking into their bedroom, she grabbed the corset and panty set determined to woo her husband tonight. Come hell or high water someone was going to see her in that corset tonight and she would get the response she was starved for.

Buzz. Lord this phone, this time from Kevin.

Um, so your hot dick on a stick is here at my karaoke driving every woman and gay man insane with his hotness. I told you; you should have come. My Spidey-senses knew someone sexy was walking in here tonight. Do you think he bats for the other side now that his wife cheated on him?

When are you finally getting divorced????

Well, Kevin didn't hold any punches, did he? He knew things had not been going well for years now. She couldn't keep things from him. He wasn't just her brother; he was one of her best friends. He and Nikki had made it their mission after Jimmy had broken her heart to try to get her laid and laid well. Years of shoving any guy in front of her until she was ready to start seriously dating. Then Hank came along.

Hank was beautiful, he had aged well and was fit. Blessed with ridiculously good genes where he never gained weight, and despite the tiny wrinkles near his eyes and just a little bit of gray at the temples, he was still gorgeous. Recently though he had been growing in some weird goatee which she absolutely hated, but it wasn't her face. Never one to hide his opinion of himself, he thought he was out of her league and the verbal assaults he berated her with made sure she knew it. The constant insults about her weight, hair color, clothes, or glasses, really anything was a target, and recently her age. Yet still she stayed in this ridiculous sham of a marriage. Not for herself; she knew she deserved better. She stayed for her boys, her world, wanting to give them a normal life and not wanting to disrupt it by divorcing Hank even though it was clear day by day that the marriage was becoming worse. Maybe Kevin had a point. Maybe it was time. Maybe it was her time; but she was willing to give it one last shot.

Buzz - Kevin

Hey Kevin said I could use his phone to say hi. Hope you are doing well.
Jim

A picture of Kevin and Jimmy taking a selfie and that smile.

CHRIST! She hated her brother right at that moment. It meant that knowing Kevin, he would give him her number. Fuck!

Buzz – unknown number

Hey, hope it's okay with your husband if I have your number, just moved back and was hoping to have a way to get a hold of my old friend. If not okay let me know and I will remove it.

This is Jim b-t-dubs.

Buzz – unknown number

Hey, did you know Nikki is here? I just saw her; I'm shocked you aren't here with her.

A picture of Nikki and Jim taking a selfie with Denise photobombing came through. The universe was plotting against her. Waiting for her husband to come home, while her best friends were hanging out with Jim. He wasn't Jimmy anymore, he was Jim. Kevin and Nikki both had big mouths, it was only a matter of time for them to tell him all about how her life really turned out, not the sugar-coated perfect one she posted on social media. Grace could feel her chest starting to get tight. *Breathe Grace, they won't say anything, just breathe.*

Buzz

She couldn't take anymore texts. Sitting on the edge of the bed trying to hold some semblance of peace in her brain, pushing away thoughts of Jim and the rest of them enjoying their evening without her, but luckily when she looked down one last time Hank had finally texted.

On my way home.

Finally, she can get back to her life, as boring and unexciting as it was. Perhaps she could shock some romance back into their lives and things could go back to the way they were years ago. But that gut of hers just kept telling her she was kidding herself. The gut. It had never failed her, but she wanted to change the fates. She wanted to win for once in her damn life. One last attempt to change things. Glancing back down to the corset and panties she had still in her hands, she went into their bathroom and changed. One last shot.

She had turned off most of the lights except for her bedside table and lay on the bed with her satin robe tied lightly around her waist. She shrugged one sleeve off her shoulder seductively and positioned herself with a book to make it look like she had been waiting for him to come in and ravage her. She heard the front door shut and the sound of his feet walking up the stairs. *Please dear God let this work because I can't do this anymore*, she thought. Adjusting once more to keep looking seductive, the door opened. He didn't lift his head, he just kept looking around and never at her. Clearing her throat to gather his attention she coyly gazed at him.

"Hey, how was your day?"

Grace asked in a sultry tone and was looking over her glasses giving him her best dirty librarian look even though she could barely see without them. Hank, however, just kept taking his clothes off and throwing them on the armchair on his side of the room. Clearing her throat again to grab his attention, he finally looked at her judgingly. The dismissive look and shaking of his head gave her a new determination to try harder. Tired of this one-sided longing, she sauntered her way over to his side.

"What is this for? Why are you wearing that and not ready for bed?"

The disgusted tone hit her stomach like a well-placed punch. Grace thought she looked great! Her breasts looked phenomenal in this corset, and it showed off just how much weight she had lost. The bikini bottoms hid some of her stretch marks but still was sexy according to the saleswoman who had practically told her she would have sex with her if her husband didn't. Mustering up all her self-confidence, Grace looked up into Hank's sneering eyes and prayed for the best.

"Well, I thought perhaps we could have some fun."

Running her fingers through his thick hair, he stood there surveying her body. *Yup keep taking it in pal I know I look hot,* Grace thought.

"It's been a long time; and since your meeting was so late, I thought I could ease some tension."

Cute, sexy, and practically desperate. But then her gut twisted as she caught a faint smell of a woman's perfume that smelt nothing like one of hers. She had carefully moved her hands down his body and was on his belt hoping to assist in getting him out of his pants when he pushed her hands away. Her face instantly went from sultry to something different.

"Not tonight, I'm too tired. I don't know why you spent money on this; you look ridiculous."

The gut. Hank disappeared into the bathroom leaving her standing there alone in their bedroom once again dejected. Grace didn't know if she was going to get sick or if she was going to throw something. Eyes filled with tears; she looked for anything to throw when she saw her phone lying on the bed.

Buzz – unknown number

I miss my singing buddy. What do you say?

CHAPTER TWO

This was nuts. Mike had sent a text that an Uber was on its way to pick her up. Apparently, he and Nikki were in no condition to drive home. Allegedly. Nikki knew Grace would do anything for them, but this felt more like a setup. Explaining to Hank about the text, he just rolled over and went to bed leaving Grace to her feelings and a chance to go. It was obvious he didn't care at all, but little did he know tonight was the last straw. The Divorce Complaint was all ready for her signature at any moment, her father had made sure of that. Being an attorney for years, he had made sure that Grace was protected, and she couldn't have been more grateful for it.

The June heat had officially arrived, and it was already unbearable, so she put a sundress on right over the corset. She didn't know why she needed confirmation, but she did, she needed to know if she looked good in it. Texting them a picture was not an option; knowing Nikki, she would send it to Kevin, who then would make sure it made its way to *someone's* DMs or worse on social media. Praying that Jim had already left, she took a deep breath as she got out of the Uber ride. Feeling vulnerable, she knew it would take just a single look from Jim. *He needs to stay in the friendzone, Grace.*

Grace stood outside of the bar and took another big breath just as Nikki and Denise came barreling out the front door. Screaming, laughing, and hugging Grace to the point where she prayed the corset was keeping her breasts firmly in place. She was so grateful to see them.

"We just came out to have a smoke, what the hell are you doing here? I thought you were going to seduce Mr. Limp Dick."

Alcohol made all Nikki's filters melt away as well as her volume control, she was practically screaming. Searching through her bag, Nikki dug out a pack of cigarettes and passed them out. Grace had quit smoking a million years ago, bad habits and all, but now seemed like a GREAT time to start back up again. With closed eyes she took a deep inhale of her cigarette as the menthol burned at the back of her throat. She missed smoking sometimes, but she would regret it in the morning.

"Is that a new dress?"

Opening her eyes Grace laughed as Denise scanned her body while she played with the straps of the dress. The sundress was black and did indeed hug her torso and then it flared out into ruffles, the greatest part of the dress.

"Yes, and it has pockets. And besides I needed your opinions, please don't laugh at me," Grace had lowered her voice so that only her friends could hear.

"I still have my outfit on that I tried seducing HANK with." She had emphasized his name to correct Nikki. "I just want to know if his comment was valid."

She couldn't even believe that she had doubted herself, but the self-confidence destroying that had gone on for years from Hank had her all twisted. Grace watched the looks exchanged between her friends and knew something was up. Crushing out Grace's cigarette for her, Denise grabbed her hand and dragged her through the heavy oak door. Thankfully, due to her height advantage, Denise speedily navigated them through the crush of the packed crowd and into the bathroom. Grace felt herself getting shoved into the larger stall and then turned looking at her best friends.

"Alright, listen he better have said, get on my dick right this minute! Either way, if you look amazing, I will fuck you right here and make Nikki watch."

Denise for the win. The tiny black and white bathroom filled with laughter and Grace just shook her head, her curls tickling her cheeks. She couldn't have asked for better friends.

Closing the stall door, she went to work unbuttoning the front of her dress, pulling it down so it fell just below her waist, showing off the full corset, and opened the door. Denise started whistling and Nikki started bowing to Grace. The catcalling was so loud she was sure other people just down the hall in the main bar could hear them despite the karaoke and crowd there. Someone had; the bathroom door opened, and Kevin walked in and stared at his sister.

"Oh my god, what the, what in the holy hell is going on, put your clothes on, hooker!" Kevin had walked in just as the girls were boosting her ego and pretended to dry heave in his mouth.

"Oh my god, get the fuck out, Kev. What the hell!!!" Grace yelled, scrambling to get her dress back on. Denise and Nikki turned to whirl him around and shove him out the door, but then they heard a knock.

"Everything okay in there?" Grace's heart dropped into her stomach. Jim stood just on the other side of the door. *This can't be happening*, Grace thought to herself as she started struggling to get the dress back into place. Denise and Nikki stood there with their mouths open and then Grace watched a wicked sneer come across Nikki's mouth.

"Maybe we should ask Jim what his thoughts are on this outfit?"

"I hate you. Help me get this dress back on, the corset is stuck on the dress."

"He has seen you naked before, what is a little black corset boosting up these gorgeous tits going to do?"

Grace locked eyes with Kevin pleading with him for some help. Luckily Kevin had seen this expression on her face for years and jumped in to assist.

"Uh, yeah, just a wardrobe malfunction and apparently they needed a gay to assist, so cliché, right?", he yelled toward the door, waving his hands like he didn't even know what to do with them. The adrenaline was still pumping and Grace's mind raced as she thought how tonight had been just one bad decision after another. She needed Mike and Nikki to leave at this very minute. She also needed to deal with the elephant in the bar, the guy on the other side of the door. Jim.

Her mind was racing. *Maybe he's a big asshole now,* she thought; but he had been so nice and respectful about not wanting to be weird about texting. *It's all in your head, your husband made you feel like crap. He doesn't want you; no man wants you.* Ugh, was this true or just years of emotional trauma?

And then it started happening, the room was becoming too stuffy, the corset seemed like it was getting tighter. She had been fine one second and then all the thoughts running through her brain, all the stupid feelings in her heart, were all going at one time, and her lungs felt like they were in a vise.

A wheezing sound started coming from Grace and just as they were about to leave, the group turned and looked at her. Her face went white, her breathing became labored, and she knew instantly it was a panic attack. The knocking at the door got their attention and Kevin ran to the door to get Jim to leave. Grace felt Nikki and Denise guiding her to sit down on the toilet so she could get off her feet and catch her breath.

"You are gonna be okay, do you hear me?" Grace looked up at her brother and slowly nodded. Closing her eyes, trying to catch her breath, she knew she just needed to get out of this room and run as far away as she could. She would be okay; she just needed to escape this room.

"Hey, what's going on?" Jim clearly was worried about what was happening in the bathroom. He was sure he had seen someone who looked like Grace and her friends go into the bathroom and then there was a commotion coming from there. It had sounded like Grace's voice, but because he hadn't gotten a good view of her he was not sure. *Why would she come here but not say hi?*

Kevin put his arm around Jim, but he knew him well enough to know that he was just trying to distract him. Always trying to protect his sister in the past, he knew this was just so that he could give his sister the opportunity to escape the bar without Jim seeing her.

"Kev, is Gracie in there? Is she okay?" Jim knit his brow, now truly worried that she was not okay. It might have been years since they had spoken, but she had been his friend, and no matter how hard he tried to forget her, something always brought her to his mind.

"Yes." He hesitated "She only came to take Nikki and Mike home, she isn't staying."

His words might be saying she is fine, but his face said otherwise. Hearing the distant creak of the bathroom door, Jim watched as Mike and Denise and the top of two shorter-statured women left it. Now was his chance.

Gravity. What was it about her even after all these years? She was like the sun, pulling him towards her. He went to start walking after them, but then a bunch of people got in his way and Kevin pulled on his arm to choose another song. Jim felt the tight grip that Kevin had on his bicep, and he shot the younger man a look clearly conveying to let him go. The four leaving had now gotten out of sight and more people were in his path. But he needed to just make sure she was okay. As he made his way through the crowd, he reached for his phone and began to text as he was walking. He pulled up Grace.

Hey, are you here? Are you okay?

He looked towards the door and that was when he saw her just ten feet away. Grace may have been older, but how was it possible that she could have become more stunning?

"Gracie!" he shouted, and everything seemed to move in slow motion as she turned in his direction and their eyes locked. Her parted rosy lips, those deep brown hesitant eyes, something hidden behind them, robbed him of his breath. She was leaving and wasn't going to say anything?

"Grace." Like a solemn prayer he whispered her name as another person stepped between them. It had been but a split second and like an apparition she was gone. Shoving his way to the door, trying very hard to avoid stepping on peoples' feet as he struggled through the crowd, he made his way outside, just as two cars left the parking lot. This was not the woman he remembered, she would have been polite and said hello after all these years to a friend.

He looked down at his phone and saw no text back. Perhaps things were worse than he previously thought, but he had been sure that everything was better now. They were friends on social media, and it was always so pleasant, so what had changed after all these years? He needed answers and as much as Kevin would protect her, Jim knew he could possibly charm him enough to get some answers. Walking back into the bar, he was now determined to get them and find out just what was going on with her.

Closing the bar had not been his intention, but he had been patient enough to wait. As the bartenders were doing their night prep, Jim spent his time helping Kevin break down his karaoke gear and bringing it out to his car.

"Kevin, I know I have no right to ask, but..." Jim broke the silence. Kevin turned to him and held up his hand.

"Things are complicated, that is all I will say. She will be fine."

"Complicated, how?" This was a loaded question, however, when Jim asked, he hadn't realized it would trigger the response he would get.

"He is cheating on her, and she doesn't know, or at least she hasn't said anything to us. She is insistent on not disrupting things for the boys by divorcing him." He sighed. "She won't see how much better her life would be without him." Kevin closed his eyes, shaking his head.

"So why haven't you told her about the cheating? She deserves the truth."

His own words echoing back to that one night. After all this time, she was still dealing with the same shit. Another man breaking her heart and not realizing she is all they ever needed. Jim knew what pain this was. Between his own betrayal back when he was just a kid to then being cheated on by his wife. Elizabeth had been someone he thought was going to be the one he would spend the rest of his life with. They had two girls together and he loved them more than anything, so he understood the rationale. Liz blamed her cheating on the fact that deep inside he was still holding a torch for someone in his past and perhaps that was true. The one who had had the strength to walk away.

"Yeah, uh, hey, your husband is cheating on you." Kevin paused. "Not exactly something I'm about to do to my own sister. How would you have felt if your brother had done the same thing to you? How devastated would you have been?"

Jim could tell this was something that Kevin had been wrestling with for some time. Looking up from putting cables in the trunk, he knew Kevin was right, it was too hard, he couldn't do that to her.

"Do your parents know?"

"My parents are not in jail, so no, they don't know. Otherwise, you know Ken would have shown up and castrated him in a heartbeat. Not like she would miss it, especially since they haven't..." He stopped.

Jim whipped around nearly hurting his neck in the process grasping exactly what he was saying. Kevin just zipped his lips and started making himself busy with other stuff, avoiding Jim's glare.

"They haven't what?"

What am I doing, how could I ask that? Kevin whirled around and was just shaking his head, humming 'nah uh', clearly not wanting to betray her trust. Jim couldn't help himself and he pressed but this time with a little bit of charm. Meandering over to Kevin, Jim threw his muscular arm around him and flashed that gorgeous smile.

"Kevin, I'm only asking because she is my friend, and I just want to make sure she is being taken care of properly."

Adding a wink, hoping that his charm would ooze enough to get Kevin to confess. Kevin's knees buckled under the pressure.

"Oh God, now I get it. Okay, take your handsome ass over there."

He turned Jim around and placed him on the back bumper and started pacing, raking his hands in his hair.

"She is gonna kill me. So just remember that at my funeral no orchids, they stink."

Jim nodded in annoyance as he watched Kevin shaking his hands knowing this would get him killed and then taking one long look at Jim, who was waiting intently for his confession.

"Oh God okay." Deep breath "It's been four years." Jim looked at him unsure he understood. "Since they have had sex." He stood cringing, scared for the reaction that would follow.

"WHAT?"

Jim growled that out much louder than he intended, but his brain had just exploded. How was this possible? Grace had been a very sensual person back in high school, he could only imagine how she could be now. She needed touch. In fact, she had said that her favorite line from any book or movie was from Margaret Mitchell's *Gone with the Wind* - *'You should be kissed and often, by someone who knows what he's doing,'* and it was one hundred percent true.

He remembered how she would melt, her breathlessness, the moans and her ease to acquiesce to his invasion. Perhaps his ex-wife was right, that damn torch was like the eternal flame, never going out. Just the thought of how she would feel and sound stirred a warmth in his loins that felt almost haunting. Disbelief left him shaking his head and screwing up his face as he tried to comprehend this for Grace. Aghast, he ran his hands through his hair and turned to Kevin.

"No," he stammered, *this couldn't be.* "Seriously, stop joking." Kevin's face said it all, he was telling the truth.

"Four years, Grace with no sex? You realize," Jim paused, "that is," his mind swirled as his thoughts couldn't seem to focus. "She, how, NO!" He was not making sense and now the rage hit him. How could this person, who promised to love her, the one person lucky enough to spend the rest of their life with her, worship her, how could he do this? Deep in the recesses of his heart he heard the truth. *If only you hadn't been stupid, she would have been yours.* Unable to control himself, he grabbed Kevin by his shirt.

"Oh God!" Kevin was beyond startled.

"Kev, you need to tell her. That is neglect, it is cruel, she" he was stuttering again, "she doesn't deserve that!"

Jim was seething at this point as his mind went to all the hurt feelings he felt as his ex-wife had pulled away from him by doing the exact same thing. The painful look he gave Kevin must have shaken him enough to know that perhaps the conversation needed to end. Kevin placed his hands on Jim's and started to loosen his grip on his shirt.

"Okay, Charming, she may be a damsel, she may be in distress, but" Jim glared at him "she doesn't need some tin foil covered fool riding up thinking that they need to save her. You should know by now that Grace is her own hero."

He was right, she would rescue herself. Jim felt his head starting to swirl a bit and knew the amount of alcohol he had drunk after seeing Grace was not the right move.

"Listen, clearly you are too drunk to get behind the wheel, so get in. I can't have someone as gorgeous as you dying on my hands."

Kevin was right, he needed to think with a clear mind and not in a buzz-filled rage. Taking a big breath, he nodded in agreement.

"Thanks, sorry I don't know what's come over me."

He could blame beer, but truthfully it was nerves. He had been nervous about coming back home because he knew her parents were still friends with his own, and they always kept him updated on what was going on in their lives. Jim handed him his keys and he put them in his pocket.

"I believe they are called HORMONES. Listen, come over tomorrow in the morning and I will drive you over to get your car. I'm sure my parents will be thrilled to see you after all this time."

Breathing another sigh of relief, he knew tomorrow would be a new day, and perhaps a chance to find out what actually was going on in Grace's life.

CHAPTER THREE

A pair of tiny lips kissed her temple, and she could only assume that it was morning. Getting in at 2 a.m. was not her norm and it felt like she had barely slept. Opening her eyes, Colin stood in front of her with a granola bar munching away.

She hadn't bothered climbing the stairs to sleep and had crashed on the plush gray couch in her office. Standing there offering a piece of his granola bar with a grin, Grace shook her head no and proceeded to carefully get up.

Magical bean liquid was required, and an ibuprofen for a headache that seemed to be living just behind her bleary eyes. Gathering herself, she headed to the warm, sunlit kitchen for coffee and several texts she needed to send off. The first one to Mike, second to the girls, and the third to Kevin-

Morning Bitch! Thanks for covering our escape. I'm assuming he had a bunch of questions. My own damn husband didn't give a shit, but Jim does? WTF?

Final text to Jim-

Hey, sorry to bother you so early. But hi. Sorry about last night, I was only there to take Mike and Nikki home. Perhaps sometime soon we can meet up at one of Kev's karaoke nights, just don't make fun of me, it's been like five years since I've sang.

Considering the time, she was sure none of them would respond right away. But then her phone rang.

"Seriously, what was last night about anyway?"

Not how are you, not yelling at her for the early hour, it had been like Kevin was up early on purpose which was completely unlike him. She heard rustling in the background and her mother's voice.

Buzz – Jim

Totally okay and I would never laugh at your singing, you should know me better than that.

"What is mommy going on about?"

Her mother's chatter was more high-pitched and happier than normal. Grace had not consumed enough coffee for that much cheerfulness on the other end of the phone. Kevin sucked in his breath, hesitating before responding, which gave Grace every indication that something was amiss.

"So, you know how I am an amazing person. I made sure that someone got home safely, and mom found out and invited them for coffee."

Someone, Kevin was not saying specifically who it was; he was avoiding, and she knew it.

"Uh huh, and that particular person is there right now? This early in the morning? Who?"

She was not avoiding anything. The noise he made clearly indicated that he did not want to say and was not ready to give in.

"Who is there, Kevin?"

Her mother's laughter was a whole octave higher than usual and then there was a rustling on the other end of the phone like he was trying to cover the microphone so she couldn't hear, but Grace had had enough of this.

"Kevin Michael Cartino, who is Mommy making a ridiculous fuss over?"

The full name card. She could still hear her mother's voice giggling in the background. Then she heard her father's voice in the far distance chiming in.

"Hey Jim, can you look at this old thing out here. I can't tell what is going on with her." Her father was talking about his old 1978 Z28 Chevy Camaro. The phone just seemed to slide out of her hand as her mind raced. She wasn't sure which god she had obviously pissed off, but this could not be happening to her. Colin looked up from his tablet to her.

"Mommy, you okay?" his tiny voice and face worried.

Looking at her sweet baby, she changed her shocked look and flashed him a smile of reassurance. But her foolish heart was thundering in her chest; Jim was at her parents' house just when she would need to talk to her dad. This could not be happening.

Grabbing her phone from where it had landed on the floor, the cigarettes that Nikki gave her, and her coffee, she stormed through the house and out onto the cozy front porch. Lighting a cigarette, she took a huge inhale and put the phone back up to her ear listening to an echoing of Kevin and her mother saying her name over and over until she finally spoke, no it was more of a yell.

"WHAT THE FUCK!" The other side of the phone went silent. Janie chimed up first.

"Morning, honey, you sleep okay last night?"

Janie's asked in that tone she used for when things were bad and she needed to make light of a situation, which was why she was using it now, and probably hoping that if she changed the subject perhaps Grace would calm down. This, however, was one of those moments where there was no calming down, Grace hit the video call button because she needed to look these two in the face.

"Mom, accept the video call NOW."

Looking at her phone, she waited until she finally saw the two traitors' faces pop up on the screen. Janie's smiling face and comforting look was in total contrast to Kevin, who looked on apprehensively.

"Good morning, my sweetness, you look like you didn't get enough sleep. Why don't you go back to bed? Is that a cigarette in your hand, when did you start smoking again?"

Grace raised her eyebrow and glared at the screen serving her best resting bitch face. She was not falling for her mother's redirection.

"I don't need more sleep, Mother." She was being a bit overdramatic. "Why is Jim at your house, Mother?"

"Okay, so like I said, I felt bad that he was drunk last night and didn't want him to drive home and smash up his pretty face." Kevin jumped in.

"Why is he at our parent's house? His car was at the bar."

"Because he walked over here so I could take him back to the bar and Mommy invited him over for coffee after. Daddy has him looking at the Camaro."

Yup, she had pissed off some deity because someone was clearly trying to ruin her life. Her boring, loveless life seemed easier to handle without him in it. She had let him go and said they would be friends; she could do this; it was just her overreacting.

That's it. Her friend. Just her friend who she had been intimate with in many, many ways and many, many times. Ways that curled toes and liquified her insides. Something she hadn't felt in twenty-seven years. But she could do this. She could be his friend. Grace after all had bigger issues in her life and that needed to be her focus.

Closing her eyes and taking a steadying breath, she looked back to the phone. She needed to talk to her dad, which meant she needed Jim out of there. So, she was going to give her brother a very simple job.

"I need to come over there today, so I am going to get in the shower and come over with the boys. I highly suggest that you do *EVERYTHING* in your power to get him out of the house and on his way."

This was not a suggestion; this was an order. Kevin just nodded his head, confirming that he heard her, and so that she didn't have to hear anymore, she hung up. Grabbing her stuff off the porch, she went back into the house to get the boys moving. Getting a teenager away from a game and into a shower was daunting, but after much yelling on her part, Calvin had finally gotten into the shower.

Stepping back into their bedroom for the first time since last night, she heard the shower running in their ensuite and knew Hank was up. He had left the bathroom door ajar, and because she couldn't help herself, she peeked in.

There right in front of her eyes was her final proof of what she had been suspecting - scratches on his ass from two hands she knew for sure weren't hers. The perfume, the scratches, the late nights – there was all the evidence clear as day. An affair. And now the thing she needed to do was get a divorce.

Walking down the stairs was difficult, each step felt like she was walking on broken glass. No tears, no anger, absolutely nothing, actually. Just a ringing in her ears making her head fuzzy, like she was wading through a sea of cobwebs. Through the ringing she could hear a muffled noise, and she blinked to see Colin looking up at her.

"Mommy, can I have something else to eat? I'm still hungry."

Making Colin something to eat was easy, she could do easy, she needed easy right now. What she wanted was to run away and never look back and then it hit her. Turning with a devilish smirk and a brilliant plan, she handed Colin a bowl of cereal.

"What do you say we go down to the shore house? Maybe I can get Grammy and Pappi to come with us?"

The beach, she needed to get the hell out of this house and this town. Colin's face lit up just as Calvin walked into the kitchen to grab his breakfast. He had caught that last part and looked at his mom with a furrowed brow.

"Where are we going?"

Calvin may be a pain to tear away from his computer, but maybe the possibility to play on the boardwalk might be something to coax him to agree, she thought.

"Well, I want to go down to the shore house and maybe hit the boards for a week. What do you say?" Grace sat there praying there would be no kickback from him. Colin, however, had practically been singing the word yes over and over. She looked at Calvin and mouthed the word 'Please,' and with that he gave a sigh knowing that his mom worked hard enough and might need this.

"Okay go up and pack, we are gonna head over to Grammy and Pappi's house in ten minutes and then hit the road." Hearing footsteps coming down the stairs as the teen headed back upstairs to pack a bag, she wasn't ready to see the liar's face, but she put on her most obnoxious smile.

"What's going on?" Hank went right to making coffee. Grace was hesitating on responding until he had taken his first sip.

"WE are heading to the shore house for a week." Grace said with enough happiness to choke a horse, which made Hank choke on his coffee. Small victories. He turned red and distorted his face, ready to protest.

"I can't take off Grace. I have meetings lined up and-" She walked over and halted his protests with her fingers over his lips and he swatted them away. She was getting to him, good.

"Oh, I know, which is why I thought it might be nice for me to take my ridiculous looking ass and the kids to the beach house. You can stay home, I know just how *important* your job is with these late nights and all."

Zing. dickhead. He looked at her with disgust and grabbed her upper arm, dragging her towards the back door and away from Colin who was still eating his bowl of cereal.

"So, this is about last night with that little comment?"

Hank seethed, gripping her arm even tighter. Yanking her arm away from his grasp, she noticed that he had left marks on it and prayed it wouldn't bruise. She made a face to clarify that things were fine; acting at its finest.

"I'd rather not discuss last night." Her face was still unwavering in indifference. "But honestly, I just wanted to take the kids down the shore. So, it's completely fine that your work is *so important to you*. But if you want to come, then come, if not, it's totally fine."

Praying that he would take the bait and not take her up on the offer, she thought, *Go ahead and bring your hooker here, just remember to smile for the cameras when you bring her in.* He straightened his back and moved away from her.

"Have fun then. I have a meeting Monday morning, and I had to work this weekend anyway."

"Of course, you do, and we will." She looked up at him with an air of smugness that she had rarely showed him before. "Right, Col?"

She had walked over to the six–year old and kissed his head, then walked up to take her shower. There she stood once again in another shower feeling numb and alone. One of these days she would get it right.

𝄢

"Grammy, Pappi we are going down the shore!"

Colin came tearing into the kitchen like a hurricane as Ken watched his wife embrace their grandson with such vigor that the two fell over rolling on the floor giving each other kisses and giggling. Calvin and his beautiful daughter brought up the rear as they entered through the side door. Eyeing Grace, she looked tired

and slightly bothered, and he had gathered from the conversations he had overheard earlier things were not alright in her world. He watched as his children exchanged odd glances and carried on an unsaid conversation the moment she came across the threshold.

Something was definitely up, and he was sure it had to do with their current guest. He watched Grace glare at Kevin, a look he had seen her give numerous times, and felt a pang of sadness for his son, knowing he would have hell to pay later. As she made her way into the kitchen, Ken outstretched his arms and gave his daughter a huge hug. There was something defeatist in her embrace and he just prayed a hug would help. Feeling her breathe in and hold him a little tighter gave him the first indication that he was right, but he wasn't fully prepared for what she said next.

"Daddy, I need those papers."

Ken stilled for just a moment before squeezing her a little harder. With a silent nod, he kissed his daughter's cheek and motioned to his office. Kevin exchanged glances with his dad and was about to open his mouth, but Ken knew Grace didn't need any comments at this moment. Giving his son a slight shake of his head to not say a thing, he followed his daughter to his office and was thankful he was able to help her.

𝄢

Jim walked into the kitchen to find that he had missed a lot in the short time he had gone into the bathroom, because he was not sure where these two boys had come from and gave a quizzical look at Kevin. He had seen these two boys in pictures on social media before, which meant Grace was possibly here as well.

"Jim, these are my extremely handsome grandsons, Calvin and Colin." With pride brimming, Janie wrapped her arms around the boys as she was introducing them. "Grace's sons."

"It is so nice to meet you. I'm an old friend of your mom's and your Uncle Kevin's."

He smiled at the two boys and held out his hand, both shook it and said hi shyly. They even had her bashful behavior, which was still adorable.

"Is your mom here, I haven't seen her in a million years, and I'd like to say hi before I leave."

"Yeah, she and Pappi went somewhere to talk. Probably about going down the shore for the week."

The teenager said as he nonchalantly stuffed another cookie in his mouth. Jim had just got back to town, and she was running already. Maybe after all these years she still hadn't forgiven him.

"We have camp in two weeks so Mommy thought it would be good to go down the shore." Colin spoke up, "It's right on the beach! We have a pool too! Grammy, you are coming, right?" Janie bent down and hugged him.

"Oh boopa, I am not sure, I think Pappi and Mr. Jim are gonna work on the car. Mr. Jim fixes old cars and Pappi has been dying to get that old hunk of junk taking up space in my garage to run. But maybe we can come down for the day one day." Then it seemed Janie had a brilliant idea and turned to Jim. "Jim, why don't you and your girls come down for the day? The house has plenty of space if you wanted to stay over."

𝄢

"Dale can file these first thing Monday." Ken was a man of few words, but he was here to protect her, and she couldn't have been more thankful at this specific moment. Grace turned to Kevin as he entered the room and walked over to her side.

She was doubting herself as she glanced over the paperwork. Was she sure that it was time to do this? Perhaps she was rushing things. As she twirled the pen in her hand, she heard her brother gasp and looked up at him. Grabbing her arm and showing it to his father he flipped out.

"What the hell happened?"

His voice was a whole octave higher and louder than he probably needed to be. Wrenching her arm away, she breathed in deeply as she clearly saw that both men in the room were seeing red. Heat on her cheeks was the dead giveaway that perhaps Hank had grabbed her just a little too tightly when they had spoken earlier.

"It is nothing, drop it."

"Kevin, I have bail money!"

"Both of you stop! I instigated it. He has never done anything like this before and he never will again."

Now she was loud and with that the house stilled. Grace could hear her mother's distinct pair of footsteps coming down the hallway and poked her head in.

"What the hell is going on in here? I have the boys and Jim in the kitchen and you three are practically screaming."

Looking around the room to the three staring back at her, Grace looked down at the papers again and flipped to the tabs for signing her name.

"Done! I want him served as soon as this is filed; this conversation is over."

Looking at her father and Kevin again, she got up from the seat, walking over to the door, and stood next to her mother.

"And to be honest I am very disappointed in both of you."

Glaring at them, her hackles up, the heat of her anger with the whole situation was now rising in her tenor. Darkness filled her eyes.

"Do you really think I would allow that asshole to cause me any physical pain apart from this morning's stupid arm grab? I may be two apples tall, but I sure as shit am able to hold my own!"

She was sure that even the neighbors had heard this, let alone her children and Jim. Narrowing her gaze she took another breath.

"Now if you will excuse me, I have my children in the other room that I need to reassure that everything will be okay and that their mother is not some battered woman."

Her sons had been entertaining Jim in the kitchen while the arguing in the office had been happening. Praying that they hadn't heard that much Grace stopped just outside the kitchen to collect herself and then she heard Calvin speak.

"So, you know my mom from high school you said? Was my mom as much of a badass as she is now?"

A badass, not sure of that kid, but then she heard Jim laugh, because if there was anyone who would know what she used to be like, it would be Jim.

"Yeah, she was."

They both laughed at that. Janie stood behind Grace placing a healing hand on her shoulder. Grace turned to see her mother's reassuring smile and knew she would be okay.

"Who is what?" Janie asked as she entered the kitchen, starting to go through her pantry to look for snacks. Grace looked at the three of them at the kitchen island and grinned at Jim.

"Mom is a badass."

"Well, she does take after me, so of course she is."

Grace lit up the room as she walked up to the island and next to Jim. Bumping his shoulder, she looked at him through slightly hooded eyes. *God, he smells good,* she thought, but he always did. *Just a friend, Grace, just a friend.*

"Hey," he said ever so softly, melting her like a hot knife with butter.

"Do I get a proper hug hello after blowing me off last night?"

With everything going on she really shouldn't, but he hadn't gotten his hello hug. Friends do that, they say hello, they stay in touch, they joke, that is what friends do. She could just do a tiny friendly hug. And maybe she needed one, remembering how comforting his arms were. Focusing on the fact that her boys were here in the room, he turned to her with arms stretched out and she allowed him to place them around her shoulders, bringing her close. Slowly she put her arms around him but didn't squeeze like she used to.

Could she just stay in his arms forever? *No, you are just his friend, remember Grace, just friends.* And now this pesky divorce. Resting her chin on his shoulder she could smell his cologne. This was not the old high school Drakkar Noir that all the guys saturated themselves in. This smelt like a mix of lemon, bergamot, and leather. He always had that leathery car smell. All those times with him sitting in the car, all those naughty things they would do and pray not to get caught. Her cheeks flushed at those memories. *Don't get too close to his body. Don't remember all the dirty things he does with his tongue or how good it feels when he pins you against the wall, or, FUCK, stop.*

Pushing herself away from him was hard, there was an old comfort in those arms. But she needed to do this on her own, and she would for her boys and for herself. She looked at them. Colin was blissfully unaware that something bigger was going on, but with one look at Calvin she knew. She knew he knew something was going on, but that would be a conversation for another time.

"Well, I have to get going, I have my kids this week and today is pick up."

Placing his hand on her shoulder as he got up from his chair, she could tell he was being careful as he moved behind her not to press his body against her. She would lose all control when he would come up from behind her, always sneaking up with his lips to either side of her neck right near the nape. He would brush light kisses there and then slowly would glide his hands up under her breasts. How her body would sink back into his and she would surrender. *For the love of God, Grace, stop it now, your children and mother are present.*

"Jim, if you have the kids why don't you come down for the day? Grace, you don't mind if Jim and his girls come to enjoy the house? It's supposed to be great weather!" Grace could feel the twitch in her left eye starting; what the hell was her mother doing, as she just continued to pack up more drinks. Grace and

Jim exchanged looks, not sure how to respond, but fortunately for Grace, Jim spoke up first.

"Oh, I wouldn't want to impose, you guys should just enjoy the week in peace and quiet, my girls can be a bit much at times. You should have family time; we would just be getting in the way."

He was being gracious, she knew that. But apparently her treacherous mother was not hearing of it.

"Nonsense!"

Grace thought her mother was speaking nonsense! Janie rattled on.

"Grace, tell him how big the house is and that there is a ton of room, we can all come down and stay the night." Then turning to her grandsons, "And hit the boards!"

Colin chimed up with a loud *Yay,* Calvin however just shrugged. She had spent years protecting the boys from finding out just how bad things really were at home, and she could only imagine how blindsided he must be feeling and her heart ached for him. Grace, still looking at her son, gave a nod to her mother to recognize Calvin and that something was going on.

"Thank you for the offer. How about Grace lets me know later on if that will work for her and the boys. I hate to intrude."

Jim had thankfully read the room and by the look on his face, Grace could see that his heart was going out to the whole family. Looking at his phone, he added "And with that, thank you again for the warm welcome back, but I really need to go. Mind walking me out?"

𝄢

"I'm going to be okay."

She was right, but *Where do I fit in?* he thought.

"I'm just worried about the boys. I am assuming that Cal has figured it out and I can only imagine how he is feeling."

"We kinda overheard what was going on."

"Well, this has nothing to do with them. It's a long story, which I'm going to take a shot in the dark here that Kevin has probably given you some details on already, knowing him."

Sheepishly nodding his head, he confirmed her suspicions. There was no point in hiding the truth from her; she deserved honesty. Her veiled gaze at him melted his heart and all he wanted to do was reach out and embrace her. Bring her tiny frame to his towering form and protect her. She shifted towards him for a second and something made him inch closer. His arm reached for hers and gently stroked over the slight bruises on her arm.

"Kev had mentioned how your husband was neglecting some duties in your marriage."

Her head snapped up to meet his smokey gaze. He then said, "And if I remember correctly, you were like a caged tiger if you didn't get what you needed." Her mouth gaped, cheeks flushed pink. "Am I right?" he asked.

She shifted closer, and he wasn't sure if it was her closeness or the summer heat, but he was suddenly feeling heated and light-headed. She broke the spell as she cleared her throat and took a step back.

Out of the corner of his eye he saw a car coming towards them. Speeding up the road, it was clearly going too fast and driving a bit too close for comfort. Instinctively he reached out, wrapping his arms around her, drawing her close to his chest to keep the car from hitting her. Dangerous, far too dangerous, but it felt amazing again to have her this close. Dangerously good.

His eyes darted to hers, then to the blush on her cheeks and her soft inviting lips. He could just lean down and capture her in a kiss she deserved, but in Grace fashion, she took a second to collect herself and checked her surroundings before fully pulling herself away. A full foot. He would need much further than that with her. Pushing back a few strands of hair behind her ear, she flashed a bashful grin.

"Yes, but that isn't why I'm divorcing him. But yes, he is…well…" He could tell she was trying to gather her thoughts, "I guess I'll eventually have to try and find someone who is up to the challenge. Eventually. I'm not in a rush."

His smile reached from ear to ear, and he nodded in agreement. *Challenge accepted.*

"Listen, just let me know if you need anything okay."

Winking and letting her hand graze his cheek, she left a flame that caused a light flush to his cheeks. Watching her cross the street, his gaze fell to the swishing of her hips and that tantalizing bottom, and he realized being around her might be more difficult than he imagined. Finally getting into his car and turning it on, he needed to crank up the air and music. Anything to distract him from that tempting creature.

He just couldn't believe that he had been back for a week already and things were different from how he had envisioned it. He was just supposed to get a job, live with his parents until he got his new place, take care of his kids, co-parent with his ex, and make friends. He had done all that, he had even made friends with old friends. But this woman came barreling back into his life with her own crumbling around her. He was not a hero, nor did he want to be. Not that she would allow it anyway, knowing her.

She was fierce, fiercer than he remembered her being; time had hardened her or at least her marriage had. But what was it with her? She was like a battering ram; that bit of quiet as it swung back and then she blasted through doors. That is how she came back into his life - quiet, and then chaos. But perhaps he needed a little bit of chaos in his life. She had that in spades, but what was needed was calm. Maybe he could be that calm. Calm and chaos. Perhaps they could be the chaotic calm or the calm chaos.

CHAPTER FOUR

The older gentleman sitting behind the huge desk looked up from his computer to see his old friend standing in the doorway to his office. "Ken, what the hell are you doing here? If I had known you were coming I would have had Connie put on a pot of coffee."

"Only you would be fool enough to work on the weekends at home."

Ken's old partner sheepishly looked up like a kid caught with his hand in the cookie jar. But if there was anyone who would help his daughter, it would be Dale Howard. As he sat down in the chair in front of the large mahogany desk, Ken handed him a folder and gave him a nod. As Dale reviewed the documents in the file, the older gentleman knew exactly why he would make the trip to see him on the weekend.

"Based on our last dinner together, I thought that perhaps this would be coming across my desk. How is she?"

Dale's concern was genuine; he had watched Ken's kids grow up right before his eyes, they had been the kids he had never had. Grace, though, had held a special place in his heart. She was brilliant, someone who, when she was younger, both Ken and Dale had assumed would become an attorney herself. But as tenacious as she was, she had other plans.

Rubbing his forehead, Ken tried to ease the headache that had started after Grace had yelled at him. However, he could only imagine how his daughter had felt in that moment.

"Devastated. He's apparently been having an affair. She is not sure for how long, but Kevin apparently had seen him out with some woman a couple of months ago." Ken just shook his head. "He told me today after she left. I told him not to say anything, at least not right now because she doesn't need to hear it."

Sighing, he took the time to look outside the window and just shook his head. That was all he could do, sigh and shake his head. How could someone do this to his daughter? He felt his blood pressure rising and the heat was flushing across his face. Dale must have realized how he was feeling, prompting him to get up and handing him his unopened bottle of water from his desk.

"I don't need you going and having another heart attack, this time in my house, so take a sip. It was scary enough when you had it in the office." Ken obliged his friend. "So how quickly does she want to move on this?" Ken finished the water and placed the bottle on the ground.

"Monday if you can. He is still in the house. Apparently, she convinced him that she was just taking the boys down the shore for the week. Listen, if you can get this filed Monday, see if you can get a process server to serve him at the office same day."

Ken wanted his daughter to be safe and secure. The sooner that scumbag was out of the house and out of her life, the better off she would be.

𝄢

Jim stood in the doorway as he watched Elizabeth trying to help the girls get their belongings together. Usually, she was not prepared or would be struggling to get the girls to listen to her, but something was different this time. Her beautiful face was lit up with one of her mischievous smiles, and he instantly knew something was up.

"You are in a happier mood than the last time I picked them up. I guess it was a good week."

Giving her the benefit of the doubt, he was hoping that things were getting better between her and the girls. They had sided with him when they found out she had been having an affair.

"It was rough," Elizabeth said rolling her eyes. "But I'm not excited to be rid of them if that is what you are thinking. We promised we wouldn't talk about it."

 He instantly knew with that last comment what was going on. She had been dating, that was all she was willing to divulge years ago. He turned and looked at the girls; Katherine "Katie" just rolled her eyes, like the teenager she was, and Vivian just kept grabbing her stuff. The teen picked up her bag and huffed.

"And with that I'm out. Come on, Viv, let's get you in dad's car."

She kissed her mother's cheek then brushed right past her with Vivian on her heels. Elizabeth sighed and Jim couldn't help but feel a bit sorry for her. Their eldest had not taken the divorce very well. Katie had been a bit of a "daddy's girl" after all.

"You know it's just a phase. She's a teen, she pulls that crap with me too."

Jim was lying and Elizabeth knew it; he was just trying to soften the blow. "Sure, it is. Listen, I'm sorry for what I did, but tell me that this, what we have now, isn't better than what we had before?"

He had been oblivious to the years that she had been unhappy. Hell, even his own true unhappiness he had been blind to. However, years of therapy had clarified a lot for him. It was truly the best thing he had done after the divorce.

"Yes, what we have now is fine. But it would have been better to be honest with me before you thought it was okay to have an affair."

He had said those exact words in his therapy session to her. Jim wasn't one to throw something back in your face, however, there was a part of him after this morning and what he just saw Grace go through that was brought back to some of that old hurt below the surface. "I know, but..." The words died in her throat. She was wrong, and she knew it. He walked over to her and gave her a hug.

"Listen, it's in the past, okay? We both knew that we would eventually move on from this. I'm okay, you're okay. I'll talk to the girls, maybe if they see that I'm okay with it they will soften."

Open lines of communication were something that his therapist had suggested, but it was clear that after years of hiding things Liz still had her issues. But her issues were hers not his; however, being a good co-parent was something they had agreed to. So, he would talk to the girls. He hadn't been the one to destroy anything, but there had been a part of his heart that he had held guarded. Like he was never truly hers. As he picked up Viv's pillow, he started towards the door, then turned.

"A friend of mine invited me and the girls down to their shore house for one day this week. I just wanted to let you know. Nothing is set in stone yet, but an invite was given, just wanted to let you know in case you can't get a hold of the girls, we might be on the beach, and I might take them to the boardwalk for some games."

She smiled and something sparked in her eyes, he wasn't sure what it was, but something was off.

"Oh, that is great, see and you were afraid that you wouldn't make any friends coming back here. Is it one of your old friends?"

"Yeah, I met up with him last night at karaoke. My buddy Kevin's mom invited us down for the day."

None of that statement was a lie, but deep inside he couldn't bring himself to say Grace's name. It wasn't that his friendship with her was a secret. It was just that Elizabeth was the one that he had hooked up with back in college that led to him and Grace officially breaking things off.

Liz had been the other woman. When he had gotten back to college that following Monday, she had asked what was wrong because it was very clear to anyone that he was upset. Explaining what had happened, Jim asked if he could have some time, but she had pressed that she was into him. Liz had pursued him, and yet she had been the one to cheat on him. There was something in his heart that knew if he had mentioned Grace's name that she would have managed to make this a bigger thing than it was.

She had her secrets, and now it seemed that he was keeping his own. So much for trust. However, Liz seemed to have bought what he had said. It was after all completely true.

"Well, that sounds fun, have a great time if you wind up going down. Maybe you can let me know and I can meet up with you guys. It might be fun to hit the boardwalk again. It would be great to meet your friend too."

That would not be happening. Waving to Liz as he got into the car, he noticed the teen in the back looking at him in his rearview mirror as he started the car. "How do you do it?" He could see the anger in her eyes as they drove away.

"Okay, first off, that is not what we talked about. I told you girls that your mother, whether I am married to her or not, that I would always love her; second,, it has been long enough for you to be holding grudges. I have gone on dates, and you don't get angry with me."

There were to be no double standards in his life.

"Well, that is because you never cheated on her. You are a halfway decent human being, as opposed to our whoring mother. Lord knows who she was with last night."

Katie was clearly not holding back, but Jim wasn't going to take this. He pulled over, parked, and turned to face the girls.

"Now listen to me, she is your mother, and I will not allow you to talk about her in that way. She does not deserve such unbelievably accurate but rude behavior." Closing his eyes, he sighed. "I'm sorry, I didn't mean that either.

Whether you like it or not, she's your mom. Please don't say things like that, okay?"

Reaching back to hold Katie's hand and then Viv's, he wanted to make sure that they understood that talking about their mom in that way was not acceptable. They both nodded their heads, and he turned back around and drove the remaining way in silence.

As they got out of the car making their way to the house, that comment Katie had made about last night made Jim pause. He stopped as they walked into the house.

"Hey, what you said a few minutes ago, was your mom not home last night?"

"She came home late, she said she had a late meeting, but I could smell some dude's cologne on her." Disgust on her face, the one she always made whenever talking about her mom. "It's the same one I've smelt on her for the past couple of years. At least she is with only one jerk. Probably the same one she cheated on us with."

The 'us' meant that Katie would never let this go. This hadn't been just a betrayal of Jim but of her and her sister. As the oldest, she had developed the role of the protector, which he understood. It always hit his heart the hardest when she would use that term, but she was just a teenager and shouldn't have to be taking on such a difficult position. As he embraced her, she sighed, letting out unspoken pain in his arms. He lifted her chin up to him.

"Listen, I've made peace with it so I'm going to ask you to do the same. Holding onto these feelings is not gonna do you any good, I promise you."

Closing her eyes, she let a single tear roll down her cheek and hugged him a little tighter. "I'll try." And he squeezed her right back.

"Um, are you two coming in or am I air conditioning the whole street!?"

His mother, Judi, stood with hands on her hips in the doorway to the house, embracing each girl as they crossed the threshold with a hug that stole their breath from them as she squeezed.

"Girls, head upstairs, put your stuff away and then help yourself to whatever for lunch."

She looped her arm into Jim's and led him to the kitchen. He knew this move; she would only do this when she had heard a bit of gossip and wanted some kind of confirmation. Her M.O. had not changed in the slightest over the years, he thought smiling slightly to himself, his mother acting nonchalant grabbing sandwich fixings out of the refrigerator and him waiting for the shoe to drop.

"So, I heard you are gonna be helping Ken with the Camaro."

Nodding in agreement to her over-the-rim-of-her-glasses stare, Jim was going to enjoy this.

"Yes. I'm gonna work up a quote and see what I can do."

Turning away from her to start making a sandwich, he stifled the laugh that was brewing by clearing his throat. *This is going to be fun,* he thought to himself, trying to see how long he could keep playing this game with his mother, who stood there with hands on hips clearly waiting on more information.

"And how is everyone else?"

Jim knew just how close his mom and Janie were, he was sure that in the amount of time it took him to get the girls and then drive home, Janie had already filled her in. But this was too much fun.

"Kevin is doing well, and Janie is the same, still as wonderful as ever."

He looked at her like nothing else had happened. She raised her eyebrows still feigning ignorance and then she lowered her gaze over the top of her glasses.

"Any other news or anyone else there?"

He watched her busy herself by making a cup of tea. He couldn't keep doing this to his own mom no matter how hysterical it was.

"Mom?"

"Okay," Judi turned spilling water on the floor to face him. "So maybe Janie called me this morning after you left and had mentioned that Grace and her sons had stopped by. And that she might have seen the two of you outside by the car before you left."

He had pulled her close when that car had almost tried to hit her, but to be honest that car would have missed her. Maybe it was just an excuse to have her close to him again, that gravity.

"She mentioned that some car almost hit Grace, and you saved her. Very chivalrous I believe was what she said. It must have caught Grace by surprised because she was all flushed when she went back into the house."

It wasn't the car; it was the caged tiger comment. Sitting there thinking about kissing her and all the places he would was stirring a warmth in his belly, his pulse quickened with the ideas of things he would do, and it was making him blush. Suddenly he realized just how thankful he was that he was sitting down because he could feel some tightening in his pants causing him to shift in his seat.

"Who is Grace?"

Vivian and Katie had walked in and started making sandwiches. Closing his eyes, bracing for whatever response the girls would make, he lowered his head.

"An old friend of mine."

Both girls turned to their grandmother and Katie arched her eyebrow towards her to get some sort of reaction. Judi mouthed the word "girlfriend" to the girls with her back to Jim so he wouldn't see, but the girls' responses confirmed that she had said it. Cocking his head, he looked at his mother. He knew he should have gotten his own place instead of staying with his parents.

"Yes, fine, an ex-girlfriend, there happy."

Old tea on their dad, this should be great for them, he thought. This was a part of his life he had never talked about because it was in the past. A past he thought he would never have to approach again, but here he was, back home, same group of friends in the same town. And now his girls would want to hear all the juicy stories. The girls looked between their grandmother and Jim waiting for more gossip.

"Grace and her sons went over to the Cartinoes' this morning apparently to get ready for their trip down the shore. Janie invited us down for the day, but I'm leaving it up to Grace to decide if it is okay."

The girls looked at each other with a mix of emotions, excitement and then disappointment at the prospect of not going down the shore.

"Anything else happen that might be interesting?"

He wasn't sure why Judi had asked because she knew already. Why was she doing this to him? To get his hopes up? Did he have hopes at the prospect of possibly starting a new relationship? And with Grace it seemed almost crazy. Almost.

"If you already know then why ask?"

Now he was getting aggravated with all the questioning.

"Okay fine, I know about the divorce. Ken is taking the papers over to his old partner to get them filed on Monday and served as soon as possible so Grace can go back to the house without him in it and finally be free of that awful man."

Jim just nodded his head already understanding that this might have been the case. Judi went on, "Apparently, there is a pre-nup and he has no right to anything except for joint custody of the kids."

Katie dropped half of her sandwich onto the plate and Viv giggled. It was more information than he was aware of. Grace had learned her lessons in life early, so she made sure that the future would be protected. He knew that she was never the type to cheat, that wasn't in her nature. When she loved, she loved forever, truthfully and wholly. But she also had that cold side to her, so she would pull the rug out from under you if you crossed her and that was why she had the pre-nup. Smart Grace, brilliant woman.

"Is she rich or something?"

Katie of course was going to ask the question that both girls were wondering, but they weren't the only ones invested in the answer to that question. Jim hadn't been fully updated on what was going on in Grace's life so this would be interesting to hear. Judi took another sip of her tea and placed the mug down.

"Well, most people see her and underestimate her because of her appearance, being so tiny and all. But she is extremely smart and has built a nice little empire for herself by making a number of smart investments. Including a number of properties. Like the house that her soon-to-be ex-husband is living in, she bought that a few years after you two had split up."

Jim noticed that inflection on the word *properties*.

"Properties? Like the shore house that Janie invited us to?"

Judi shook her head, but it didn't make any sense. Why would Janie think it was okay to invite them down if she didn't own the property?

"It's in Ken and Janie's name but Grace bought it with her money so that Hank wouldn't go after it."

The concern in his mother's voice made the hair on the back of his neck stand up. He had a lot more questions, but the girls were sitting there finding all this too thrilling and he was not about to allow them to get sucked in.

"Alright, enough talk of Gracie." he said.

"Gracie? Seconds ago, she was Grace, now she is Gracie. So, she was a serious girlfriend."

If Katie or Vivian were genuinely interested in finding out more about *his Gracie,* the girls would find out why they broke up and might change their opinion of him.

"That is a story for another day. I am going upstairs to work on the estimate for Ken's Camaro." Turning to his mother, "No more tea spilling unless I'm around to clarify."

She hadn't moved from the sink but uncrossed her arms and held them up gesturing that she was zipping her lips leaving the girls to sound their displeasure. Ignoring their protests, he made his way up to his room to start researching all the parts he would need for Ken's car. But he kept going back to what his mother had said: *'nice little empire for herself by making a number of smart investments. Including a number of properties.'*

Running a business and keeping track of her parents' work was something but not what he would consider an empire it was more theirs than hers. But to own a house on the beach in New Jersey was incredibly expensive, it would take her years to save up for it, plus she owned the house here in town. Two homes, two mortgages as well as the taxes that go with it. If she had done all that while being a business manager, then her parents' book sales would have to be through the roof, and they would be paying her handsomely. But he wasn't sure it would have been enough money to be able to afford all that she has. What was more unsettling was that she didn't trust her husband enough with the knowledge of her owning the beach house. Trust was not given with her; it was earned, and it was clear that she was still guarding herself.

Was it his fault all those years ago that these walls that she erected to save herself had gone up? It must have been. She had trusted someone who betrayed her, he did that. Had he really meant so much to her that such a childish betrayal should shape her future and any relationships? He knew that she had love for him back in high school, but was it that grand, deep, and mature that he had missed it?

Running his fingers through his hair, trying to massage some of the thoughts of her and her pain from his brain. Closing his eyes and lowering his head. He realized there was no point in sitting in front of the computer. He wasn't getting anywhere on his estimate. All he could do was sit and think of Grace when he noticed a slight padding of feet on the hallway carpet letting him know he wasn't alone. A tiny tapping on his door and Katie appeared in the doorway. He smiled, and as she crossed the length of his room to his desk, she bent down and wrapped her arms around his neck.

"How is the estimate coming? Or are you thinking more about *Gracie*?"

His daughter was too sassy for her own good. Craning his neck around to see her smiling as she asked, scrunching up his face in a questioning look, he turned so he could see her straight on as she had moved to the bed to sit to chat.

"Are you happy to hear gossip about your dad's old love life? I mean I'm kinda boring."

"I guess it's nice to hear that you had a life before Mom, I guess."

He knew that as a teenager herself dating was bound to come up at some point. Their relationship was much different from what she had with Elizabeth. The girls knew they could always come to him with stuff like this, not because they were daddy's girls but because he always held a strong line of communication with them.

"My life before your mom was not all good. I did some stupid immature stuff. Stuff that caused pain and I regretted it, so I don't share it with you girls because I don't like what I did."

He remembered that honesty with Katie was the key, he had to be honest so that he didn't severe any lines of communication with her.

"Yeah, but Dad, don't all teenagers do stupid immature stuff in high school in order to date?"

Jim snapped his head up on that comment. Oh god, Katie could have been dating at this point. She continued, "I mean I can honestly say the boys in my old school were pretty dumb, it's why I didn't bother dating anyone."

No dad was ever truly ready for their teenage daughter to start dating, especially if they had been fools when they were younger. But it was a blessing in disguise that his daughter had realized that her fellow teens were morons.

"So, is this an inquiry about my teenage years? Or should I be worried about you dating sometime soon?"

He was gauging just where this conversation was going. Katie had a way about her. Her bright green eyes fluttered as if she wasn't quite sure how to answer the question.

"Yes and no, yes to what dating is like as a teen, and no, Dad, there is no one I'm interested in, but it's a new school and if I meet someone and they are nice and ask me out I just want to know what to expect. I mean of course I know no means no and you've taught me enough defensive moves that I could take a guy, but" she paused and cautiously continued, "with what happened with you and Mom, dating seemed to be the last thing I wanted to talk about or even attempt. But hearing about this Grace person, I just thought it was something I might consider. I mean, I thought you and Mom were high school sweethearts all these years."

And then he realized, the girls had thought that their mom had been the love of his life. High school sweethearts, but that wasn't it at all.

"No, Mom and I met our first week at college. Grace and I" - his voice stopped as his heart ached, Grace had been his high school sweetheart, first loves have a way of staying in the deepest parts of someone's hearts and minds. "We dated in our senior year. But we had been friends for years before that."

The softness in his voice must have given her a brief indication of the fact that he had hurt Grace, and he had regrets.

"Look, being a teen is not easy," he said "Dating is far more difficult because you have all these emotions and hormones going on. But when you are ready, I am happy to help you out no matter how weird that is to hear from your dad. All I will say is have fun, just be safe about it."

She leaned onto his shoulder, and he bumped her back. Another pair of soft footsteps had made their way to his door, and they turned to find Vivian standing in the doorway.

"Grandma said dinner will be at 5 p.m. She also said you broke Grace's heart all those years ago because of Mom."

A voice from down the hallway yelled up the stairs, "Vivian Leigh Wooley, I told you not to say anything!" After all these years he realized his mother still couldn't keep a secret. Katie's mouth had dropped and now all was starting to make sense.

"Thanks, Mom!" And now he had a lot of explaining to do and he still had all this work. So much for the estimate.

CHAPTER FIVE

The warmth of the sun and the sea breeze always made Grace feel better. The salty air somehow made her equally hungry and sleepy at the same time every single visit they were down at the house. There was something about being here that made her feel centered.

The boys had made themselves comfy on the outdoor couches while they ate lunch. The sea breeze brought a caressing chill against the warmth of the sun and considering just how hot it was, it was much welcomed. Colin's lunch had disappeared faster than it had gotten onto his plate.

"Mom, can I have some chippies?"

The sweet smile on Colin's face could melt any cold heart, but he owned hers. Smiling, she walked towards the kitchen from the deck with Colin in tow. Thankful for her mom and the cooler she had packed with goodies, she grabbed a bag of chips and opened them for him. A tiny 'yay' escaped his lips and he turned to the deck before going back to his seat.

Busying herself with unloading the cooler and taking stock of what she needed from the store, she realized that after spending months away from the house she was in desperate need to restock. If it was going to be her and the boys it wouldn't be that big of a list, but her parents would be down and now that her mother had invited Jim and his kids, she would have a few more mouths and bodies to accommodate for.

"Cal, I am going to run to the market and get what we need for the week, we may be having some people come down."

Grace was speaking quickly so she could blow over the whole situation, but Calvin's head popped up when she had mentioned people coming down.

"Is your friend Jim coming down?"

His questioning tone was soft, and she had half expected him to have an attitude which was not there. She wasn't sure, did she want Jim down right now?

"Would you guys mind if he came down? Grammy did invite his daughters too. Maybe we can make them feel welcome."

Smiling, Calvin nodded and Colin wasn't even paying attention, too focused on his tablet. Grace realized that whatever impression Jim had made on Calvin was a good one. He had mentioned that he had spoken to him about divorce and maybe he wanted to continue talking to him about it. Considering how the shit was going to hit the fan within days, it was probably best to be prepared. Locking the house behind herself, she got into her car and started to make her calls. Might as well make it a conference call.

"Shut up! So, this is real, this is End Game!" Denise screamed.

"That's right! Now get your ass laid!!!" Nikki cheered and began wooting on the other end.

"The single parent life is not all that bad, just look at me!" Denise chimed in again.

"That nasty piece of shit deserves to get gonorrhea or syphilis or something nasty." Nikki wasn't drunk but she wasn't going to hold back any longer, Grace imagined.

"Are you home or at your parents? When does his ass get served?" At this point Grace couldn't figure out if it was Nikki or Denise talking as they were speaking over each other. So, she just let them drone on.

"I'm gonna make some popcorn to watch him get served, are they gonna serve him at home or work? Oh, I hope it's at work and he loses his shit and craps his pants."

"Why didn't we get cameras installed in his office, I said that years ago, you could have been getting busy for years if we had gotten that done. You know it's some nasty skank from his office because no one who really knows him would have had sex with him."

At this point, the conference call had wound up being just Denise and Nikki carrying on about how awful Hank was and that he deserved all of their vitriol, Grace hadn't been able to get a word in edgewise due to their tirade.

"Guuuuuurlzzzzah! If you two can settle down long enough I can try and answer some of these questions. Yes, we are in End Game."

Cheering erupted on the other side of the phone.

"Snap those fingers, girl!" Grace snickered at that one.

"Let's slow our roll on getting laid, as lovely and much needed as that may be." Grace was not about to try and jeopardize the whole divorce proceedings by getting someone else involved in this mess. It was bad enough that Hank had been sleeping with someone, but she didn't need to stoop so low as to go and sleep with the first person with a dick just to get her rocks off.

Nikki made a sound of annoyance and Denise chimed in.

"Oh, much needed! Do you know that a woman is supposed to have sex for their vaginal health?"

The guttural laugh that came out of all of them was loud enough for the occupants in the car next to her at the light take notice and look at her. At this point she didn't care; it was the kind of laugh that could heal anything.

"I honestly don't think that is true."

Grace was the kind of person when Denise said something so sincerely like this, she couldn't tell whether she was joking or telling the truth, so she would Google if it was true.

"What does it matter, you have needs and that corset is sitting around collecting dust."

Nikki had a point, although she had just worn it last night, it would now be sitting around collecting dust without someone to see it. Considering she bought it for Hank perhaps she just needed to burn it.

"Hmmmmm, let's see, do WE know anyone who would be accommodating to help out our old friend here, Denise?"

Oh no, Grace knew where this would be going. Grace had to shut this down. "No."

"Hmmmm, I may have just met someone last night. Tall, handsome, divorced and I believe he is very good friends with someone we know."

Biting her lip, Grace laughed because she wasn't stupid, so she repeated herself.

"Nooo."

Denise and Nikki were just having far too much fun with this. Nikki chimed in.

"Someone with muscles, that could lift her up and bang her against a wall. Oh, wait even better," she paused and then carried on. "Someone who comes up from behind her, attacks her neck and ravages her from behind."

Red light, thank God for the red light because as Nikki had been speaking, she remembered the exact time that Jim had done that to her in his parents' house while they had been out. Her knees feeling very weak and the flush of heat spreading up from her chest to her face made it very clear that this conversation needed to end.

"Alright, enough, I love you two and I now regret telling you that story, but seriously, I'm not sure I am ready for anything. So can we please drop it?"

There was reluctant grunting and "Fine" being said on the other end of the line.

"Dad brought the paperwork over to Dale today so he will be filing the Complaint Monday. He said he is gonna pull some strings and get a process server to serve it as soon as possible. Dad wants to change the locks on the house while I am not home, but I am not sure that is such a good idea. I am down the shore right now and can stay here until Hank clears out."

"Do you think he is going to be an ass about this?"

Denise had gone serious. Luckily Grace knew the answer though. She was sure he was, but just how much of an ass he was going to be was yet to be decided.

"Probably. He knows I'm down here. This can go many ways, he can be relieved that he can be with his girlfriend and go celebrate with her that night, or he can be civil and just text me or call me to let me know he was served, or" she stopped because she was sure that this was what he was going to do, "he will feel blindsided and drive all the way down here to rip me a new one and continue to berate me and tell me just how useless I was as a wife or some stupid shit like that."

She was blindsiding him, but turnabout was fair play. He was the one who had given up on the marriage and had an affair, even if it was just one time, it didn't matter, she wanted out.

"Okay so what you are saying is Denise and I should come down. We can share an Air B&B nearby or we'll get a couple of rooms at the B&B around the corner from you for the week, so you aren't alone."

Although she had the best friends in the entire world and no one could change her mind, she had hoped it would be a quiet week. Yet, there was a part of her that was afraid he would come down and make a scene and she couldn't handle that. Then she remembered that her parents would come down, but that an invitation had also been made to someone else.

"No, Mom and Dad said they will come down, I'm not sure about Kev, but Mom went and invited someone to come down to spend the day one day this week."

Immediately she regretted giving that last bit of information as she had pulled into the grocery store parking lot and parked her car. Closing her eyes for the anticipation of the insanity that was about to erupt on the other end of the phone she braced herself.

"Really? Who did she invite?"

"A friend and their kids."

"Graciella Marie Nereid, who did she invite?" Nikki pulled the full name card.

"Jim."

The cacophony of screams made Grace pull her shirt collar up over her head to cover her reddened face. This was the exact reaction she knew she would get from this information, divorce or no divorce. There was heavy breathing, and both Denise and Nikki were trying to calm down as they knew that with Grace's silence that she was just beyond words.

"Okay, okay, hmm, well that was very nice of your mother. Clearly just wanting to introduce Jim's kids to some others in the schools and of course welcome an old friend back into your lives."

Nikki was trying her best to behave, but Grace could hear her hitting Mike in the background because it now sounded as if Nikki was on speaker. She heard a faint 'oh my god' in a male voice and instantly knew Mike was now in on the conversation.

"Yeah, well considering how the invite was given after mom saw me sign the divorce papers, I wouldn't have put it past her to shove me right back into his arms again. I don't remember who took the break-up worse, me, her, or his mom. I was sure those two had been planning the wedding since the beginning."

Grace joked, it had just been a high school relationship after all, but she did remember that Janie and Judi had gotten extremely close while they had been dating.

"They were."

Nikki wasn't helping, but she did remember that their moms had been upset, and they were probably secretly hoping they would get back together. Mike whispered, "You are not helping."

"Hi Mike."

"Gracie, I'm so sorry you are going through this. If you need anything you just let us know."

Nikki truly was the luckiest woman in the world, Grace had thought every time Mike would come to her rescue or just be there for her as her friend. Her brother from another mother, he was the best and there was nothing anyone could say differently.

"Thanks, babe, I appreciate it. Honestly right now I just need to go shopping for groceries and spend time with the boys."

Grace was trying to figure out how many people would be descending upon the house before she walked into the grocery store. Denise chimed in.

"Just get two of everything, if we need to bring anything down or run out we will."

"So, you guys are coming? You really don't have to."

Grace prayed that Mike would step in and convince Nikki and Denise to reconsider, she really wasn't sure she wanted that many people at her house.

"Of course we are."

"Oh okay. Well, Jim told me to let him know whether I want them to come down or not. I mean Mom invited them, but not for the whole week, just for a day. So which day should I have them come down?"

Her friends knew the house was hers, she never once kept that secret from them.

"Okay so your mom invited them, just call him up and say, hey, come down for the week and hang on the beach with us. Besides Mike and Jim can go off and do other stuff if being around him is uncomfortable for you."

The week? The whole week? Grace thought. She still felt a bit uncomfortable about the whole thing and now this group of people were planning on invading her space. For a day was one thing, but a whole week with so many people seemed a bit overwhelming and she felt a tightening starting in her chest.

"Okay so the B&B has 3 rooms available, I'm booking them now. We are coming. Denise, just Venmo me the amount. See, done."

Nikki booked the rooms without even a question or hesitation. Grace knew her friends were amazing and super supportive but did either one of them ask her if it was okay? She loved them, but it was supposed to be about her and her boys, yet she hated denying their help. People who would drop their whole lives to support her. But now she had to scramble with ideas to entertain them all.

"Fine, we can do one night at the boardwalk and get food up there, we can figure the rest of the week out as we go because this is supposed to be about relaxing. Sound good?"

Nikki, Denise, and Mike all agreed, and Grace hung up the phone. She then texted her parents and brother about what was going on, so they knew what was happening. Butterflies had started to flutter about in her stomach as she realized she had one more call to make. Why was she so nervous? She was just going to call her friend. Taking another deep breath, she scrolled through her contacts and hit the call button.

𝄢

"Hey Grace, what's going on? Everything okay?"

Jim had been surprised to be getting a call from her so soon after seeing her just a few hours ago. He had finally got to work on the estimate for Ken's car and was about halfway through his searches for parts. Two sets of padded feet came to the open door to his bedroom. Both his girls' faces had a look of shocked delight on it. "Is that Gracie?" Katie joked, causing Jim to cover the speaker end of his phone. He gave them both a face that clearly meant for the two of them to be quiet.

"Hey yeah, everything is fine. I'm sorry I didn't know you were with someone. If you are busy, I don't want to bother you, I just wanted to call you about mom's invite."

She sounded nervous, why did she sound nervous?

"No, it was just my girls being nosey." He smiled and he could hear her snicker on the other line, "Oh yeah, it was sweet of her but with all that you have going on, you don't need a couple of strangers around the boys taking away from your time with them."

He didn't want her pulling away, but he knew what she was like when she felt caged and considering how her morning had gone, he was sure that she just wanted to run away. The girls both had matching frowning faces now, he felt bad to let them down but giving Grace her space was the right thing to do.

"Oh, I was just going to say that you and your girls should come down. It might be nice for them to meet a couple of kids in the school system. Mike and Nikki and my friend Denise, you met last night, they are gonna come down for the week and obviously all their kids so, if you guys want to come down you are more than welcome."

She had rushed through that whole tiny speech as if it was hard to get out. Grace had always been one to speak slowly, choosing her words carefully, so hearing it so rushed was something that took him totally by surprise.

"Wow that is a lot of people to be staying at the house. We could just come for the day instead of staying overnight like your mom had said."

Comfortable, he needed this to be on her terms not anyone else's. Katie gave him a look to insinuate that she hadn't realized that they could possibly be spending the night down the shore.

"Oh no, um, they are gonna stay around the corner from us, they aren't staying at the house."

Jim's eyebrow went up, so they would be alone with the kids in the house and everyone else was staying somewhere else. Viv and Katie inched closer so they could hear the conversation more clearly and both were now motioning to him to tell them more as he waved them off. Being alone with Grace could be a problem.

"Oh, uh um, are you sure you have enough room for the three of us to stay over? We wouldn't want to inconvenience you."

The girls were now losing their minds on the idea of staying at a beach house, something they had only ever seen in a movie. Vivian now on her knees was being over dramatic and praying with her hands up to the sky and Katie was just mouthing the word 'please' over and over.

"Well, if the girls don't mind bunking with the boys, the one bedroom has 2 bunk beds in it so it sleeps 4 and you can take Kevin's room. He rarely comes down."

There would be space. Watching his daughters' theatrics was impressive, but something in her voice through this whole conversation gave him the indication that she actually didn't want to be there alone. Considering that she had called him, someone she hadn't seen in a million years, to spend that time with was weird but important all at the same time.

"Well, let me see what the girls want to do, can I," both girls now burst out, "Yes, yes, yes." And at the other end of the phone came a sound he hadn't heard in a long time, Grace's laugh. He could hear her smile as she laughed. God, that smile.

"I'm gonna take that as a maybe?"

Grace was now poking fun, and he couldn't help but start laughing at himself. A woman hadn't made him smile as big as she had the ability to. Katie and Vivian both looked at their father and couldn't quite believe how happy a single sound of Grace's laugh and a comment could make their dad. He had finally told them the story about what had happened all those years ago, about what transpired with Grace and both girls could sense the sadness he had felt. The girls had given him a huge hug, realizing that he had done what he had thought was the right thing to do back then, but deep inside he wondered if the girls knew just how deep his feelings for Grace ran.

"I think it's a yes." Jim winked at the girls who were now dancing in his room. "When would you like the Wooley invasion to commence?" Best to allow her to make all the calls on this.

"Whenever." She hesitated for a moment. "I will text you shortly with information. I'll leave it up to you to decide the rest." It was cryptic but with his girls still in the room, he understood she had a lot more to say.

"Gotcha, well, I'll check my text shortly then."

Not sure what to expect in the text was causing his stomach to churn. She sighed on the other end, she was breathing a sigh of relief, he knew it was relief just from the tone.

"Great, okay well, let me go, I'm grabbing supplies, but we'll see you guys soon."

And she hung up. It took a few minutes to convince the girls to get out of his room before the text came through.

Buzz – Grace

I didn't want to say anything with the girls listening but Hank is gonna be served the divorce papers this week and it was suggested that I surround myself with as many friends as possible. So, if you guys want to stay the week, you can. It would be nice to catch up with my bud after all these years. 😊

A growing warmth started in his chest, her bud, he would take being her bud again. To see how life had treated her despite all that had been going on recently would be great. But knowing that it was possible that things could go south for her with the impending divorce complaint being filed, he would take this time to spend with her. He had never met her husband but after seeing the slight bruise on her arm this morning something stirred in him. Jim never considered that someone still had the balls to put their hands on their wife. Even after all the lying and cheating that Elizabeth had done, he had never once gotten angry enough to harm her. If this Hank person had behaved in such a manner, Jim was getting more worried as to how he would react once the papers were served. The warmth that had started in his chest went from something sweet to now turning into something primal, hot and boiling, protective. No one would hurt Gracie, no one.

He looked down at his phone and started replying.

I completely understand and whoever thought that is very smart. You should surround yourself with people who support you. We would love to stay the week. Let me know if you want us to bring anything down. The girls don't have any food allergies, so we are easy.

Knowing Grace, he knew she was bound to ask.

Buzz – Grace

LOL I was just going to ask! Great minds still think alike I see.

He wished their minds were thinking alike. Jim knew that she didn't. Deep inside he knew that she had placed him into just the friend's box once he had broken her heart and that was where he was going to stay. She would never know just where she lived in his. Would never know that Elizabeth had been right, he had always loved Grace and Liz had been playing second fiddle their whole marriage. His phone buzzed again, and this time Grace had sent him the address to the shore house. He typed the address into his GPS to see how long it would take them to get down and it was just a 45-minute drive. Getting up from his chair, he looked around for an overnight bag. A couple of days' worth of clothes and his bathing suit were going to be needed. His mind wandered aimlessly as he went through his closet, not sure if he should bring a more formal shirt in case they went some place nice one night, he made sure to pick a sweatshirt out because he knew nights can get cool with the sea air. Almost like it was perfectly timed, Judi seemed to know and appeared in the doorway.

"So that is an awful lot of clothes for an overnight? The girls are excited." He was going to play this cool and calm to not get his mother too excited.

"Well, we have been invited down for the week, not for an overnight. So, I have to tell them to pack for more than one day."

Jim's blasé comment gave his mom no indication as to how he was nearly jumping out of his own skin and he turned to watch her stunned look spread into a huge smile.

"Stop, whatever thoughts you have going through your brain, stop them right now."

He didn't want to give her any hope that something could happen between him and Grace. Closing the door behind her, she pulled him towards the bed and sat him down.

"Jimmy, this is the one person in the whole world, next to your girls, that you have truly loved. And now you have a chance. She is going to be free. Please, please, please don't let her walk out of your life all over again."

Judi had known, of course she had, she was his mother. It may take him years to get her back but hearing his mother's words made him take notice that he needed Grace just as much as he needed air to breathe. Maybe that is what this pull was towards her. She was an element for him to be at peace, to live, to exist.

He had not felt that way about Elizabeth for sure. But Grace, there was always something about Grace.

Looking up into his mother's sanguine face, she could tell by the desperate look in his eyes he missed Grace, he needed her. They embraced and he could feel her pour all her love into it with an ever-so-gentle kiss on the top of his head, hoping that it would help.

"She just has so much going on. I don't want to confuse her or rush her."

The pain in his words coming through and choking him. Carefully lifting his chin up so she could look him in the eyes, his mother whispered, "Then take your time, you've waited this long. Just remind her of what being loved is truly like. Grace hasn't been loved in years and it's about time someone showed her."

Kissing his forehead and then giving him a sly wink, she walked out of the room. As she exited, Katie walked up, giving her grandmother a quizzical look, then turning the look to her father.

"We will be leaving in 15 minutes, and we will be staying for the week. Make sure you girls have a nice dress each, I would like to take Grace and her boys out for a nice dinner one night so that we can thank them for hosting us. Also, make sure you each have a sweatshirt because it can get cold at night."

Katie's feet couldn't seem to move fast enough for her as she nearly tripped over herself screaming to Vivian that they would be staying longer than one night. The cheering from the other room just made Jim smile and shake his head. He was packing up the rest of his things when the phone buzzed.

Buzz – Kevin

Hey, Grace just texted. You guys are heading down for a few days. That's fun.

Jim waited for the shoe to drop.

We are heading down tomorrow afternoon. Mom wants to be down the shore with Grace when he gets served, which if her attorney can swing, it the paperwork will be filed and served all in one day.

Wow that is insanely fast, normally it takes weeks to go through the whole mailing system and then have it sent back to the attorney's office, but if he was personally taking care of it and knows someone in the Clerk's office, then that could explain the speed with which this was being handled.

Buzz - Kevin

Lord knows how the asshat will react, so we are preparing for him to possibly come down there to throw a hissy fit.

He wasn't sure just how big this Hank was, but Jim was no shrinking violet. She had also mentioned that the rest of her crew would be there so that would be good. Not to mention if this guy had any sense he wouldn't react around a bunch of kids, especially his own boys. But he didn't know this man who had married Grace. Jim texted back:

Well luckily, she has all of us to help her through this difficult time.

It was best to keep things short and sweet with Kevin. He could go on forever. His phone buzzed back.

Buzz – Kevin

Well, Moscato "helps" her take her pants off. There are condoms in the top drawer of my right nightstand if you want to "help" her out.

His mouth dropped; Kevin was not subtle. He wasn't going to do that. There was a part of him that felt a bit rushed, and as great as it would be, he just felt like there was this intense pressure on him. He decided that he wasn't going to respond. Let Kevin believe whatever he wanted, he knew how to handle Grace, he would bide his time. With a sly grin spreading across his face, he thought bringing a bottle of wine as a gesture of thanks wouldn't hurt. Two stops before they headed down the shore was just what he planned on doing.

CHAPTER SIX

There was no way this was the right house. The three Wooleys sat in the car staring at the massive cedar-shingled coastal colonial home in front of them. Having grown up in New Jersey, Jim knew that properties like this were normally owned by people with generational wealth, not someone like Grace's family. However, there was a black Jolly-Roger flag right outside the front of the driveway and Grace had said to look for that.

Sweeping out of the front door came Grace beaming and waving. Glancing over his shoulder at the girls whose jaws were still hanging open he noticed Vivian elbow Katie as they caught sight of Grace.

He hadn't told them what she looked like, she was the complete opposite to Liz, he was sure that they hadn't expected this tiny creature to be someone their dad had been interested in. And then she smiled, and it seemed to be brighter than the sun. It was genuine, there was no air of fakeness to it, brimming from ear to ear, he could tell how happy she was to see them. Two steps behind her, the boys followed her out of the house making their way down to greet their guests.

As their hosts made their way to the car, Jim turned to his girls. "I don't think I need to tell you to be polite, but I want you on your best behavior. They have a lot going on right now."

"So why did you agree to come down?" Vivian asked.

"Because he still has the hots for *Gracie,*" Katie taunted as the girls giggled and Jim glared at them.

"I..." he stopped, they were seeing right through him. "I accepted because she is a friend and is going through something right now and friends should stick together and support one another."

The girls looked at each other, Vivian lowered her head and whispered rather loudly to Katie, "I bet I know something he wants to stick-"

Jim swatted his arm towards Vivian, not wanting her to finish that statement, and the girls burst into laughter as they started grabbing their bags to head out of the car. As he turned to get out, he caught his reflection in the rearview mirror and saw his cheeks were flushed and realized this was going to be a difficult week.

"I wasn't sure if I had the right place, this is incredible."

He still couldn't believe this house and where they were. He went over to the passenger side door and grabbed a bag and one last thing before turning to Grace.

"You should have seen it before the remodel. It was tiny."

Finally making her way over to his car, she caught sight of what he had in his hands. An enormous stunning bouquet of all her favorite flowers - lilacs, baby's breath and pale pink roses with white tips. Her reaction was just what he was hoping for as her breath stuck at the back of her throat and her hand flew up to her mouth, not sure exactly how to respond. Jim looked down at her with the sweetest smile.

"Are they still all your favorites?"

Lifting her sunglasses to enjoy the bouquet, it seemed that all she could do was nod her head in confirmation. He was so thankful that Grace was such a creature of habit and that her tastes were timeless but then again so was she. Meeting his eyes in a tender gaze of thanks, he had forgotten how Grace had these amazing flecks of amber in hers that only illuminated when the sunlight caught them. He couldn't quite tear himself away from looking at her.

The sound of the girls elbowing each other and Katie clearing her throat snapped Jim from his trance and he acknowledged them. Grace's sons had finally made their way to her side as well.

"Grace, these are my daughters, Katie and Vivian. Girls, this is Grace and her sons, Calvin and Colin."

There were shy hellos from the kids. Grace turned back to Jim and gave him a quick hug.

"I can't believe you remembered," as she looked down at the flowers. "You didn't need to do this, honestly. We are just happy that you could arrange your schedule to join us this week."

"Well, I don't start teaching until September, so it really wasn't an inconvenience; besides I thought it would be nice for the girls to meet someone who would be in school with them, and they haven't been down the shore in years. But this," he paused and gestured to the house clearly shocked. "This was not what we had been expecting."

"Like I said, it was tiny before, but then Hurricane Sandy came through and just destroyed it, so we rebuilt, bigger and better. We couldn't pass up the opportunity to go bigger, what kind of a Jersey Girl would I be?"

Jim watched as Grace gave a wink to the girls, who were just enthralled by her. Even when the world was crashing down around her, she was gracious and welcoming.

"Alright you two, the ladies have bags, they don't need to carry them, they are our guests." She turned back to the girls. "Well, first time you are guests, any time after that you are family."

Without hesitation both boys grabbed the girls' overnight bags and started walking towards the house. Motioning her stunned guests to follow, the three

Wooleys looked at each other and again at the house. Jim smiled and motioned for them to follow.

As they crossed the threshold, Jim couldn't believe this was all real. It was gorgeous, the whole home was something out of an interior design magazine with all the light blues, tans, and cream colors you would expect in a coastal home. The wood trim throughout the house was the same gray as the cedar shingles on the outside, something he was sure Grace had done on purpose. Everything was just perfect and yet it held no airs of being overly haughty or fake. As she took them on a tour, he could see touches of Grace and her love of the shore in everything. She had built paradise.

"I feel like I'm in a movie, this house is insane." Vivian looked at Grace who just smiled.

"Well, this is my family's refuge. My parents and I travel a lot for work so when we want to relax, we come here. It's nice to have the comforts of home, but with a vacation feel."

Standing on the deck outside of her bedroom, Jim watched as his girls looked around and as Grace waved at someone on the beach. This Grace was different from the one he had seen this morning. She was at peace here; he could hear it in her voice and see it in her movements.

"I don't think I would go anywhere else if we had a house like this."

Katie looked up at Jim and there was a part of him that felt bad that he couldn't give them something like this. He knew it wasn't meant to be a mean jab. Ushering them back into the house and down the stairs, Grace turned to them smiling.

"Well, anytime you want to come down, just tell Dad and we will make it happen."

Both girls practically squealed, and Jim had to give them a quieting look, to say don't overstep.

"That is very nice, but-"

He started stepping into the kitchen when he was instantly quieted by the look and two small fingers Grace had placed over his mouth. The shocked look on his face caused her to laugh and then she narrowed her eyes and glared at him over the rim of her glasses.

"Girls, the next time you want to come down, let me know directly and I will make it happen."

Grace's eyes never left his and he wasn't sure if the sensation of her fingers on his lips or her glare was making him feel a bit dizzy. Blinking to break the gaze, he just stood there unable to speak as Grace smirked at the girls and gave them another wink. Calvin and Colin sat there laughing as they just watched their mom, they knew better than to mess with her. Calvin looked at Jim.

"Mr. Jim, I thought you said you knew Mom was a badass? You should know by now that when my mom has her mind made up there is no changing it," Calvin muttered through a mouth full of chips.

"Can we go onto the beach yet?" Colin stood waiting at the deck door in the kitchen, ready to go.

"Yes, but since it's almost dinner time we are not doing our bathing suits, we can just go down to the water to show the girls." She then turned to Katie and Vivian. "The water can be a little chilly at this time of day, well, year really. Usually, the best time is the end of July, beginning of August. But I still put my toes in the water, I'm part mermaid after all."

Jim had forgotten that she was a Capricorn, the sea goat. She may be an earth sign, but he was remembering something she had said over their last summer together about how she felt whole when the waves washed up over her toes in the sand.

Chuckling to himself as that memory came into focus caused Grace to turn her head towards him. Jim just shook his head to dismiss any questions she may be starting to formulate in that pretty little head of hers. As they started walking out, Jim remembered the wine he had left by the front door.

"You guys head out onto the deck; I have another gift for allowing us to stay for the week."

"You really did too much already with the flowers. You didn't even need to bring these," he called out to him from the kitchen as she got a vase from under the sink to put the flowers in. He walked in with the gift bag and carefully placed it on the counter in front of her. Her expression changed so quickly from appreciative to suspicious in the blink of an eye and he prepared for her wrath.

"A little birdie might have mentioned you might enjoy this."

He was hoping that Kevin had been right. Arching her brow with a quizzical look, she pulled away the pretty pink tissue paper from the bag and peered inside. Narrowing her eyes and pursing her lips, causing him to snicker, he knew what was coming next, the interrogation.

"Which snitch was it? Because you don't know about this wine. Was it Nikki or Kevin?"

She pulled out the beautiful blue bottle of Italian Moscato and then started strumming her fingers on the countertop. Walking towards her, Jim decided to play it cool.

"Kevin. In his defense he just wants to see you relaxed, he said this might help you get there."

Jim glided right up next to her and lowered his head to look at the bottle. A wafting of her soft perfume reached his nose; she smelt like a fusion of vanilla, amber, and some kind of musk, and it was intoxicating, but in truth so was she. Pretending to be more interested in the bottle just so that he could be close to her, he took the bottle out of her hands.

"So, is it any good? I've never tried it."

"It's sweet and smooth." He couldn't keep his eyes off of her lips as they puckered on the "oo" sound, and it seemed she had noticed.

"So, it tastes like you."

Jim couldn't believe he had just said that out loud. Stunned into silence, Grace stood there with her mouth agape as a heated blush rose on her cheeks making him realize he had just embarrassed her but worse, himself.

"Uh, I am so sorry, I don't know why I just said that." Jim knew why he said it. Realizing that if he didn't move away from her, he would do something he would regret, he scratched the back of his head and moved away from her to give her some space as he pretended to read the back of the bottle. "So, you enjoy the wine?"

"Um yup, great wine. We should probably get this in the fridge and get the kids onto the beach."

Had he just said that she tasted sweet and smooth? Placing the bottle of wine in the fridge, Grace turned to face him but couldn't make eye contact. S*hit, I took that too far didn't I, and now I've made her uncomfortable*, he thought. Watching her back up toward the hallway, Jim knew he had messed up.

𝄢

"I'm just gonna go to the bathroom and I'll meet you on the beach! Just watch Col, he gets a little out of hand sometimes."

Grace was sure she was going to slip on the tile as she practically ran into the hall heading to the bathroom. Her mind was going a mile a minute. Was he flirting with her? No, it had to be just a throw away comment. Did she taste smooth and sweet?

It had been years since they had been intimate with each other, would he even remember something like that? The idea of him remembering something like that made her knees a bit weak.

Glancing at herself in the bathroom mirror she noticed just how red she had gotten.   She felt ridiculous, she wasn't a teenager anymore. *It didn't mean anything. He was just being kind; he is just a friend, for crying out loud.*

Taking some deep breaths, she took herself in; the redness was gone, and she decided to brave the outdoors. They were all there to have a good time, to relax and enjoy the beach. Just her, the kids, and her old ex-boyfriend who was flirting with her. *How am I gonna get through this week?*

The water felt like a cold shower as it crested over her toes, it was a small blessing as she really needed a cold shower. But she couldn't resist the waves. It was heaven, she was here in her favorite place watching her boys, standing right next to her friend and his girls.   Katie and Vivian had been running from the surf after they had felt just how cold it was. Calvin had been watching them and smiling, but Grace was sure it was Katie that he was smiling at. He was a teenager after all, and Katie was beautiful so she hadn't been surprised that her son was trying to steal glances at her when he could.

The boys had busied themselves looking for shells and it seemed Calvin had found a nice one. She watched as he called Colin over and whispered something in his ear and handed him the shell. Colin then went and gave it to Katie who gushed over how pretty it was. Grace turned back to the ocean, biting her lip trying her best not to laugh out loud. She stood there for a while watching the ocean and the ships as they sailed so far off in the distance.

There was peace in it all. The coolness of the sea breeze and surf; the sea air mingled with a mixture of scents, the saltiness of the ocean, her own perfume, and suddenly she caught a new scent. It carried on the breeze, and she knew exactly what it was. Jim's cologne.

He had been with his daughters not two seconds ago and as Grace looked over her right shoulder to where they had been standing, he was gone. Her pulse quickened as the warmth of him moved closer towards her; heart thundering in her chest, she turned her head towards him and saw he had something himself in his hand.

"I remember a certain mermaid who liked collecting shells. Would this be a good one for her collection?"

Gently skimming the inside of his palm to grab the shell, she felt just how rough his hands had become over the years. Curling his fingers, capturing her hand and the shell before she was able to move away, he squeezed ever so slightly. Neither one dared move. Grace looked up into his eyes and there was something there, it wasn't just kindness, it wasn't just friendliness, she had seen this look before. It was want.

"Hey girl, trouble is in town! What's for dinner? Hey kiddos!" Denise called down from the top of the dune, and the magic was broken. Denise and Jodi came running down the beach and started hugging the boys.

"Jim, are these your kids? Hey, I'm Denise, this is my daughter Jodi. You guys are finding shells, now's the time. Grace, you are gonna freeze your damn feet off in the surf."

Grace hadn't noticed but her feet had sunk into the sand at the surf and to be honest, with the amount of heat and wanting that Jim had stirred in her she didn't even notice just how frozen they were. Denise smacked Jim and held her arms out giving him a quick hug.

"You're family, and I give hugs."

Despite Denise's outward intimidating appearance, she had a heart of gold. She looked at Grace, who was still in a trance.

"Gracie, you sexy thing you!"

Denise bent down, yanked Grace right out of the sand and whirled her around. This was helping, her mind was already spinning, physically doing this somehow was making her mind come back to reality and grounding her. Grace hugged her best friend right back.

"Denise, that is Katie and Vivian, Jim's daughters. They are gonna be staying with us for the week."

"Sweet, nice to meet you! Nikki and Mike were right behind me. They were just dropping their bags at the B&B. So, what are we doing for chow?"

Grace hadn't realized they had been out on the beach for so long as she looked down at her phone. There was a murmur coming from the direction of the house and she heard Nikki screaming hello.

"I guess we should head back; I hadn't realized how long we had been out here."

Grace truly could lose all track of time here. The group of them started heading back to the pathway when Mike appeared at the top of the dune.

"We were wondering if you had been swept out to sea. The kids are complaining they are starving so Nikki is raiding your fridge."

Mike was pushing John back towards the house as Grace was bringing up the rear with Jim. She couldn't believe just how slick he had made her with just being close or the faintest touch. However, with every step she got closer to the house, she realized just how much trouble she was in and that being alone with Jim was a bad decision, a very bad stupid decision.

Once all sand had been dusted off, Grace entered the kitchen to find the McCarren crew going through the refrigerator and pantry looking for something to eat. Nikki was swatting away her children when she reached into the fridge and pulled out the bottle of wine Jim had brought. Nikki's expression was priceless, and Grace braced for the onslaught of comments.

"Well, well, well. What have we here?" Nikki looked at Grace and Mike in total shock. Grace screwed up her facial expression, clearly indicating to Nikki to keep quiet. "Um, who brought this little treat? This is a bit dangerous, don't you think?"

Everyone was now inside the house; Jim had moved into the TV room area to sit down with some of the kids. Denise saw the bottle and moved directly next to Grace, who was trying to swat Nikki to get her to put it back.

"It is a thank you gift." Whispering as softly as she could so the kids didn't hear. "From Jim for hosting them this week." Mike craned closer to listen as well and just started laughing. That bottle was a trap for Grace; she was not a big alcohol drinker, but she did enjoy this wine.

"Do you think he knows that if you drink that, all your clothes fall off?" Denise whispered, glancing over to make sure Jim hadn't heard what she had said. "If it is going to be difficult for you, I can drink the whole bottle so that you don't end up naked riding him like a mechanical bull."

That was an image she hadn't imagined, but now all Grace could envision was climbing on top of Jim, with his head buried in her cleavage and her grinding on top of him. She stood there rubbing her eyes, not sure whether it was exhaustion or the prospect of sex with Jim that was making her lightheaded. *Focus, Grace, have them put the bottle away.* She walked around the island, grabbing the bottle out of Nikki's hand and shoving it back in the fridge.

"Well, we can't feed the kids wine, so why don't we just go grab something and get everyone out of the house." Thank God for Mike, Grace thought to herself, thankfully he was the voice of reason. Food was the last thing on her mind, but this was too big of a crowd not to worry about such things. Fortunately for her, Mike had come up with an easy game plan and she was happy to go with the flow instead of having to make all the arrangements for once. There was a peace at being down the shore and despite her constant need to control everything, she let someone else take the lead for once.

Jim sat on the deck staring at the night sky as if he had never seen it like this before, as the candlelight glowed casting tiny streaks of light around the table while the five of them sat enjoying the evening. Looking into the house, all the kids were either watching a movie or working on a puzzle. It felt almost unreal.

Seeing his daughters surrounded by new friends and possibly the happiest he had seen them in years was hitting him a bit harder than he had expected.

The dimness from the candles luckily hid his tears as he took a swig of his beer and swallowed hard. Grace, sitting next to him, had noticed and gently touched his hand to insinuate that he wasn't alone.

"They seem to be having a great time. I hope the rest of the week holds up to the hype."

It was nice to hear Grace joke; it was nicer to be with her. There was a calmness being here that he hadn't felt in a long time, but he wasn't surprised that he would find that with Grace. This older, mature Grace was not so different from the one he remembered. Obviously, things were different, years had gone by, hardships had been weathered, but still she was herself. She was resilient.

As soft music was playing on Grace's phone, he sat looking around the table of new and old friends. This was what he was supposed to have for years. He had friends back in Pennsylvania, but not like this crew, this was family and they had welcomed him in without hesitation.

A love song he had never heard before came on and he noticed that Grace and Denise rolled their eyes as Nikki and Mike got up, starting to dance. Taking a sip of her beer, Denise looked unimpressed whispering to Jim "It's their wedding song." Nodding in approval, Jim thought it was sweet that after all the years of marriage and kids that they still stopped everything to dance with each other. Turning to Grace, he saw a glimmer of sadness in her eyes as she reached for her phone.

"If you want good dance music, I've got something."

Suddenly changing it to 90s music, all three women got up and started dancing. The commotion of them having fun spurred the kids inside to take notice as they all started to wander out to the deck.

"Oh God, they must be close to being drunk because they're dancing."

Denise grabbed her daughter's hand, dragging her around attempting to dance with her while Colin charged forward barreling through the door to dance with Grace. Jim and his girls merely stood there not sure what to do. Working her way towards them, Grace pulled them into the group so that they could join in on the fun.

Looking on, Jim watched this scene of love, happiness, and just knew, this was the woman he should have married, this was the woman he wished he could love for the rest of his life; and then his phone buzzed in his pocket.

Buzz – Kevin

Don't show Grace, but I got a picture of Hank and his girlfriend. How is someone so pretty with such an asshole?

The attachment buffered for a few seconds and then there it was. A picture of who he was assuming was Grace's husband Hank, and then he looked at the woman and dropped his phone. "Oh my god."

Frozen in place, unable to move, Jim realized that all eyes were now on him, and he didn't know what to do or say. Bending down very slowly, picking up his phone, he just kept staring at the picture in front of him. Quizzical worry came across Grace's face as she turned off the music and his girls came to his side.

"Jim, you okay? Did something happen?"

Still stunned, he looked back at his phone twice to make sure it was real and then held it to his chest, knowing the girls couldn't see this picture. Denise and Nikki looked at each other and started to whisper to the kids to start going into the house.

"Jim, are your parents okay?"

His mind was blank, he did not know what to do. Does he show her, should he break her heart again? Because deep inside him, something was happening that he had not realized he could feel again. His heart was breaking. Only this time, he wasn't sure if his heart was breaking for himself or for Grace.

𝄢

"My parents are fine. Kevin sent me a text. I-I can't."

Something in her gut told her it was about her. What could it have been that would make Jim react this way? But she knew Kevin was aware of what was going on. The realization hit her then. It was proof of Hank's affair, but why would he send it to Jim, why not send it to her?

If it was proof, then she couldn't have the boys see the picture. Jim still held the phone in his hand, not willing to show anyone. He looked at Mike and without having to say a word he knew.

"Guys, let's go grab dessert." Mike started ushering the kids into the house.

The kids stood there looking at their separate parents and both Jim and Grace motioned to them to head inside. Before heading in Calvin tugged Grace's hand and squeezed it. For someone so young to have such intuition to know that something was going on, it broke her heart. Finally getting the kids inside the house, Mike closed the sliding glass door behind him.

Taking a deep breath in as she went back to the table, she decided that sitting down was best because she really didn't know if she was going to be angry or upset at this point. She could pass out, she could wind up having another lovely panic attack and knowing how well she handled those, she opted to sit. Walking over to her, Jim sat down and held her hand before he proceeded.

"Grace, I don't know why Kevin sent it to me. Maybe it is fate or I don't know what, but this picture concerns me as well. Is this your husband?"

There it was: a picture of Hank with a gorgeous blonde woman. She was stunning, of course he would be dating someone who looked the complete opposite of herself. She was practically a supermodel. But there, clear as day, was Hank holding the hand of this beautiful blonde creature in a restaurant. Grace slowly bobbed her head yes and looked up into Jim's eyes. Etched in his brow and in his steel blue eyes was a pain, something she hadn't seen in years.

"The woman your husband has been having an affair with, her name is Elizabeth, my ex-wife."

CHAPTER SEVEN

ikki stood there gaping at the picture and couldn't quite look away. Hank with another woman. However, this woman was gorgeous, how was it even possible that Hank could be dating her? Denise and Mike slid closer, bookending her to see the text.

Looking up, she realized that Katie and Calvin had heard the sound of her getting the text as they started walking towards her. Nikki knew no good could come from Cal seeing this but then she looked down at the picture. There were several similarities between the woman in the photo and the young woman heading towards her. Katie looked far too much like this woman. Could the woman in the picture be Jim's ex-wife?

As they approached the kitchen island, Nikki knew just what he was going to ask for and deep inside she knew it wouldn't be right.

"Nikki, show me. Please."

Although he had asked politely, the tenor in his voice made it sound more like a polite command than a request. He was not going to take no for an answer. She couldn't do this; it wasn't her place.

"Cal, this isn't a picture your mom would want you to see, sweetie. I can't."

Nikki had never seen Calvin so serious and firm, but he didn't move. Instead, he held out his hand for the phone.

"Miss Nicole, please let me see what has our parents so upset. I already know Dad is having an affair, I'm not stupid."

He stood firm, not giving up, and gestured again to hand over the phone. Every bit of Nikki's heart broke. Calvin was like her own son, she remembered when Grace had brought him home and now who stood in front of her was no longer a child, but a young man.

"Sweetie, we know you aren't stupid, we love you guys; I just don't want to get you more upset than you need to be."

"Take it from someone who knows what this is like, show him." Katie chimed in.

Nikki looked at both teens and placed the phone on the counter within their reach. She was going to allow them to decide if they were going to look or not. Calvin stared at the adults in front of him and took the phone. Breathing deep, he turned the phone over and she watched the two teens look at the picture.

"Mom." Katie uttered as they stood dumbfounded. Nikki couldn't believe what she had just said; the woman that Hank had been having an affair with is Jim's ex-wife, the same woman who had stolen Jim from Grace all those years ago. After all these years, what were the odds of this happening again?

Gently putting down the phone, Calvin hung his head in disbelief. Embracing him was all Nikki could think of doing. Not only was her best friend hurt, but now her kids. She wanted to hug the pain right out of them, to make them know that they were loved and she would be there for all of them. Cal moved towards the glass door and opened it, only he wasn't the only one standing in the doorway. Katie stood right next to him staring at their parents.

Nikki was behind the kids waving her phone towards Grace and she knew. Fucking Kevin. Grace only imagined what they were feeling. Betrayed, hurt, angry; however something in her was more relieved than any of those emotions.

Placing her hand on Jim's, giving it a squeeze, she got up from her seat and walked over to Calvin, tightly hugging him. His embrace was intense; she could feel that his breathing was getting ragged. Making a tiny shushing sound she kissed his scruffy cheek, quietly praying that he would be okay. Pulling back from him she clasped his face, looking into his bleary eyes.

"Hey, it's okay. Everything is gonna be okay. Alright? We are here, we are surrounded by people who love and care about us."

The calming nature in her tone was remarkable. Grace should have been upset, enraged, devastated, all the big feelings, but she was remarkably mellow. A tear or two had been shed but not because of sadness; it was more that Jim had been shown a picture of the man who had caused his marriage to fail.

Running to her father, Katie embraced him, burying her head in his chest. Grace watched as he very gingerly brushed the top of her head and put his arms around her. He was such a great dad, she thought to herself, far better than Hank had been with the boys.

As she hugged Calvin, Nikki's phone rang; holding it up, the screen showed Kevin's name on her caller ID, and she walked away from them to take the call. Grace knew how her brother was. No one had gotten back to him and he hated suspense, she would leave it to Nikki to fill him in.

Denise and Mike came out as Nikki had walked away. "You guys need anything?" Grace had a litany of things that she needed, but there was one thing in the house that she desperately needed.

"Wine. Open the bottle." Mike and Denise looked at each other.

"Babycakes, that is a bad decision right now." Denise was right, it wasn't a good decision. It was a great decision. Grace needed a drink and if it meant that her clothes might fall off, she wouldn't care. Nakedness be damned, she needed a drink.

"Well, can it be a Bad Decision Monday?"

"It's Saturday, darling."

"Shenanigan Saturday, then?"

Grace was determined to drink that wine, the whole bottle if possible. She needed to find a cohort to assist her, or at least someone who would take pity on her. A pleading glance to Jim for some kind of assistance was met with a curt nod. He did after all bring the wine.

"Listen, it's been a long, interesting day. I'm thinking it is best the kids head to bed, and you and I can share a single glass of wine." He turned to Denise, who was clearly going to start protesting. "Just one and we share."

The day had been long; considering the time and what had just occurred it probably was best that everyone went to bed anyway. However, the stream of protests from the teens went from "It's still early" to "How can you expect us to sleep after this?" But Grace looked at Jim and nodded her head in agreement.

"Alright kids, time for bed, we got a long day tomorrow and it's late. Colin, give me some squinches, no snuggles tonight with mommy, right to bed mister, we will see you in the AM," Mike said, as he did his best trying to wrangle his own kids to leave.

As the group left, the two emotionally exhausted adults started ushering their kids up the stairs as they closed the front door. Grace had made the boys change into their pjs in her room to allow the girls their privacy; they were their guests after all. She stood watching from the doorway as Jim was taking his time tucking in his girls.

"Everything okay, Dad?"

"Yeah. Just a long day." Grace knew that was a lie, but a necessary one. It touched her heart how gentle he was with his daughters as he kissed Vivian on the forehead and then went to Katie.

"Katie Scarlett, you okay?"

Snapping her head up to look at Jim, Grace couldn't believe what she had just heard. He had named his oldest after one of her favorite characters, Grace's favorite character. What were the odds of this, or that his ex-wife also loved that character?

"Yeah, we'll be alright. Do you think it would be possible to go to the boardwalk tomorrow?"

Trying to focus on the question, Grace merely winked to confirm that they would indeed head over to the boardwalk. As Colin was already half asleep and mumbling about breakfast, she placed a tiny kiss on his forehead. As Calvin settled in, she brushed his hair away from his face. He was such a handsome young man whose whole world got turned upside down in the course of one day. With an aching heart and misty eyes, she kissed him, praying that he knew that she would always protect him and Colin till her dying breath.

𝄢

Jim's feet felt like they had lead weights on them as he walked into the room he was going to be staying in. Scanning the room, he saw the lone nightstand next to the bed and remembered the text from Kevin, however he didn't plan on taking him up on the offer.

Opening his bag to change, there on top of his clothes was an old baseball cap. Positive he hadn't packed it, he pulled it out realizing which hat it was, the baseball cap that Grace had tried to give back to him the night they broke up. Turning the hat over, in it was a tiny note with his mother's writing on it with only three words: *Win her back*. And he knew just what to do.

There, at the bottom of the stairs, Jim froze as he stared at Grace. His gaze swept across the short greenish-blue nightgown that hugged her body perfectly as she fought perilously with the bottle of wine. Was she intending on torturing him? He couldn't quite figure her out right this moment. With all that had just happened today, was she trying to seduce him to get revenge on her husband? And then deep inside, Jim thought it might be best to turn right around and go back upstairs to sleep. But she looked too damn tempting in that nightgown.

Managing to finally get the cork out of the bottle with a pop, he watched as she huffed and mumbled to herself as she realized the wine glasses were up on a shelf that she couldn't reach. Bemused by her attempts to reach them, she stood on her tiptoes and her thin gown began to rise just a few inches higher, hugging her round bottom and displaying her soft curvy legs.

The need in him started to creep up and he could feel his pulse quickening with all his rationale being tossed right out the window. *Win her back.* His body was getting hotter as he moved closer, smirking at how she just kept trying to get the glasses, the fruitless attempts causing her nightgown to perilously rise higher as he stared at the back of her milky soft thighs. Thighs he enjoyed all those years ago wrapped around him, and the indescribable sensation of how they would shake right before she would climax. He needed to help her get those glasses or he was going to lose himself right here. Thoughts of him lifting her onto the counter and having his way with her racing through his mind.

He was really having a difficult time trying not to think of her in such a way. He had promised himself he would take things slow. But his growing need reminded him of something else he could do slowly, sinfully slowly. Closing the distance between them, startling her as he pressed his body directly up behind her, his body pinning her against the counter as she let out a gasp of surprise.

Brushing his lips past her ear, "Need some help?" he whispered. The sigh that escaped her lips was something he missed.

"Um, yeah. I was..." Distracted, he had distracted her by his mere presence and his proximity was making her lose her train of thought. He watched the back of her head as she shook it, trying to clear her mind. "GLASSES, I couldn't reach the glasses."

"I'm sorry it took me so long to get here to help."

With every glass he reached for, his arousal brushed against her bottom and he could feel her push back just a little. She would always push back against him when they were younger, begging, pleading, always hungry for more. Her nightgown rode up with every inch, making her breath catch in her throat. She needed to know someone wanted her, that he wanted her, even after all these years.

She stole her hands on the counter, and he knew it was because she was holding herself back. He was so damned close, and this was a slow torturous seduction. But like a good whiskey or bourbon, it needed to be savored. Jim then noticed the tag on her nightgown sticking out; gently tucking it back in, he lazily skimmed one of his fingertips up her spine.

𝄢

"What are you doing?"

"I'm just wondering if the wine is as smooth and sweet as you say?"

His lips dusting against her ear, then her neck, and her body shuddered, the wine, *smooth and sweet like me*, she thought. This man was her kryptonite, she needed to breathe, no matter how turned on or how slick he was making her. He had been so tender and kind earlier, and now it was like there was a fire lit in him that she didn't understand. Where did this come from?

She was refusing to turn around to face him, afraid to see it was all some joke, that this wasn't real.

"Jim, what are you really doing?" She had her eyes closed, waiting for him to just laugh at her, that his arousal wasn't real, that this whole thing was a cruel prank or that it was just some erotic nightmare. But she remembered that comment he made earlier in the day about how she was a caged tiger.

"I told you, the wine."

"Is this really about the wine? Do you have to be so-" slowly moving his hips again against her now nearly exposed pale pink satin panties, she was having a hard time breathing normally but she had to finish her sentence. "Incredibly close. You are practically on top of me."

"Would you like me to be?" The feel of his lips skimming along her neck and that question made her shudder. *Dear God, yes please*! Did she really need to drink the wine with him grinding against her?

Steeling her nerves, Grace gathered herself, pouring the glass of wine. Jim now had both hands placed on the counter locking her in place but had lowered himself down so that his lower half was away from her, which was good because the lounge pants he had changed into really made everything a lot more evident.

Grabbing the glass, taking a deep breath in, she turned to face him. Staring into the depths of his steel gray eyes for a few seconds, she brushed past his cheek and whispered against his ear so that her lips touched his earlobe.

"Well, you did say we would share a glass, yes? You will just have to have a glass and let me know." Allowing the "O" sound in the word *know* to leave a puckered lip imprint on his ear, leaving him to shudder. She brushed her face past his, allowing the very corner of her mouth to graze his.

Bringing the glass to her lips, she took a long sip, her heavily lidded eyes never left his heated gaze. Holding out the glass for him to try, he took it but placed it down on the counter. Grace looked up at him with a quizzical look which melted away the moment his lips came down on hers.

And the whole world blurred away. Electricity shot through her as Jim wound one hand around her waist and the other through the hair at the nape of her neck. And for the first time in a very long time, she felt alive.

Sliding his tongue along the seam of her lips, hoping for access, Grace, without any hesitation, opened to him. Moaning into his mouth as he tasted her, she instinctively reached for his hair, pulling him in.

"You were right." He whispered as he sucked on her lower lip.

"I usually am." Her eyes glazed over from such an intimate kiss. "But what was I right about this time?", kissing him yet again. Her hands continued playing with the hair on the back of his neck and it was driving him a bit crazy.

"The wine does taste like you, smooth and sweet, just like I remembered." It may have been cheesy, but she was going to allow it. Pulling him down to kiss her again, this time he ground his hips against her causing her to moan, her fingers tightening their grip in his hair.

"You remembered? Did I leave that much of an impression on you that you remember what I taste like?"

The one thing she hated about the two of them was the height difference. She struggled to move her hips closer to his and then feeling his arms running down the length of her body and without notice, he lifted her up and placed her on the counter. The coolness of the marble hitting the back of her thighs and bottom was in total contrast to the heat that was emanating from her entire body, and it caused a gasp from her lips. Now she was the one with the height advantage.

Her breasts were perfectly lined up with his eyeline, she knew they were his weakness. Placing himself between her thighs, his hands roamed over them feeling, their lush softness. These were not the same hands from when they were teens. They were rough and calloused, but he was so incredibly gentle, and the sensation was overwhelming. She wanted him to touch her.

The hem of her nightgown and barely-there underwear just covered her soaked core. All it would take was for him to pull her towards him and she would be exposed, but at this point she didn't care. Almost as if he had read her mind, he moved his hands towards her round ass, moving her to the edge of the counter.

"I don't know what you did to me all those years ago, but I could never forget any part of you." His fingernails gently scratching her outer thighs. "The feel of you." Brushing his nose against the pulse point on her neck, kissing and lightly sucking at it, he then breathed her in. "The smell of you". He bent his head down and licked a stripe in between her cleavage. "The taste of you, why would I want to forget?"

Her whole body was a smoldering fire, and she never wanted to be extinguished. Gripping his shirt, she pulled him towards her for another kiss and he let out a slight growl releasing his hold on her thighs and then gripped the back of her night gown pulling it out from under her.

Working his way down from her lips, kissing her jaw, then peppering tiny kisses down her throat again as he worked his way down to her clavicle, sucking hard causing her to moan as she wrap her thighs around him.

"We shouldn't be doing this." She said breathlessly, but he only shook his head as he made his way down, kissing a trail down to her cleavage.

"Grace, someone needs to kiss you" he looked up from her breasts that he had been enjoying "every day, every night, and I" he grabbed her breast kneading it causing her breath to catch as he thumbed her pert nipple through the fabric "am willing to make such a sacrifice." Bending his head, he sucked at her nipple through the thin fabric. The sensation sent another round of electricity through her body and down to her core. She knew she was soaked but her legs and arms pulled him closer, unable to restrain herself.

The intense pressure was making her run her nails along his back and she was thankful that he was wearing his shirt because she was sure she would have left marks. He continued kneading her breast, but she knew he wanted the real thing, not through the dress. He took his other hand and as he lowered the strap of her nightgown, they heard a creak coming from the upstairs hallway.

Suddenly jerking them both back to reality, Grace looked towards the stairs and held her breath for two seconds. None of the kids had come down the stairs, but they could hear tiny feet moving in the hallway and what Grace could only suspect was the upstairs bathroom door closed, and they both looked at each other. They both looked like shambles. Silently laughing, they hadn't been caught, but the kids were still in the house and the idea that any one of them could have walked in on something made them both feel like teens all over again.

Jim ran his hand through her hair to soften the curls that had gotten on her face and then tilted her chin down to him. His kiss was soft and tender, almost reverent. She sighed into him, closing her eyes to allow the kiss and the feeling of relief washing over her.

"Why does this remind me of the time Chris walked in on us making out?" Jim was remembering the time his brother walked in on them in the living room with his hand-up Grace's shirt.

"Because that is exactly what would have happened just now. Only it would have been one of the kids." She smirked at him. "Our kids. Not sure how I would have explained that one, I can't bribe them to keep quiet, unlike your brother."

She wound her arms around his neck and played with his hair. Sliding his hands down her back to her hips, he scooted her closer to him again, her bottom barely on the countertop. But now, being this close, she felt his throbbing member aching to be closer to her, to her wet center, and she was desperate for him. She ground her core against him and he stifled a groan as he gripped her tighter, but then they heard the upstairs door again. They both held their breath until they heard footsteps hit the top of the landing and heard a tiny voice.

"Mommy, are you down there?" Colin was up. Grace looked at Jim trying to plead with him to release her and he dropped his head on her chest. She may have been his temptress, but she was a mom first. Scooping her up off the counter, placing her back on the ground, Grace's legs were a bit wobbly when she placed her feet on the floor.

"Yeah, buddy, I'll be up in a second." She looked up at Jim who had been holding her hands, and he kissed them. She went to leave, but he pulled her in for another kiss.

"What was that for?" she asked as he pulled away.

"I told you. You deserve to be kissed often, so I volunteered. I also have twenty-seven years of stupidity to make up for. Now if you will excuse me, I need to go take an ice-cold shower before I can even consider going to bed. Can I use the bathroom down here?"

She blushed at the idea that he was that turned on by her after all these years. She nodded her head yes and watched him go down the hallway before she attempted to climb the stairs. Sitting patiently at the top was Colin in a dreamy state, looking like he was going to fall asleep against the wall.

Grace got to the top of the stairs and helped Colin, walking him back to his bed, and tucked him in. Walking into her own room she stood there thinking a cold shower wasn't such a bad idea. She closed the door behind her and went immediately into the bathroom, looked at her disheveled state and laughed.

CHAPTER EIGHT

There were hushed noises coming from outside her bedroom door. Young voices. "Mommy never locks her bedroom door." It was Colin's tiny voice. "Mommy, we can't find Mr. Jim."

Grace stirred as the sound of Colin's voice, although muffled, was coming from the crack at the door. Reaching for her phone, she saw it was 7 a.m., and all she wanted to do was sleep. Last night had been a bit insane. The picture, the realization that Hank was indeed cheating and not just cheating but with Jim's ex-wife, and then what had happened between her and Jim.

Looking up at the ceiling, she laid there remembering it all, the wine, the kiss, the feel of him and how amazing she felt. She had wanted more. Hell, she wanted all of him. It was the sex deprivation for years that was spurring this need, it couldn't possibly be because she was still in love with him, she thought. She heard the sound of heavy footsteps in the hall and then a familiar voice.

"Hey midget, what are you doing outside mommy's bedroom? Where is Mr. Jim?"

"We can't find him and mommy's room is locked." Colin was now knocking at her door. Denise's voice grew closer and Grace realized that she was trying to pry Colin away from the door to let her sleep.

"Um, sass pot, if it is locked, she may have a migraine. Remember how she needs sleep, let's go. Why don't you guys get dressed and we can go out for breakfast. Where is your sister and your brother?," she said to Colin, and Jim's younger daughter who was standing there with him.

"They are in the TV room. We couldn't find my dad though."

"He must have gone for a walk on the beach. Why don't we get you ready and we can get chocolate chip pancakes." Denise called down to the older kids and got them all dressed and sent them down the stairs before checking on Grace. Carefully she knocked on the door and whispered, "It's me."

"Thank you." She said sheepishly and the pink in her cheeks was far too funny for Denise.

"Sure. You got someone in there with you?"

"No, just me and my lonesome self. Why?"

"The kids can't find Jim, you sure he isn't in there with you? You are all flushed." Grace shook her head and then felt her cheeks; they were indeed flushed and hot. God, she would be awful at poker, her face would give her away in a minute.

"Yes, I am sure. I just needed some privacy."

Jim walked up the stairs glistening with sweat. He was wearing shorts and a shirt that was soaked, clinging to his body. Looking him up and down, Grace and Denise just smiled as he took his ear buds out.

"Hey, everything okay?"

God I could eat him for breakfast, Grace thought as she just stood there admiring his muscles. Feeling his gaze on her, she realized she must have looked a mess and was probably regretting last night. Clearing her throat, Denise must have realized that Grace and Jim were just staring at each other and had forgotten all about her.

"So, I think you," she turned to Grace "should stay here and relax and enjoy some more privacy." And then she turned to Jim who was still unable to peel his eyes away from Grace and his body was clearly reacting to the sight of her. Denise cleared her throat again. "I think you may want to take a cool shower of some sort, unless you know of another way to relax. I'm just gonna steal your kids for an hour or two so you guys can unwind." Patting Grace on the shoulder, she walked past Jim and smiled and called down the stairs. "Alright team, let's go get breakfast, Mom is staying here to deal with her migraine and all that and Jim is staying to make sure she is okay. Let's vamoose."

They finally heard the front door close and then utter silence. They were still standing in the hallway looking at each other, when she finally took a step towards him.

"Last night was lovely" was all she got out before Jim had her pinned against the wall. He held her face kissing her with an intensity she hadn't felt before. It was messy and she didn't care, as she kissed him; his lips tasted of coffee and salty sweat. Snaking her arms up around his neck, wanting him even closer, it was as if he read her mind as his hands slid down her body like he had done the night before.

She felt his hands wander along the outside of her form, lightly grazing the outer curve of her breasts, down her waist, and then he grabbed her hips and ground against her. One to two hours, she could get a lot done in an hour or two.

She felt dizzy from his actions, every touch or brush of his bare fingers on her body leaving tiny fires that needed to be extinguished, and he was the only one who could. She wanted more, more of his touch, more of these feelings, just more. Hungry for him, she slid her tongue along his lower lip, and he opened his mouth to her, allowing a moan to escape his throat as he enjoyed her soft tongue's invasion. Their intensity caused his arousal to become even harder as he rutted against her, again causing her to pull away allowing a deep moan in her throat.

Sliding his hands back up her sides, he palmed her breasts and allowed his thumbs to pad against her nipples, causing Grace's head to roll back, exposing her neck, and he took the opportunity to attack it. Grace's knees were getting weaker, and she wasn't sure she was going to be able to stand on her own feet for much longer.

Grace started pulling at his dampened shirt, trying to pull it off of him, which caused Jim to smirk. Pulling it off over his head, he dropped it on the floor and Grace couldn't keep her eyes off his torso. He clearly had taken very good care of himself; this was not a dad bod! Reaching around to his back she brought him close again as she kissed his chest and then for fun sucked on his nipple, and this time he shuddered and moaned.

Slowly moving her hands down to his ass, she dug her nails in and gripped hard, causing Jim to thread his fingers through her hair and pull her head back, kissing her all over again. This was fast and messy, but she didn't care, they had an hour or two to take their time, but right now she needed him, and it was clear that he wanted her.

CHIME - the front door alarm chimed off. Jim and Grace froze. Someone opened the front door.

"Hello?" Hank called out. "Where is everyone?" The panic on Grace's her face told Jim everything.

"Fuck me!" Grace whispered as she listened to Hank move around the first floor.

"Honestly! I've been trying but we keep getting interrupted."

His cheeky response was met with a breathless sigh as Jim started kissing her tense jaw and working his way to her ear.

"He said he wasn't coming down. Quick, get in the shower," she whispered. Now it sounded like Hank was in the kitchen, and then the alarm chime for the back door went off.

"I don't think finding us in the shower is a good idea," Jim quipped; Grace shot him a look of frustration. She grabbed his arms, shoving him into the bathroom.

"You, shower here; I will deal with this."

Shutting the door quietly and then softly padding her way to her bedroom, Grace looked out the sliding glass door to see that Hank was walking around outside. She had at best another two minutes before he was back inside. Quickly running into the ensuite, locking the door, she stripped down and hopped into the shower. She knew if he saw her this minute he would know. She had caught a glimpse of herself; her lips were swollen and red and the blush across her chest was enough to know she had been aroused. She turned on the water to as high as she could take it and scrubbed. She needed to scrub off any hint of Jim from her body, his sweat, his smell, his taste.

The handle on the door shook. "Grace, are you in there?" Hank said from the opposite side. And reality snapped back into place. Fuck, he was still here.

"Yeah, I'm almost done."

"Where is everyone and who is in the other bathroom?" he was still jiggling the door handle.

"Kids went to breakfast with Denise and the McCarrens. They should be back in an hour. I'm assuming Kevin's buddy came back from his run. Mom, Dad and Kev are gonna come down later." She was working extremely fast to get out of the shower. Finally, she wrapped towels around herself and her hair. Unlocking the door, she braced for all of his bullshit. "What?"

As he looked her over, her stomach churned. She couldn't believe he even came down. She should tell him to turn right around and go home, but then she caught how he was looking at her arm and the bruises he had left. Was that regret she was seeing? Could he possibly be sorry?

"Listen, I-" he was cut off by a knock at Grace's bedroom door. Hank snapped his head to the tall man standing in the doorway and that brief moment of regret and the possible apology she might have gotten was whisked away the moment Jim had knocked at the door.

"Who the fuck are you?"

"Hey, sorry, I heard a strange voice, and I wanted to make sure someone wasn't trying to hurt Grace. I'm Jim, an old friend of Kevin and Grace's."

Grace stood there naked except for her towel, praying that Jim didn't just punch his lights out. Instead, he was walking towards Hank with his hand outstretched. Watching this crazy play unfold, Hank looked down at his hand and then up to Jim's face as he took it.

It seemed that the two men in front of her were doing that weird handshake showdown of who was stronger. Hank was an accountant who pushed papers; Jim restored cars and taught mechanics; it was clear who was going to win this. She bit the inside of her cheek to keep from smiling at how Hank needing to shake his hand to get feeling back in it was hilarious.

"Hank Nereid, I'm Grace's husband," he said firmly. Grace wasn't sure why he was suddenly sounding so possessive. The two men stood there in a stand-off of sorts.

"Nice to meet you. This is a great spot, my girls are loving it. Grace, thanks for watching them this morning while I went on my run. I'll go grab a spot on the beach for us. Great to finally meet you." It was a lie, but Grace was thankful for the act.

Hank turned to her. "Get dressed, I'll be downstairs." He walked out of the room leaving Grace standing there not knowing what would happen. She shut the door and tried to collect herself. Her thoughts were whirling, but she needed to calm down. Jim had acted, and she just needed to do the same thing.

She went through her closet and realized that she didn't have a bathing suit that would fit, everything was huge on her now and she hadn't had time to get a new one. She knew one of the stores in town would have something. Throwing on a pair of shorts and an oversized t-shirt, she grabbed her phone to let the team know that Hank had come down. She didn't need the kids losing their minds in front of him and since they were eventually heading down, she needed her parents to know as well.

Hank had made himself a coffee and was sitting at the island. "So, your friend, John." She turned and looked at him confused.

"You mean Jim? What about him?" She was afraid of how this line of questioning was going to go. She walked over to the coffee machine and made herself a cup.

"I've never met him before." His eyes never left her as she made her coffee and she could feel it. She was a terrible liar, and he could sniff it out in seconds. She did keep secrets from him, but when it came to her heart there was no possibility of hiding the fact that just outside stood someone who cared about her, and she was thankful for it. So, she would need to be just as cold as she was yesterday to throw him off.

"Oh, his family just moved back. Mom invited them down so his girls can make some new friends. She figured it would be nice to welcome Jim back."

It wasn't a lie; every single word was the truth. Just then Jim walked in, and she saw how Hank was inspecting him, trying to size him up. It was almost laughable because Jim could squash Hank in a heartbeat if need be.

"Okay, we are all set up with chairs and an umbrella down on the beach. Do we need anything else?"

"Nah, not till the gang gets here. I need to run out to get a new suit, all my old ones don't fit anymore."

"You don't need a new one, what's wrong with the one from last year?" Hank's annoyed tone made Grace whip around and shoot him a look and the air in the room seemed to change.

"Because that one is six sizes too big."

"You didn't lose that much weight, just wear the old one. You only lost what, ten pounds?"

Grace was sure she was seeing red at that exact moment. Ten pounds? How was it possible to live with someone for years, make nasty comments about their weight, and then when they lost weight you didn't even notice. Taking a sip of coffee and then a deep breath in, she turned to Hank.

"Ten? Try sixty last year and forty the year before! You know what, I'm not having this conversation with you. The crew should be back any minute, so just ask the girls what to do. I'm going for a walk."

Grace couldn't seem to get out of the house fast enough. Luckily as she got to the gate, the rest of the team was making their way in. Letting them know what was going on inside, she turned right and walked to town. She needed to get away. Hank showing up had taken a perfectly delightful and tempting morning to awful and dismal. Why the hell had he come down? Just last night he was with Jim's ex-wife and now he is what? Trying to play husband and dad? She had literally come all this way to escape him and now he is trying to ruin her peace.

𝄢

"For the love of God Grace, what the hell is wrong with you? What are you wearing?" Hank looked at Grace in her new green two-piece bathing suit. Nikki made a sound of disgust at Hank.

"Hey asshole, you may want to get your eyes checked because all I see is a sexy bitch ready to sit next to me or on my lap, whichever you prefer!" Nikki said as she patted the beach chair next to her. Jim wanted her to sit on him - right on his face. She looked amazing and he was finding it difficult not to look at her. The water, he needed to get into the ocean otherwise he would be pitching a tent in his shorts.

Denise looked at Jim; clearing her throat and raising her eyebrow towards him, she leaned over so that only he could hear her. "When I left you this morning, I thought you took care of that?" she said, moving her gaze down to his pants. Quickly draping his towel over his waist so no one else would notice, he watched Grace as she sat down next to Nikki, his eyes enjoying the way the cut of the bathing suit bottoms hugged her perfect curves. Denise gently touched his arm to bring him back to reality.

"It was interrupted." He motioned his head towards Hank and Denise just rolled her eyes.

"Well, if I were you, I would get in the ocean and cool that jet, sir."

They both looked around and realized they were surrounded. The only way that would happen is if he just ran and dove into the ocean. He looked at Denise and prayed she would run in with him. She completely understood and stared at the water.

"You owe me. That water is freezing."

"I'm good for it. Please?"

He knew if he stayed on land and had to watch Grace get torn down by her husband one more second, they would have to get the cops involved. Hank sat on the other side of Nikki glaring at him for some reason.

"Hey, what are you guys talking about over there?"

"How small your dick is." Denise replied, smiling at Hank. "None of your damned business. You weren't even supposed to be here, so just sit there and shut the fuck up. You're ruining our day."

She got up, leaving Hank to sit and stew, holding out her hand to Jim.

"Come on, stud, let's go." Jim looked up and knew he really did owe her, as they ran right into the ocean. A huge wave came in and they both dove. The water truly was freezing but it was what he needed. They both came up gasping for air and rode the waves out a little farther just trying to get away from shore and keep their bodies moving.

"I hate you, you know that!" She called over to him and he was sorry but as he swam to her, his hard-on was definitely gone. The water was far too cold for him.

"I'm so sorry but thank you. We can get out now if you want." She just shook her head.

"Nah, I grew up in Wisconsin, lake water is much colder than this. And besides, I can't talk to you with all of them around. So, what do you think of Hank now that you have met him?"

He looked at her and his face said it all. Looking towards the shore, he realized Hank must have said something again to anger Grace, prompting her to get up from her chair and make her way into the water.

"I hate him. Not just with what happened between me and Liz, but the way he talks to Grace and treats her. Did you know he thought she had only lost ten pounds? She said she lost one hundred pounds over the last two years, how, how do you miss that?" He watched as she waded out into the water, taking her time as if the temperature wasn't bothering her. "And why does he need to berate her all the time?" Denise just smiled, letting him get it all out. "Doesn't he know just how funny or brilliant she is, did you know that she used to write one act plays in high school?" She just looked at Jim, searching his face and then she laughed as he just treads the water around him.

"Oh, this isn't just some physical thing, is it?" He turned to her as the tide pushed him forward a bit. "You, you're in love with her. Shit, here I was thinking she was just gonna get her ass laid after all these years, but you, sir." She was laughing again. "Wow, you two are idiots. Listen, I need to know the truth. According to the stories, you are the one who got away."

He looked back to where Grace had been, and she was gone. Jim turned to Denise and that was it, she saw it all over his face. He had set her free, she was the one who got away.

"She was the one who was strong enough to walk away and I let her."

A huge wave came in, and their bodies just seemed to go with it, they were moving back to the beach. When they came up, they both looked around realizing they weren't far from the shoreline and Grace seemed to be getting closer to them in the surf.

"She thinks you are the one who got away, that you wanted to end things. So, after tomorrow if you want her, then you need to-"

"Win her back."

His mother's note. Denise's line of sight shifted just past his left ear as she saw Grace swimming towards them.

"Well, stud, now is your chance, you got your little mermaid on your six so I'm gonna try and get Mr. Limp Dick back in the house to leave her alone. Don't freeze your balls off out here, you may need them later. Go win your girl back."

Denise dunked him under before swimming back to the beach. Jim had not been expecting her to do that and between the pull of the tide and the surprise, he didn't know where he was until he came up for air. A small hand on his arm steadied him, and he looked at Grace, who truly did look like a mermaid.

"You okay there, tiger?" Grace's smile was brighter than the sun.

"Yeah, just wasn't expecting Denise to dunk me like that. Aren't you cold out here in that bathing suit?"

"You want to be dunked again? I came out here to escape the comments about my suit."

The top of her breasts was practically acting like buoys in the water, and he knew he was staring, which at this point he didn't care. about Alone floating in the ocean, Grace took her leg and slipped it between his, her foot sliding up his legs, past his knees and to his thighs, but he clamped his legs together trapping her foot and she giggled. He knew what she was doing.

"I would prefer that suit on your bedroom floor and you just wearing me."

Jim smirked as he could see the fire dancing in her eyes, and she swallowed hard at the idea. Loud yelling from the shore tore their attention away from each other. Detangling themselves, they could see Denise yelling at Hank, and Jim knew she needed to get back.

"Why do you have to be such an ass? We know you don't want to be here, so why come? Did you get bored and think, oh, it might be fun to go bully my wife so more?"

Denise followed Hank into the house as she continued her tirade. She was taller than him and everyone knew she wasn't afraid of him. But she wasn't the only person who had followed him. Grace, Jim, and Mike had been right behind them. Grace had been trying to stop the argument from the beach.

"I thought I would come down and spend time with my family, not that it is any of your business," Hank spat at her as he tried to put some distance between them in the kitchen.

"They don't want you here," she said a little too quickly.

"Guys, please can we just calm down." Grace was tired and there was a part of her that just wanted him to leave.

"Well, last I checked this was still my family's house and I have an open invitation."

"Grace's family's and we can get that invitation rescinded," she bit back. He just laughed.

"I'm here forever, you think Grace is gonna do better than me?" Hank just kept laughing.

And there it was, thought Grace. He doesn't think she can be a whole person without him, and he doesn't care who knows. She turned and saw that Mike had a solid grip on Jim's arm, trying to remind him that he couldn't jeopardize her divorce. However, Denise moved too fast, and neither she nor Mike grabbed her in time. Denise charged right up to Hank and towered over him.

"YES! We all know she can! You are just a narcissistic misogynist with a self-entitled God complex who thinks that simply because you are good looking, you are better than her. But the laughable part is that you don't even deserve to wipe her ass, let alone get to fuck her, and you haven't even been doing that!" She said looking down at him.

Grace knew well enough not to get close; she had seen Denise knock a full-grown man out and she was not planning on taking a trip to the ER to save the utter garbage that was her soon-to-be ex-husband.

"I am not going to take this from some sad lonely bitch who can't even keep a relationship longer than six months." Hank tore his eyes away from Denise and looked at Grace and Mike. "One of you want to control her?"

Hank knew better than to try and even push Denise away, but Grace just looked at him and whispered softly, "No, stop, don't" in her best impression of Gene Wilder in *"Willy Wonka and the Chocolate Factory."*

Surprisingly it had been Jim that walked up to Denise and gently placed his hand on her arm to let her know to step back. Positive he was just calming her down; it wasn't until Grace saw him pull his right arm back and punch Hank in the nose that she realized things just got messy. Hank yelped in pain as he crumpled to the floor and all Grace could do was stand there in disbelief, while Mike and Denise just smiled.

"Fuck, what the hell man. What is your problem?" yelled Hank, who must have been seeing stars as he was trying to grab anything to stop the bleeding from his nose.

The kids and Nikki had made their way up from the beach to see what was going on in the house and had all started piling in. Calvin had moved directly next to his mother and saw Jim standing over his father, who had a bloody nose, and smiled. Katie had walked up from behind and was about to head towards her dad when Grace blocked her way with her arm. If her father's actions were any indication of what she might do, she didn't need a teenage girl fighting her husband.

"My problem? My problem is that you have a wife that you could have loved and cherished but instead you treat her as something to just toss aside."

Her heart pounding in her chest, not sure how to feel as she watched Jim tower over Hank, Grace just listened on. His eyes narrowed and he started crouching down to get right into Hank's face, which was scaring Hank, causing him to fall back and scoot away from him on the floor.

"My problem is that you married someone who deserves to be loved and shown that and told that every single second of the day you get with them, but instead she is barely a second thought."

Grace's breath caught in her throat. *Oh my god, what is happening?* Calvin took his mom's hand in his and squeezed. She could feel the tears pricking her eyes as they all just stood there watching this unfold around them.

"My problem is that you have the greatest woman in the world, but you would rather fuck Liz, MY ex-wife. Yeah I know all about it. But my real problem is that Grace is stuck with you, and you don't deserve her."

Hank scrambled to get up to his feet and was checking his nose to see if it was still bleeding. Looking around the room, he must have realized he was outnumbered. Grace felt a tiny hand slide into hers and she looked down at Colin, seeing tears in his eyes, causing her own to start as well. Bending down to pick him up, she held him in her arms kissing him, letting him know it would be okay.

"Fine, I've been cheating on you, there! But if you think she is all so wonderful, then you marry her." He mustered up whatever conceited anger he had in him and looked directly at Grace. "I want a divorce."

There was a collective gasp amongst everyone in the room. She couldn't believe it; it was too good to be true. Placing Colin back on the ground, she squeezed Calvin's hand to let him know it was okay. Calmly and carefully walking towards Jim and Hank, she looked up to Jim to let him know that she had this.

Looking into Hank's enraged eyes she said, "If that is what you want, I won't fight you." The boys had moved and stood beside her, each holding her hand, her true loves. The anger and dejection in Hank's eyes worried Grace as she moved the boys behind her, ready to protect them at all costs. Glancing around the room Hank must have realized he had crossed into enemy lines.

"Fine," he spat.

Grabbing his bag, he headed to the front door, Grace and the boys following. He was going to grab the door handle when it twisted under his hand and the door flew open. Kevin pushed the door open, causing Hank to fly back and land on his back. Calvin and Colin both laughed. Ken and Janie were walking up the steps when they saw the whole thing happen and Grace bit her lip, attempting to stifle her own laugh to not make the whole thing worse. Struggling to get up, Hank grabbed his bag and looked at Ken and Janie as they stood on the top step.

"You can have her back. Tell Dale he will be hearing from my lawyer!"

Ken just smiled and stopped Hank on the steps.

"Will do! But just remember there is a pre-nup and that house you are thinking about going back to is hers. So, you pack your shit, you're out."

Ken patted him on the shoulder and walked into the house to see his daughter and grandsons.

"Well, I wasn't expecting this. What the hell happened?"

Janie placed her bag down and embraced her daughter and grandbabies.

"I'll tell you in a few minutes."

Janie touched her daughter's face before she kissed her cheek. Then she walked into the kitchen and announced "Grammy Janie is here! Where are my huggies?" and she held out her hands to everyone and all the kids except for Jim's daughters ran up to her for a hug. Grace and the boys still stood in the doorway and watched as Hank drove off. Jim walked up behind her and placed his hands on her shoulders, allowing her to lean back against him. The boys just stood there hugging their mom, not saying anything, no tears, no sounds. Ken walked over to the four of them and shook Jim's hand causing Jim to wince when he did. Ken looked at Jim's knuckles.

"What happened here?"

"Hank's nose ran into my fist." The boys laughed at that one.

"That's a shame, it was such a pretty nose. How many times did it run into your fist?"

"Just the once." Jim smiled at Ken and the older man patted him on the back for a job well done.

"Shame it was just the once. You may want to ice that, one-punch." Ken then turned to his grandsons. "Now I came down to go on the beach and the boards. So let's go, I need sand in my toes!"

Grace smiled and hugged her dad as he took them back to the kitchen. Turning around, she took Jim's hand into hers and looked at it and placed a kiss on his bruised knuckles.

"You didn't have to do that you know."

Grazing her lips against the slight bruise that was starting, she kissed him again.

"I know, but I couldn't help it. Either I did it or Denise was going to."

She looked back into the kitchen and saw Denise retelling the story as Janie had started to mop the floor with her Wet Jet. Kevin's facial expressions and the pride on Katie's and Vivian's faces as they heard the story was priceless. Katie looked over to her dad and Grace and a single tear rolled down her cheek and Janie went over to give her a hug. Grace's own eyes glazed over as she could feel the tears welling up in her water line as she looked up at Jim. Lifting her chin, he bent down to place a soft kiss on her lips. He had promised her kisses and now that Hank had declared he wanted a divorce, she didn't care who saw or who knew anymore. All she wanted was Jim.

𝄢

Grace had been correct; a Sunday was the perfect night to bring the kids to the boardwalk. There were no big crowds, and it was mostly families. Grace's parents had bought all the kids game cards at the arcade and all the ride tickets despite many protests.

It had been very warm during the day but with nightfall and the sea breeze they had needed sweatshirts, and Jim was thankful that he had told the girls to bring them. Everyone had truly made them feel welcome and he was thankful that the earlier events of yesterday evening and this morning had not put a damper on their time. Both girls had started to make friends, which was what he had been hoping. Vivian had taken to calling Janie "Grammy Janie" and Ken "Pops." Katie was a different story; she was a little more formal, still calling them Mr. and Mrs. Cartino.

"So, I heard you got to try some wine."

"Your sister got to enjoy some wine."

"Oh nice, did it produce the results I had told you about?"

Kevin and Jim were walking ahead of the group so as to keep their conversation a bit more private.

"No." Jim pouted; Kevin huffed and hit Jim's shoulder.

"Boo, that makes me sad."

"I gotta know, what is the deal with all of you trying to get Grace laid?"

Jim looked at Grace in the distance, who had been talking and laughing with the girls. She seemed to have such easy conversations with them, as if they had known each other for years.

"Um, because she needs sex, she has been operating on autopilot for years now."

Kevin and Jim hadn't noticed that someone was close by until a male teenager cleared his throat causing both of them to turn to see Calvin standing there.

"Uncle Kev, can you not discuss my mom's sex life, it's gross."

The adults looked like deer in headlights. Cal just walked away shaking his head. Janie had spied the interaction and gave both men a questioning glare as she made her way over and into the conversation.

"What was that about?"

"Cal overhead me say that Gracie needs to have sex."

"For the love of God, Kevin, after all that happened earlier, you bring up Autopilot Grace?"

"Oh my god, can we not discuss this at all?"

Jim couldn't believe what he was hearing; turning away from these two he decided to find Grace. It wasn't hard, he merely followed the sound of her laugh as she and the girls watched Nikki completely embarrass her kids by dancing right there on the boardwalk.

Taking in his surroundings, he felt a wave of joy and nostalgia rush through him. The bright lights of the game booths, the smell of pizza, cotton candy, and fried Oreos, the sounds of the bells, popping balloons, music - but it was the laughter that hit his heart. He looked around some more, watching his group of friends and their kids all laughing and having a great time. Something deep in his throat was causing a small choking feeling as he realized that this was all he had ever wanted.

And he then realized that all those years ago he knew she needed a man who would need to have his shit together, who would treat her the way she deserved, to take care of her and not want to waste a second without her. A fall for Grace. He had fallen and he never wanted to get back up.

Bending down to pick up his dirty clothes from the day before off the floor of Kevin's room, he looked towards the door, hearing the laughter coming from her room.

"Ah snuggle time. It's a ritual. She spends five minutes making them laugh and getting all their energy out and then a quick meditation to get Col to relax."

Kevin smiled at the notion of how long she had been doing this. Jim heard mumbles and then roars of laughter. She was a great mom, and the boys couldn't have gotten a better one. He thought of his own girls. Elizabeth had never really been very maternal; he had had to step in and not just be their dad but their mom at times. It was something he didn't mind, but there was a nagging feeling that just bothered him about the whole situation with Elizabeth and how she treated the girls. But then it came to him that Grace's boys were in the same position. Their father was no better. Hank and Elizabeth deserved each other.

"You okay there, pal?"

Kevin looked at Jim and noticed a tear running down his cheek. Kevin grabbed a tissue and handed it to Jim.

"Yeah, wow, I don't know where that came from, sorry," Jim said as he wiped his face and cleared his throat. Kevin walked over to Jim and held his arms.

"Trauma sucks, but you know, you and Grace are gonna get through this, right? You are gonna be fine and she is gonna be too. She is tiny but mighty." Squeezing Jim's arms and then giving him a hug, he said "God, you are cut like a statue, aren't you?"

He grasped Jim's biceps and Jim batted him away, grabbing his bag as he headed to see if the girls were in their bunks. As he passed Janie and Ken's room, he heard Ken call his name and decided to poke his face in the doorway.

"Jim, we hope you and the girls had a nice time tonight."

Ken looked over his glasses as he was sitting in bed reading a book and Jim noticed it had his name on the cover. He found it weird that Ken would be reading his own book.

"I believe it was the first time in a long time that they had that much fun. Thank you both, the girls and I really needed this."

Beaming, Jim noticed Janie place her book across her stomach, spotting that she was reading one of her own books. He was puzzled as he didn't think authors would take the time to read their own works, but maybe they enjoyed re-reading it to get ideas for new projects.

"I don't want to interrupt your reading, enjoy the rest of your evening and again thank you both for a wonderful evening."

Jim exited the doorway making his way to the kids' room only to find it empty. Then something magically happened, an echo from his past came from Grace's room. Whirling around he knew exactly what it was, soft, almost angelic, no, not angelic, it was like a siren's call, and he was sure the whole world had stopped moving. Grace was singing and it sounded like the sweetest thing he had ever heard.

Standing in the doorway he looked down the hall to see Kevin, Janie, and Ken at their doors. Janie had tears streaming down her face and Kevin was softly walking towards Jim to not make a sound. Ken just embraced his wife and closed his eyes to listen.

As he stood next to Jim, Kevin whispered, "She hasn't sung in five years. I don't know what you have done, but don't stop."

Jim looked at Grace's bedroom doorway and closed his eyes, listening to her finish singing, doing his best not to cry. Ken turned Janie around to get her back into their room, and a thankful smile washed across his weathered face as he joined his wife.

Jim didn't know what to expect before he entered the room, until the sight of the kids lying with Grace on the bed left him astounded. Stroking Colin's hair as his head was in her lap, Vivian had snuggled right up to Grace resting her head on her shoulder and Katie right next to her as Cal was lying at Grace's feet. As Grace looked up at him, he felt another tear starting to run down his face. He wiped it away, and she smiled at him and his heart stopped. He wanted to take a picture of this moment because it was everything to him.

"I can't believe they fell asleep. We really tired them out today."

Walking over to the side of the bed, Jim bent down and kissed her. He wanted this very second to last forever. Resting his forehead on hers for a few seconds before he realized that the oldest two had not fully fallen asleep, he glimpsed over to Katie, who gave him a little wink knowing that she must have seen him kiss Grace. His heart leapt a little knowing his daughter was happy for him and she apparently approved of Grace.

"I think you guys should go to bed; it's been a busy day. Tomorrow, we do nothing!"

Both Calvin and Katie gave him a nod, reluctantly pulling themselves off the bed. Katie walked over to Jim giving him a hug goodnight and then surprised them both as she went and hugged Grace. Closing her eyes Grace leaned into the hug and then allowed Katie to pull away.

"Good night, Gracie."

She turned back to her dad. Jim couldn't help but hug her a little tighter; he knew exactly what she had just done, she had given them her blessing. It wasn't that two adults needed their children's blessing but considering how Katie had felt for the past few years about Liz, it warmed his heart to know she was okay with this.

Walking to the other side of the bed, he scooped up Vivian who had passed out for sure. Grace kept brushing Colin's hair until Jim came back and picked up Colin, bringing him into his bed.

Grace had changed for bed and waited for Jim before turning off her bedside light off.

"Hey roomie."

"Hey," she said with a smile.

"Are you as tired as I am?" Jim said as he changed into his lounge pants.

"Is there a word that means 'beyond exhausted'?" Grace was truly trying to think of anything, but words were lost to her at this point.

"Pooped."

"Zonked."

She had to have a thesaurus in her brain to think of that one. They both laughed as she pulled her blankets up. The moonlight illuminated the room, and she settled in. Curling up behind her, he pulled her warm soft tiny form towards him.

"Can I ask you a favor?"

"Sure," he replied, kissing the back of her neck, which made her sigh.

"Can we just sleep tonight? I know we have been leading up to something more but after everything today, can we just lay here?"

He pulled her closer and held her tightly. "I am able to restrain myself." The friction of their bodies being so close had Grace wiggling closer and her bottom brushed against his groin. "Ah, see, I held back, and you are being a temptress with your ass. Do we need pillows between us, or can you behave?" She had been giggling, her body just instinctively did what it really wanted, which was him.

"I'm sorry, I was just getting comfortable. I will behave." Grace sighed and closed her eyes.

Jim kissed the back of her head, knowing that her neck would cause her to grind against him again and that was not what they needed right now. "Alright, now say goodnight, Gracie."

"Goodnight, Gracie."

CHAPTER NINE

It had reached 92F and not a cloud in the sky; Grace sat in the beach chair trying to relax, but every second that ticked by just made her more uncomfortable. She needed to refocus, relax, and be patient, but knowing that it was just a matter of time until the storm hit had her on edge. Around her were her friends and family and although they would have her back, she still couldn't settle.

Grounding her feet into the sand, she watched as the tiny grains stuck to her toes and legs. Relishing in the cool breeze coming off the ocean, she tried to think of nothing but the sand, the sun, and the soft sounds of conversations and waves.

Nikki and her oldest sat next to her applying sunscreen to their fair Irish skin so they wouldn't get burned, while Janie and Denise were enjoying the shade of the beach umbrella, reading. Her dad had been a saint and was being buried in the sand by John and Colin, doing his best to avoid getting sand in his mouth because the boys kept throwing the sand up into the air. She was about to readjust her chair, hoping to find comfort in getting some Vitamin D when Amanda came running over.

"Miss Grace, where is Vivian? I was going to fly a kite with her today."

"Oh, sweetie, I'm sorry Mr. Jim wanted to spend the day with his girls alone, so he took them to Breakwater."

Grace felt bad because she knew all the kids would have wanted to go but it was important to Jim to have some fun with just his daughters and not this whole group of crazy people. Grace didn't want to admit it, but she found herself a bit jealous that Jim was taking time with his girls. This was just supposed to be a week with the boys. She was kicking herself in the ass for not speaking up before.

"Why can't we go to Breakwater? I want to go," Amanda demanded. Nikki looked at Grace and made a snarling sound to make known her displeasure.

"We have the whole week! You get to go every year, they have never been, so go fly your kite with Jodi," and she tapped Amanda's bottom to get her to go with Jodi. Nikki turned to Grace.

"Thanks! You know she is going to be a pain in the ass the whole week until we take her?" she said, placing a large hat over her head to cover her face. Grace rolled her eyes; she didn't need someone else's kids, making her feel guilty that they wanted to do something, and she had chosen to stay at the house.

"They are all going to be a pain until we do," Denise added, looking up from her book. Grace knew they weren't trying to annoy her, but she didn't care anymore.

"Then take them! I don't need to be babysat."

For someone normally so easy-going and calm, her annoyance caught Nikki and Denise off guard. But with everything going on that day she didn't want to hear about their kids or what they wanted. Her family was far more important right now and if they hadn't been there, she would be able to relax a whole lot more.

She had been checking her phone to see if the paperwork had been filed or if Hank's attorney had reached out to him yet, but there was nothing. Nikki and Denise looked over to Janie who just shook her head at them to not say anything.

"Grace, that is a great idea. Sweeties, why don't you take the kids? Mr. C and I are not big fans of the water park anyway, so you guys all go and enjoy yourselves!" Janie looked at Nikki to take the hint, and before she could open her mouth to say something Denise got up.

"That sounds perfect, right, Nik? Just text us if you need anything, okay? Come on crew, let's go, we are gonna head out." Denise looked at Nikki, motioning for her to get up.

"Fine, just let us know if you need us."

Grace nodded as their crew collected themselves and left. Looking over at her mom she merely mouthed the words *"Thank you"*, and Janie's knowing wink let her know she had her back. She had a lot of emotions going through her at this moment and watching the waves crash in called to her. Getting up from her chair she walked over to Calvin and sat down next to him. The waves softly lapping at her toes, she could feel that the water was a little warmer than yesterday. Bumping his shoulder, he turned to look at her.

"Hey, you gonna sit here all day? You want to go in the water with me?" She could see that there was a sand bar they could walk on not far due to the tide being out farther at this time of the day. He just shrugged his shoulders.

"Is it wrong that I don't even want to be on the beach right now? Do you mind if I go back? Uncle Kevin is back at the house."

She could see that he was not himself. Grace didn't want her kid to be unhappy and forcing him to do something he didn't want was not the kind of parent she was.

"It's not wrong. I actually have to make a call so I'm heading back up to the house, you want to talk about it before we do?"

Calvin just shook his head no; he wasn't ready yet and she could tell.

"Well, when you DO want to talk, I'm here, okay? Or if you want to talk to a counselor, we can find you one if you want." All Calvin did was bob his head in agreement this time, but still no words came out. She didn't want him holding in his feelings or think that it was okay to keep them bottled up. Helping her son up off the sand, the two made their way to the top of the dune and could see Kevin sitting on the deck with his laptop. Stopping for a brief moment, Calvin turned to her and she could see his mind working, so she gave him time to formulate his feelings.

"Do you really think we are gonna be okay?"

"Hopefully; maybe not right this second, but eventually, yes." Grace lifted her son's face so that she could look into his eyes. "I know I have kept a lot from you boys, but I did it to protect you. Maybe it was wrong, but I didn't want you boys to get hurt. You should know by now that I will always protect the ones I love the most, even if I have to throw myself in front of a car to protect them, I will always put the ones I love first."

Hugging her son, she went inside to check her phone. Grabbing water from the refrigerator, she picked up her phone and saw several texts and missed calls. She looked at the missed calls and saw Dale Howard, Hank, and Chelsea at the publisher's office. She figured work was the first call, at least it wouldn't be bad news. Walking into the office, she sat at the desk and opened her laptop. Chelsea was an easy call, just confirming tour dates, locations, and that all travel arrangements had been made. This was a no pressure conversation and work took her mind off the heavy stuff.

Next was Dale. As she called him on speaker, she pulled up her texts. Several angry rambling texts from Hank about how she was a coward, a shrew, and a hateful frigid bitch.

"Hey kiddo, how you are holding up? I heard it was eventful day yesterday." He laughed.

"You could say that. Just out of curiosity, has he officially been served?"

"About an hour ago. Dad asked me to have him served at his office, According to the process server, he was in the middle of a meeting."

"Ah, well, that explains these texts."

"All pleasantries I'm assuming. Send those to me will you. Other than these lovely texts, any other communication?" he needed to know.

She checked her phone log and voicemails; it seemed Hank had been busy. "I've got three voicemails from him. I haven't checked them or called him back." Dale would know how to proceed.

"Alright kiddo, let me do my job, you will not communicate with him unless it is about the boys, understand? Send me those messages and I will take care of them; and do yourself a favor, don't listen or read them, it will only get you upset. I'll speak with his attorney about this communication issue he has decided to start."

Checking the time on her laptop, she realized it was just before lunch. He had done all this before noon; she should have been impressed. It felt like it was going rather quickly but having Dale in their lives for so many years she knew that he most likely had called in a bunch of favors to expedite this whole process.

A sense of regret fell over her for a second. There was a part of her that would have loved to see his face. The cameras at the house would have captured it in color. Suddenly it dawned on her - the cameras in the house, she hadn't even thought of checking them the entire time she had been down.

"Should I check the cameras in the house to make sure he hasn't destroyed anything?" Grace was remembering the rage in Hank's eyes before he left and suddenly was afraid to look. "I can check it from my app on my phone."

"It might be best to have your dad check but have the video sent to me, have Kevin help. I love your dad, but, man, is he technology-stupid." He wasn't wrong, she thought to herself.

"Okay, well, he is being buried in the sand right now, so I will have him look at it once Colin digs him back out."

"Sounds good kiddo, I'll keep you posted."

Grace prayed that the mediation they would go through would be amicable, and considering how the negotiation of the prenuptial agreement had gone so well, hopefully this would too. But Hank had been so furious it was almost a guarantee that he would try to pull some kind of stunt to fight her.

It was killing her to know that the texts and voicemails were right at her fingertips and Dale had told her not to touch them. She knew he was doing it for her benefit, but it made it no better to know it was just there. Staring at her phone, she heard Kevin knock on the door before walking in.

"So, what did Dale say?"

"He's been served, which explains these texts and voicemails. Dale said not to engage unless it is about the boys, and I've got to send him what Hank sent. Dale doesn't even want me reading or listening to them," she rolled her eyes, knowing that the suspense was killing her.

"Alright, so give me the phone and I will send them."

Kevin bent over and grabbed the phone out of her hand. He knew her far too well; her tiny fingers were always so quick typing that he was sure she was just another second away from looking. He opened the texts first and he tried to make his face unreactive to what he was reading. The texts were vicious; it was best that she didn't read them. He then sent them to Dale and deleted them, then turned to her.

"He wants the voicemails too."

Sitting there feeling helpless was not her strong suit as he made a few clicks on her phone and then handed it back to her. Kevin had deleted the texts from Hank and the one that he had sent Dale so she didn't see them. She had to trust Dale. Grace only hoped that the calls would stop once his attorney got wind of his actions.

Resting her head on the desk, Grace tried to enjoy the coolness of the wood against her aching head. Kevin came over and started massaging her neck and back, causing her to groan.

"Lord, woman, you are a rock. Now that this is done, why don't you go sit in the jacuzzi and then I want you back on that beach, got me!" Releasing his grip on her shoulders, he tapped the top of her head, and she looked up at him. Her brother was the best.

That afternoon she spent probably far too much time in the jacuzzi, but she had really needed it. She was starting to feel a bit better as the sun and sand recharged her. Kevin and her dad had been checking her phone on a constant basis so that she didn't have to. But by 3:30 the whole gang was back in time for discussions about dinner.

Calvin had joined them on the beach and was in a much better mood, now that Katie had come back. Not sure exactly what was going on there, Grace was just grateful that he was not internalizing things. She had watched them go off on a walk and they had spent a good half hour chatting.

Listening to the group drone on endlessly about the water park and how much fun they had and were already planning on going back later that week, Grace was truly grateful for the quiet she had experienced earlier. She felt like a rubber band that was wound so tightly that she wasn't sure if the tension was going to cause her to snap in half or if she would just spin out of control.

Needing to escape the incessant talking, Grace made her way down to the water, to feel the roll of the waves to relax her. The water had been extremely clear for NJ waters, and she hadn't seen any jellyfish on the beach or in the waters so she knew it would be safe as long as she didn't swim out too far.

It was cool at first but amazingly refreshing. Wading through the cresting tides, she found a sand bar and stood there surrounded by the water. The surf was not rough, which was perfect, and she found a spot where she could just sit and enjoy the water. It felt like home. She heard nothing but the sound of wind and crashing waves behind her. Her own little world, away from the nonsense, the stress and chaos, just her and the ocean.

9:

"How long will she stay out there you think?" Jim turned to Mike who was admiring his wife's cleavage in her bathing suit.

"Hm?" Mike pulled his view from his wife and turned to Jim, who had opted to sit under another beach umbrella. "Grace? Oh, if you let her, she would probably just sit there all year depending on the tides. It is very peaceful out there though, so probably until she becomes a prune."

"I would leave her be for a while. Barring a shark attack, but even then, she would probably kick its ass considering how tense she was earlier." Kevin added and he wasn't wrong, - a shark versus Grace, Jim would take Grace any day. Jim knew today was when they were filing the paperwork, so he didn't want to bring it up.

"What happened earlier?" Jim asked because he wanted to know just how much room he needed to give her or if she needed him.

"The short of it, Grace snapped. I was surprised it took this long. I've been waiting for years, Nikki got all butt-hurt over it, but Denise and I got her to chill out once we got to the water park. I'm surprised we didn't run into each other."

Pressure was never good for Grace and when she felt it, she either cracked or shut down. But using her voice instead of internalizing it was good, and he was rather impressed that she had set a boundary. Since he had not been around in years, it seemed that she was not really one who did that, but maybe this new Grace would.

A buzzing noise from his bag indicated that he had a message on his phone; reaching in, he pulled it out and saw it was Elizabeth. This was not the person he wanted to speak to, but he knew that it was possible that she was calling to check on the girls, but it was also possible that Hank had told her where he was and with whom.

Kevin glanced over and saw the caller ID and gave Jim a look of concern. Jim shut the ringer off and put it back in his bag. Kevin and Mike exchanged quizzical glances and then turned to Jim who had taken his sunglasses off and gotten up from his chair.

"Peaceful you said, right?"

Looking over his shoulder at Mike, his friend just nodded in confirmation. Making his way through the surf he found Grace sitting on the sandbar. The tide had gotten a little higher and the water had risen from when she had initially gone out there. The warm smile and relieved look she gave him let him know she was happy to see him. Even in the late day sun she looked as gorgeous as she did in the moonlight. Finding a spot next to her, he sat in the water wincing at the cold.

"Planning on joining a school of fish or walking on land soon? You could do both I suppose."

"If I didn't have the boys I would say the fish, but as they are not mermaids like their mother, I will opt to grace the land with my presence."

Grace dipped her head back to wet her hair and Jim was blessed with a beautiful view of her ample cleavage. His eyes drifted over her breasts which had been sprayed repeatedly by the tides as they glistened with tiny droplets of sea water that seemed to sparkle as the sun hit them. Hungrily, he looked up to her throat and took every pain not to lunge across and kiss her right there in front of everyone. He needed to control himself, everyone was currently on the shore, and he didn't need to come out of the water hard with desire. Closing his eyes and dipping backwards into the water, he needed the coolness to wash over him and calm his nerves and so he submerged himself with the next wave, allowing it to rush over him. When he came up, he wiped his face and saw Grace standing up next to him.

"I'm gonna head back, but you are welcome to stay, just not too long because the tide is coming in and this sandbar won't be here much longer."

Turning to the shore, she body surfed her way back and made it look effortless. He was just in awe of her, but then he remembered why he went out there. He still had to deal with Elizabeth and that was a conversation he didn't want to have. He was afraid that she would find out about what he had done and said to Hank.

𝄢

"How do you want your steak? I usually only cook them medium rare."

Grace stood over the grill as she was turning over the marinated chicken making room to cook the ribeye steaks. She loved grilling, the marinated chicken had been soaking in her chimichurri marinade for a few hours and smelled amazing. Food was love to her and she always cooked with her heart. She had looked at Jim, who still hadn't answered as he seemed distracted.

"Or perhaps I'll just make them into hockey pucks and grill them well done?"

Grace looked in his direction again and she noticed that he was staring off into the distance and just kept turning his phone over and over in his hand. Something had happened, she didn't know what, but she had a feeling it had to do with Elizabeth.

"Well done? What is wrong with you? Are you trying to kill us?"

Janie had walked out to bring the ribeye steaks to her to throw onto the grill. Grace motioned to Jim and Janie made the connection. Her mother decided to play along.

"Oh, you know the best way to eat a well-done steak is to smother it with ketchup, right, Jim?"

Janie bumped Jim on the shoulder, and it shook him out of his trance. Blinking up at her, Janie could see the forlorn look in his eyes and gave him a little squeeze.

"I'm sorry, I was somewhere else. But a well-done ribeye is a crime against nature and smothering it with ketchup just gets you right into Hell." Janie and Grace just giggled.

"Just checking to see if you were listening. You disappeared somewhere; you want to talk about it?" Grace already knew the answer was no, but she wanted him to know that she was still there to listen. Denise walked out of the house with a large empty platter for the chicken.

"The herd of cats inside are apparently all dying horrible deaths from starvation and are threatening to call child protective services. Is the chicken ready? I can take them in and get the ingrates started at least." Grace took the platter and loaded it up. Stopping next to Jim, Denise turned and said, "Come on you, I need help herding cats." Jim smiled at her and left his phone on the table, walking into the house.

Janie walked over to the grill and rubbed her daughter's back. Sighing and closing the lid to allow the heat of the grill to come up to temp for the steaks, they stood there in comfortable silence and looked around the deck.

"You are going to be okay." Janie was not just speaking of her daughter. She was talking about many more people than just Grace.

"I know, why does everyone need to tell me that? The boys are gonna get through this once Hank pulls his head out of his ass and we can have a civil conversation about co-parenting." She had been avoiding her phone as much as possible.

"I know, sweetheart. I think people are saying it to just reassure you."

Grace had craned her neck to look inside and watched as Jim helped Vivian make a plate of food and all the kids were making their way into the dining room since there were so many of them.

She was starving but something was gnawing in her gut causing her to be nauseous. As if on cue, Jim's phone started to buzz and Janie looked down to see it showing the name Elizabeth. The look in her eyes told Grace exactly who was calling. They didn't know what to do, but fortunately Jim had heard the buzzing and this time he answered it as he walked towards the dunes. It was clear he would need some distance.

Grace went back to cooking, checking every so often as he talked, unable to hear the conversation. However, by the way he was running his fingers through his hair and waving his arms it was clear this was not a pleasant call to see how the girls were enjoying the shore. Because he had his back turned, she couldn't tell if he was talking or not and then he turned and just held the phone away from his ear and he rolled his eyes.

Grace really needed to mind her own business and cook the steaks before she did over cook them. Focusing her attention on the grill, she finished up and then turned off the heat, placing the steaks on a clean platter, and walked into the house. She knew the steaks needed to rest, and she took two and put them on two separate plates, placing them aside.

Turning to the other adults in the room, she let them know to start without her as she made her way to the deck again. Did she dare to walk closer? Her heart was pounding as she could see him getting angrier, and then he yelled.

"Well, now the two of you can go live your happily ever after then. Congratulations, Elizabeth, on ruining not just one marriage but two! I hope you have a wonderful life together!"

With those final words he hung up the phone. The rage that was running through him was so intense he let out a guttural yell and threw his phone into the sand dune. When he turned around Grace was mere feet from him and her closeness must have taken him by surprise. Her dusky-colored hair blowing in the wind framed one side of her face as her chestnut eyes stared up into his pain-streaked face.

Grace stood there feeling utterly helpless, his words ringing in her ears. The intensity and fiery tone had taken her aback; it had all been so brave. It was incredible. She wasn't sure if he spoke to Elizabeth like that in the past, but this seemed charged, it was as if it was something he had been holding in for years. It was closure. She envied him and was not sure that she would ever be so brave.

Grace would avoid confrontation, which was why she hadn't divorced Hank years ago. She inched closer and just stared into his stormy eyes, no malice, just pain. Storms out on the ocean were gorgeous to watch, the electricity of the lightning and the water funnels that would rile up during the height of the chaos, it was exquisite to behold. So were Jim's eyes. He moved closer, bent down, and embraced her. Grace listened to his breaths that had been ragged from him yelling finally starting to slow down, so she squeezed him to let him know he was okay.

Jim pulled Grace closer to him, her body melding into him and the scent of him made her weak. He pulled away for a second and looked into her eyes and she saw sadness.

"I think I screwed everything up for you."

"You? You have no blame here. I should have left him years ago." But he shook his head no.

"No, Grace, they think we have been having an affair for years." Grace knit her brow. It was preposterous.

"Was she drunk or high when she said this?" The sarcasm in her question had finally caused a tiny laugh to escape his lips. "Jim, we know that isn't true. Everyone else knows that isn't true!" Placing a hand on his face so that she could look into his eyes, she said "You and I know the truth and that is all that matters. So, let's just go and eat something. If we stay out here much longer everyone will start to worry."

Grace went over and retrieved his phone from the dune and then placed it in his hand. She smiled at the thought that Liz and Hank thought that they had been having an affair considering how long they had been carrying on. She found it even more laughable that Hank and Liz thought that she would have stayed with Hank when she could have been loved without question by Jim.

The stars shone brighter in the night sky and Grace wasn't sure if it was the shore, the company, or that she was taking her life back that made her feel that way as she nestled deeper into Jim's chest, the two of them lying there on the lounger on her bedroom deck. After the phone call, Grace had felt Jim's whole demeanor change. For some reason he felt guilty when there was nothing there for him to be guilty of and Grace just couldn't seem to wrap her head around it. Why would he feel guilty? Because he punched Hank, because he exposed him right in front of everyone? It all made no sense, but she didn't want to think about it.

What she honestly couldn't believe was what had happened in such a short time. But when she thought about it, she had felt like her life had been on hold for so long, stagnant and unmoving, and now everything she had ever wanted was finally happening faster than she could take a breath.

She sat there holding her wine glass and staring up at the stars without drinking.

"You just enjoying the smell of the wine or are you going to drink it?" A slight smile crossed his lips, and he kissed the top of her head. Taking a sip of the wine and a light inhale of her cigarette, she then looked up at him.

"Is it wrong I don't want to do anything again?"

"Did you do anything today besides sit on the beach?" Jim didn't know what she had done while he and the girls spent time at the water park.

"Yes, I worked, I talked to Dale, ignored Hank, sat in the ocean, cooked, made sure you and the kids were okay, got Kevin and Colin their ice cream. Averted disaster. All the normal daily stuff. But what I mean is really do nothing, nothing that requires me to wait on someone or entertain or worry about someone else's feelings before my own." He shifted her so he could look at her. Grace wasn't sure what he was thinking. "I'm sorry, I don't mean that, I don't care, it's just..." she stopped herself from maybe saying something wrong.

"Gracie, I understand, and you don't have to wait on us or entertain us. The problem is that you care about everyone before yourself." Grace looked at him and motioned in agreement. "So, stop. You know what, don't worry about tomorrow. You want to go swimming, then go swimming, you want to go and get a pedicure down here all by yourself, then go, you want to take a nap on the couch, then do it." Jim just smiled at her and kissed her forehead.

"But what about everyone else?"

"What about everyone else? They are big kids; they can take care of themselves and their children."

"Yeah, but what about Cal and Colin?"

"I'm pretty sure I can handle two more kids."

Grace didn't believe this whole conversation was taking place. She thought back to the twenty years that she was with Hank and never once had he ever offered to give her some time alone.

"Are you sure?"

Jim took the cigarette out of her hand, took a drag and then crushed it out before removing her glass, placing it next to his beer on the table next to them. Gathering her up in his arms, she snuggled across his lap, laying her head on his chest.

"Grace, I'm so sorry" he whispered, his hands running over her body, and she felt her body relaxing releasing muscles she hadn't even noticed she had been tensing. "I'm sorry that it wasn't me. I'm sorry I had been a coward."

Grace understood what he was saying. She didn't want words, the sadness and regret in his eyes told her all she needed to know. Moving their heads closer together, their foreheads meeting each other and the warmth of their breath mingling together was making her insides flutter knowing that his delicious lips were about to be on hers.

And then the moment was gone, the echo of banging coming from the front door could be heard all the way up and outside on her balcony. Scrambling off his lap, she checked her phone to see if perhaps something had happened with Denise and Nikki, but there had been no texting, except one from Hank.

She wasn't supposed to read them. There was more banging, and then she heard commotion in the hallway. Following her out of the room, Jim went to see what was going on. Janie and Ken, who had retired for the night, were suddenly coming out of their room as Grace pulled on her robe as she passed them in the hallway,

"Stay with the kids. And if we need to, prepare to call Dale."

Dashing down the hallway, Jim bolted down the stairs with Kevin on his heels to find out what was going on. She had gotten to the top of the stairs and looked back to see Janie standing next to a half-asleep Katie and Calvin.

The sound of the front door chime going off let her know that whoever was outside was now in the house. The resonating sound of a male voice berating Jim and Kevin and then the thud of a fist hitting someone's body immediate shot a chill through her body. It was Hank and he wasn't here to be nice. Before descending the stairs, she screamed out to her father "Dale! Now!"

By the time she got to the bottom of the stairs, Jim and Hank were already in the throes of a fight. Kevin was holding back a drunken alcohol-laced Elizabeth from trying to jump on top of Jim as Hank had got the advantage and was on top of Jim throwing punches. Propelling herself forward, Grace tried to peel Hank off Jim, but just as he took another punch his elbow collided with Grace's cheek, and she fell back. It felt like her eye had exploded and it had thrown her off guard, but she had had enough.

Elizabeth's slurred screams and the waft of vodka coming from Hank gave the indication that neither one of them was of their right mind. Grace got back up and ran over to Hank again, this time putting him in a choke hold to knock him out. It was a move she had learned in a self-defense class that Denise had forced her to go to and amazingly it seemed to be working.

The object was not to kill, just knock your opponent out. His fists weren't even connecting anymore, allowing Jim to wiggle out from underneath him as Hank became more still. Grace remembered the amount of pressure and as much as she wanted to increase it, she didn't. It took a few seconds, and she was able to lay him down on the ground. She checked his heart rate and breathing and knew he was just unconscious.

Elizabeth was still carrying on, trying to wriggle free from Kevin's grip but that didn't seem to be happening. Grace snapped her attention to this once-stunning woman, the person who had stolen Jim away and then Hank, drunk and instigating a fight.

Every fiber in Grace's body burned and all she wanted to do was tear this woman to shreds. What was her problem with her? Why did it seem like this person was out to destroy Grace's life?

Grace's nerves of steel and rationale kicked into high gear. Despite wanting to pummel this woman into the ground, she took the high road. Saying nothing, she went into the kitchen, returning with a clean cloth in one hand and extra-large tie wraps in the other.

Still silent, which Kevin knew was more deadly than anyone could realize, Grace grabbed two folding chairs from the dining room closet and put them in the front foyer. Ken made his way down the stairs and looked at the scene.

"Oh my god. Is he dead?"

"Grace knocked him out." Jim smirked holding the clean cloth Grace had handed to him for the cut above his eye.

Grace continued her hardline stare at Elizabeth. The look of disdain and disgust on Grace's face was so intense that her eyes could have melted steel.

"Sit down," Grace hissed. "NOW."

It came out as a low growl. Kevin moved Elizabeth into the chair and Grace went over and took each hand and securing them separately to the sides of one folding chair; she did the same to her legs. She did this so that if Elizabeth attempted to get up, she would instantly fall over.

Once she was secured, Jim and Kevin hoisted Hank up and did the same to him in the other folding chair. Grace's eye and cheek were killing her, she was sure that Hank had given her a black eye because of the throbbing. She was fortunate that her glasses had not broken. She touched her cheek and based on the blood on her hand, her glasses must have cut her when Hank hit her. Looking at her dad she said "Call the cops."

"So, you are gonna send us to jail, you are holding us against our will and you knocked him out." Elizabeth let out a hiccup. It always amazed Grace how stupid people are.

"Liz, you came here drunk, uninvited, harassing us and then assaulting us out of nowhere. What did you think was going to happen? I think jail is well deserved, in fact if I were you, I would start praying I don't consider taking your custody of the girls away from you."

Jim's voice was low, calm and menacing, causing Elizabeth's eyes to widen. Kevin had gone upstairs to check on his mom and the kids and brought down a first aid kit. Grace was still incredibly quiet, her scowling gaze never wavering.

"Of course you will." Liz turned and looked back at Grace. "So that's it, huh? I steal your boyfriend and your husband, so you are gonna take my kids away. Always winning, aren't you? But look at you, you are nothing, you have no talent, you are nothing but a thief."

Stalking her like a cat with a mouse, Grace stared down into her eyes; her facial expression never changed. Cocking her head to the side, Grace said, "Winning? Not sure that is the word I would choose."

The red and blue lights of the cop cars pulling up outside let her know that they were all now safe.

"Oh, come on Grace, you always win, don't you? Always thinking you are better than everyone else? Like some queen. It's why when I met Hank it was even more delicious that he was yours too. Because if I could steal one once, I could steal the other."

There may have been tears falling from Elizabeth's eyes but there was a level of lunacy in them that was haunting. Lowering herself to get nose to nose with the woman restrained in the chair, Grace ever so gently whispered to her:

"You know what, you have one thing right, about being a queen. The fact is I am a queen, I've always been, but you - you've always been the spare, just the runner-up, enjoying my sloppy seconds."

The wicked smile that spread across her face made her whole body feel a heat she had never felt before. That last mention of being a runner-up caused Elizabeth to scream at the top of her lungs and charge forward in her chair towards Grace. Calmly Grace stood up and looked down at the mess of a human in front of her. There was no remorse or pity for this creature, she needed mental help, Grace thought, and lots of it.

The cops had been speaking with Ken on the porch and were taking his statement. EMS came in and checked on Hank, who was starting to wake from his stupor, and another was checking Jim. Grace made her way out to the porch and sat on the top step just trying to breathe when Kevin came over and handed her a cigarette.

"I grabbed them from upstairs. I thought you might need one. I also thought you might need something else."

She looked up and saw Nikki and Denise running up the pathway, both with tears in their eyes and relief spread across their faces as they ran up the stairs and practically tackled her to the ground. Another officer had pulled up and walked up to Grace.

"Mrs. Nereid?"

She hated that last name, but it translated to another word for siren or mermaid, so she liked it for only that reason, but she wanted to be called Cartino again. She nodded her head yes.

"We need to take your statement, ma'am, and have EMS check you out as well."

Nikki and Denise just sat there rubbing her back, which with all the chaos was now making her feel sick. Her stomach churned again and this time, she ran past the cop and luckily found the garbage can to empty her guts. Denise ran over with a bottle of water in hand, and she swished the water in her mouth and spit it out. Amazingly, she felt a lot better.

"Ma'am, have you been drinking?"

Grace just started laughing. "I had two sips of wine, I just don't do well with stress. I also got knocked back in the fight."

This was not how this was not supposed to go; she had expected him to be annoyed or angry but not idiotic or irresponsible. Nikki had gone inside to grab another bottle of water and gave Grace the heads up the cops were bringing out Elizabeth. This woman could have had anyone, could have found happiness, but she had chosen a life of loathing and hate for her. But for the life of Grace, she couldn't remember ever meeting this woman before tonight.

Ken and Jim walked out onto the porch as they all watched as Elizabeth was put in a police vehicle and taken away. Two officers then brought out Hank who was mumbling and slurring curses towards Jim. Grace felt incredibly bad for the officers as Hank was really giving them a hard time getting into the car.

As the adrenaline started wearing off she felt like she needed to pass out. Trudging over to one of the porch chairs, her whole body seemed to crumple into it and all she could do was close her eyes.

The sound of gasps from Katie and Calvin stirred her to open them, as they stood in the door frame with complete and utter shock on their faces at the sight of their parents. Running to their respective parents, embracing them, she knew that the tears streaming down their cheeks were of relief.

After the tears came hugs and the kids swapped to the other's parent, making sure they were okay and saying how grateful they were for what they had done.

"Your mom is the real hero, she put a sleeper hold on your dad to get him for almost knocking me out. I would look much worse if it wasn't for her." Calvin turned to his mom and laughed.

"I keep telling you, she is a badass, why is no one listening to me?"

Grace didn't feel like a badass, she felt like a beat-up piece of wood and all she wanted to do was sleep. Gently hugging Katie again, she was sure that Katie would let go, but she didn't, she hugged her harder, only making more tears emerge in her eyes.

"Okay, well this badass is beyond exhausted, I would like to sleep. And you two are supposed to be in bed anyway." Turning to Nikki and Denise, she said "Thanks for coming. We'll see you in the morning."

Completely understanding, Nikki and Denise gave her another hug, thankful for the fact that she was safe. Sighing, Janie helped Grace get up the stairs and into her room. Her mother hadn't tucked her in since she was a kid, but it was extremely comforting to know that she would always be there to help her.

Ten minutes later, as she had finally settled and was about to doze off, Jim carefully crawled in the bed and gingerly took her into his arms. She didn't have the energy to ask what had taken him so long to come to bed, all she did have the energy to do was kiss his bruised hand and fall asleep.

CHAPTER TEN

The sting and radiating pain in her cheek was not what had stirred her from her restless sleep. It had been the coffee. Opening her eyes she looked at her nightstand; sitting right next to her glasses was an oversized mug with steam escaping it, and two pills. Coffee and some pain pills were just what she needed.

The house sounded eerily quiet. Grabbing her phone and coffee, she made her way down the stairs to find no one in the house. It was as if everyone had vanished, and then she heard a rustling on the deck. Peering outside, Jim was sitting there at the table reading an actual newspaper and drinking coffee. Wincing as he placed the mug back down, the bruises on his hands and arms from the fight had darkened overnight.

"Hey, what are you doing up? I was hoping you were gonna get some more rest. You were rather restless last night."

He groaned as he turned in his chair so that he could angle himself to look at her as she took the seat next to him. Hank had indeed gotten some good punches in based on how he looked and moved. The two of them must have been a sight. Grace's beautiful pink skin had purpled under her eye and across her cheek, but she had been fortunate that it had not swelled. Despite all the cuts and bruises Jim had on his face, arms, and hands, Grace thought he still looked handsome.

"Well, someone left a cup of coffee on my nightstand. I will always get up for magical bean liquid." Smiling as she took another sip of her amazingly perfectly made cup of coffee, she said "Thanks for the ibuprofen. You should probably get on ice pack on that jaw though."

Running her hand across his stubble-covered swollen jaw, Jim slightly recoiled from her touch. Sighing, he put down the newspaper and held her hand.

"Your dad called Dale this morning. They both said we need to go down to the station and it's best that we file a restraining order against them as soon as possible."

Grace's mind raced causing her head to spin as she recalled that the events didn't just affect her, but Jim and his girls. He could see it in her eyes; reaching across with a groan and capturing both her hands, he continued.

"Okay, let me start with good news; my parents are coming down today. They are gonna hang with yours and the kids while we handle this. But Grace," he hesitated, "the not so good news is that Dale said this is going to complicate things, but I know you know that already. Your dad asked him if he had spoken with Hank's attorney, and he had. He sent him everything, all the texts, calls, voicemails, and the attorney said he would talk with Hank. So, either he didn't or Hank just ignored him."

Hank was losing his whipping girl, that was the only logic behind his behavior. Even though he had loudly announced he wanted the divorce, he still was acting like she had to obey him. Like she was supposed to not want this for herself. As if he was the only one who had rights in this marriage. And then she realized she had been married to a narcissistic sociopath who had emotionally and verbally abused her for years.

Tears pricked her eyes as she realized how she had failed. Her mind raced about how she had allowed it for years, she had taken the abuse, and all for what? For the boys? That wasn't it, she knew she should have left years ago. And then it hit her - it had been fear. It had been years of abuse demolishing her self-confidence and resolve. Some badass she was, she had been living in fear of another human.

The tears ran down her cheek, stinging the cut below her right eye. She should just take today hiding in her room and deal with all this tomorrow. But then he wins another day, he robs her of joy and happiness. This Grace wouldn't allow. She was not going to put this fight off any longer. She needed to take her life back and protect not just herself but her children, family, and friends. Grace didn't trust that Hank wouldn't go after her boys especially now that he didn't have her to berate, and it would be over her dead body that she would allow him to hurt them.

"What about you and Elizabeth, what are you going to do?"

"I called my attorney, he said he is gonna start the paperwork to petition for full custody. She'll fight it, but I can't have the girls around her if she is going to act this way. Dale and Andrew, my attorney, both said we need the police report from last night and then we have to go back home and file the restraining order up there. I told them I'd call them once we leave here."

So much for a day of doing nothing. She felt better knowing that the kids were with her parents and being occupied as well as his parents coming down for his girls. It was just a lot to take in all at once. Getting up, she grabbed what was left of her coffee and kissed him on the top of his head. She guessed she needed to get this awful day started.

𝄢

The landscape blurred past them as they headed back down the shore. It had been an incredibly long day, and he realized that neither of them had eaten a thing all day. They had met with Dale and Andrew and had pictures taken of their injuries that had resulted from the altercation and then waited for the petition for the restraining orders to be filed. The stress had made them both not just mentally exhausted but physically as well.

"Mom said to meet them at the Shrimp Box. I hope that is, okay?"

"Well, I was thinking about us ordering dinner in, but if you want lobster, I won't stop you!"

Jim kissed her hand while keeping an eye on the road. But if Grace was anything like himself, he didn't care what he ate, he only wanted one thing.

"I just want to be with the boys right now." The sadness in her voice choked him, because deep inside all he wanted was his girls. He wanted to hold them tight in his arms and never let them go. Knowing how Grace felt about her own children, she would hold them tighter tonight and that snuggle time would perhaps wind up being much longer. He was happy to sleep on the couch so that she could sleep in the same bed as her boys.

These two young men had fixed her broken heart; they were the truest loves of her life and the swelling in his heart warmed him to his core. Jim was pretty sure that Calvin and Colin knew just how lucky they were to have such an unbreakable love and bond with her. In his book, they were the luckiest two guys on the planet, and he wouldn't want it any other way.

"I understand, kinda don't want to be with anyone but the girls. Present company excluded."

That had gotten a giggle out of her as she wiped away the tears, wincing as she brushed her right cheek. Pulling into the parking lot of the restaurant, he saw their parents and kids waiting outside for them. Jim's body had stiffened up from the car ride and had him moving a little slower. As they made their way to the entrance, their families noticed them and ran up. The enthusiastic embrace caused him to yelp, startling both girls, who had not realized that he had been that injured.

Grace was embracing her boys, and both sets of parents were not far behind. Judi and Mark gave Grace a hug and then carefully embraced Jim, trying very hard not to cause him any more discomfort.

"I still think you should have gotten an X-ray," Judi said as she pulled up the sides of her son's shirt to look at the bruises. Jim was swatting away her hands so that the girls didn't see but it had been too late. Vivian and Katie saw the bruises and stood aghast at the sight. They had both been upset by the cut and bruise on his face, so he had made sure they hadn't seen his ribs; he didn't want them to know he was more seriously injured than that.

"I told him the same thing on the way back but he is refusing, saying that he is just bruised." Grace looked at his family with concern. "I'm so sorry, this was not your fight." Turning to the girls, "Ladies, I'm so sorry your dad got hurt." Both girls looked at her with such sadness and there was silence until Katie spoke up.

"This isn't your fault. We are just glad you and our dad are safe now." Katie left her dad's side and went over to hug Grace and then she shocked both him and Grace by kissing her cheek. Tears welled in Grace's eyes and Jim's heart swooned.

In such a short time, this tiny creature had become someone special to his girls. She had won their hearts; he saw it with every interaction, and he couldn't have been happier. Grace exchanged a caring glance at Jim, and he knew with unspoken words that she cared for them deeply.

Making their way into the restaurant they found they weren't alone; the rest of the crew were all inside waiting for them, allowing them time with their parents and kids before they descended on them.

After all that had occurred it was no wonder that their children insisted on sitting on either side of their parents so that they could spend all their time with them, and no one stopped them. Not wanting to rehash the entire day, they asked the kids what they had done all day. Jim's own parents helped by talking about all the fun things they had done that day. Apparently they had gone down to Seaside Heights to the boardwalk, go-karts, mini-golf, and then Amanda chimed in.

"We were told we couldn't go to Breakwater because *you* weren't there." the sassy blonde chided.

Grace tried suppressing her laugh at the sheer perturbed attitude of someone so tiny, but Jim couldn't hold in his own snicker. Mike had warned him about Mandy, that she was exactly like Nikki.

"Listen, sass pot, I appreciate your sacrifice. It means a lot. But we had some stuff to do, 'kay?"

"Because of that bag of dicks?" Amanda said with a straight face.

That got several responses, between laughs from the kids, a few adults spitting their water out, "Hey" and "Language" out the other adults' mouths. Something deep inside of him snapped and he just couldn't stop. The laugh started in his throat and then spread through his sore body. Jim looked across the table to Grace who had been biting her lip and then the flood of laughter started. He was sure that it was just delirium, but they needed this. The entire table had joined in and he was hoping they weren't disturbing anyone else's dinner but they all seemed to need this laugh.

Staring down the length of the table at the amazing people surrounding them, it hit him. This was what he had always wanted. This was the life he had craved for years and the love he had yearned for. But most of all the woman sitting across from him. It had taken him what felt like a lifetime to figure it out, but she was always his destiny.

𝄢

"How long does it take for a divorce to be finalized?"

Judi cocked her head and turned it to try and look at Vivian, who had asked, but sitting in the front of the car was making it a little difficult to look at her.

"Well, your dad's was done in a month but it was very amicable. Why do you ask?" Judi looked at Mark as he drove, and he gave her a sliding glance to keep his eyes on the road.

"I'm just trying to figure out when he is going to propose to Grace. Are things with Mom going to complicate things?"

"Wow. Okay. Well, there is just a lot going on with Grace, I'm not sure she or the boys would be ready for her to get into a serious relationship with your dad."

"Not that you would mind," Mark chimed in. "You and Janie were practically planning the damn wedding back when they were kids."

Judi smacked her husband and he just laughed. Devasted, she had been completely devastated when they had broken it off for good. Grace was supposed to be her daughter-in-law, she had known that before they even started dating, but then Elizabeth happened, and she had never forgiven her for ruining things.

"Gram, *everyone* can see how they feel about each other. Even Colin knows and he is six; he told me, "*I hope they get married because I always wanted sisters, and I think you and Vivian would be good ones.* "" Katie said.

Judi looked out the window trying to gather her thoughts. She didn't want to get their hopes up or mislead them in any way, but deep inside, it was what they all wished for both Grace and her son.

"Girls, I know how your dad feels and yes, it is very apparent that Grace cares very much for him, but we *all* must be patient, especially now with the events of yesterday. Your dad and Grace have a much harder battle to fight now. Hopefully they know that they have each other during the whole process."

The girls made a bit of a huffing noise to express their displeasure at the idea of waiting. Glancing at her husband for assistance was all he needed. Mark looked at the reflection of his granddaughters in the rear-view mirror and spoke up again.

"Girls, as your dad's dad, all I would ever want is someone to care for him as much as Grace has, but let's remember they haven't seen each other in over twenty-five years. Their relationship back in high school was complicated and unless they can work out previous issues and get through the current ones, I personally think *no one* should be forcing them into anything too finite. Let everyone, including yourselves, get settled back into a normal routine and see if it works then."

Mark was not one of many words, but when he did speak, the wisdom he imparted was great advice. Judi knew he didn't want to see their son hurt again, but now the girls were becoming invested. The rest of the car ride back to the shore house was somber and silent.

𝄢

Bristling past Kevin, the girls had not shown such dismay and annoyance before, and he looked back to see Judi and Mark walking slowly up the stairs.

"What was that about? I haven't seen that much female teenage angst in a million years. Did something happen?" Kevin was holding the door and patted Mark on the shoulder.

"I am a killer of their romantic dreams."

Kevin shook his head and furrowed his brows unsure how to respond. Then Judi leaned in to whisper to Kevin "He told them that Jim and Grace need to take it slow and not to rush them into marriage."

"Yeah well, that is solid advice, but this is a steam train with an unlimited amount of coal here, babe, so good luck with that. Let's just hope they don't derail this time. I've been a passenger on this runaway locomotive since '95, I can't deal with another derailment."

Judi gave Kevin a squeeze as they walked into the house, leaving Kevin on the porch. Speaking of the devils, Kevin turned and saw Jim pulling his car up the drive and getting out. Jim walked around the car, grabbing Grace's hand and kissing it as they headed up the stairs. It looked as if the two had been doing this their whole lives and it gave a small tug at Kevin's heart. Only wanting to see his sister happy, he knew that no one else in the entire world could make her feel so free and alive as Jim.

"You two are quite the topic of conversation today," whispered Kevin as he looked behind him to make sure no one else was listening. They could hear laughing from the house and he shut the door so he could let them know what was going on.

"Okay so what did we miss?" Jim knew Kevin well enough to know he couldn't keep secrets.

"Your kids apparently are shipping the two of you now. I mean, we all know the parentals have been on this crazy train, along with me, since day one, but now your kids have boarded at the station."

Kevin could see their faces turn from smiles to concerned glances between the two of them. They knew there was a bit of danger in all this. He stood there watching his sister's eyes darting around the porch and knew that Grace's mind was everywhere. She went to pull her hand from Jim's, but he only held it tighter, causing her to look at him. Kevin, knowing his sister too well, walked over, placing his hands on her arms and holding her in place.

"And maybe it;s my delulu, but I will always be Team Grimm. I just wanted you two to know that this team has four new players and breaking their hearts will be something that you may not be able to come back from if things go south." Bending down so he was staring right into her eyes, he added "So it might be time someone tells some truths before Team Grimm gets in too deep."

𝄢

The poor thing didn't have a clue, thought Grace as she watched the puzzled look spread across Jim's face. Kevin had been cryptic enough, but she knew what he was getting at. This was the one thing that she had kept from her husband, but worst of all this secret went back to when she and Jim dated in high school.

Kevin let go of her and walked into the house. Grace attempted to pull her hand away again but this time Jim didn't just hold her hand, he moved and stood in front of her, lifting her chin so she could look into his eyes.

"Gracie, don't pull away from me again. Please."

The heartache in his voice was killing her. Taking a big breath and formulating her next words, she decided to take a leap.

"You need to sit."

"Oh God, that bad?"

Jim was still not releasing her hand, but he realized he needed both hands to lower himself down into the chair due to the ache in his ribs. Wincing, he moved in the chair to get comfortable. Looking down at him in the chair, she kissed his forehead.

"I will be right back, hang on."

Grace ran into the house and Jim just sat there waiting for her to come back. It hadn't been very long but when she came back, she had two books tucked under one arm, a glass of water in one hand, and a pain pill in the other.

"First take the pill, I can't stand watching you wince every time you move."

Taking a huge breath, she took the two books and handed them to him as she sat down. Lighting her cigarette, she took a big inhale and blew it out as if it was helping her breathe. He turned the books over and saw she had given him the first books that her parents had written, and he looked at her unsure why he was holding these books.

"Your parents' books. Your secret is about your parents' books."

Slowly she leaned her head to the side avoiding his gaze.

"They aren't my parents' books. They are mine."

Taking another drag, she shifted her gaze down toward the ground, bracing for the yelling.

"Your books. These books have your parents' names on them, but they are your books. You wrote them?"

The fact that he wasn't freaking out and his tone stayed steady and calm was freaking her out. Slightly bobbing her head, she sat waiting on the expected rage, but nothing happened. The rage never came. Instead, there was silence. She turned her head and looked at him, searching his steely blue eyes.

"Every single one. I wrote them all."

She took another drag from her cigarette and let it out. He still said nothing, so she continued.

"Initially it was just so I could get published because no one would publish a teenager's book, so I asked Mom to get the first book published, then I wrote a horror one and asked Dad since they were two different genres. It worked, but then they did exceedingly well, and the publisher asked for more stories, so I wrote, and we just kept doing the same thing. I thought maybe one day I would use my own name but then I met Hank, and he made fun of the romance novels, which honestly are my favorite ones to write, and I thought it might be best to not tell him and just keep publishing under Mom's name."

The comment about Hank made him make a tsking sound, but she kept explaining.

"The two books in your hands are about us." He looked down and read the back of the book. Great loves who find each other through the storms of life and could work through everything no matter how hard things were. And there it was, their current reality. Here in the present, she was telling him that she had written their love story, what it felt like a million years ago. Her main character Caroline being scared and how she would run when it was all too much, but how she would finally find the courage to find her love. Even as her world was crumbling around her, she found the strength to fight.

She watched as he looked at the other book, it was a horror story, it had been her revenge story. Grace remembered the anger, depression, and pain she felt as she wrote and wondered if he had not read it and did now, would it change things.

"I have read this one. I didn't get it back then; well, I did but... I get it now." He held up Caroline's Lost and she smiled; it was her first book and the fact that he liked it made her heart leap. It had been her favorite. She had written it before they had started dating, when she was interested in him from a distance. It had been before their first kiss.

"But this one I haven't read yet. A horror?" He didn't sound upset just wasn't sure how it applied to them. She finished her cigarette and blew out the smoke a little longer than she needed to.

"Yeah, I wrote it when we were coming out of our relationship our senior year. So, it might be from a weird point of view. But if you read it, it might make sense why I would pull away from you. I had been dealing with bouts of depression, going to therapy, and writing was helping with it. I had gotten about halfway through the book before we got back together for the summer, and then after the breakup, well, the book sort of wrote itself. So, I'm apologizing now before you read it. In my defense, you had broken my heart, and I was really angry." It was a fair statement.

"So does my character die?"

"Painfully and grotesquely. Sorry not sorry, it's a horror, not a romance."

"Ouch. Does the hero or heroine wear the villain's skin like a trophy or something?" He laughed. She was feeling more and more relief as they talked.

"You will have to read it to find out." She gave him a snarky smile.

"So, you wrote all these books, so what does that mean, you're what, a millionaire or something?"

"Well, not because of the books, I mean they make really good money because we're with a publishing company who pushes them out, but it's complicated."

Grace watched as the realization hit him. She had been a published author using her parents' names with over thirty books published and a number of them being bestsellers. It was clear that he was trying to do the math.

"So let me get this straight, you are some kind of millionaire, but not just because of the books? Because of something else?" She titled her head before he continued.

"And your current husband has no idea?" She nodded. "So how does this work?"

"Well," she stopped and squinted again waiting for an outraged response. "The books are under Mom and Dad's name, so the money goes into their business account that I have access to so that I can use it. I'm essentially their ghostwriter. They go to all the conventions, book launches and stuff like that, so they do work. But I do most of it. Writing, promoting, travel arrangements, marketing, working with the literary agent and publishing company. Hank has no idea about the writing; after he made fun of the books when we started dating, I promised myself that I wouldn't tell him, and I never published anything under my own name. Which is why there is only a tiny group of people who know the truth, and the fact that I have been keeping it from my husband since the beginning is because I could never trust him."

There it all was, her truth was out there now. He sat there and took a sip of water, and she was wondering if he was wishing it had been something much stronger. She knew she wished she had a shot of something right now. It had been a lot to unload, but now he truly understood what Kevin meant.

"Okay. Well, thank you for trusting me."

He sat there still silent and she was shocked. She had been expecting him to freak out, or call her a liar, run right inside to pack up and leave with the girls; but he just sat there.

"I'm sorry, did you not understand what I just said? I mean, that's it, no screaming about lying or keeping things from my husband or that I wrote about you and killed you as a character in a book? Just 'Okay'?" she asked, dumbfounded by his cool behavior. Grabbing one of her cigarettes, he lit one and decided to actually smoke, bobbing his head yes.

"Yeah, what you did in your past doesn't change what you are doing with me right now."

Grace wasn't sure if she had fallen asleep and she was having one of those dreams where everything went perfectly or if this was real life. But when Jim reached over and grabbed her hand, she knew it was real. He was real.

"I mean, I get it. It's a lot to take, but this doesn't change anything between us. Yeah, you kept important information from your husband, but he is a bag of dicks, so that makes sense."

They both laughed at that one as he rubbed his thumb over her hand. She didn't know what to say, but he slowly got up from his chair and walked over to her, pulling her to her feet.

"And since you confessed something important about yourself, it's my turn, and you do with this information whatever you want." He pulled her into his arms and lifted her face so he was staring into her eyes. "I don't know why I gravitate to you, but I do. It's like some magnetic pull and I cannot escape it for the life of me. But then I realized I don't want to." He paused to brush her cheek, admiring her soft skin. "I am in love with you. I always have been, and I never want to stop."

Brushing his lips over hers he left a whisper of a kiss on her mouth. She pulled away and, grazing her nose against his and through her heavy-lidded gaze said, "So don't." And she poured all the love she had into the kiss, and in her heart, it roared with joy.

CHAPTER ELEVEN

The sunrise was a few minutes away. Standing there in the sand, the water cresting over her toes, Grace couldn't help but feel a wave of relief flooding her soul. She had confessed everything to Jim, not in full detail but enough for her to feel better about keeping this from him for so long. There had been no anger from the deception; in fact, he seemed impressed.

As the sky's color was changing to a bright red before the sun came up, she wondered if it was a warning. Red skies in the morning, sailors take warning. Red skies at night, sailor's delight. It was a warning.

Watching the sea as waves tumbled in a bit harder, kicking up seafoam, it wasn't too bad, but it might be best to get out of the surf. Moving back a few feet, just watching the wind spray the water as the waves crashed and looking at the clouds in the distance, she knew they might want to batten down the hatches and stay put for the day. Technically it was hurricane season but there hadn't been any developments this early. Today would just bring a bad storm.

Two large hands with the ends of a blanket in them were wrapping around her and the sensation scared her. Glimpsing behind her, Jim stood there wrapped up in an old Toselle Park sweatshirt, gazing down at her.

"What are you doing out here without a coat this early?"

"It's only 70 degrees, its comfortable, besides the sunrise is in a few seconds so it will start warming up."

Her eyes alight with utter joy as she angled her head up to welcome his sweet kiss, she embraced the warmth of the sunrise creeping over the horizon, just wanting to remember this moment forever. They stood there in silence as they watched the sunrise in the distance, breathing in the scents of the ocean and each other.

"I put on a pot of coffee; it should be ready."

She whirled around and threw her arms around his neck.

"God Bless you, James Wooley!" Showering his face over and over with kisses as if he had offered her a million dollars. Laughing as she was not missing a single inch on his face to pepper kisses.

"Is there anything you love more than coffee?" She pulled back from her onslaught of kisses. Pursing her lips, she looked up at the sky, being coy.

"More than coffee?"

She was being cute and giggling, but he looked down at her and there she found nothing but heat in his gaze. Grace knew he needed to hear the words that she loved him, but the words had not come out of her mouth yet. She could feel his heart pounding in his chest, but he was not the only one.

Truthfully, she was afraid. Having said it too many times in her life for that person to rip her heart out as if the words held no meaning. But his eyes said what she knew was true. He was hers to destroy, hers to toss aside, but all she knew was he was hers, body, mind, and soul.

"Gracie, please."

His voice caught in his throat and he swallowed hard. Grace touched his cheek and kissed his lips, as his arms tightened around her, deepening their kiss. Bringing his hand up to the nape of her neck, his lips placed tempting kisses on her chin and down her throat. Slowly tangling his fingers in her windblown curls, pulling ever so gently, causing a moan from her lips.

"Please tell me I'm not alone. That I'm not the only one feeling this way."

He brought his face back up to hers and stared into her dreamy chestnut-colored eyes, his eyes begging her for three simple words.

"Please?"

"I do love you. But my heart can't take losing you again."

A single tear rolled down her cheek.

"So please be careful with it this time, because it's not just my heart you have. My boys adore you and I can't have you breaking their hearts too."

Tears flowed from her eyes and through her misty gaze she saw that he was tearing up as well.

"Same, my love. So, I promise you here and now, I will not break anyone's hearts and know that mine is yours, always has been, always will be." And she knew this was a promise he intended to keep.

𝄢

"When do we leave for the launch?"

"Right after the Fourth of July. I can always catch flights back and forth if I need to."

Grace had made all the arrangements and sent an email to her dad. Although she was busy working, she could feel his concerned gaze bearing down on her.

"We could always push this back if you want. I'm not sure we need to do this right now." Grace ignored that comment and just kept typing. "I see, so our game plan is to avoid everything. And here I was thinking you had gotten better about avoidance?"

That hit the nerve he must have been hoping for. She stopped typing and arched her brow, giving him a look and then without even looking at the computer she just kept typing.

"I'm not avoiding, I have a job to do." She went back to looking at the screen, typing away.

"Yes, and you are great at it. I just don't want you disconnecting again and avoiding things that are too hard. You have the family, your friends, Dale and now you have Jim." He paused and watched her face at the mention of Jim. "You have a massive support team ready to help you in this fight, so for once don't try and do this all on your own. I don't want to see what happened to me to happen to you."

Father's guilt was a good mechanism especially when it was the truth. She stopped typing again, closing her wearied eyes, resting her head on the back of her chair, and didn't move. She knew he was right, her health was better, but it didn't mean that her stress wouldn't cause her to have a heart attack.

"Mommy isn't supposed to come with us, maybe she could watch the boys once we figure out this stupid custody thing. Can you ask Dale to have something set in place before we leave?" Ken just nodded and then it dawned on her about the house and Hank needing to get out. "Oh, and can you go over to the house and make sure everything is okay. I could check the cameras and the video from here but honestly, I just can't."

"Do you want me to check it now before we leave?"

"Yeah. I'm leaving now anyway; we promised the kids the boardwalk just to get them out of the house before the storm."

"If there are any issues, I'll let Dale handle it, but I will stop by the house either way to make sure everything is okay in person. We've got you, kid!"

"Thanks, Daddy."

𝄢

Rain had neither hindered nor deterred this crew and it seemed that every single child or teen was going home with either a stuffed animal or a massive box of candy. But as the day went on hunger had finally hit and fortunately Grace's favorite stand on the boardwalk for cheesesteaks and pizza was just next door. Considering the size of this army, Mike had suggested they get a bunch of food. Two pizzas and three cheesesteaks. Later they all ravenously tucked in. Although Jim was moving around a lot better, getting into the tight booths seemed to cause some discomfort. Digging in her bag, Grace pulled out a bottle of ibuprofen and handed it to him, forcing a laugh out of Katie as she ate her pizza.

"God, Dad, Grace didn't think she would be getting another kid when she started dating you."

Both Grace and Jim spit out their sodas at that. Were they dating? Is that what they were doing? Their reaction got everyone's attention. Nikki, who had been sitting next to Grace, was hitting her thigh because it seemed that Grace and Jim had not responded past the spit take.

"Sweetie, we aren't dating, or at least I haven't asked anyone yet," Jim said as he wiped soda off his shirt and Grace watched as a massive smile ran from ear to ear on Katie's face. Nikki's pinch on Grace's leg caused her to yelp and rub her thigh, narrowing her eyes at Nikki.

"Yeah Mr. Jim, I already gave you the go-ahead on telling her you love her, did you do that yet?"

Calvin called from a different booth and Denise, who was sitting next to him, just smacked him. *What is happening?* Grace thought. Calvin had spoken to Jim behind her back and let him know that it was okay to confess his feelings. Was this her life, not yet divorced and already her child is marrying her off?

"Oh my god, what is wrong with you kids. Poor Jim's eyes look like they are going to bug out of his head and I'm sure your poor mother is losing her damned mind right now because none of us need to be talking about this. Bunch of sass—pots, the lot of you," Denise said, again smacking Calvin in the upper arm and then handing a napkin to Colin. Sitting there unable to form coherent thoughts, Grace needed to shut the conversation down, now before it got too out of hand.

"Well, I feel so honored that such a large group of people that I care about cares about us, but I think the smartest thing is to leave it to us to make these decisions." Everyone had turned and was glued to her as she spoke. "But I will make you a promise, IF we decide to divulge any information about a relationship, we will be happy to inform you all once it is agreed upon." There was utter silence and then Amanda spoke up.

"So, are you dating or not?" The loud exasperated tone out of one so tiny just baffled Grace

"No, Mandy, not yet, I'll let you know when we do," Grace called towards the tiny blonde.

The kids all seemed incredibly disappointed by this news, and she even heard a tsking from Nikki. Turning to her best friend, batting her on the shoulder, under her breath Grace muttered "You're a bag of dicks, you know that." She knew that Nikki had put Amanda up to asking that, she was sure of it. Batting her lashes at Grace, Nikki just kept eating her sandwich.

Glancing up at Jim, whose mouth had curled up to one side in a sly smile, Katie stuffed more pizza in her mouth and rolled her eyes out of disappointment. Grace caught Katie's eye and just smiled giving her a knowing wink, causing the teen to smile. Grace hoped that she could understand. She remembered being that age and romance seemed so exciting. But everyone just needed to be patient.

Gathering their large gaggle and walking out of the building heading towards the water balloon game, there was a massive flash of lightning and Grace started counting. Ten seconds later there was a rumble of thunder and Jim turned to Grace. "Ten miles" he said. She let out a laugh; did he really remember? After all these years.

As the clouds released their deluge, the six of them all piled into Jim's car and headed back to the house soaked to the bone. Mike had called out to Jim to let him know they would follow just in case there was an outage. Pulling into the driveway there was another flash and at this point the thunder roared eight seconds later. Everyone scrambled into the house and Grace immediately went to work delegating different tasks for the adults in case they needed to spend the night.

Grace came down from upstairs and confirmed with everyone that they were okay. They hadn't lost power, which was good, but the wind was definitely starting to escalate and quickly. Letting Nikki know that she was just heading outside for a second, Grace snuck out to sit on the front porch. Jim followed her to make sure she was okay.

Grace always loved rainstorms, especially lightning. The way it lit up the sky like fireworks, the electricity splitting the sky in half was such a marvel to her. She had fond memories of storms. All but one.

"Mind if I join you?"

The last time they were together during a storm, things between them were so different. Another bolt of lightning flashed in the sky, her eyes watching it, the electricity in the air making the hair on her arms stand up. Sitting there in silence, Jim and Grace watched the lightning and listened to the thunder.

"Did you know that, that night, I thought you were controlling the weather? It was so angry and you, you were so calm, I was sure that whatever was going on inside that brain and heart of yours was just surrounding us and that was why you were so calm." She bit her lip at that comment and just snickered. If only she had actually had that power, but he wasn't wrong, she had been calm and the world had raged around them. Grace reached over and grasped his hand, squeezing it ever so gently.

"I'll be honest, it's because of that night that I learned that little trick of yours with the lightning and thunder. I even taught the girls." Another bolt of lightning and she started counting. She was sure it was getting closer. Four seconds later, thunder.

"It's moving fast."

"Us or the storm?" He asked with a sly grin. She got up, putting out her cigarette, and sat down on his lap.

"Maybe both."

"Asking you to marry me is moving fast."

She stilled in his lap and looked up into his eyes. It was still early but the storm had darkened the skies so much that his eyes had that denim color to them. Her heart was pounding at that comment.

"I have been thinking about this. Technically I can't date you without at least taking you out on a date." The smoothness in his voice was almost as good as that wine she liked. She played along with him.

"True, I have not actually been out on a date with you since '96, which means the statute of limitations on our courtship is up, so you will need to take me out on a new date. But fair warning, my expectations for what constitutes a date have risen since '96 so I wish you luck on your wooing of me." She was not going to let him get away with a simple date. He needed to impress her this time.

"Hmmm, any place you can recommend?"

Although he had lived in New Jersey most of his life, he knew that places open and close all the time and most of the places he would take her to were up north. The lightning had been flashing and there was another roll of thunder, this time two seconds away.

"Nope, you've got to figure this out yourself. Or at least, I will not be the one making the choice."

She was giving up control, allowing someone else to plan. It was hard, she could list a bunch of places, but her dad had told her to trust people, not control everything, so she did. More flashes and one second later, *BANG*. The flickering of the lights on the porch meant that this was going to get worse, and then as if on cue the rain picked up. More lightning and this time a bolt hit a transformer down

the street, and they saw the green sparks before everything went out. Screams came from the house.

Turning to him, "See this is what happens when I give up power!" she laughed, getting up and going into the house to check on everyone. The lightning and thunder were now in synch, and he went into the house because the rain and wind were becoming intolerable.

The storm had been strong the rest of the day and into the evening. Due to the electricity being out they were doing puzzles and playing cards by candlelight. They had made sandwiches in order to avoid opening the refrigerator and Grace was thankful she had a pantry filled with drinks and snacks.

Mike and Jim were working on a puzzle with John and Colin when Jim had a brilliant idea. He would ask the boys. They knew her best and if he was going to be serious about dating her, he wanted them to help and know that he cared about them as well. Jim called Calvin over to the table and asked them for suggestions. They had a number of places in mind but one stuck out for both of them.

It had to be a real date and the more he thought about it the more nervous he got. What if the date went badly? He didn't think that could happen. What if something happened to the kids while they were out for the night? He was sure that his fellow adults here would be able to watch the kids.

Jim wasn't sure what had made him feel so unsure suddenly and then he thought about the past four days. It had been a whirlwind to be sure. He had heard stories of people going out on two dates and then getting engaged and at the time thought it was crazy. But this was Grace. He had dated her before and despite the time they had spent apart, deep down inside this was the same, incredible woman he remembered. Just older and wiser.

Jim looked at both boys and smiled, then Colin did the one thing he hadn't been expecting. Colin jumped up and gave him a hug. Compared to Jim, Colin was tiny but this hug from one so small crushed his heart. He had made her a promise, he wasn't going to break her heart or the boys' and as he squeezed Colin back, he intended to keep that promise. No broken hearts this time.

The storm had finally started to slow down as midnight approached. He had dozed off until Grace started shifting in the bed, attempting to nestle herself closer to him, and he realized that she was still up.

"Can't sleep?" Jim said, his voice rough with sleep. She craned her head, accepting his soft kiss.

"No, yes, I'm sorry I'm keeping you up."

Attempting to pull away was fruitless as Jim only strengthened his grip on her waist. Her soft curves were warm against him, and it was heat he was not willing to let go of. Inhaling her scent was intoxicating and he wasn't sure how he was going to handle being in bed all alone again once the week was over. The thought only made him frustrated, and he pushed the idea from his mind.

"You aren't.," he whispered, placing a kiss on her enticing neck, causing goosebumps to run down the length of her back as she let out a sigh. He enjoyed the little sounds of ecstasy that escaped her lips, and he could tell how his own made her feel. The heat that radiated off her skin when she was aroused set his own skin on fire. He could feel his own arousal starting and he knew physically he was not able to perform with his ribs being bruised so he needed to stop this before they were both too far gone.

Painfully he turned and laid flat on his back so he could pull away from her and tried to focus on nothing but sleep. However, the whimper that emerged from her throat was making it difficult to not continue.

"Baby steps."

"I think in this department we are well past baby steps, sir."

Turning over, she curled up to his side and took his hand towards her lips and kissed his rough knuckles. The cuts and bruises on his hands were starting to heal, but the whole situation and events were really what kept her up. He could see the pain and frustration in her eyes.

"Stop stressing. I can feel your shoulders tensing up. Stop avoiding. Talk it out."

"I'm not avoiding. Fine, it's just everything. We have the book tour starting in two weeks, and all this other bullshit, scheduling coverage for the boys, waiting around for court dates and the mediation for the divorce. And-" His steel gray eyes looked over her face and read the "And."

"Grace, you don't have to do all this on your own. I'm gonna be working on your dad's car this summer so I'm around. If you need help, just ask." He lifted her chin and grazed his lips across hers. "And since you enjoy checking off boxes you can put a check mark in one thing I have control over." Grace looked at him, not sure what he was going to say.

"I'm not planning on going anywhere, so check that off right now." Grace sighed as his lips came down on hers for a gentle kiss, and this time when she settled her head against him, she finally fell asleep.

CHAPTER TWELVE

Usually after a storm like that one, it would have been cooler, however they woke up to much warmer temperatures, which made for the perfect day at the kids' favorite place. Grace sat under one of the blue cabanas next to Denise and Nikki looking at an overly excited Amanda.

"Are you happy now, sassy pants?" Amanda couldn't stay still as Nikki struggled to apply sunscreen to her youngest.

"Best day ever, GURL!" The three adult women were taken aback by someone so tiny. Grace looked over the top of her glasses, looking at Nikki and commented, "Was your poor husband even present at conception? Or was this just a cloning?"

Nikki stuck out her tongue and shooed her daughter off to Mike, who was standing near the kids' area. Finally getting a moment's peace, the ladies sat there enjoying the kids being out and about throughout the park. Jim had taken Vivian and John to go to the wave pool, while the teens had gone off to do the rides.

Although surrounded by screaming and loud families around them, Grace took a moment to take it all in as she enjoyed all the scenes unfolding around her. Denise and Nikki were talking about the upcoming fundraiser for the marching band, but Grace was only half listening.

"I believe she has finally learned how to sleep with her eyes open. Grace? Are you listening?" Denise was doing everything to get her to pay attention. Grace didn't even blink. Nikki and Denise just kept looking at her in awe.

"I think she did learn how to sleep with her eyes open. I feel bad for Jim, that would freak me the hell out." Nikki was waving her hat up and down to get Grace's attention. However, Grace's sight was fixed and unmoving as if in a trance.

"I have not learned how to sleep with my eyes open. I would do six poker tables, two roulette wheels, and two craps tables based on the attendance."

Grace turned to them, batting her eyelashes. Nikki gave Denise a look and threw her hat at Grace. Grace looked down, placing the hat on her head.

"So if you were listening then why didn't you say something?" Denise said, turning to Grace who was still staring off in the distance. Grace reached down and took a magazine out of her bag, holding it up so she looked as if she was reading it. Denise could see something was wrong with the way that Grace was behaving and decided to follow Grace's behavior. She took a book out of Grace's bag and put her sunglasses back on her face.

"Two o'clock: blue shorts, gray hat, sunglasses; he's been using his phone to take pictures of us."

Denise, without moving her head, caught sight of who Grace was mentioning. Nikki had her eyes closed and was just listening. Lowering her chair so that it was reclined, she turned over to lay on her stomach so that she could participate in their conversation without drawing attention.

"Do you think they are here for you?" Nikki asked.

"Are any of YOU embroiled in a messy divorce?" Grace turned a page in the magazine to continue to look as though she was reading.

"Yeah, but are you sure? Maybe he is just some creeper checking out my perfect breasts." Grace glared down at Nikki, who just giggled.

"My gut is telling me he is here for me, so just watch him. I'm going over to Mike and then I'll come back. If he moves to follow me, then I'm right."

Grace walked over to where Mike had been standing in the kiddie pool. Just as she had predicted, the young man she had pointed out moved so that he could get a better shot of her.

"Hey, what are you doing over here?" Mike seemed surprised to see Grace over in the water.

"Testing a theory, and I was right."

"Do I ask?"

"Probably best you don't know. But thanks for participating in this segment of Grace's life is crazy. Stay tuned for the next episode of Grace is losing her mind."

Mike gave Grace a questioning look, and she just smiled at him before walking back over to the cabana. Sitting back down, she picked up her magazine, looking like nothing had happened.

"So?" Grace asked.

"You need to harness that talent; he totally followed you. So, what do you want to do? You can go tell security." Grace thought that might be best and would be the easiest way to handle things.

"Why don't you call the cops and have them check his phone, this would be considered harassment, right?"

Grace wanted to know just who this guy was working for and whether they were there for her or for Jim. Who knew if there weren't more than one of these guys following them around. But then she remembered a little trick Nikki could do.

"I could, or we could put those old skills of yours to work and see if you still got that light touch." Grace closed the magazine and looked down at Nikki. "I'm gonna go to the lazy river, want to join me?" Nikki looked up and sighed.

"Don't you dare tell my kids I did this. They don't know I was a criminal in my past."

"I don't think lifting your dad's wallet to take $20 out makes you a criminal, he always found out," Grace said, facing the opposite direction so the guy couldn't see what she was saying.

Grace knew she could just go to security and complain that the guy was taking pictures of her, and that this might complicate things, however she was done playing nice guy. Nikki and Denise both got up and they started walking to the lazy river. Out of the corner of her eye she could see "blue shorts" had begun moving and following her movements with his phone.

Nikki was walking a bit behind her and Denise headed off in the direction of the wave pool. As Grace got closer to "blue shorts", she noticed him put his phone in the back pocket of his trunks. Perfect. He hadn't realized that he was standing near the entrance of the lazy river, and his only option was a dead end or to get on the ride.

Nikki spotted a large group of teen girls clumping together on their way to the lazy river and straggled behind them. Grace turned, pretending to look for Nikki but knowing that she was going to use the girls as buffers, and a tiny smile went across her lips. "Blue shorts" was a few people ahead of her and looked like a deer in headlights as she approached. Walking another two feet, Grace bent down and yelled.

"Oh God, my toe."

Crumpling to the floor grasping her foot as if she was in pain caused the group of teens behind her to slam into "blue shorts." Getting twisted around and practically being rubbed up against by hot teenagers, the young man hadn't noticed the petite older woman taking his cell phone out of his pocket. The whole chaotic scene was a lot of "I'm sorry," "Ma'am, are you okay," "Do you need first aid,", "Ew don't touch me, perv," "Ew gross," and 'Watch where you're going, bruh." Nikki made her way over to Grace, and luckily, she had chosen to wear her two piece that had shorts with pockets. Stuffing the phone in her pocket, she ran over to Grace and winked.

"Oh my god, are you okay? Come on, let's get you up." Nikki took Grace's hand and helped her up as Grace faked a sound of pain and screwed up her face.

"Yeah, I just think I need to go sit back down. Help me over there. Sorry, everyone, sorry."

Grace kept up her act as they made their way back to the cabana. Once there, Nikki helped Grace onto her seat and as she lowered her down with her other hand she dropped the phone into Grace's bag. Nikki sat down next to Grace and put the bag on Grace's lap so she could inspect the phone. Grace could see that "blue shorts" was not smart and had apparently unlocked his phone after using greasy sunscreen because there was a clear greasy fingerprint trace on the lock screen.

"Amateur," she said to Nikki, who started laughing.

"Or too dumb to remember a code or use his face ID." Nikki just shook her head. Grace rolled her eyes. Taking her finger, she traced the lock screen, and it opened.

"Oh, come on, this is too easy. Just keep a look out."

Nikki had her sunglasses back on and had taken Denise's visor and placed it on as she scanned the area discreetly. Grace made it look like she was looking for things in her bag with one hand and using her other scrolled through and went to the messages. There was a group text with a number she recognized and she read it. Apparently, Liz and Hank had hired "blue shorts" and another person to take pictures to catch Jim and Grace in the act. Grace took her phone that had been in the bag, went to the sharing program on "blue shorts'" phone, and shared the texts and the photos they had taken to hers. She then wiped the phone clean with a towel and rolled it up and placed it on the floor along with her bag. Nikki watched as she realized that Grace was one of the smartest women she know.

"You know you are scary, right?"

Grace was holding her phone and looking at the pictures. She then sent them to Dale along with the texts that had copied to her phone from "blue shorts." Placing her big hat back on her head and looking at Nikki, she said "I thought I was adorable actually."

"And? What did you find?"

"That I'm always right. He was hired by Liz and Hank to follow us and get pics. I sent them over to Dale, just waiting on him to respond."

Grace just kept looking around and watched to see if "Mr. Blue Shorts" had figured out his phone was missing yet. She didn't see him, instead she saw their group of teens heading back to them. Catching sight of them as well, Nikki placed Grace's phone back in her bag. Cristina walked up and sat on the chair her mom was on.

"Hey, we are kinda bored already, we really would rather go back to the house." Cristina pouted. Nikki huffed knowing that her two younger kids had been looking forward to this. But Grace took this as an opportunity.

"Nik, listen, you stay, I'll take this group back, that way I can wait for that call."

Grace knew the best thing to do was not be around if they wanted to get pictures of her and Jim. Plus, she really wasn't into big crowds and there was already a huge line of people trying to get into the park. Nikki made a sound to start protesting but Grace gave her a look which immediately stopped any protests she was going to start.

"Fine," Said Nikki, sticking her tongue out at the kids. Grace collected her things, including the phone in the towel. She wasn't cruel, she would just place it somewhere no one would think, like the ladies' restroom. She smiled to herself;

she would let another woman find it and bring it to the lost and found. Cruel yes, smart absolutely, because why would a man leave their phone in a women's room? What was this young man doing in there, especially when there were a bunch of pictures of women being taken on his camera?

The herd of teens followed her towards the exit. On the way, she stopped briefly to let them know she just needed to pop into the restroom before they left. Once inside, Grace left the phone in one of the stalls and then walked out. She had been fortunate that no one else was in there at the time. Washing her hands because bathrooms are gross, she walked out with her mission accomplished and took the teens home, but not before taking them for ice cream first, because she earned that one.

Grace realized that Dale didn't charge her enough for all this crap. After receiving the texts, he asked where she got the information, and she said it was best she didn't answer that question, which got her a huge laugh out of the old man. All he said to her was that he would take care of it. She would need to grab him a fantastic bottle of whiskey while they were on tour in Tennessee.

Sitting on the deck and enjoying a bit of quiet as the teens hung out in the pool, this was really what she had wanted. Jim had promised that she would have a day to herself but with all the circumstances it hadn't happened. He also had asked her out, but now with this new situation with a private investigator following them, maybe it was best to delay whatever this was she had going on with Jim.

The idea that she would need to ask Jim to wait for her made the pieces of her heart ache, but deep inside she knew he would understand because of their connection.

That gravity he talked about. He wasn't the only one who felt it. They were magnetically connected; she felt it all those years ago and it had never stopped. If he was in the room she needed to gaze in his direction, her hand pulled towards his, to feel his closeness, his warmth, his embrace. To feel whole. She felt whole with him. Grace knew she didn't need to pretend anymore or hold her tongue with him. Completely lost in thought, she hadn't realized that the kids were talking to her.

"Grace, Ms. Grace, you okay?" Jodi was waving her hands in the air from the pool. Grace turned her head and smiled.

"Sorry, Jojo, I got lost there for a minute. What's up?"

Grace took a sip of her water and absent-mindedly took a bite of a chip as she looked at the teen. Jodi was coming out of the pool to grab a chip and shoved some in her face, wiping her fingers on her towel.

"Do you mind if we walk down to the sub shop and get sandwiches? We can grab you one," Jodi said, shoving more chips in her mouth. Grace had actually been wanting to take a nap after barely getting any sleep the past few days. Just a quick power nap should help.

"Yeah. Cal, just bring your phone. I'm gonna go upstairs and take a power nap." Calvin concurred. "Be safe and if you decide to eat there just text me if you want me to come pick you up, alright."

The chorus of "thank yous" coming from the teens was sweet. But exhaustion was setting in. Every part of her was tired, her brain, muscles, and heart; it had all been so much so quickly. As she climbed onto the bed and pulled a blanket over her, she could feel her eyes burning. Closing them, she allowed herself to drift off, and her last thought was that she just needed a half hour.

𝄢

The adults looked at the teens as they shushed them while they entered the house. Jim realized something was up and as he looked around, he noticed it was clean and quiet.

"What happened here? Did Grace clean?" Mike said in a hushed tone. The teens just smiled.

"No, we thought it might be nice to help Grace out, so we cleaned up and organized," Cristina whispered. Jim looked among his friends, who were all shocked at their own kids' initiative.

"You did good, kid. How long she been out?"

Calvin wore his worry for his mom across his face and whispered "Two and a half hours, she doesn't sleep this long unless she is sick or going to bed."

Patting his shoulder, Jim gave him a knowing nod and glanced at Nikki and Denise before walking up the stairs. The late afternoon glow of the sun coming into her room made it almost dreamlike. She had left the windows open and there was a soft warm breeze coming in. He looked over to the bed and the sight of her was reminiscent of a Renaissance painting.

The streaks of light that were coming through the window were highlighting her cheeks and her soft curls seemed to glow as they spread across the sheets. There was a soft rosy glow on her and on her lips. He crawled up onto the bed to lie behind her. Her body barely moved but it seemed to settle into his as he lightly touched the nape of her neck to pull the hair away, allowing her to breathe even more deeply. He wanted to kiss her, but he was afraid to disturb her.

Jim inhaled; her scent filled his nostrils, stirring a need in him. He wanted to wrap her up and protect her for the rest of her life, to never allow anyone to cause her harm. Knowing what she was going through, the exhaustion from the depression, the trauma, it was all too much. But he would be there to help her through it.

None of her friends knew what this was like. Jim knew that she could sleep for hours due to all the stress, and he would let her. Getting up from his place next to her, he swore a slight whimper escaped her lips, then he went back downstairs.

The concerned gazes that met him as he entered the kitchen touched his heart. Everyone stood around the island waiting for a report. He walked over to Calvin and Colin, patting them on the shoulders.

"She is okay, she just needs to rest, that's all. I think it's all just overwhelming, especially with all of us being here."

Mike and Denise nodded. Perhaps the group of them being there was just too many people, as great as it is to be surrounded by loved ones, too many could be too much, Jim pondered.

"Listen, why don't we take our kids and let you guys enjoy the rest of the week yourselves." Mike looked at Nikki, understanding what Jim had been trying to explain politely. Nikki, however, was not hearing it.

"I have been here for years, I know what this looks like, she just needs someone to go wake her up and tell her to get her ass moving. She can't let this overtake her like the-" she stopped herself and looked at Mike. Jim didn't need her to finish that sentence.

Like the last time, like when he broke her heart. Nikki was her rock during that breakup, he didn't need anyone to tell him that, but this wasn't just a breakup; divorces were much trickier, especially when it came to kids. Nikki looked at Jim and he saw for the first time a bit of pain there. Breathing in, he walked over to her, knowing that somewhere deep inside of her she resented him.

"You are right, you were there, when I should have been." Nikki rolled her eyes as he stated the obvious. "But I was a kid, so was she." He added, hoping that would help his case. Nikki apparently didn't want to hear it. She held up her hand so she could say her peace.

"You know what, you don't get it. The love she has for you now is the same as when you broke her."

There it was. Grace had been in love with him all those years ago, a mature love, not some childish teenage romance, true love, and Jim's heart broke all over again. This was why she never shared the truth with her husband and why she held her heart so tightly.

"After all these years and all the pain, she never stopped loving you. Listen, I'm thrilled that you finally pulled your head out of your ass and have realized what she realized years ago. But losing you devastated her for months." Her words choked her as she stammered on. "Her mom and I held her hand for fucking months. It took her years before she dated again. You know her dad's first book is-"

"About me. Yeah, she told me. But so is her mom's."

Nikki and Denise looked shocked; he guessed she hadn't told them about their conversation. Jim hadn't realized just how their break-up had devastated her and deep inside he knew he didn't have to earn just Grace's trust but her friends' as well.

"Nik, I'm sorry that you had to even do that, but I was a kid. Grace was always years ahead of me, but I'm not that kid anymore. I've been where she is now, I know the heartbreak, the pain, and the exhaustion she is feeling." Wiping away a tear, Nikki looked at him.

"Please, I wasn't there when I should have been, so let me be here now."

Jim knew it was a long shot with the way Nikki's behavior had changed towards him after what she had said. But something in her demeanor changed as she looked at the boys. There was hope in their eyes as they looked at Jim, and she sighed knowing that she would have to trust him.

"You break even the smallest part of her heart." Nikki looked back at Jim, and he nodded.

"I know, you'll break my face."

Denise patted his shoulder and started grabbing her things, motioning to Jodi to grab her stuff, and with much coaxing on Mike's part, Nikki followed suit. His girls and the boys stood there looking at Jim. He held his arms out and to his surprise they all came to him looking for a hug. He had just expected his girls but clearly her boys needed the most hugs at this moment, and he would never deny Grace's boys anything. It amazed him just how close they had been getting over such a short time, but for some reason it felt more like they had known each other their entire lives.

"So, what do we do now?" Colin asked. Jim hadn't thought that far ahead. All that he had wanted was to get everyone out of the house because he knew it would be overwhelming once Grace woke up. Too many people, with too many questions. He looked at the time and realized they had another three hours before dinner, but he knew based on spending time with Colin this past week that he would be asking for a snack any minute.

"Let's do this, let's have a snack, then go sit on the beach for two more hours, then we'll come back and figure something out for dinner."

Jim was already starting to get some snacks out for the kids as he was talking. It wasn't fair of him to expect Grace to want to cook or even think about dinner. He could always cook something, but then they would have to clean up. What he really wanted to do was take Grace out for their date, but after pissing off Nikki, it was highly unlikely that she would agree to watching the kids. So, he thought of the next best thing. Winning over the boys would be the way to go on this. He would take the whole lot of them out on their date. He had three hours to really impress her so he had some calls to make.

𝄢

Something was tickling her cheek, something rough but not too rough. Taking a deep inhale as she stretched, smelling that leathery soft cologne that made her insides warm, she opened her eyes. Jim stood at the edge of the bed wearing a pair of tan dockers and a form-hugging button-down sky-blue shirt that made his muscles look like they were going to rip the sleeves. His tanned face smiling down at her, she wasn't sure if she was awake or asleep still.

She had dreamt of him, holding her and reassuring her that everything was going to be okay. He had kissed her and set her on fire with his touches. It had been extremely hard containing her desire, and she knew he was struggling as well, but with his bruised ribs she hadn't pressed him for more than just stolen kisses. Bending down, his soft lips reverently kissed hers; it was real, she was awake.

"Hey, feel like going to dinner?" His lips brushed hers again as he placed a quick peck on her lips. Dinner? It had been lunch when she laid down. Grace reached for her phone and glasses, looking at the time.

"Holy crap, I was only supposed to sleep for a half hour. How did I lose five hours? Are the boys, okay? Is everyone pissed? Fuck!"

She was scrambling to get up, but the light green crocheted blanket had woven itself in her legs. Jim sat down next to her, calmly helping her with the blanket.

"Hey, hey, Super Grace, take a breath." Grace glared at him. Jim carefully measured his next words. "Breathe with me. Everyone is fine. The kids are all dressed, and we are taking you out." Grace sat there stunned. "On OUR date." She furrowed her brow, unable to comprehend.

"OUR date?" Jim laughed at Grace's expression.

"Yeah, well, I thought about it. And I realized that I'm not just trying to get your approval for us to date, we kinda have a package deal going on. So, I thought that perhaps the kids should come along. You and I will have plenty of time to go on dates alone once we are back up north, so I thought it would be okay to include them."

Grace didn't know whether to cry or throw her arms around him for being so perfect. Of course, he had realized just how important her boys were to her, he was such an amazing dad to his own kids. Although she had been hoping for a one-on-one date, this was great, and she loved the idea.

Smiling, she hugged him and scooted off the bed. Running to her closet and realizing that all her summer dresses were now too big, her face dropped. Sauntering over to the door he held out a bag by the tip of one of his strong fingers, smiling, and she looked at him.

"I know you have lost some weight and after the bathing suit debacle I figured you may not have something to wear, so the girls helped me pick this out at the store down the street. I hope it fits. I had to guess your size."

She must have looked like a dead fish with her mouth open in total shock. Hank had never bought her clothes and here Jim was standing in the doorway to her bathroom with an outfit for her.

"Oh my god! Are you for real right now?"

Grace stood there pinching her arm to make sure she was really awake and then looked in the bag. Jim shrugged his shoulders and placed a kiss on her cheek.

"Just get in the shower, we will be waiting downstairs."

Closing the door behind him, Grace just stood there still in total disbelief. She couldn't quite believe all this was happening. Hopping in and taking the quickest shower known to man she rushed through and put on some make-up, did her hair, and then took the outfit out. It was a stunning white sundress with faint hints of icy blue accents that flowed down to her ankles, hugging her curves. Looking at herself in the mirror for the first time in a very long time, she felt beautiful. It was hard not to cry because this was the way she wanted to be seen, not just by herself but by others. Taking a deep breath, she exited the bathroom and went downstairs.

𝄢

Standing at the bottom of the stairs were Jim and the kids. His back was turned to her and the kids were bickering about how much longer they were going to be when Colin noticed Grace coming down the stairs.

"Wow Mommy, you look beautiful!"

Grace smiled as she took her time coming down the stairs. Five pairs of eyes were on her and Jim's mouth dropped as he looked at her. She truly was a vision. He had seen her before all dressed up, prom, plays, but this was something else. He hadn't noticed just how fast his heart was racing until he could hear the blood pumping in his ears. The kids were all giving compliments and Grace was smiling and thanking them, but he couldn't hear any of it. He walked towards her and held his hand out to her as she came down the last few steps. Grace put her hand in his and smiled.

"So, who picked this dress?" Grace asked, and the girls pointed to Jim.

"Dad picked it out and we just confirmed it was a good choice. Dad is great at this stuff. Right, Dad?" Vivian spoke up but Jim just kept staring at Grace. She stood there blushing under his gaze, he couldn't seem to help it, she was just stunning. "Dad? Earth to Dad?" Vivian tapped him on the back, and it seemed to snap him out of his trance.

"What?" Jim snapped and everyone laughed.

"You are very good at picking out dresses, thank you this is lovely. However, I am more impressed that you got the boys ready, I was sure I was returning to chaos."

"Okay, let's get going. I'm sure Colin is going to die of hunger soon, right, kiddo?"

Colin stood there bobbing his head continually. Making sure the kids were out of the house, he stood patiently waiting for Grace to lock up the house. Snaking his arm around her waist, he spun her around, pulling her close, then crushed his lips down on hers. Grace instantly dissolved into a puddle in his arms but then he pulled himself away.

"Just a taste for later."

Grace's eyes widened as she saw the heated look in his eyes and his words weighed heavy in the air. *Just a taste for later.*

His intentions were to woo her, and he seemed to be doing a fabulous job at it. Dinner had been a success and now he surprised them all by taking them to watch a band and karaoke. Grace's smiles and laughter brought him such joy after having seen her in such a state earlier that day. He wanted to bring a little bit of light to her, to erase the pain a little even if he knew that only she could do that for herself.

Colin got up and went to Katie to ask her to dance to a fast song and she happily obliged; however, seeing Vivian looking a little dejected, Calvin got up and asked her to dance and they went to the dance floor. Sitting there Jim and Grace watched the kids as they enjoyed themselves, but then his gaze moved to the creature sitting next to him. She had aged beautifully.

Her once completely chocolate brown hair now was mostly streaked with sparkling silver and when she smiled tiny lines appeared at the corner of her eyes. Some men might think she looked old but God help him, she was a work of art. The sun and sea air had brought out her freckles and the slight reddish hue on the bridge of her nose and cheeks gave her a healthy glow. Jim wondered if she had gotten tan lines over the past couple of days since they really hadn't done anything since their first night and morning together due to all the insanity, so he hadn't seen her yet, but he was determined to find out tonight.

He had to stop himself, the kids were here, and he still had to get her up to sing and he was hoping to dance with her as well. Then the band started playing *"Shut Up and Dance"*, the kids waved to their parents and Grace got up and held her hand out to Jim. How could he refuse to dance with the prettiest woman in the world? Everyone was singing and having a blast and then they began to play Ed Sheeran's *"Perfect"* and Jim turned to Grace. The kids sat down and watched as their parents danced.

Gazing down at the incredible woman in his arms, he started singing to her. Realizing how much the words encapsulated their love and lives, his eyes couldn't pull from hers, he was completely hers. Everything around them seemed to wash away, it was as if they were the only ones there and it felt only right for him to kiss her. She had been a siren pulling him in with the way she moved and her scent that tugged him in all night.

"Oh, come on, can't you wait till after the date?" Vivian said loud enough to make everyone there laugh and applaud. Opening his eyes, still locked in their kiss, he realized they had been left alone on the dance floor. Struggling to break the enchantment of their kiss, he noticed a blush across her cheeks and couldn't help but grin.

Fortunately, the band shifted their set and started playing one more fast song before finishing and then turned it over to the DJ for the karaoke. As they sat back down at the table, the kids had all started thinking of songs to sing; mostly it was the girls and Jim who were coming up with songs, the boys came up with one each just so they could do it as well.

"So what song are you going to do?" Jim asked, but Grace just shrugged. "Oh no, don't do that, what are you going to sing?" Jim wasn't going to back down.

"Probably just enjoy watching this time. I can't sing anymore."

All at the table looked at her like she was crazy and a chorus of compliments on how she sang the other night came flying at her. While they tried to convince her to sing, she sent Jim an exasperated glare as he just shrugged. He had no intention of allowing her to not sing. If there was one thing that Jim remembered about Grace, it was how applause after a song was always the best feeling in the world for her.

"Fine, I have a couple of songs I could do but let me think about it." Jim raised his eyebrow; he knew she would do this, so he had asked Kevin for some of her songs. He got up and she looked up at him. "Where are you going?" Grace asked.

"Well, I want to sing so I am going to put in a few songs with the kids."

They had all made their selections, but Jim had a special song he wanted, it just wouldn't be him doing the singing. As they all took their turns Jim realized that they had all needed this, they needed to sing out their emotions, something he had learned years ago, which was how he and Grace had met in chorus.

The boys and Vivian had done great jobs, clearly they all had talent from their parents. But as Katie got up and started singing, he was grateful that Katie had a singing voice like Elizabeth. It was very beautiful, and despite her protest of not wanting to continue with chorus and lessons she stuck it out. She was a bit shy but had true talent.

As a proud dad he turned to Grace to see what she thought of her singing, but there was something in Grace's expression he couldn't quite read. It was as if something was off; she looked distant and almost unsure. He watched her close her eyes as Katie kept singing, and he knew something was going in that brain of hers.

"Katie, your voice is just beautiful. Jim, why didn't you tell me that she took after you?"

"Actually, I can't take credit, her singing voice came from Elizabeth. She used to sing; apparently, she was in plays back in high school too."

Grace's heart stopped; Elizabeth used to sing. Her mind raced to when Elizabeth and Hank were in the house and she had made that comment, the one about winning. She hadn't understood what she had meant by it, but perhaps somewhere in her past Elizabeth had met Grace. It was something about winning, so it would have been one of the many competitions that Grace had done as a kid, but she was just a kid, and she didn't win all the time. But Katie's voice had been so eerily familiar, like an echo of her past.

Jim must have noticed Grace's face change when he had mentioned Elizabeth, and she just spaced out for a bit. Grabbing her hand to bring her back to reality, she just looked at him and smiled. It had been quick, because her smile faded as she heard her name being called up to sing. Her eyes went wide. She hadn't put anything in. She looked around praying for another Grace to go up but no one went. They called Grace again and Jim turned to her.

"Looks like you are the only Grace here. You should go up." Grace narrowed her eyes at him and then got up. The crowd cheered as she went up then stood there not knowing what it was that she was going to sing. She stared at the screen praying it was something short and easy. And then the song title came up on the screen. It wasn't. She had sung this song a million times, but not for over a good ten years. It was an updated version of *"Can't Help Falling In Love"* that had been done for a recent movie. She closed her eyes and waited for the words to hit the screen, and then she sang.

Her vision was focused only on Jim. He had after all picked this song. But as she sang, she realized just why he picked this song - because he must have known deep down inside, this was how she felt. Throwing themselves back together so quickly and rushing through this; but they couldn't help this, could they? This feeling, this love they had for each other was something they couldn't hold back.

A single tear rolled down her cheek as she finished singing and she was brought back to reality with thunderous applause. Wiping away the tear, she felt the blush had returned to her cheeks, and she took a tiny curtsy, quickly walking back to the table. As she sat down she wasn't sure if she wanted to kiss him or smack him. She opted for a playful punch.

"Aw, what was that for?"

"Because I know you put that in. I wasn't sure I was even going to sing." Grace took a sip of her coffee; Jim just smiled and rubbed his arm. He leaned in and kissed her cheek.

"What can I say, I like showing off my girl's talents."

He was being adorably coy and looking for a kiss, but after he had made her get up and sing, she shook her head and stuck her tongue out. Jim looked at her tongue and then into her eyes before bringing his lips to her ear to whisper.

"If you are gonna stick your tongue out, I'm gonna make you use it."

Her heart leapt at the idea of what he was insinuating. She looked at the kids to make sure neither of them had heard him. Luckily, they sat there immersed in their conversations, oblivious to what Jim had just said. Taking another sip of her coffee, scanning her surroundings, she then turned back to face Jim and stuck her tongue out. Inclining his head to the side, he sat there aghast; she was calling his bluff, and she knew that she had him. He couldn't exactly suck on her tongue in public let alone in front of the kids. Never one to back down from a challenge a sneer spread across his lips as he leaned in one more time and whispered in her ear "Later".

This was the second time he had mentioned later, she thought. His ribs must be feeling better if he is willing to risk some pain in order to enjoy himself *later*.

The evening flew by with a few more rounds of the kids getting up and just as she was going to suggest that they get the check, the DJ called up Grace and Jim together. Not pleased to be getting called up once more and incredibly nervous about what he could have picked for them, he walked her up onto the stage. As the DJ handed them the mics the song title came up; it was a duet version of *"You Are The Reason"* she had been listening to recently.

As the music started, it seemed their surroundings faded away around them, she felt as though they were the only people standing there. Like no time had passed between them, they sang as if they themselves had written these words, that this was their declaration of love, and no one could hear them. But they hadn't been alone, and as they finished the song the crowd at the restaurant erupted around them, it seemed to bring Jim and Grace back to reality and both blushed as they walked back to their seats.

𝄢

Bombarding Grace with a mix of compliments and questions about how great they had sounded the kids were buzzing with excitement. Something deep in his body stirred, electricity just from a single glance from her. Grace's gaze was turning his blood to honey and a heat spread from his heart. He cursed the dress he bought because it clung to all her curves and the cut to her bust line was so incredibly low that he wanted to bury his face in her cleavage. Fortunately, the waiter was quick and as Jim looked at the bill he pulled out more than enough money to cover not just the bill but to over-tip the server.

"Okay guys, let's get going. It's getting late." Grace turned to Jim wondering just what was causing this immediate desire to leave. But then she must have noticed how he was breathing and how there was a flushed hue rising from his chest up his neck, as well as the way he was looking at her decolletage, causing her to smile. Trying to suppress a giggle, Grace calmed the kids down and told them that it really was late and that she was very tired. Considering how she had passed out earlier and how concerned they had been about her well-being they didn't press the matter any further. Begrudgingly they started walking ahead of them and as Grace walked in front of Jim, he reached out his hand and goosed her round ass causing her to utter a tiny yelp since she had not expected it.

"Hey guys before we leave do you need to use the restroom?" Jim asked as they were about to walk past the hostess station.

The kids turned and figured it might be best to do so, and as they went into the respective restrooms, they left Grace and Jim waiting outside in the hallway. Just as the doors shut, he pulled her in close and kissed her with a ferocity he had never kissed her with before. He felt Grace's knees buckle instantly, and he held her even closer. Grace sighed and pressed her body to his; the heat radiating off of them was intense, as her arms flew up to his hair and she pulled at the hair at the back of his head causing a growl to escape his lips into her mouth. His hands had settled on her round ass as he pulled her even closer to his body and he tore his lips from hers to start kissing down her neck. When they heard someone clearing their throat.

"Um, you couldn't have waited till we got home?" Calvin said as Colin came out of the men's room, Katie and Vivian just standing there shaking their heads.

"Seriously, worse than the kids in school, Dad," Katie tsked as she walked past them. Looking at each other, it was hard not to laugh; they had been caught. Calvin stood there with his arms crossed shaking his head and Jim was not sure if he was going to punch him or leap into a lecture.

"No, you guys in front of me, no funny business, she is a respectable lady, and you don't need to defile my mother anymore in public mister," said Calvin. Pointing at the exit, he was not taking no for an answer. Walking behind them he made sure they acted properly, causing Jim and Grace to both smile.

The ride back to the house was quiet and short. Luckily with all the excitement of the day it seemed that the kids were all very tired. Both Vivian and

Colin had passed out, Katie and Calvin seemed to have heavy lids and were slowly leaning towards each other to the point where Katie's head eventually landed on his shoulder, causing him to become alert, but then Cal was too tired and put his head on hers, closing his eyes. Jim looked in the mirror to see the kids asleep.

"I guess it was a successful date then. Take a look." Grace turned to see the kids sleeping.

"If only it was this lovely every day."

"I know, but I'll be right here when it isn't." Grace rested her head against the headrest and just looked admiringly at him.

"I know."

Life had been so weird in the few days since he had marched back into her life. Their connection, their feelings for one another, as if all those years apart hadn't existed between them. That they had picked up exactly where they had left off, before he went off to college, before Elizabeth, before Hank. How different would their life have been if things had happened the way she had wanted it to with him if he hadn't been so stupid?

𝄢

Jim pulled up the drive and parked the car. Slowly the kids woke up and Colin had complained he was too tired to walk, so Jim picked him up and carried him. Vivian clung to Grace's arm as they walked up the stairs, and she was just going to turn the key when something in her gut didn't feel right. It was as if she could feel someone's eyes on her. She stopped and looked around before turning the key. Jim noticed and shifted Colin in his arms, looking behind them. He wasn't sure what she was looking at.

"You okay? He is getting kinda heavy."

Grace kept looking as if to see if she saw something. Very slowly a dark car with darkened windows drove past the driveway, almost stopping in front of it. Squinting, she could see a figure driving but couldn't tell if it was a woman or a man. Someone had followed them. To not alarm the kids, she flashed a smile and unlocked the door.

"Yup, everything is fine," Grace said as she watched the car finally pass the house. Jim walked into the house and headed upstairs, and she made sure the kids had gotten upstairs before she let the panic set in.

Someone had been following them, she was sure of it. Her heart racing, she double locked the front door and then set the alarm, but something wasn't working right and she still needed to say goodnight to the kids. The alarm would have to wait. Grace came up slightly winded, kissing her boys goodnight, and wished the girls sweet dreams before vanishing from the room.

CHAPTER THIRTEEN

Jim wasn't sure what was going on, but he needed to talk to Grace to see what was happening in that little pretty head of hers. He walked into her room, but she wasn't there. Then he heard something downstairs,. It didn't sound menacing, it sounded more like a panicked Grace pacing. Taking two stairs at a time, he arrived downstairs to see her back at the front door looking out towards the front gate.

"Grace, what is-" was all he got out.

"Someone followed us home. I am trying to get the gate to close remotely like it is supposed to but it's not working. I don't know why, it worked last year with no issues, but now it is like it-" She was shaking.

Jim had made his way to her side and reached for her hands to hold them, but she recoiled. Flexing her hands, looking up at him, panic and fear flooded her eyes. For someone who had never shown an ounce of these emotions before, he knew it must truly have been something very real for her to react in such a way. Cool, calculated, seductive, he could list a million more things, but never panic or fear.

Stepping back, he held his hands up to her, allowing her to come to him if she wanted, but she seemed glued to her spot.

"Okay, I can go out and fix the gate and get it to close. Do you want me to do that?"

It wasn't a big deal, but he knew if he said that, she would probably flip out and he promised her he would be there to help not make light of her feelings. Grace's eyes and brow softened just a little and she looked at his hand and then looked him in the eyes.

9:

Grace had never been this scared in her life; she had suffered many traumatic moments in her life, and it never fazed her, but this eerily cold twist in her gut had her scared. It wasn't that she was afraid of something happening to her, it was the unrealistic fear that something would happen to the kids and Jim.

But the two eyes looking back at her were safe. Jim's steel gray-blue eyes reflected love, concern, and protection, she didn't say anything, just took his hand and. Sheed as he brought her close to him, enveloping her in his arms. The moment she let herself be cocooned in him her resolve snapped as the tears came and she started to crumble, only his embrace tightened so she wouldn't fall. Scooping her up in his arms, walking over to the blue and white striped couch, he sat down allowing her to just cry in his arms.

"You have to go close the gate," she said into his shirt through her tears. "It has to be the guy who followed me today and I can't have them trying to get on the property." Kissing the top of her head, he bowed his head.

"Okay, but I will have to let you go to do that. Is that okay?" Bobbing her head against his powerful chest, still gripping his shirt, she confirmed that she needed him to do this, but she wasn't ready to let go just yet. So, he waited for her to loosen her hold on him before he pulled away.

As he moved back, she saw what a mess she had made of his shirt. He wiped away her tears from her face and placed another gentle kiss, this time on her lips, and whispered "I'll be right back, I promise." Scooting off his lap, she walked with him to the front door and undid the code.

She wasn't willing to let her eyes off of him; she wanted to make sure he was going to be okay. Standing guard at the door, she never lost sight of him the entire time. As he closed the gate and locked it, she let out the breath she hadn't realized she had been holding. Her heart rate started to go back to normal the closer he got to the house and when he was finally in with the door closed and locked, she was able to breathe properly again. She set the alarm as he went to the back door to close the blinds to bring her a bit more comfort.

Grace started turning off the lights around the house, trying to keep her mind off of how she was feeling. Thankful was one feeling, she stood there realizing just how incredibly grateful she was to have him back in her life.

Walking over to her, Jim touched her hand again. This time she didn't shy away and he entwined his fingers in hers and pulled her close again, and it seemed her tears were not done.

"I'm so sorry, I'm not normally a fucking mess." She pulled away, wiping her tears away.

"You are not a mess, you are a normal person going through some serious bullshit right now." He cupped her face in his hands and kissed her nose. "Fortunately for you, you have an extremely handsome, fairly sane man able to help you with whatever you want." Grace furrowed her brow.

"Fairly sane?" sniffled Grace.

"That is what you took away from that, not the extremely handsome part?" Jim looked down at her.

"You know you are extremely handsome, unlike me, all blotchy face and running nose."

"I happen to think you are very beautiful, always have, always will."

Grace rolled her eyes but as she looked up at him, she saw that he was looking into her eyes. His heated gaze moving over to her hair as his hand ran through her curls that had come free from the hair style she had worn earlier, his eyes wandering to her cheeks, then to her lips and then back up to her eyes.

Her blood had slowed, it was as if the world's axis had slowed, and everything was moving at a tenth of its normal pace. But she could feel her heartbeat increasing, this slow acceleration, and as he brought his lips down to hers, her heart felt as if it was going to leap right out of her chest.

Jim's lips brushed languidly against hers, setting them aflame, easing all the tension she had been holding in her body. Her eyes fluttered to his and the heat she saw there was so intense that it stirred something deep in her belly. Grace had been kissed many times by Jim but this kiss was possessive. His hand that had been lightly playing with her curls was now entwined at the back of her head, pulling her hairpins out, dropping each one on the floor until he had a fist full of her curls in his hand and he pulled on them to coax a moan out of her. Her arms wrapped around his neck, trying to bring him closer, and she felt him moving her up against a wall.

Releasing her hair, he reached down and grabbed her ass with both hands to lift her up. Jumping up to make it a bit easier for him, she was now resting her hips against his and she could feel just how hard he was as he ground against her center. A soft moan escaped her lips as he kissed his way down her chin and neck and from his new vantage point had easy access to her cleavage.

Jim's strong hands kneaded her ass as he began to nip and suck at her collarbone and then languidly grazed his tongue along the seam of her cleavage. Her torridly gyrating against his length was going to send them over the edge before they even made it to bed. Grace had laced her fingers into his hair and went immediately to his ear, nipping at it, then sucking on it causing him to rut his hips into her again, a low groan escaping him.

"We need to move this upstairs, otherwise I'm hiking up this dress and letting you nail me against the wall." Grace nibbled his earlobe again. His hands on her ass gripped tighter as he lifted her away from the wall and started towards the stairs. She was startled as she realized that he was determined to carry her upstairs so that he could have his way with her in the comfort of her bed.

𝄢

"Hold on."

They stayed as quiet as they could but at the top of the stairs, he let her down so she could walk the rest of the way. The smile across her face was a welcome sight, he hated seeing her crying and this was the way he wished to see her always. A wicked, tempting smile, pleased and happy, was the only way she deserved to look. He watched as her curvaceous hips swished in the dress and he was tempted to reach out and pinch her ass right then, but he knew she would make a sound and waking the kids was not what he needed at this moment.

Locking the door behind him, he ran to her, unable to wait any longer to take her, and they instantly started pulling the clothes off each other. She carefully took off his shirt as she looked at the purple bruises across his chiseled abdomen, her fingers grazing his flesh, and he winced only slightly, the ache not as bad as it had been a few days before.

She kissed his flushed neck as he worked on the buttons at the front of her dress, slowly revealing that she had not worn a bra. He bent down, kissing her shoulders as he continued working on the buttons. He hadn't realized just how many there were and he was beginning to hate this dress, or at least this many buttons.

Meanwhile Grace helped him out of the shirt and started trailing kisses from his neck down to his powerful chest then gingerly over his bruises. He sucked in his breath as she worked her way around to the side where most of the bruising was and then made her way to his back while kissing and running her nails down it. The sensation was odd, he had never been kissed on his back before, but it made the hair on his arms stand on end.

Jim unbuckled his belt and tore it out of the loops with a snap that made Grace stop for a few seconds but then he found her hands traveling to the front of him while she stood behind. She continued kissing and nipping at his back as she gripped his pectoral muscles, scratching lightly then slowly moving her hands down to his pants.

Jim wasn't sure if he should help, as he went to undo the buttons himself, but Grace swatted at his hands causing him to crane his neck to look into her lustful eyes.

"Uh-uh, that's my job," she commanded from behind him as she continued her torturous attack on his back. With every nip she made a fire on his tanned skin ignite and he was sure that he would incinerate right there on the spot. Dexterously undoing the button and unzipping the fly on his dockers, Jim looked down at the foreign hands slowly gliding along the waistband of his underwear, pulling both his pants and boxers deftly down at the same time.

As she moved back up, one tiny hand slithered along the inside of his right leg and her other hand skated along the outside of his left leg. It was a slow methodical torture he had never felt before in his life and he would let her do it every day going forward, he would get on his knees and beg her to if he had to. This was not the girl he remembered; this was a woman who knew what she wanted and how to get it.

As her hands went higher, she kissed the back of his thighs, causing him to moan. He had been trying so hard not to make a sound, but this was too exquisite of a feeling. And then her right hand was cupping his balls as the other was rhythmically stroking his engorged erection just as she bit his ass. Closing his eyes so forcefully that he saw stars, he bit his lip because he was going to lose it right then. The prospect of blowing his load before he even got to touch her was making him insane and, snarling, he knew that despite this glorious sensation, this needed to end.

He needed to touch her, to caress her soft skin, to make her moan and squirm and writhe beneath him. To watch her breasts bounce as she rides him, anything but the pain she was putting him through. But first to get his feet out of these pants. He grabbed her hands and pushed them away, making every attempt to escape so that his legs were free, and then he whirled around to face her.

Picking her up, he would have loved to have slowly undressed her the way she had. To slowly torment her in the same fashion. But he had no patience for that. As he nimbly worked with the buttons to undress her, she continued to play with him, her hands barely able to wrap themselves around his girth.

"If you don't stop doing that, this will be over far too quickly and that is not what I had intended for this evening, Miss!"

Yanking down her dress over her hips to find she had no underwear on at all, he realized she had gone out wearing no panties or bra, and with the kids! His eyes went wide in confounded disbelief as he looked at her body.

"Do you mean to tell me that you had nothing on but the dress?"

Grace's seductive smile said it all. "Well, you gave me the dress and said you picked something out for me to wear, so I wore just what you bought me."

She licked and then bit her lower lip, and he didn't know whether to spank her or kiss her, so he decided to do both. Drawing her close he crashed his lips down on her wet lips and then spanked her ass very hard causing her to yelp into his mouth as he squeezed the ass cheek he had just spanked.

"Do that again," she begged with a smile, looking up at him through heavy-lidded eyes. He squeezed her ass, and she shook her head. "No, I meant the thing before that."

Jim had a bit of a shock. Tiny Grace, sweet kind sexy Grace, liked to be spanked. He looked down at her with a raised eyebrow, as his hand rubbed her ass gently. "You want me to spank you?" A crimson bloom tinted her smiling cheeks, and her eyes told him yes without her uttering a sound.

Reaching back his enormous hand, he spanked her again with such force their bodies smashed closer causing her damped folds to brush against his thigh. The impact had stirred a carnal moan from her lips and the scent of her arousal wafted up, mixing with her perfume, making the headiest scent. Scooping her up, he placed her onto the bed, causing her to bounce, but in doing so he hadn't realized that all this moving around had caused his ribs to hurt causing him to make an "oof" sound.

He hadn't meant to break their magic by hurting himself but she immediately scrambled over to him to make sure he was okay.

"Why did you do that? You carried me twice already, which was twice too many." Even naked she went into nurse mode and was checking him as he climbed up on the bed. He took a deep breath then gathered her to him.

"For the love of God, woman, I will carry you with broken ribs, arms, legs, whatever part of my body, as long as I can just make love to you. Is that okay?"

He pulled her on top of him not caring about the soreness from the bruises. But she knew it was bothering him so she slid off.

"No, I am too heavy. You could seriously injure yourself."

Grace didn't understand why he was willing to risk more injury. Jim creased his brow, not understanding her.

"Grace, who said you were heavy? You are like what 125 pounds, at most 140. I work with big metal car parts, trust me, I can toss you around and it would be like nothing."

Hank had really done a number on her head; she had lost so much weight and although her body showed it with loose skin, Jim didn't care. It was only flesh, flesh he planned on worshipping, and if he needed to remind her of how sexy she was on a daily basis he would. The woman she was now went deeper than skin and bones; she was his queen, his siren, his love. But as he sat there watching her mind racing, he placed a hand on her soft face to look at him.

"Hey, listen to me." She wasn't looking at him. "Gracie, look at me."

Fixing her pained eyes back on his, he brushed away a stray curl that had fallen in front of her eye and cupped her cheek.

"I'm not him, it's just you and me. Same old Jimmy Wooley from a million years ago. Only now I get to love you the way I should have."

Tears gathered in the corners of her eyes, and she moved her lips to kiss the inside of his palm.

"I love you, and no amount of weight or hair color or whatever is going to change the amazing woman who is in bed with me right now." A tear fell from her eye and his thumb brushed it away. "Now stop crying and make love to me.," he breathed as he pulled her down for a kiss.

𝄢

Her body seemed to gravitate to him, and she moved back on top of him, gently lying, there and she could feel his heart racing as he crushed her to his chest. Her legs straddling his hips as she ground against him caused them both to gasp and moan in delight. His hands trailed down her curves and spanked her again, taking her by surprise, making her bite his lower lip as they kissed.

"Again," she whispered and he was happy to oblige as his large wide hands this time smacked both her ass cheeks and gripped them hard, squeezing them, leaving tiny nail marks. Grace smiled at the exquisite electricity it elicited and whimpered in delight, but she needed more. Sliding down his hard body a little more, she settled his thick shaft between her slick folds causing Jim to sigh. She did it again getting his hardness wet from her arousal and teasing her clit, causing that sensation she loved. There was a swirling inside her demanding for release, but she was going to need him inside her first.

She didn't hesitate this time as she poised him to her entrance and then allowed only the tip to slide in as his girth was much larger than she had remembered. Placing her hands on his chest, she lifted herself up and braced for the punishing stretch as he slid the rest of the way, in taking their breaths away.

She had forgotten just how wide and long he was and after four years with no dick in her at all she needed a moment. She sat there for just a second before moving slowly, excruciatingly slowly as she adjusted to him, tipping her head back as she moved up and down on his hard cock. While her eyes were closed, he reached up, grasping at her breasts, kneading them and brushing his thumbs against her nipples, teasing her even more. The thrill of his tantalizing thumbs and the pressure from his dick hitting her cervix, she quickened her pace; she was close but not close enough.

𝄢

Jim moved his hands down her soft sweaty body to her hips and then thrust up as hard as he could just as she came down so that he was now buried to the hilt in her, a strangled cry escaping from her lips. Jim laid there watching Grace take complete control and watching her enjoying herself over and over again. This was definitely not the young girl that he had shared his first time with; this creature on top of him was a woman. A woman who knew her own desire, her own lust and need, and was willing to enjoy it with him.

Releasing her hip with one hand, he slid the other between the two of them and started to strum her overly-stimulated clit in a circular motion causing little sounds to escape her throat. With every thrust he made in her, he placed more pressure on that bundle of nerves and the deep breaths she was taking indicated that she was getting close. But then she surprised him as she reached behind her with one hand and was able to play with him as she ground against him, and he played with her. It was a feat of multitasking at its best, but they were both close and he could feel it as her drenched pussy pulsated around him.

"Babe, please I need you on top."

Without even pulling out he rolled her over and was on top of her in one swift move. Never one to argue with a horny Grace, he realized she wasn't wrong and he had needed her underneath him as well. Curling her fingers through his hair, she pulled him in for another kiss as he moved in her, feeling her walls engulfing his thick shaft. Snaking her hand between them, she found her engorged clit and started her own ministrations, and he was loving watching her face as she surrendered to ecstasy of it all.

"Why do you feel so fucking good?" he groaned into her ear, sucking hard on it, and she let out a sound from her throat he was sure was a moan, but this was more primal. It was pure pleasure, rare unadulterated pleasure. It was a sound he had never heard from Elizabeth, so he had plans of making sure he heard this sound over and over again from Grace until his last days on this earth.

"Harder!" she pleaded. If she wanted more, he would give her more. His thrust was deeper and harder this time as Grace threw her head back. Grasping at his back and wrapping her legs tighter around him, she picked up her pace and just as he thrust again it came. The world around exploded as her climax rolled over her. The undulating power of her whole body shuddering and pulsating around his drenched cock induced his own pleasure. The eruption of his own release was the strongest he had ever experienced, leaving him feeling a sensation he couldn't describe. Gasping for air, he collapsed on her and rolled to the side, taking her with him. A tangled mess of hot and sweaty limbs trying to breathe as they looked at each other, Grace and Jim could do nothing but laugh.

"Holy-" Grace was barely able to speak and still catching her breath.

"Shit," Jim finished her statement and kissed her nose in between breaths, causing her to giggle again.

"Okay, that is a very weird feeling." He was finally breathing normally again, as Grace wiped away sweat from his brow.

"What is?"

"Me being in you as you laugh, you are clenching me every time you giggle."

Grace pulled herself closer and squeezed her pelvic floor causing that clenching feeling, causing Jim to shudder and laugh.

"Alright, enough torture." Then he closed his eyes. "Fuck." He looked around for something, but Grace looked at him. "What's the matter?" she asked, then she realized.

"We forgot a towel. Hang on, I got an idea."

"Am I going to like this idea?"

"It's worth a shot,. You trust me?"

"I don't think I have an option here." Jim smiled back at her and grabbed her bottom.

"Hold on!"

Jim rolled her back on top of him and then wiggled towards the edge of the bed. Grace gripped his neck as he lifted them both off the bed and walked her to the bathroom laughing quietly the whole way there. Once there, he walked them into the shower and finally dislodged Grace from his body.

"Well, I guess we should clean up while we are here," he said looking at her, but something was different. Her face showed she was uneasy. "You okay?" Sheepishly she looked around and found anywhere to look but at him. "Grace, I've seen ya naked, I was just in you, we can take a shower together."

Grace took a deep breath. "I know it's just-" she rolled her eyes and huffed. "We had the lights off and-" she hesitated "I've never taken a shower with someone." She looked at Jim who just stood there dumbfounded.

"So, you have suffered a crime against humanity?" Jim's serious tone made her laugh. "Oh no, no, no, no, this is unacceptable, these tits and that ass have not been soaped down by another person?"

"Do maternity nurses count?"

"Absolutely not! Get out of the way, I'm remedying this immediately." Jim moved Grace behind him, running the faucet first, then had her move out of the way before he turned the shower head on.

He was going to make this completely enjoyable for both of them. But at this moment, this time, he was determined to make her feel phenomenal when she walked out of this shower. Worshipping this woman, bathing her and making sure she knew she had absolutely nothing to feel insecure about.

Drawing her under the water, he started by running his fingers through her wet hair. As he massaged her scalp, she leaned back into him and instantly he felt whatever muscles she had been tensing were slowly releasing. But he didn't stop there; grabbing her magical-smelling shampoo, he started with washing her hair.

"You could take the soap and start washing me if you like."

Her head was tipped back under the water as she was helping him rinse the soap out of her hair. Tiny water droplets clung to her lashes, and she looked like a water nymph, causing him to smile. His little siren. Reaching for the soap, she started washing his muscular chest and chiseled abdomen carefully as the light made the bruising more clear, cautiously washing him and then carefully turning him so she could do his back. She had been avoiding his ass and his growing erection.

"Won't all this cause things to...um...start over again?" she questioned, raising her eyebrow. The sly smile on his lips let her know it was what he was hoping for. He slowly walked her back under the water and then bent down to kiss her as he ran his hands over her wet skin.

"That is exactly what should happen, only you get to leave nice and clean."

Soaping up her breasts and then pinching her taut nipples to produce a sharp intake of air out of her mouth, it was the exact reaction he was looking for. There was no roughness or hurrying. It was like a slow dance. Methodically he soaped up every part of her, teasing her breasts, ass, and quim as he took the time to place wet kisses on her body. She was sighing and goosebumps were forming on her skin despite the hot water raining down over them.

Resuming her turn to wash his body, this time she opted to start with his shoulders and work her way down to his abs. Then she surprised him. Sitting him down on the shower bench, Jim watched as she turned her back and then lowered her soapy ass onto his lap and started grinding against him.

"You are a dirty little siren, aren't you?" he whispered as he grabbed her hips and thrust his now fully erect dick between her folds. Her breath was now coming in short pants, and he knew she was ready for him all over again. She continued her grinding by doing a very wet lap dance. When he had had enough of this, he took her hips and easily guided himself back inside her quivering, slick core.

Letting out a gasp, she settled back and he continued thrusting into her from behind. The water was making the movements sound lewd and filthy as their skin slapped against each other. Reaching around, he slid his hand down over her mound and found her clit again and started playing her like a guitar. She just leaned back on him and allowed him to have his way with her. The sounds she was making were music to his ears and he only had to shush her once so that she would keep her voice down.

"Shhh, I can't have you waking everyone up, so you need to be quiet, or I will stop."

He felt Grace's body tense at that threat, and she instantly quieted down. Peppering her neck with kisses and even a few bites on her neck, he noticed her breaths just kept getting shorter as the build of her climax was coming in fast this time around. Several quick hard thrusts and swirling of her clit later, their climaxes hit at the exact same time again.

He kissed her ear and whispered, "Now that is how you take a shower the right way." She giggled once again, craning her neck to kiss him on the lips before removing herself. He sat there enjoying watching her wash herself; it wasn't fancy or enticing, he just enjoyed watching this woman do anything really. Once she finished rinsing off, she bent down, placing a sweet kiss on his lips, and left the shower, leaving him to do his own job. He still couldn't believe all of this. They were together. Yes, they had a number of obstacles in the way, but here she was.

He found her on her deck wearing that delightful green nightgown from the other night, looking at the moon, and he joined her, wrapping his arms around her waist.

"Thank you," she said, leaning against him.

"For what?" He looked out at the ocean, which looked so unbelievably peaceful.

"For loving me, taking care of me, putting up with all this shit for me." He turned her towards him this time and looked her in those deep brown eyes.

"You should have stopped after the first three words in that statement." She snickered at that one, but Jim was serious. "Grace, if I have to say it every day I will, I was an idiot as a kid, but I'm just thankful I get to be right here, next to you, now." She looked down at the ground and it pained him that she couldn't look at someone who loved her so much, that she had been so mistreated for so long that she didn't think she was worthy of love and affection. "Gracie, I love you. I made you a promise, I'm not leaving." She looked at him again and kissed him.

"I love you too, always have," she whispered.

"Always will." He kissed her right back.

CHAPTER FOURTEEN

What do you mean Jim kicked you all out?" Kevin said as he put Nikki on speaker so his mother could hear.

"He kicked us out, telling us that we don't know what she is going through and he does and how he changed, and he isn't going to break her heart again and that perhaps we were all overwhelming her." Nikki only had one speed and octave when she was pissed, fast and high. Fortunately for Kevin, he had had many years of practice listening to her screeching.

"Well, okay but he is the one who has recently gone through a divorce, and with the woman who Hank is having an affair with. Which is super cringe," Kevin said. As much as he loved Nikki, she could be a little overwhelming.

"Yeah, but-" she started, but Kevin went on.

"And he isn't that kid from high school. This is the guy that Grace knew he was gonna grow up to be. He took a massive beating for her, who would do that? I'm her brother and I wouldn't have."

"I would have. But to say we are overwhelming? Come on that is fucked up and you know it." Nikki tsked but there was silence. Kevin and his mother just looked at each other, not sure how to respond. "Your silence speaks volumes, Kev."

"Listen babe, I love you but when she left here on Saturday I was under the impression that it was just gonna be me, Mom, and Dad going down for the week, and Jim and his girls joining for a day. I don't even know how a day turned into a week." Kevin didn't want to ask it outright, but he had been a bit confused when it all went down. Then he heard Mike in the background.

"See, I told you. Also, I was the one who suggested we should let them have the rest of the week to themselves."

"Shut up Mike, so you are telling me, we were wrong for coming down and telling her to invite Jim for the week? If it wasn't for us, she would have been there all alone with no support for the week and we'd have let her be there to deal with Hank and that psycho." Janie and Kevin covered their mouths. No wonder she had been entertaining everyone - because they invited themselves. Well, all except Jim.

"Nicole, sweetie, you know she loves you guys and would never tell you "No, don't come," but even I felt bad later inviting Jim and now that all this has happened, I'm glad he is down there taking care of her, and that you guys are supporting her, but it is a lot for her to handle right now. Especially with all of Hank's shenanigans. So maybe Jimmy is right. Maybe just call or text her before you go over, okay?" Janie was the voice of reason sometimes and Nikki would hopefully listen.

"We can do that Mrs. C. Right, Nikki?" Mike said in the background as Nikki sighed heavily.

"Fine." She huffed again; she really was not happy with this decision. "I'll let Denise know too."

Kevin wasn't worried so much about Denise; she had a good head on her shoulders most days. Kevin knew it would be okay, but Nikki would fly to Grace's side in a heartbeat.

𝄢

Ken walked into the room having heard some of the conversation and started making himself a cup of coffee to go. He checked his watch; he had an hour before he needed to make sure that Hank was out of the house and the locks were changed.

Kevin had suggested a friend on the police force, George Nicols, who had the day off, to make sure the transition was a smooth and peaceful one. Ken was too old to be in a fight, especially after seeing how Jim had looked. Jim could handle himself and it was a good thing too, but he did worry about Grace.

As her father, he didn't want to see any harm come to her, but that meant emotional harm as well. A small voice in his head thought she and Jim had been moving too quickly back together, but Janie had said that it was wonderful and finally the right time. Her romantic nature was one of the things he loved best about her, but he just didn't want this to end badly again.

As Nicole's chattering droned on, he kissed Janie and patted his son on the shoulder, waving goodbye as he left the house. He had woken up a bit too early and was wrestling with nagging nervous energy all day. He had tried to busy himself around the house and with the car, but nothing seemed to be helping. Just as he turned the car on, his Bluetooth connected, and Dale was calling.

"How's it going, Dale?"

"Could be better. Have you talked to Grace this morning?"

"No, should I have?" Ken pulled over and parked his car. The tone of Dale's voice now had him worried.

"Apparently someone is following them. She sent me texts yesterday that Hank and his mistress hired someone to follow them to get photos of her and Jim together. I'm assuming they want to paint it that this has been going on for years so they can go after them."

"You have to be kidding me?" Ken was now pissed. "When was she supposed to have time to carry on an affair? She's been suffering in that marriage with that asshole for years." He spat; he would murder Hank. Spiteful rat bastard, he was glad he asked George to be there with him because he was going to skin this dipshit. His heart rate was up too high, and his phone was letting him know. He took a breath and tried to calm down.

"Did you get a hold of George? I don't want you over there by yourself."

"Yeah, he is meeting me over there. You know what I don't get is, why is he doing this? Why can't he just move on? Like he has this other woman, just go be with her." He didn't know this woman that Jim had been married to, but he had zero respect for her after meeting her the other night.

"What I want to know is what the odds are that Jim's ex-wife is the one that Hank is having this affair with? And how did they even meet?"

Dale raised a great point. First she stole Jim away and now Hank - but to be fair she could keep him. It all felt fishy to him, like there was something they were missing.

"I'm not sure. I'll have to check with Jim to see if he knows anything."

"Well, I have to say, Ken, I'm really glad he and Grace did reconnect. She deserves someone to make her happy."

"Yeah, he is a good kid. Kid, shit, he isn't that anymore. God, that is weird. I see them together and I see the two teenagers ready to take on the world together, not the two adults whose lives got fucked up by awful partners." Ken had a thought, but he was afraid to say it out loud. Maybe if he said it to Dale, it would just stay between the two of them. "If only they had gotten married to each other, this wouldn't even be an issue."

Dale laughed on the other end. "Don't let Janie hear you say that she would be saying 'S*ee, I told you, they should have just worked it out and gotten married like Judi and I wanted*'.'" Dale did a pretty good impression of Janie. Ken roared with laughter; it was just what he needed.

"Well, don't tell her I said it and I can still live my life in peace. But seriously, this wouldn't have been an issue. But then I wouldn't have my grandsons, so I guess that is the upside of all this." He thought of the two boys, and he couldn't think what his life would be like without them. As crappy of a dad as Hank was, Grace had raised such amazing young men, and he couldn't be prouder of her and them.

"How are they doing in all this? I'm sure this has been rough; Cal has to know what's all going on."

"They are okay for now, it's gonna be a long road for them, but luckily, they know they are loved, and they seemed to understand this is for the best. Cal is more worried about Grace than anything."

"Well, hopefully we can get this all situated for her in the next few weeks. If we can get his Answer, then we can schedule the meeting while you are away." Ken heard a knock at Dale's office door. "Listen, Ken, let me go, keep me posted on the move and the locks. I gotta take this."

"Yeah, I'll text you." Ken hung up and pulled his hands from the wheel. He hadn't realized that he had been gripping the steering wheel so tightly. Flexing his fingers to get the blood flowing back in them again, he took another deep breath. She was going to be okay, he kept telling himself. He hadn't realized that he was not far from Grace's. He looked at the time and decided to head over a little early. George should be there in a few so he would just go and park in Nicole and Mike's driveway and watch from a distance since they lived a few houses away.

He backed into the driveway and watched Hank with a few other men taking bags and boxes from the house and putting them into a small moving truck. It was one of those one day rentals and he could see that there was a recliner that Grace had bought him for Christmas in the truck, storage tubs with Grace's handwriting on it saying Hank's winter clothes, a couple of lamps he remembered him moving in with, a box that had a TV in it, another chair, one he remembered seeing in their bedroom, and more suitcases. He just shook his head, then he saw Elizabeth. She was calling Hank to come over to look at her phone. She was showing him something that clearly was upsetting him. He heard Hank yell *"Hope they fall off that damned deck"* and she hugged him to try and calm him down. A car pulled up in front of the house and it was the cleaning service that Dale had given him the information for.

Elizabeth went down and met the women coming out of the car and started giving them instructions. Ken couldn't hear what she was saying but he was sure that it wasn't anything useful. Fortunately, George pulled up and got out of his truck. Ken then walked over to let him know that it seemed that Hank was not done just yet, but the cleaning crew had just arrived.

George Nicols had been one of the defensive linemen on the football team back when Grace went to school, and it seemed that he was still just as extremely intimidating as he was in high school. His dark chocolate complexion, broad shoulders, and a scar on his face that he had earned from an attack from an assailant he was apprehending in a foot chase gave the opposite impression of what he was like in real life, a big mushy teddy bear.

Elizabeth heard their footsteps as they approached the walkway and ran to the house. Hank appeared two seconds later with another box and Elizabeth right on his heels.

"It's not 11 a.m. yet, Ken. Tell your little bodyguard to back off." Hank's face had looked better, and his knuckles were multicolored now.

"Oh, I know, George and I are just making sure nothing that belongs to my daughter and my grandsons is missing or destroyed. Have you met George? He's an officer here in town, he graduated with Grace, so he wanted to make sure that nothing was being taken that wasn't yours. We would hate to add larceny to that list of charges you seem to be racking up here lately." Ken took a sip of his coffee and smiled.

"Everything in there is mine."

"Including that recliner that Grace bought in the back of the truck?" Hank turned at the mention of the chair.

"That was a Christmas present for me, so it's mine."

"Enjoy it. I'm sure it will serve as an excellent bed for the time being." He winked at George, who stifled a laugh.

Elizabeth turned to George. "So, you know Grace?" George smiled a wide smile and nodded. Elizabeth looked him up and down as if she was inspecting him.

"Then you must know James Wooley, he graduated with her too, right?" Ken wasn't sure what she was getting at with this line of questioning. But she was up against one of the best investigators in town so this should be fun.

George looked unimpressed with her. "Jimmy Wooley? Yeah, I heard he just moved back home a week or so ago. How do you know Jimmy?"

Hank was trying to move boxes from the house and ignore the conversation, but it seemed he wanted to hear more so he pretended to organize boxes in the truck. Elizabeth looked uncomfortably over at him and then to George.

"I'm his ex-wife," she whispered. Ken took another sip of his coffee and looked at George, then pretended as if there was something very interesting in Grace's hydrangea bushes and walked over to admire them.

"Ah, I see." Ken was doing everything in his power not to laugh as he knew that George was about to launch into his interrogation. "You don't look familiar, we didn't graduate together, did we?" Elizabeth shifted in her spot and shook her head.

"No, we met in college." George kept his eyes on Elizabeth, never breaking his gaze.

"Huh, well that makes sense. Ken weren't Grace and Jimmy dating back in our senior year? I remember I asked her to prom, but she turned me down because Jimmy took her." Hank squared a look at this tall, dark, menacing- looking man who seemed to be moving closer to Elizabeth. Ken kept looking at the plants in Grace's front yard as if they were far more interesting than the conversation.

"Yeah, they were on and off during senior year, nothing serious though. I can't remember why they broke up." He reached down and admired a bloom and then pretended the thought hit him. "Oh right, now I remember." He squared and looked at Elizabeth, Hank a mere foot away from her. "He apparently had hooked up with a girl that first week in college. Jim had come home the weekend after and told Grace and they broke it off."

Elizabeth shifted her gaze to the ground as George feigned a surprised reaction. Hank looked a bit surprised, and Ken thought he had only expected to be there to change the locks to the house and not get a front row seat to such wonderful entertainment. He thought that perhaps Grace had never spoken about previous relationships with Hank and now Hank was getting a history lesson about the woman he was married to, but also the woman he was having an affair with. Ken watched as Hank took a step back from Elizabeth and walked to the front steps to take another box.

"Huh. So, when in college did you meet Jim? Were you guys in the same year?"

Elizabeth glared up at George. "Why do I feel like I'm being interrogated? I'm just here to help my boyfriend move." George crossed his arms smiling.

"I'm just curious about what happened with Jimmy after he left and went to college. I haven't had the chance to meet up with him to catch up, I figured the woman who had been married to him wouldn't mind filling me in." He put on his best smile to try and calm her down. He looked over to Hank, who seemed rather interested in the line of questioning. Elizabeth looked at Hank and sighed.

"Fine. Jim and I met at freshmen orientation, and I was the one he hooked up with. Okay?" She shot a look at Ken, who put on his best shocked face. She turned back to Hank and continued "He said that he had a girlfriend, but that they had some stupid agreement to keep things open. But when he came back from the weekend, he was a mess, going on about how we shouldn't have hooked up and how she dumped him, and I was pissed because he pushed me away."

"And you are not used to losing, are you?" George whispered, as he had moved rather close to her. Her face soured, looking down at the ground, and she just shook her head.

"But you still ended up with Jim in the long run, you won your prize so what happened?"

She had smiled at the word *won* but then changed back to the same sour expression. Ken looked at Hank, who just stood there stunned, and could see the wheels turning in that pretty little head of his. He and Dale had just been talking about Elizabeth and what her deal was, but now it seemed a little clearer that she for some reason had a vendetta with Grace. Going after a boyfriend and then years later her husband - something was off.

"I'm not going to stand here and be grilled. I'm going to wait by the car." Elizabeth threw her hands up shaking her head and stood by the car. Hank looked at George and then Ken.

"You missed a very interesting conversation the other night after Grace knocked you out. It seems you may not know the woman you are seeing as well as you may realize," Ken said looking at Hank, who probably felt as if he had just had the rug pulled out from beneath him.

"Wait, Grace knocked you out? Did she do that to your face too? It seems my self-defense classes were not in vain."

"Jim broke my nose, I was-" he trailed off. Ken could list a litany of things he was, an ass, an idiot, a moron, the list could on and on, but there was a part of him that just felt bad for him. It was clear that he had been kept in the dark on a lot of things. Observing Hank look back towards the house, down at his knuckles, then to Elizabeth, Hank did the one thing that could ever shock Ken. He realized he was wrong. "I'm sorry."

Looking at George, Ken didn't know what to say or do but Hank kept going. "Look, just let me know how much the damage is, I'll take care of it. And make sure they do a good job cleaning; I don't want the boys coming home to my mess."

Still in utter disbelief, Ken turned to Hank and gave him a nod that he would make sure that it got taken care of. *There might be hope for you yet.*

Walking over to the movers, Hank gave them a piece of paper as he got into the car with Elizabeth and drove off. George and Ken looked at each other. George gave Ken a wink.

"You didn't ask Grace to prom," Ken said as he started making his way into the house.

"No, but he didn't know that." Patting Ken on the back, he walked up the stairs with the older gentleman and started looking around the house. Ken straightened a few things up that Hank and Elizabeth had knocked over in their rampage and looked around.

The house looked like a hurricane had torn through it, and he stood there just shaking his head. It seemed emptier, as he piled up the picture frames of Hank and Grace which had been destroyed, placing them on the edge of the hallway table. George walked around looking at broken items and the mess.

"That chick really did a number on his head, didn't she?" All Ken could respond with was a tiny tilt of his head and walked to the front door. Sitting in one of the oversized rocking chairs on the front porch, he waved to the locksmith who had just pulled up. He knew he would be there until the cleaning crew was done so he settled in and closed his eyes.

He was going to take George out to dinner for being such a huge help, he decided, as he walked the locksmith through the house to show him which doors to change the locks to.

Taking out his phone, he texted Dale that it all went smoothly and then to Grace that he was at the house. His phone rang.

"Hey, sweetie. How are you this morning?"

"Hey, I'm okay. Everything alright?"

"Amazingly, yes. Hank is going to pay for any damage and the cleaning crew. He took the recliner and the chair from your bedroom." Taking the last sip of his coffee, he needed a refill. Luckily, he knew how to operate Grace's machine.

"That's fine. How much damage is there? Do I need to come back up?"

"Not really, it's mostly small stuff, knick knacks and picture frames. Nothing that can't be replaced. Just stay there and relax, if you can with that whole crew you got down there. Although I heard this morning that Mike is keeping Nikki at bay, Mommy told her to call or text first before they come by."

𝄢

"Oh, I was wondering why they hadn't come by yet. I just thought they went to breakfast without us." Grace looked over to Jim who was sitting drinking his coffee, reading something on his phone. He looked up like he had missed something.

"I don't know exactly what was said, but Mommy and Kevin did tell Nicole to back off and give you some space and that it had been wrong of her and Denise to invite themselves down since you wouldn't say no to them."

"Yeah, well, they were only trying to help." She took a sip of her coffee. She hadn't really wanted to be alone. Well, she did and she didn't. Grace had gotten swept up in their call and just went right along with them, something she seemed to do a lot. It had been peaceful this morning, just their kids who had been enjoying the house by themselves and not having to make arrangements for so many people.

"I know, sweetie, but they haven't been through this. The good thing is you have someone who sadly has some insight on this sort of situation and he is there with you so lean on him."

She heard some muffled talking in the background and then her dad got back on the line.

"Gracie, let me go. Stop overstretching yourself and just relax, okay, and stay a couple more days if you need it. Gotta go; I'll text you later." Ken hung up. Grace placed her phone on the table and closed her eyes.

"So was it really Mike's idea to keep their distance or did you talk to him?"

She glanced over to Jim who was mid-sip, narrowing a glare on him that left him looking like a deer in headlights. He softened his face and then went back to sipping his coffee.

"All I said was that they didn't know what you were going through and I did. I told them that you were most likely feeling beyond overwhelmed, which don't deny it, you were yesterday for sure, and that they needed to take a back seat and let me handle this. More or less." Looking up, he smiled at her.

"Handle this? I need to be handled?"

She wasn't sure how she felt about that wording. He realized immediately he had used the wrong words.

"Grace, no, that wasn't what I meant. I meant that I could help you through this, coping through this is hard, I only had my parents who had never been through a divorce, so I really didn't have someone who understood my feelings. But in this situation, I believe, I understand what you are feeling better than they do."

He reached for her hand and laced his fingers into hers. Whether she wanted to admit it or not, she knew he was right.

"Okay but they don't need to keep their distance."

"Oh, absolutely they do. Hurricane Nicole and Typhoon Denise are intense. My head spins with those two." Grace laughed and her phone buzzed.

It was Nikki

Hey, we are on the beach and Mandy needs to use the bathroom, can we come to the house?

"Speak of the devil. They are on the beach and Mandy needs the potty. I'm letting them come."

Grace wasn't going to deny anyone the use of her bathroom; she wasn't a heathen. Two minutes later Nikki and Mandy were on the deck brushing off their feet before Mandy went in. Nikki stood there with her hands on her voluptuous hips staring at Jim.

"Happy?" Her attitude clearly indicated she was still pissed at him.

"Nik, please. He is only trying to help."

"What the hell have I been doing your whole adult life? I've been here this whole damned time, where the hell has he been? Oh, that's right, off with the chick he cheated on you with."

He didn't say anything only because it was best not to antagonize her. Grace closed her eyes, sighing; she didn't understand why Nikki couldn't let it go. She was the one who had been wronged, but her best friend was the one who was still harboring hurt feelings. None of it made sense.

"Nik, look at me." She waited until Nikki had cut her defiant stare at Jim turning to look at Grace, "Yes, you have been here, and you have been amazing to me and the boys. But you and Mike have this amazing marriage, he has never made you feel the way I have been made to feel. He will love you for the rest of your days together, I-" She stopped, shaking her head. "I don't have that." Nikki looked at her and pointed to Jim.

"Yes, you do! He is right here! For crying out loud we are all taking bets on how long it will be before the two of you are actually married!" Nikki cried throwing her hands up in the air, but Jim just blushed at the idea.

"But that doesn't heal years of neglect and abuse. Nikki, you are right, I am here, now. But that doesn't stop the feelings of being out of control." Jim finally needed to chime in on this conversation. "I wish you guys could have seen the mess I was before. It was the worst feeling in the world, and I still had to be a dad for my kids. Trying to hold myself together for them and my job was one thing, but in order to heal you need support, therapy, and to be honest, I didn't feel heard or understood even by my own family. I walked around, functioning for everyone but myself, until I found a therapy group for spouses who had been cheated on. There is just an unspoken thing that I can't express or explain."

Grace just sat there watching a flood of emotions come over Jim as his eyes teared up, and then she understood. He really did know how it felt. He had so eloquently described how she had been feeling all these years. How if she shared a brief moment of her own feelings, she would be a burden. Sure, she would complain about the treatment she had been receiving from Hank to her friends. But that didn't make up for the constant feeling of failure and loneliness she struggled with.

As she sat there watching Jim blink back tears and wipe his nose as he cleared his throat, something in Nikki's brain must have suddenly clicked.

"I'm sorry, I just want to help." With tears in her eyes, she looked at Grace. She reached out and hugged her friend.

"You are helping, but sometimes I may need some space, and I won't be able to ask for it so I may need someone to remind me and right now that is Jim. I need you to be okay with that."

"Well, I don't like it, but I'll be okay with it." Nikki sighed. "You know the rules, break her heart-"

"You break my face, I remember."

Jim gave her a knowing look and Nikki nodded. Grace rolled her eyes, and Amanda came out with Colin in tow.

"Mommy, can I go on the beach with Mandy? She wants my help finding shells." he asked, and Mandy put her hands together in prayer. Nikki looked at them and then Grace.

"I can watch him if they are gonna be looking for shells. Do the other kids want to come too?"

Nikki was offering to help, not that the kids had been difficult, in fact they had been amazing by occupying themselves all morning. Jim got up and went inside to ask. He came out a few minutes later.

"It would seem they would like to join you guys. I'll be down in a bit. You gonna join us or hang here?" he asked Grace, who had mentioned she really didn't want to go to the beach today.

She felt safer after last night being near the house, so she just shook her head no. Nikki bent down giving Grace a quick peck on the forehead, ushered the kids off the deck, and walked onto the beach with Jim in tow.

Scanning the deck, Grace couldn't decide if she wanted to just lounge in the chairs, sit and read, or soak in the hot tub. Turning her neck, the loud cracking noise it made sealed her decision. Closing her eyes, she thought she should just shut out the world, but her mind just wouldn't stop.

All the balls she was juggling just seemed to be getting out of hand, she couldn't do it all herself anymore. After all these years it might be time for her to hire an assistant. She just had so much gone on personally that professionally it might be best for her to finally give in.

Her parents had been trying to convince her to hire someone for the past six years but because of the ghostwriting she had been refusing. Now the more she thought about it though, the more it was starting to make sense. *It's okay to ask for help*. She couldn't tell if it was her dad's or Jim's voice she heard in her head, but whichever one it was, they were right.

Then there was the issue of dealing with Hank. He had been absolutely unbearable of late and she was sure based on how Elizabeth had been that it was all her doing. She still couldn't understand what her deal was. Why was she so insistent on trying to ruin her life?

In fairness, things with her and Hank had been awful before Elizabeth had entered the picture, but perhaps they could have worked it out in therapy. Grace knew deep down though that Hank never would have gone, he wasn't the type, he thought it was a waste of money which was why she hadn't let him know that she had been going. It wasn't worth the argument. She had avoided problems for so long and now they were all out there for her to face. But she didn't have to face them alone, she knew that now.

Opening her eyes she saw Jim walking up the path and onto the deck. Waving to him, he smiled back and walked over. "How long till Grace soup?" She skewed her head to the side and made a face.

"Lord, now I will have to listen to bad dad jokes. No Grace soup, I forgot to add in the veggies and spices. Just boiled Grace."

"Well, I have been told I can be spicy but after listening to the nonsense down by the ocean I'm feeling more like a vegetable. Feel like company? We can make Grim stew." Jim wiggled his eyebrows and Grace let out the loudest laugh.

"Oh my god, that was awful. But I will have to tell Kev you stole his ship name!" She shook her head and uttered "Grim awful. Come on Im."

Jim looked at her. "Im, really? Is this what our relationship is going to be, awful dad jokes being one upped by each other?"

"Would you rather me be a hot mess like last night?" she said as he slid in right next to her, his arm wrapping around her waist. He nuzzled his face against hers.

"Well, I can deal with a hot mess, if what comes after is what we had last night." He kissing her cheek and then the shell of her ear. Despite being in hot water for so long, the shiver that ran up her spine from his kissing chilled her, leaving goosebumps on her arms and legs.

"Good God, man, we are outside, and everyone is on the beach, haven't you had enough of me already?" Turning her face to his, he brushed the tip of his nose against her, slowly shaking his head no as his gray eyes gazed longingly into the depths of hers.

"Of you? Never, I will never have enough of you." He kissed her soundly on the mouth and she melted. Grace would always melt in his arms, and she was happy to do so. But she knew that this thing between them, as great as the romance and sex was - and it so was - needed to be more if this was to work.

It was a serious conversation; one she needed to have with him. The only problem was that his tongue was currently preoccupied with her own.

In the distance a throat was clearing, pulling the two of them apart. Mike was standing there smiling. "Just need to use the restroom, didn't mean to interrupt. However, a few others are heading back to go in the pool. So thought I would give you two a heads up."

Grace could feel a blush starting on her cheeks and she decided to pull herself away from Jim. Perhaps it was best to just remove herself from the jacuzzi all together. Grabbing a towel as she got out, she looked over her shoulder and saw Jim checking her out, causing her to grin. She didn't know why he was so infatuated with her, but she was going to enjoy the attention anyway.

Heading into her office, she checked her phone to see she had a text. She did, from Hank. Dale had said not to look and just send it on to him, especially now that there was the restraining order. Turning around, she went to find either Mike, Jim, or someone else to read it and re-send it. Luckily, she found Mike coming out of the bathroom.

"Mike, I have a text from Hank. I'm not supposed to read them or answer them. Can you send this to Dale and then delete it?"

He looked at her phone and pulled away so he could do as she asked but after he opened it, he didn't move.

"Oh God, what? Why are you not doing anything?"

Grace didn't understand what was so awful that he was now fully stunned. Looking back down at her phone, Mike seemed to be re-reading the text just as Jim walked in. Mike, clearly contemplating his next move, started walking over to Jim. All the while Grace felt herself going in and out of annoyance alternating with nervousness.

"I'm gonna let Jim read this and I'm gonna leave it to him to decide what to do."

Grace hated not knowing. All she could do was watch Mike hand Jim the phone and let him read it. It was torturous, as Grace didn't know where to look between the silent conversation happening between the two of them and the phone.

"One of you say something!" she yelled, jarring the two men to turn stunned to her. Walking over, Jim handed her the phone.

"I think you should read this one."

Grace looked down at her phone and opened the text. It was three simple words. Three words that she never thought she would ever hear or see from Hank, but there they were.

I'm so sorry.

What the hell had happened? In twenty years of marriage, he never once apologized, EVER. Perhaps he hadn't meant to send it to her. It had to have been a mistake. He had found joy in making fun of her, putting her down at any opportunity he could find. Always blaming her for everything that went wrong to the point of even making her apologize to him for him bumping into her. Clearly the text was not meant for her.

"Okay, so this was not meant for me. Hank never apologizes to me. So, I'll just send it to Dale and let him deal with it."

She smiled as she sent it to Dale and deleted it. Mike and Jim kept looking at each other then back to Grace. Too deep in denial, Grace just shook her head at them.

"Hank doesn't apologize to me, okay, ever, never ever does he-" She stopped herself.

Jim leveled a gaze at her, and she wasn't sure what he was trying to convey. She thought she saw a tinge of remorse, but she couldn't tell. Grace was expecting him to agree with her, but how could he know, he didn't know what Hank was like. In her mind that text had not been for her, someone else perhaps, probably Elizabeth, but certainly not her.

"Grace, is it possible that it was?" Mike started to say, but the way Grace snapped her head to him caused him to stop whatever he was going to continue with in that statement. Shaking her head, not sure whether she was shaking her head in denial or just not wanting to hear the rest, Grace was not having this conversation right now. She just needed to check in with her dad and see if everything was done. Jim and Mike had no intention of following her as she went into her office.

Closing the door, not wanting to talk to anyone, she walked over to her desk and sat. Her heart was racing. Why would he apologize now, things were over, they had been over for years, he had broken her down and treated her so terribly. And if this apology was really for her, why? Why now? Was he finally realizing what he had lost or that he was in jeopardy of losing the boys? She looked back down at the phone and held it in her hand when it started ringing. Dad. Thank God.

"Hi Daddy" Her tone was cold and short.

"Hey peanut, you okay?" His concern was not lost on her.

"Uh, yeah," she lied.

"Gracie, what's going on?"

She didn't answer right away, she didn't know how to answer. He had sat right in this office and told her to be careful, that he was concerned for her health. If she couldn't talk to him, then who could she talk to?

"Hank sent me a text."

"Did you read it? Did you send it to Dale?" He spoke slowly to not push.

"Yes and yes."

"What did it say?"

"'I'm so sorry.'" Her voice caught in her throat. "That's all it said, I'm so sorry."

"Interesting. Well, it's about time. Perhaps-" He hesitated. "Perhaps some things have been brought to his attention, and he came to an epiphany of sorts."

"Highly doubtful, I'm going with the idea that it wasn't meant for me."

"Yeah, I don't think that is the case, I would go with what I said." His voice just a little too light as if he knew something.

"What happened? What did you do?"

"I didn't do a single thing. George came with me to make sure that things went smoothly and perhaps someone got an impromptu interrogation."

"Who, Daddy? Who got interrogated?"

"Elizabeth was there, and George wanted to know a little bit more about the woman. That's all."

Now she felt like a cat and the curiosity was going to kill her. But honestly there was a part of her that didn't care, whatever it was that had been found out had softened Hank or at least that is what it seemed like to her dad. If that was the case, perhaps the text had been for her. And since she wasn't in the habit of looking a gift horse in the mouth, she was going to take this win and run with it.

"Well, then thank George for me. Is everything okay on that end?"

"Everything is fine, I have the new keys, and the cleaning service just finished so you will have no mess to come back to. Hank also said if there is anything that needs replacing, he would pay for it."

Who was this person named Hank that her father was speaking about, because it was not her soon-to-be ex-husband. Did the Grinch's heart actually grow a size bigger? She wasn't going to believe it till she saw it with her own eyes and heard it directly from the horse's mouth. Running her fingers through her hair, she still couldn't believe any of it.

"Thank you, I appreciate it. I'm thinking we will probably head back Saturday so I'll call you before we leave."

"Sounds good sweetie, try and enjoy the next two days, please."

It wasn't so much a question as it was a command, and she wasn't about to argue with him. Considering all the work she had lined up for the summer, she needed this time.

"I will. Talk to you later."

Grace sat there looking around her office and at her laptop. She could be working but that wasn't why she had come down in the first place. Calvin and Colin were the reason. They were her whole world, and she knew just how much she was going to miss them while she and her dad were on the tour. Not that she wouldn't miss Jim, but her boys came first.

I don't want to see what happened to me to happen to you. Her father's words swirled in her mind. He had spent years working and driving himself to the point of a heart attack at work because he hadn't taken the time to relax or spend time with his family. He had been fortunate though; it hadn't landed him in an early grave, but it had forced him into an early retirement, and she couldn't imagine leaving the boys behind or giving up what she loved to do.

Realizing that all she wanted in this world was to spend time with her boys, she knew what she would have to do, whether certain people liked it or not.

CHAPTER FIFTEEN

Janie sat wide-eyed as Judi read the text from Jim out loud. Grace asked them to leave the beach and house for the rest of the day. Judi's phone buzzed again with another text, but this time she didn't read it for Janie and it was slightly killing her to know what it said. Sitting there on tenterhooks, Janie bit her fingers and waited patiently for Judi to take a sip of her tea.

"They're fine. Grace just wanted to spend time with the boys by herself. Which was the whole point for her anyway, wasn't it?"

"That's what she said. Ugh, I feel like this whole thing is my fault, I was just so excited when you told me Jimmy was coming back and that maybe they could pick up where they left off. But it wasn't supposed to be the whole week; not that I mind of course, you know I love him, and his girls are delightful."

Janie did feel bad; the whole week had been a disaster. She hadn't expected the whole crew to be down there for the entire week and then for Grace to invite Jim and his girls as well. It was just supposed to be one night and the boardwalk. Judi nodded, making Janie feel a bit better. At least they were both of the same mind.

"Here is my thing, who invited the rest of them down there, not that they aren't great, but you know how Nicole gets. I'm surprised Jimmy has had any time with Grace at all."

"Nicole, she and Denise just sort of invited themselves down after Grace told them that she signed the divorce papers. She admitted she was the one who told her to invite Jim down for the whole week." Judi threw her hands up in the air.

"What is she, new? Slow and steady with Grace, Hell even I know that." Judi turned to make herself another cup of tea. Setting the kettle back on the stove, she then went over to another cabinet and pulled out a bottle of Irish whiskey. Janie stared at her friend and the bottle.

"It's for my tea. I have a little cough." Judi proceeded to fake cough as she poured a little of the whiskey into her mug and took a sip, shivering a bit from the harshness of the alcohol.

"Isn't it a bit early to drink?" Janie scrunched up her nose to the smell of the whiskey. Judi's unamused look gave every indication that it wasn't.

"It's five o'clock somewhere, right?" Judi took another sip and shook her head. "Well, I'm just glad that Grace actually spoke up." Janie added a few drops of the whiskey to her own mug and waved her finger as she took a sip.

"Oh, that is your son's doing." Janie sipped her tea a little too long. Judi stood there shocked for all of two minutes and then shrugged.

"Good for him, and I guess that Nicole didn't take that too well." Janie just shook her head no. "Oh well."

The women both laughed at that last comment, and Janie wasn't sure if it was the whiskey or if Judi just wasn't holding her tongue about Nicole anymore.

Nicole was a great friend, but she was rather overwhelming at times. Janie thought about how she was when Grace and Jim had dated when they were younger, a bit of a third wheel even though she had her own boyfriends.

"Well, at least now Gracie can relax. No offense to Jim of course. Did he say what they were doing? Are they heading back?" Janie pushed her cup forward as Judi made her another cup of tea.

"He's taking the girls to one of the bay beaches. Grace said that they would meet up for dinner and then they are gonna go crabbing. She said she wanted to make the crab sauce tomorrow. I'm almost tempted to ask him to bring back some of the sauce."

Their conversation was interrupted by Mark walking in, looking between the two women and then at the whiskey bottle.

"Oh God, what happened now? Wedding called off already?" he said as he held up the bottle. Judi shot him a disapproving look causing Janie nearly to spit out her tea.

"God forbid, don't even put that energy out there, Marcus Wooley. They are fine," Judi said as her husband gave her a quick peck on the cheek and she smacked his arm. Mark went to the sink and started washing all the motor oil off his calloused hands.

"You know the two of you have nothing to worry about. If they are going to make it down to the altar, they will get there in their own time. In the meantime, you two meddlers just need to be patient." Janie giggled at that because she knew he was right. "And make sure to tell the girls too, because they are just as bad." Janie turned to Mark in shock. What did he mean, did Jim's girls want them to get married too? Oh, this may help them if that was the case.

"Wait, Katie and Vivian want them to get married? Does Jim know?"

Janie couldn't quite contain her excitement. The girls had been very nice to Grace from the time they had spent together, but she hadn't realized that the girls actually were entertaining the notion of their dad and Grace being in a relationship further than just dating. And then a wonderful thought crossed her mind; she would finally get granddaughters! Mark must have taken notice because he was giving her a look of dismay.

"No, Janie! Absolutely not, you two will not rope them in. God help us if they let that slip to Elizabeth, she's already off her rocker. Hopefully Jim can get full custody after that little stunt she and your son-in-law pulled."

"Ex-son-in-law."

The disgust in her voice was sharp; she had never truly liked him, but she never let Grace know. Hell, she remembered the last six months of Grace's engagement to him asking her *"Are you sure?"* whenever Grace would make a complaint about little annoyances that Hank would do. She could remember him making a comment about whether Grace's gown would fit the day of the wedding and after he walked out of the room where Grace stood teary-eyed, asking her *"Are you sure?"* Even the night before the wedding at the rehearsal he wasn't taking it seriously and Janie stood at the back of the church with Ken and Grace, asking her *"Are you sure?"* They would have eaten all the money on the whole deal if she said no. Even as they exchanged vows, she prayed Grace would come to her senses.

"Either way, you four better cool your jets until all this shit blows over. For crying out loud, Grace's divorce isn't even finalized."

He wasn't wrong but hopefully it would be done quickly. But now with the custody issue for Jim it only meant that it was possible that things would get pushed back even further. Judi went over and started to push him out of the kitchen.

"And you want to know why I'm putting whiskey in my tea this early, you are a Debbie Downer! Get out of my kitchen, goodbye. You are bringing down my buzz."

She kept pushing him out of the kitchen but as he was leaving, he took the bottle of whiskey with him. Murmuring that she was cut off, he headed upstairs.

𝄢

For the first time since Saturday, Grace sat there enjoying the boys. It was nice to have the two of them not bickering with one another. In fact, since she had signed the divorce papers, the two had been getting along. She wondered if the tension she had been carrying in the marriage had crossed over to the boys and that was why they were always bickering. She took a deep breath, shutting her eyes to the idea that it was even possible.

Listening to the sounds of a quiet beach not filled with a ton of people complaining or wanting something from her felt wonderful. She did love her friends, but she needed to feel like herself. She wasn't sure what that felt like anymore.

But then it dawned on her, she knew where she truly felt like herself. It was with the boys. It was the times that she volunteered at their schools, or rides to the park or even a camping trip where she got all covered in mosquito bites. But the one thing in the whole world that made her feel like herself was snuggle time.

Perhaps tonight she would make time for the boys before bed. It was lovely with the girls joining them. They had heard Grace and the boys being silly, with bad jokes and just messing around. And then she sang the lullaby. She hadn't sung that since Colin had been a baby. In truth, she hadn't sung anything since then.

Until yesterday she hadn't felt compelled to. Music brought her happiness, but it also let her get out her frustrations. It was her release. She thought about the song that Jim had picked for their duet, and the words hit directly to her heart. Every line in that song had been about them. The original writer didn't know their story, but it was theirs.

Her thoughts turned to Jim and just how she felt about him. Physically, she felt amazing and almost energized when she was with him, yet she felt herself emotionally still reserved in a way. It wasn't so much her that she was afraid of getting hurt; it was the children.

They had truly started to care for Jim in such a short amount of time, and then she wondered. Were the boys caring about him because of the way she was when she was with him? Were they invested in this relationship because she was incapable of hiding her attraction and feelings for him? If that was the case it wouldn't be Jim she would be angry with, if this didn't work out and the boys got hurt, she would be angry with herself for allowing it.

Even though her eyes were still closed, she could feel the burning from tears starting to form. She just needed to get through this next week, because then she would be away. Away from all of this and focused on the book tour with her dad. Her voice of reason. One more week to get through and then she was free. Too busy for anything and anyone except the boys and her dad. Hell, she didn't even have to deal with the divorce, Dale had that all well in hand, which was a complete blessing. And if Hank really was softening then it truly would give her a moment to breathe. She just wanted everyone to get along and everything to fall into place like she wanted.

Calvin looked up from making the castle with Colin and watched Grace as she wiped away tears that had escaped despite her best efforts to not cry.

"You okay over there?" He stood up and sat down on the sand next to Grace as she fixed her glasses back on her nose. Smiling weakly, she gave him a tiny nod.

"You know you don't have to be brave for us, right? It's okay if you just want to fall apart sometimes, we aren't gonna think less of you." Her brave boy. Grace reached over and hugged him.

"I know, it's all just hitting me at one time. I'll be okay, I'm just worried about you boys." She was going to be honest with him, hiding the truth was just not something she was willing to do anymore. Calvin looked at his mom and smiled.

"We will be fine if you are. But even when you aren't, we know that you love us and that is enough for us."

She was not sure when this boy sitting next to her had grown up into such a smart young man, but she thanked the heavens that she had him. Her brilliant young man. Colin looked up and flashed a stunning smile and just kept working on the sandcastle.

"Daddy texted me earlier." Calvin and Colin both looked at her waiting to hear what he had written. "He said-" a lump suddenly catching in her throat as tears pricked at her eyes behind her sunglasses - "it said, I'm so sorry."

The boys shot glances at each other in disbelief. Tears escaping from her eyes and her nose running prompted Colin to come over and sit on her lap, causing the tears to come faster. Hugging her youngest was a bit of comfort because she realized that as much as she had been trying to protect them from Hank's ire towards her, they hadn't been so blind.

"Do you believe him?" Calvin spoke up.

"I want to," she confessed.

She did want him to be sorry, but not just for this past week, for all the years of abuse, the affair, all of it. That would have to be a conversation with him but not today. Taking a deep breath, she hugged Colin a little tighter.

"Listen, I am enjoying it just being the three of us, but why don't you finish the sandcastle and then we can go join everyone else. I told them that we would go crabbing tonight and I will make sauce tomorrow." Colin leaned back to look up at his mom.

"Mommy, can it just be Jim and his girls? I just want to spend time with them."

"Well, I think that the rest of them are down till tomorrow, but if that is what you want, I can let them know."

Dinner had been cheesesteaks and hot dogs at a local spot that the boys loved and for the sake of the kids Jim and Grace had behaved themselves. Grabbing everything they had needed to go crabbing before they had left the house, she had tossed it all into the trunk of her car. Luckily the spot for dinner happened to be right on the bay with a long pier on which other families were crabbing as well.

Grace opened the cooler to take out the bait she had brought, and the girls just stared at her. Thawed uncooked chicken legs. Both girls looked up at Grace, unsure of what they were going to do.

"I'm assuming your dad has never taken you crabbing before."

The disapproving look Grace gave Jim clearly indicated that she believed that the girls had been deprived of the privilege they needed in their lives.

"Okay, so we bait the traps with the raw chicken, and it lures the crabs in. My granddad used to have us crabbing with just legs and twine for years, no traps, but that takes a lot of practice and time. But I'll show you girls."

Lowering the empty bucket into the water, she made sure she collected just a few inches worth of water, dumping it into the now empty cooler. The girls watched intently to learn exactly what to do. Jim took a trap and baited it then carefully tossed it into the bay, holding the string to keep it from being lost to the bottom. The boys then baited another trap, and the girls watched the whole process all over again, carefully learning as Calvin lowered it into the bay right next to the pier.

Grace went to work on another piece of twine and then handed it to Colin, who instinctively lowered it in the water a little farther down on the pier to not be so close to the trap and sat down waiting. Vivian and Katie just looked at their dad expecting him to not make them participate.

She looked up at the girls. "You don't have to, you can just help your dad and Cal bring the pots in. But I have one ready if you want." Aggressively shaking their heads no, Grace wasn't surprised by the lack of wanting to touch raw chicken or a live crab. "It's cool, you can sit with me, and you can see how we do it this way and if you change your minds, you can do it too, but no pressure."

Jim and Colin were sitting at the end of the pier, and it seemed that Colin had a bite. Jim grabbed the bucket as Colin slowly brought the string up to triumphantly show that the crab was still eating his chicken leg. Carefully they got it into the bucket and Colin went right back to work with Jim by his side. The girls sat wide-eyed and, unable to say a thing as they were just mesmerized by the whole spectacle. A few seconds later, Grace called them over to watch as she herself had something on her string and they were shocked to find not one but two crabs on her line. The girls, now giddy, grabbed the bucket so she could put hers in.

"Holy smokes, that is crazy, those are huge," Vivian said. Grace shook them from the chicken leg, then tossed it back into the bay. "How do you know when they are on the line?"

"It's the same as fishing, you can feel them tugging the bait." They gave her another bewildered look and she turned to Jim. "You haven't taken them fishing?"

"These two would never want to go even if I had a license," Jim remarked as he started to haul in his crab trap. Colin indicated that he had another bite. Vivian went and brought the bucket over to him and watched as he very slowly brought the trap up. Grace looked at Katie and motioned for her to sit.

"Come here, take the string. When you sit real still, you can feel a small tug as the crab is biting the chicken leg." Katie looked at Grace as she explained it and positioned her fingers just so that she would be able to feel it.

"Mom doesn't do stuff like this with us," Katie confessed. Grace turned to her shocked, not sure where this had come from, but she was not surprised that she didn't do stuff like this. Elizabeth seemed too bougie.

"Oh, um well, what kind of stuff does she do with you girls?" She didn't want to pry, but deep inside she wanted to know more about the woman who was their mother. She had to understand why Elizabeth hated her so much.

Katie sat there looking over the water, watching a flock of seagulls hovering on the bay breeze looking for food. "Nothing fun like this. She is more about how we look and our talents."

"Oh well, you do have an amazing singing voice and both of you are both blessed to have great genes. But I get it. I used to do pageants when I was younger. My mom used to put me in them." Grace still had that nagging thought in her head about how Elizabeth had harped on the word "winning." Katie looked at Grace and just nodded.

"It's like my mom is obsessed with them." Katie rolled her eyes. "Apparently she used to do them when she was younger."

"Really? Did she ever say what kind of competitions?" With her years of doing singing competitions, it had been possible that they might have competed against one another. She had only won one but that had been a really hard statewide competition.

"She had done a lot of beauty pageants; but she did a couple of singing competitions too."

There it was, the door Grace was hoping for. Katie went on "But you can't even talk about it with her, apparently she lost to some other girl who wasn't as good as she was, and she decided she was never going to do another one again."

Now her mind was racing. Was it possible that Elizabeth had been in the same competition she had? Being in the state competition was hard, there had been a whole audition process, and they had grouped the competitors together based on age and talent. But that had been over thirty years ago now.

"Yeah, well, losing is hard especially when you work so hard at it. But my mom always used to say, just go have fun, you win you win, you lose there is always next time." Grace was trying to be nonchalant about the whole thing despite her mind now racing trying to figure this out.

"See, that is what a good mom does. We are told to win, there is no second place. Dad made her stop making us do it because she becomes insane."

"Well, your dad is a good guy, he isn't one for competition. Too laid back." Katie looked at Grace and then back to the string. She must have felt a nibble. Looking back up to Grace with the widest smile she had seen on her all week, Grace couldn't help but smile back. Helping her bring up the crab, they shook it off into the cooler.

"I did it!" Katie screamed, "Dad, I did it, I caught a crab!" She turned and hugged Grace who was beaming ear to ear. Jim turned shocked, almost dropping the line for the trap. Everyone on the pier cheered. "Can we do it again?"

"Absolutely, I need a lot of crabs to make the sauce so let's get that cooler loaded!" Grace smiled.

She had a lot more to celebrate than Katie's success. She had her first clue about Elizabeth. Had this bitterness started over a competition loss? Seriously? When they were just kids, was she that unhinged?

Grace didn't want to bring down the rest of the night, she wanted to enjoy it with the kids and Jim. But first thing in the morning, she was calling her mom. Janie saved everything that her kids had been in and knowing how sentimental she was, she would still have the program.

CHAPTER SIXTEEN

Janie was mumbling in her closet on the floor going through old boxes, rifling through old photos and pamphlets from performances the kids had been in, when Kevin found her. He stood there holding two mugs in his hands, looking down on her like she was a crazy lady.

"Um, are we having a mental breakdown, because I am woefully unprepared for you to go through another menopausal freak out." Kevin had startled her as she looked up at him, a stray picture stuck to her curly gray hair. He slowly passed her the mug, and she took a sip, plucking the picture from her hair and looking down at it.

"I will have you know, I'm not having a menopausal freak out; your sister called me and asked me to look for something. I'm helping her with her investigation, but I'm not supposed to say anything."

She whispered that last bit hoping that Ken wasn't nearby. Kevin just shook his head, closing his eyes. She was sure he was trying to keep to himself any awful comments he wanted to make.

"Okay *Nancy Drew*, when something is a secret, you shouldn't share it with other people. And what, what investigation?" She glared at him and took another sip of her tea.

"I don't like your whole snippy attitude so, I'm not going to tell you. It's a secret." Smiling at him very proud of herself, she wasn't about to divulge any information to the town's king of gossip.

"What secret?" Ken walked up behind Kevin, scaring both him and Janie, causing him to smile.

"Oh my God, where did you come from? *Nancy Drew* over here is helping Grace with an investigation. But it's a secret."

Kevin took another sip of his tea and laughed. *Gossip King,* Janie thought to herself as she contorted her face in disapproval at him for spilling the beans. Putting down her mug on the floor, she started going through the boxes she had piled up on her right side again, trying to ignore the two men staring down at her.

"Janie, what does Grace have you looking for? Does this have to do with the divorce?"

Janie just ignored Ken's questions and kept going through everything. Ken must have noticed some of the old loose papers she hadn't put back yet and started going through the paperwork and pictures.

"Janie, if I guess it, will you tell me?" Ken asked, and she thought about it. He was a great litigator years ago; he had litigated his way into her heart, after all. So, he would know just how to steer his witness into getting the right answers. She would have to bring her A game.

"Is it about when Grace was in the plays?" he asked. Janie shook her head no. Kevin giggled and Ken just shot him a look.

"Is it about when Grace did the beauty pageants?" Kevin asked. Janie smiled and shook her head no again.

"Is it about when Grace used to do the singing competitions?" Ken felt like he was getting closer, and he knew it because she had stopped what she was doing. *Damn it!* Looking up at him she blinked twice and went back to look through the programs. Kevin sat down and started going through the boxes with her.

"So which competition are we looking for?" Janie just shook her head again.

"Lord, woman, how are we supposed to help if you won't say anything?" Kevin started throwing the programs up in the air and Janie huffed. These two were becoming too annoying and perhaps two other pairs of eyes could help.

"Fine, Grace thinks she competed against Elizabeth years ago and that is what started this whole insanity. The only singing competition that Grace won first place in was that huge statewide one. Remember it was her and two other girls in their category. Grace thinks that Elizabeth was one of the contestants based on a conversation she had with Katie yesterday. Katie had said that Elizabeth claimed that the girl who won had a terrible voice, and we know Gracie has a beautiful voice, so it just seems like she is suffering from sour grapes."

Kevin sat there with a look of shock on his face, while Ken just stood in the doorway to the closet drinking his coffee, watching his wife and son going through the boxes.

"You are telling me that Grace thinks that this whole Jim and Hank stealing business with Elizabeth is because Grace beat her in a singing competition? I have to call Grace, she needs to call her therapist, because this just sounds too far-fetched to me."

Ken pulled out his phone to call Grace, but Kevin reached out and grabbed his pant leg. In Kevin's hand was the program from the competition that Grace had suspected was the issue and sure enough, under the same category as Grace's name were two other girls. Elizabeth Winton was one of the other girls.

"Um, Grace may have been on to something, look." Ken and Janie looked up at the same time as Ken plucked the program from Kevin's hand and looked down to see the names. His face, which was normally rather reserved, was in total disbelief. Janie scrambled up to look, almost tipping over her tea, and she grabbed the paper out of Ken's hand and gasped. "Is this Elizabeth's maiden name?" Kevin asked, looking up at his father who just shook his head unsure of her maiden name.

Ken put his cup down and pressed his phone, putting it on speaker.

"Hey Kenny, what can I do for the Cartinos today?" Dale's voice was much more chipper today.

"Dale, what is Elizabeth's last name?" Ken's tone was in stark contrast to Dale's and Janie knew exactly how he felt; they were now more worried about their daughter than before.

"Um, let me see. Ah, Elizabeth Winton. Why?" The three Cartinos just looked at each other.

"When you filed for the restraining order, did Grace get one on Elizabeth or just Hank?"

Janie held her breath, praying that their daughter had been thorough and had gotten it on both. The rustling of papers on the other end of the phone only made the fear stretch out longer. Squeezing her eyes tightly and muttering a prayer to the Blessed Mother, Janie just prayed, *Dear God keep my baby safe.*

"Both. Grace had asked for both, she said she had a gut feeling on something. Why what's going on?"

There was a collective sigh from the three of them. Grace and her gut. She had gone into the wrong field, she could have worked for a CSI team with that gut instinct of hers.

"It's a long story. I'll come by, do you have time for me?" Ken said before finishing his coffee. He leaned over and kissed his wife. Kevin and Janie just stood there in the closet watching Ken leave.

"Good job, Joe!" Janie patted Kevin on the shoulder. But he just turned to her to see who she was talking to.

"Who's Joe?"

"Seriously, *Joe Hardy, Frank Hardy,* the *Hardy Boys.* '*Nancy Drew and the Hardy Boys.*' Oh my God, get out of my closet."

Janie shoved him out, shaking her head and mumbling to herself about the *Hardy Boys* and what an awful child he was for not knowing that.

9:

Grace had been sitting quietly at the kitchen island picking the cooked crab meat out of the shells for the sauce when the call had come in about what her family had found. She didn't want to ruin the perfect morning they had been having but she knew she had to tell Jim. It still felt completely unreal that she had been right about Elizabeth.

She wasn't happy about being right; she was afraid. This woman has made it her life mission to ruin every good thing she had in her life. Grace knew that it wasn't fair to keep this knowledge to herself, she needed to tell Jim. Breathing deeply, she got up and went to the door just as Jim was making his way into the house, but he must have noticed something was wrong by the look in her eyes.

"Hey, hey, what's going on?" He looked behind her, no one was in the house. "Grace, look at me, what is wrong?"

"I can't tell you with the kids around." She whispered "I, uh, I need to tell you something and I don't know how you are gonna take it."

"Graciella Marie, look at me." His voice was deep and firm and her eyes snapped up to his. He had never used her given name. His breathing coming in shorter breaths, he said "If you don't love me, tell me now, if yo-u" Grace's rapid blinking and confused face gave him the indication that that was not what she was freaked out about.

"What? Jim, what are you talking about?" she said. He pulled her inside, but stayed in the doorway so that he could keep an eye on the kids.

"What are you talking about?" he said. "What has you so freaked out, you were white as a ghost two seconds ago."

She shushed him so that the kids couldn't hear. He looked over his shoulder.

"Hey Kate, can you just watch Colin, Grace and I need to chat about something."

She just nodded her head yes, and he then shut the sliding glass door. Grace had gone back to the island, sitting and picking meat out of the crabs, trying to stay calm.

"Okay, so last night while we were crabbing, Katie and I got to talking and the subject of Elizabeth came up." Jim arched his eyebrow, probably wondering where this was going. "Something that Liz said Monday night stuck with me about the whole winning thing, do you remember?" He nodded. "Then I heard Katie sing, and it reminded me of someone I had heard years ago. Like I had heard the exact same voice."

"You lost me again." He was trying to follow her train of thought, but she realized that to someone else it was kind of all over the place, although to her it made total sense.

"Katie's voice sounded just like Elizabeth's when she was younger."

"Grace, somewhere in this mixed train of thoughts, could you put together a story I could understand." Jim raked his fingers through his hair, trying to figure her out.

"Okay, short version. 1993, Elizabeth and I both competed in a statewide competition and I won." That was the easiest, fastest most nondescriptive version of the story, but there it was.

"Wow and you write for a living? That's like me saying your car was broken and I fixed it. This is going to be the one time I need the full story, because that doesn't give me much here."

He had gotten up and pulled out a beer to sit down and hopefully get a full story. Grace sighed as she finished picking the last piece of meat out of the crabs, washed her hands, then rubbed lemon all over her fingers and washed them again. Grabbing the bottle of wine out of the fridge, she poured herself a glass and sat back down.

"Alright, in '93 there was this competition, it was several days' worth of auditions that people would get a number and wait in this ridiculous line for but if you wanted it bad enough, you did it. Each category had an age group division so that it was fair but there would only be three contestants per age group. I had picked a very popular song from a musical, I will not mention which one because you will make fun of me, but I digress; apparently the two other contestants that were chosen also sang that song, but because I was chosen first, I got to sing the song from the audition at the actual show. The two other contestants had to pick other songs, and they had two weeks to learn whatever song they had to perform. This competition opened doors for so many people, there were talent scouts from TV, Broadway, movies and even colleges like NYU. My mom told me she overheard that one of the girls was pissed because she had heard my audition, and she thought she should have sung the song and not me."

She looked out the window to check on the kids and saw everything was fine. Jim was sitting on the edge of his seat waiting for her to finish.

"I won; I won that competition. I was the girl that the other girl was pissed at because I sang 'her' song. Elizabeth was the girl who was pissed. I stole her win."

Jim took a swig from his beer; it was clear to her that he was not really sure how to respond. "So, you pieced all this together from a comment and Katie's singing?"

"It was the trigger of when I said that she came in second place to me that stuck out. Like she completely lost it, weren't you right there? Then Katie's voice, and Katie and I chatted last night about her putting the girls in pageants and stuff like that and how they needed to win. That kind of sparked a gut hunch I had. And saying this all out loud does make me sound nuts, but I was right. Mom found the program and Elizabeth's name was on it. Elizabeth Winton was who I was up against." Jim's jaw dropped; it was Liz.

"This has been a vendetta because you beat her at a singing competition. Then why me, why Hank?"

"Because she is sick! She is hung up on winning. What I'm still trying to figure out, was it complete dumb luck is that the two of you met, like what are the odds that you both went to the same college?" Grace was still trying to figure that out. "And how would she know you knew me?" Jim closed his eyes.

"We met at freshmen orientation the first day, I was wearing my Farmers hat." Grace looked up at him; she remembered that hat. He held up one finger and ran up the stairs. She watched as he came back down the stairs and then saw what was in his hands. Grace's eyes started to tear up remembering the last time she had held that hat. "This has always been your hat, not mine." He placed the hat in her hands, squeezing them. She looked at the hat in her hands and remembered what she had said, and the tears started to fall. He palmed her cheek, thumbing away the tears. With his other hand he took the hat and placed it on her head backwards so that he could kiss her. Her hands rested on his chest and, placing his large hands over hers, he said "Just like this, it's always been yours."

Grace kissed him with a hum. "Wow, the first line was great, but that last bit was cheesy. Thank God you fix cars and don't write." She giggled as she kissed him again. This time he pulled away.

"Alright, I'm not finishing my story."

He yanked the hat off her head and placed it on his own head, sitting back down to drink his beer. Grace fixed her hair and walked over to him, nuzzling up against his neck.

"I'm sorry, it was sweet, cheesy but sweet. Please continue," she cooed, placing a kiss on his cheek.

Jim took another sip of beer and continued. "Well, that is when she came over to me. They did a round of getting to know you questions and I let it out that I was in theater. I just remember how she was suddenly very interested in talking with me after that. We hung out the next day and talked about school. On the third day, we talked about dating and that was when I let her know about you." He sighed a long sigh before taking a sip.

"Did you tell her my name though?" He just nodded.

Grace sat there, her mind going a million miles a minute. The odds of her and Jim going to the same university were, well, insane. But then to find Hank twenty-some-odd years later was just blowing Grace's mind. Jim looked over at her and it was clear that he still had a hidden talent for reading her thoughts.

"Okay Gracie, stop. Listen, she is nuts for sure, and although this all kind of makes some sense, why would she want to break up our relationship?"

"Because she has to win. She has been hyper-focused on winning against me for years. To her, I probably took away her chance to be in the entertainment industry or something, who knows. Jim, when she talked about stealing Hank away she said it was 'delicious.' Who in their right mind describes stealing someone's husband away from them as 'delicious'?" Grace was getting loud because she felt like Jim wasn't taking this seriously.

"Okay so the good thing is that we have the restraining order, okay?" Jim just pulled her back into his arms and kissed the top of her head as she sighed.

Colin then knocked at the door, yelling "*I have to pee*" from the other side of the glass, causing them to giggle. Grace opened the door and told him not to run since he was still wet. Katie stood at the doorway. "Are you two still making out?"

"We were not making out at all, thank you very much, we are able to control ourselves," Jim said and then whispered to Grace under his breath "Most days." Grace smiled.

Katie made a sound as if she was going to be sick, but Jim got offended.

"Oh, now I can't wait till you start dating, I am gonna bust your chops every single second I catch you and someone else having a PDA, all the vomit sounds and gagging. Can't wait!"

Grace just laughed as Katie fought not to laugh right with her. It was funny to think about. Katie walked over and kissed her dad on the cheek. She looked around and saw the crab meat.

"So, is that for the sauce? Can I help you make it?" Grace was shocked. The boys never asked to help, but she was happy to show Katie.

"Sure, but not right this second, I think I am gonna go get my suit on and join you guys outside for a bit."

Giving Katie a wink, she put the shredded crab meat in the fridge and went to get her bathing suit on. When she came back down, everyone was back outside. Jim was in the hot tub and the kids were back in the pool. There was a part of her that felt better.

She had found Elizabeth's trigger, she had figured out why she was hell bent on trying to destroy her, but it didn't make it any easier to take. She would be forever tied to this individual because of Jim, if they were to stay together. Now that he was back in her life, she couldn't imagine it without him. If she had to deal with Elizabeth, she would.

Perhaps taking the time to sit with her to hash things out would make things better. Like how therapy works, although she highly doubted that Elizabeth would ever consider therapy, even though she needed it. Because who holds a grudge like this?

Grace sat in the sun trying to warm herself with its heat, trying to shake off this weird nagging feeling she had about this other woman. There was a part of her that felt incredibly sad for her. Pity, she pitied her. Elizabeth couldn't move on; she couldn't let go of one single loss.

Needing to move on from this awful business, she closed her mind to all the thoughts and just listened to all the wonderful sounds around her. Here and now was all that was important. Taking in a deep breath, she listened to the waves on the shore behind her; letting out the breath, she listened to the kids playing in the water. Another breath in, this time listening to the sound of seagulls calling in the distance and then on her breath out she heard Jim in a hard tone say "What are you doing here?"

Grace opened her eyes to see Hank standing in the doorway of the kitchen, with white roses in his hand. Jim got out of the hot tub as the kids just stayed in the pool. Grace saw Jim start marching up to Hank looking like he was going to break his nose all over again and she thought it best that she got up and intercepted him.

"I came to tell you both I'm sorry. I'm not here to start trouble, but I sent you a text yesterday and I wasn't sure if you saw it." He held out the roses for her to take but she hesitated as she looked at them. "I thought maybe white roses would be better than a white flag. Roses are the least I could do."

The kids had gotten out of the pool and Jim was standing behind Grace. They all stood there not saying anything for what felt like an eternity. Grace looked up into Hank's bruised face and then back to the boys. This wasn't like him to be this nice. She had to know what the heck was going on.

"Why don't you come inside and we can talk."

"Dad, you aren't supposed to be here. Mom has a restraining order on you, now go away," Calvin barked, his teenage voice cracking at times from his anger. Everyone's heads snapped to him, unsure of where this bravery had come from. Marching up to his father, he stood between Hank and Grace, who had covered her mouth. Hank nodded his head in agreement.

"You are right, and you could call the cops right now and I would go to jail. But I was hoping your mother and that unfathomably forgiving heart of hers would give me at least ten minutes to talk."

Hank had backed up from his son. Grace noticed something rather interesting in the way he was looking at Calvin. It wasn't anger or hurt, it was pride. Grace placed a hand on Calvin's shoulder and patted him.

"Cal, give me ten minutes okay, just me and Daddy."

Calvin had turned, looking at his mother, and gave a shallow nod in agreement. Grace pointed to the kitchen island and Hank decided to sit down. Shutting the door on everyone so that it could be just Grace and Hank, she had questions, and she was determined to get answers.

CHAPTER SEVENTEEN

I t hadn't been ten minutes; it had been two hours of talking. Jim and the kids had only interrupted to use the bathroom or to get something to eat. In those two hours, Grace had finally yelled at Hank, and he just sat there and listened. He had explained that he had started therapy, which nearly knocked her off her chair. He had confessed to the affair and told her how he was going to work to be a better dad for the boys. It was a conversation twenty years in the making. She was shocked at such a quick turnaround in his behavior.

"I don't trust you; you know that." She glared at him. He sat there sheepishly nodding his head. "You have so much work to do, you abused me like I was some toy to toss around like I was nothing. And the boys, do you have any idea what this has done to them?" He nodded again.

"Grace, I fucked up, I get it."

"No, you don't. Do you really think one therapy session is going to bring you clarity? I've asked you for years to go, do you realize that if you had gone once during our marriage that perhaps this ALL could have been avoided? That we could still be happily married?" Hank just looked at Grace.

"Grace, we have never been happily married. You have been in love with someone else our whole marriage. Your brother told me at my bachelor party that you would always hold someone else in your heart over me."

Grace's mouth just dropped; she was going to kill her brother. She avoided Hank's eyes knowing that if she looked at him, she would only be confirming it.

"See, you can't say he is wrong. Even your face can't hide it, you are blushing right now."

Grace touched her face, and it was warm, very warm. She looked out onto the deck looking at Jim, while Hank looked at her.

"I didn't know who it was, but the second you introduced him, I could see it in both your faces. Liz just confirmed it."

Grace scoffed at the mention of her name and looked back at him with disdain. "Please don't even mention her name right now." Hank held up his hands.

"I won't say it again, I have no reason to, the therapist told me it is best to cut ties. According to my therapist, her behavior is toxic." Grace spit out her water.

"Ya think?" Grace said, wiping water off her chin and the counter. "Who is this miracle worker of a therapist that brought you so much clarity so quickly?" Grace asked, refilling her bottle of water.

"I'm not telling you their name, but I am required to see them for a certain amount of time based on the restraining order."

"The restraining order you wouldn't have against you if you hadn't listened to HER."

Grace had to make that zinger, he deserved it. Grace rested her head in her hands, shaking it back and forth. She thought of all that had transpired in their conversation and what she hoped would be an amicable divorce. She took a deep breath in.

"I still want a divorce. Because I can't do this anymore. I am happy to be your friend, and co-parent our boys, and be happy for you when you find someone to date, that isn't a psycho, but I can't be your wife. It's not fair to you, and it's not fair to the boys, but mostly it's not fair to me."

She breathed out and he reached for her hand to hold it. His movement was slow so that she knew he wasn't going to hurt her. She looked at his hand and reached for it and he smiled at her.

"Can I apologize to your boyfriend at least?"

He rolled his eyes on the word "boyfriend" and Grace bit her lip as she blushed.

"See, you can't deny it, you are blushing again. God, Grace, don't play poker, you would give your hand away every time."

He laughed and gently pulled her towards him and gave her a hug. As someone he had cut off from all touch, it was an odd sensation to hug him again. But perhaps the reason he was now reaching out for her for contact was that perhaps he himself needed it. He needed to be comforted after realizing just how much he screwed up his whole life, she thought.

"I may not be happy about it now, but I'm okay with you finding your happiness."

Grace's eyes started to well up with tears. She felt like all she had done all week was cry at the drop of a hat, which was not like her at all, she had nerves of steel, she was not this hot mess she had turned into in one week. He kissed her on the top of her head and walked to the door, opening it. Grace followed behind him, wiping away her tears just as she reached the doorway. Jim and Calvin had both turned and saw her crying and were about to charge Hank when Grace stepped between them.

"Stop, everything is fine. He came out here to say something."

𝄢

Hank wasn't that surprised by their reactions. He had been an awful person this week; in truth for years. But after his meeting with the therapist to do the intake information, it was clear to them that Hank had a lot of work to do to make amends. He went into that meeting hoping the therapist would see his side, but that had not been the case and it stung. But after an additional hour, they had given him homework. If he wanted to rebuild the relationship with his boys, he needed to apologize whether he wanted to or not.

Looking at the man who loved Grace unconditionally, he realized he could never be this man. Hank took a deep breath and extended his hand to Jim.

"I'm sorry, I was misguided by someone and am no longer listening to them. You seem to make Grace happy and that is all that matters."

He hoped that, without mentioning Liz's name, Jim would understand that she no longer had any influence over him. Jim gave a curt nod, took his hand, and held it tightly.

"If you hurt her again..." Jim began and then Grace cleared her throat, raising an eyebrow at him to just accept the apology. "I accept, sorry about the broken nose, I couldn't stand listening any longer to you treat Grace the way you did." It was a back-handed apology, but Hank accepted it. Hank then turned to the boys.

"Um, before I go, I owe you two an apology as well. I'm sorry. I know that I will have to work harder to be a better dad. Just know I will do my best to do whatever I need to in order for you guys to forgive me."

And then it was Hank's turn to cry. He realized in the way they had chosen Grace the other day over him and how Calvin talked to him earlier that he had been a terrible father. His own son needed to defend his mom against his father. That had hit him harder than Jim's fist. Colin got up and ran to embrace him; Calvin, however, just stood by Grace and scowled at him. All completely fair. Hank knew he had a lot of work ahead of him with Cal.

"Would you like to stay for dinner? It's crab sauce with linguini," Grace said, but he knew she was just trying to be polite, even though he didn't deserve it. Hank just shook his head no.

"Thank you for the offer, but I'm gonna head out. I'll leave the key on the counter. Thank you for listening today."

He turned and nodded to everyone then walked through the kitchen, leaving the key to the front door just like he said he would. Hank turned at the front door and looked around, realizing the last time he had come through it had been a terrible night, fueled by alcohol and bad decisions. Decisions he never wanted to make again, knowing the damage it had done between him and his family. He closed the door behind him and walked down the steps to his car when he heard the front door open and there stood Calvin.

Calvin's face was red, his eyes filled with tears and rage. There stood not their son, but a hurt young man.

"You did this! You fucking broke all of this for what? FOR WHAT?" Calvin's voice cracked as he screamed. Hank could feel a sharp pain in his heart as the anguish in his son's voice rang in his ears. This agony felt as if he had come running out with a knife and plunged it into his chest.

"For some bitch who would suck your dick and tell you how great you are?"

The words twisted that knife and Hank realized that this was what they had been feeling. Grace had been feeling this way for years, but he didn't know how long Calvin had. Apparently it had been long enough. Hank inched closer and as he did, he saw the anguish in his son's eyes as tears started to fall.

"You had us! You had me, and Colin, and mom. We loved you, and you didn't care. We thought you were great before she came along. But you chose her. You chose her over us. You chose her over me."

Hank had walked back up the stairs to Calvin and caught him just before he collapsed. The two sat there on the front porch crying and Hank held him, rocking him as he had done when he was a child.

"I know, I'm so sorry, I'm so sorry buddy. I was an asshole. I am gonna do everything I can to make it up to you, I promise. I'm so sorry. I love you, please, I'm so sorry" was all that Hank could articulate. They sat in a crumpled mess on the front steps for what seemed like hours, and finally after all the tears and their breathing had settled down, Hank hugged his son goodbye and drove home. He needed to do better, not for himself, but for his young men.

$$9$$

There was something inherently comforting and familiar about how Jim felt whenever he was around Grace. Like it was home. He wasn't sure if it was how she felt in his arms, or the way her laugh could inspire a smile, or how just sitting in silence brought peace. He had been so lonesome for so long, never understanding why, even when he was married, he still didn't feel right, until he sat here with Grace in his lap.

But his tranquility was a bit on edge due to Hank's arrival earlier. He had come to apologize, and Grace had given him the opportunity, however that wasn't the issue that he had about the whole thing. The issue was that now that Hank and Liz were no more and Hank was getting therapy, would Grace consider going back with him? Would she try and save her marriage for the sake of her boys, or was she really ready to let go and be with him? He had made her a promise that he wouldn't break any of their hearts, but would Grace renege on this?

"Grace, I need to ask you something." Hesitation was laced in his voice, and she hummed, her neck craning to look up at him with a warm smile and love in those deep brown eyes. He took a breath, not sure exactly how to ask, what words to say so he didn't sound desperate. "Are you happy?"

Grace sat up, creasing her brow in curiosity and blinking. "What do you mean?"

He shifted and positioned her so that he was looking at her straight in the face. "Are you happy, with me?"

He held his breath, but then she started laughing, which was only making his insecurity worse until she cupped his face and kissed him gently on his lips.

"Elated," she kissed him. "Ecstatic," another kiss. "Thrilled, euphoric, delighted. Do I really need to keep going?" She kissed him again, resting her forehead on his.

"Why would you ask me such a question?" His eyes must have given him away, he didn't know why he was so nervous with her and she must have seen it. Grace crawled up higher onto his lap and held his face in her soft palms. "Hey, there is only one person in the whole world that I have ever wanted to spend my life with, to share my bed with, to sit on this deck with." She giggled. "And that's you. It's always been you."

Relief flooding through him as this amazing creature just smiled, it was the same smile she had given when he met her for the first time and every time since. He didn't know why he was so worried and then he realized it was fear. Fear of losing her again.

He brought his fingers up to the back of her neck and pulled her in for a kiss, his heart racing as his thoughts swirled with the images of them living together, growing old with one another and raising their kids together. His other arm snaked around to her back and pulled her even closer, her soft welcoming body against his. She moaned into his mouth as he deepened their kiss, knowing it would cause her blood to turn to honey. Jim tugged at her curls causing her head to tip back as he kissed her jaw and then her neck. Her pulse point was her weakness, and he smiled at it just before he started kissing and sucking on it. She was twisting her body to now straddle him to allow him full access to her neck but also a better view of her amazing breasts.

Jim slowly pulled away from her neck, which he had left a tiny mark on, and started kissing along her collar bone. He thought about how he couldn't imagine spending another night or moment away from her. She had asked for baby steps, but he would be damned if he didn't take a shot at forever.

"Grace?" he said, his breathing ragged. "There's something else I need to know."

Her lusty gaze met his and she kissed him fiercely; apparently, she didn't want words, she wanted his passion. As she slid her tongue along his lower lip, her teeth pulled at it, setting off a chain reaction throughout his whole body, and he groaned, thrusting his hips up against her again. She was going to be the death of him, one he was willing to surrender to. She wasn't responding to him; she just continued to kiss him, only now she was working her way to his ear. His eyes rolled back as she kissed his earlobe and then took a nibble. Electricity shot throughout his body and without even realizing he was saying it, he blurted "Marry me?"

Grace stilled. She had been sucking on his earlobe as he said it, and she released his ear with a pop. She looked back at him, and he had a smirk on his face. "Come again?" she said, unsure she had heard him correctly.

Slipping a hand between them, he brushed it against her center, feeling just how wet her shorts were, and he trailed his fingers back up, then, with a smile said, "Well, I haven't yet, but you might be close."

She ground her hips against him. He knew she was soaking for him and the fact that she only wanted him caused a low growl to escape his throat and she looked deep into his eyes.

"No, no, no, before, what did you just say, and James Marcus Wooley, you look me in the eyes when you say it." Her tone was firm, commanding even,. It was a different side to her. Jim ran his hands up and down her body then, looking into her eyes, he said the one thing he had been wanting to say for years.

"Marry me." His face was serious and unyielding; he wanted her forever. She blinked, unable to utter a sound. "I won't lose you again." He brushed away a stray curl. "And if I am the one you want to spend forever with, then marry me. I wasted years and tortured myself because I should have never let you walk away." His misty eyes filled with regret. "So, marry me, marry me because I can't live without you. I can't breathe without you. You have and always will be my everything. Don't make me spend the rest of my life without you."

Her face had softened, and tears threatened to fall from her eyes. They had wasted years, they both knew that it was a possibility that they would eventually get there, they both loved each other. Hell, even their kids wanted them married. He watched her mind racing behind her eyes, calculating everything, the fact that the divorce needed to be finalized, that this was incredibly fast, the kids. The longer she took to answer, the faster his heart pounded in his chest.

And then a tiny whisper escaped her lips. "Yes." He looked at her, not sure he had heard her, so she said it again, "Yes," and a joyous roar erupted in his chest. Capturing her beautiful tearful face in his large hands, he drew her in slowly and kissed her ever so reverently. She was to be his, forever, and he would be hers until his last breath, and that was all that mattered. His arms enveloped her, smashing her against him, causing a tiny pang of pain from the bruising, but he barely felt it. His head swirled and he just started laughing, causing her to laugh right along with him.

With Grace still on his lap, he scooted towards the edge of the chair and maneuvered her to wrap her legs around him. Grabbing a hold on her bottom, that bottom that would be his forever, he lifted them both off the chair and carried her into the bedroom as she peppered kisses on his face and neck as he walked them to the bed.

"I wonder who won the bet?" He laughed, placing her down on the bed, slipping her shorts and panties off. She sat up and pulled at his shirt, helping him get it off, then yanking at his belt to free him of his pants.

"Well, I think it is more about the date of the wedding than when you would pop the question. Although I highly doubt anyone would have considered it to be by the end of the week considering the divorce," she said as he let her unbutton his pants then, slipping her hands under the waistband of his boxers to help him out of his clothes, his hard erection sprang free and her eyes hungrily gazed at his nakedness. Jim couldn't help but feel amazing.

This woman was a siren and all she needed to do was gaze at him; that was, until she reached out and grabbed his hard cock with both hands and started licking the tip. Her soft tongue swirled the tip as she stroked him and then began to suck. As amazing as this felt, she was still half dressed and that was not going to do. Jim pulled back from her and heard the pop from her mouth, causing him to smile down at her.

He climbed onto the bed and pulled off her top, freeing her breasts. Leaning down, he took one of her pert nipples between his lips, sucking hard, causing her to shudder and gasp, arching her back so that he could take more of her into his mouth. He enjoyed worshipping her breasts, teasing her with his exquisite heat, knowing that every movement he made on her body would drive her closer to her unraveling.

Grace whimpered as he pulled on her nipple with his teeth. Years may have kept them apart but he knew just how to make her beg for more. He moved to her side, propping himself up so he could skim her body with his other hand. Bending down, he kissed her as his hand moved from squeezing her breast, then to her stomach, all the while feeling her squirm from his slow movements. Now this was a torture they would both enjoy, forever.

Kissing her cheek, then the line of her jaw, his hand wandered to her perfectly trimmed mound. His touch as soft and light as a feather making her reach for his head, pulling him in for another feverish kiss, her breathing ragged as he slowly moved his hand along her folds, which were already wet.

"Ready for me already?" he said, as he broke free from her lips, his own arousal twitching against her warm thigh. Jim was trying to hold it together, but he knew that all it took was one touch from her and he would be done. Jim stopped his ministrations, causing her to lift her head up in protest. Moving her legs apart, kissing down the length of her body, he had something he had been wanting to do for some time. With a sharp intake of breath, Jim positioned her legs over his shoulders, kissing her inner thighs, inching ever closer to her core.

"If memory serves me right, you might need that pillow behind you." he said with a smile, watching her lift her head, his eyes locked onto hers, and then slowly he started swirling his tongue around her bundle of nerves. He smiled at the guttural moan that came from her throat and gripped harder onto her thighs.

Covering her face with a pillow to bury all the sounds she was making was the right suggestion. His tongue and lips pulsing and swirling on her swollen clit, he watched as she only moved the pillow in order to catch her breath. He loved the way she tasted, moved, and sounded and as close as she was, he wanted to drive her to a brink she hadn't reached before. Jim moved one of his hands up to her core and slid one finger in as he sucked her clit, a muffled moan from behind the pillow making him smile. On the next glide in, he added another digit and curled it deep inside her, evoking a muffled squeal of pleasure. Her thighs started to shake, and he knew she was just on the edge.

"So, I was thinking-" he pulled away but kept gliding his fingers in and out of her slowly, as she moved the pillow to catch her breath again - "we can have the wedding here, next June."

He said, as he bent down licking a stripe from his fingers that were moving in and out of her to her throbbing clit and then sucking on it. She had thankfully covered her face back up before he had sucked.

"What do you say?"

He picked up his pace and her hips started to buck. She was saying something into the pillow that he couldn't understand. He was watching the pillow, waiting for her to come up for another breath, and then he swirled and sucked her clit.

"What was that, love? I can't understand you behind that pillow."

Her one hand found the top of his head, grabbed a bunch of his hair and kept his head steady as she ground against his tongue. She moved the pillow with the other hand so she could breathe.

"If you don't make me cum soon, there will be no damned wedding!"

Her eyes filled with lust and rage was the most intense stare he had ever seen. He thrust his fingers deep inside of her and sucked as hard as he could and that was it. She was pulsing and vibrating around him as she buried her face again in the pillow. The deep moans and squeals coming from behind the pillow made him smile and his own erection leaked a bit of pre-cum onto the bed.

He pulled himself up to the pillow that was hiding her face and peeked underneath, her breath coming in ragged spurts as she tried to collect herself.

𝄢

"That was dirty pool old man," she spat, still trying to get her bearings.

Jim smiled and kissed her. She had forgotten what she tasted like; it was tangy but a little sweet. So, he was half right on what she tasted like. But she needed just another second and then his torture would begin. Two could play this game.

She rolled him over onto his back and climbed on top of him. Lining up his hard member against her core, she slowly lowered herself down onto his thick shaft and felt that glorious stretch of his cock inside her. Lifting herself up so that he could watch her breasts bounce as she rode him, he buried himself deep inside her on the next thrust and it caused him to groan loudly.

"Looks like someone else needs a pillow. You may want to use mine." she quipped, and then reached behind her, cupping and massaging his balls as she rode him. He instantly grabbed the pillow and covered his mouth just as she ground down harder on him and squeezed his balls. She picked up her speed, and while one hand played with him, her other hand played with one of her breasts. He reached up to play with them as well, but she swatted his hand away.

"Since I was pre-occupied-" she took the hand that had been playing with him and was running a stripe with one finger massaging his perineum. He tilted his head back as she increased her pressure and ground against him. "I couldn't respond, but-" she stopped moving and he looked up and then she squeezed her pelvic floor causing her core to pulse around him - "I wouldn't mind a wedding here next year."

And then she was moving again, this time picking up her speed. He looked up at her as she lowered herself down to kiss him. Her warm breasts brushing against his chest, he moved her hips down harder on him as he thrusted up into her. His breathing was ragged, and she knew his climax stood on the edge of a knife just far enough away to torture him, then he wrapped his arms around her and rolled her onto her back.

Giggling, she looked up at him. "What'sa matter, looking for something?" He crushed his lips onto hers and finally sunk himself deep inside her. Throwing her head back, closing her eyes at the force, she allowed him to use her body. A low growl erupted from his throat as he buried himself deep into Grace's wet quim and his climax hit him. His breathing was coming in short breaths, and when he opened his eyes again, there lay Grace with a seductive smile across her lips.

"Find what you were looking for?"

He bent down to kiss her soundly before collapsing on top of her. He brushed her hair away from her sweaty brow, nodding, and said, "Yeah, my soon-to-be-wife."

CHAPTER EIGHTEEN

Standing in the front doorway of her home up north, she waved to Jim and the girls as they drove off. He had been determined to make sure that she got back in okay. Her parents had met them there and Ken was helping the boys settle back in while Janie made Grace a cup of coffee. But Grace couldn't seem to want to walk over the threshold. Her life had changed exactly one week earlier. The house she stood in held great memories, but if she was honest there were more bad ones than good.

Taking a breath, she put one hesitant foot in front of the other and walked into the house, closing the door behind her. Silently walking through, her eyes fell on the dents in the wall and permanent scratches to the hardwood floors from the havoc that Hank and Liz had caused. Hank's recliner was missing, leaving an empty space in the living room, and in the hallway, someone had piled up the broken picture frames that held family photos over the years. In all they were just things, items to be replaced, but it was the memories. She felt violated; some other woman had entered her home and destroyed her property, all with the consent of Hank.

Despite Hank's contrition and efforts to make amends, she was still hurt. Grace knew it would take many months and hours of therapy to help her work through it. And then there were the boys. She was going to ask Calvin if he wanted to go, especially after how he had reacted, she knew he needed it as well. Walking into the kitchen, Janie's compassionate gaze as she handed her the coffee let her know she wasn't alone.

But despite all the awful things that had happened in the past week, one wonderful thing had happened. Jim, she had Jim. He had shown up and been a knight in shining armor more than just once. Grace hadn't needed saving; she was perfectly fine with doing that herself. But if he hadn't been there Monday night, who knows what would have happened when Elizabeth and Hank had shown up. Elizabeth was a loose cannon and Grace wondered just how unhinged she would be now that she had lost both Jim and Hank and now possibly her custody of the girls.

"How did the pack up at the shore house go? Calvin came in so quiet." Janie's tone was hushed and worried. Grace looked at her and she could tell just by her glance that Calvin had been a bit upset.

"I told him we needed to come home, we can't hide down the shore all summer."

Calvin had begged her to see if Janie would meet them down there so he could stay down the shore. Ken walked in from getting Colin all settled in his room and made himself a cup of coffee, patting his daughter on the back.

"He's gonna be okay, kiddo, you all will. You want us to go food shopping or anything? I had the cleaning ladies clean out the fridge so you only have the basics." Ken looked at Grace, but she shook her head.

"No, I placed a grocery order to be delivered, it should be here soon, so we are okay." Just then there was a knock at the door. She smiled. "Perfect timing." Walking to the front door, she opened it to see her bags of groceries and another delivery that made her smile. Hank waved at her from his car, took a bag of the boys' favorite fast food out of his passenger side, and walked up the stairs.

"Thanks for letting me spend time with the boys. I got their favorite." Grace was happy that he wanted to work at being a better dad for the boys. She had spoken with Dale in the morning to let him know she wanted to cancel the restraining order against Hank but not Elizabeth. Elizabeth was too nuts to take that away. Grace just nodded and smiled, grabbing some of the groceries, and surprisingly Hank grabbed one as well, helping her get them all in.

She called up the stairs "Boys, you got a special delivery for lunch." Janie and Ken stared wide-eyed as they watched Hank walk into the kitchen helping Grace with the groceries. Hank put down the bags and held his hand out to Ken, who looked at it hesitantly but then shook it. Hank nodded to Janie. Grace knew if there was anyone he should really be afraid of it was Janie. She would be the one to rip his head clear off his shoulders based on the glare she was giving him.

"Ken, Jane, I just want to apologize to the two of you for my behavior and how I have treated your daughter. She deserves better. I'm sorry."

"Damn right, she deserved better," Janie snapped. "And you better change your act for those boys, or I'll kick your ass from here to Broad Street, Newark," she barked. Hank nodded, affirming that he would do better.

Both boys came down and looked at Hank and Grace, not sure what was going on. Grace smiled at them. "Daddy asked if he could bring you boys lunch and hang out together. I thought that was a good idea. He brought your favorite." Colin walked over to the bag and pulled out the package.

"Tacos! Cal, Daddy got you nachos! Can we eat outside?" Colin was smelling his taco like it was the greatest thing in the whole world. Calvin walked over and looked in the bag as Grace started putting groceries away. Hank moved closer to him.

"I can go if you don't want me here. It's okay, I just wanted to spend some time." Calvin nodded his head and turned to Grace, who gave him a wink and a smile. Ken and Janie started helping Grace take groceries out of the bags and kept to themselves while Calvin, Colin, and Hank went outside to eat on the deck.

Janie, never one to hold her tongue, was trying desperately not to say anything. But today was not that day. "Do you really think that bringing lunch is going to change anything? He isn't asking you to call off the divorce, is he?" Ken and Grace both looked at each other like she was nuts.

"Mom, he wants a divorce. But this right now, what is happening, is what I wanted, he and I working amicably for the boys, to co-parent with no issues."

Grace knew Janie didn't trust him and it was written all over her face. "You were not there yesterday, okay, I was. I yelled, he listened, do you understand that I have never yelled at him, and he has never once listened? EVER! I'm taking that as a win. I am going to take the victory lap and milk it for all it is worth. So, hush your mush."

Ken was trying to hide his smile; this was the Grace he knew she could be. Strong, independent, and with a voice. Janie sat there with her mouth agape, not able to say anything.

"Well, I am glad to hear that things are going much better. Right, Janie?" Ken elbowed his wife as he picked up another item of groceries and put it in the pantry. Janie shot her husband a look, and then looked back to her daughter. Grace held her shoulders back and held up her chin, and Janie's face eased.

"Well, as long as he fixes things with the boys and helps out like he is supposed to and doesn't give you anymore shit, then fine." Janie looked out the back door, watching the boys with Hank. They were laughing.

Grace knew her mother had to have the last word, and it was best to let her. Sighing, she finished putting away the groceries and then went outside to sit with the boys and Hank. Ken took it as a silent sign to leave and he turned to Janie, motioning to the front door.

𝄢

Judi couldn't wait to hug the girls and Jim; she was practically dancing in the doorway when they got home. "Oh, my babies, did you have a good time? Did you bring back any of the crab sauce?" The girls each hugged her and as they walked through the door Jim pulled a quart-size container out of a cooler bag that Grace had given him that contained the sauce. Her eyes lit up. "Oh that little Grace, she is such a doll. So how did the rest of the week go, I mean besides what you had texted me about Hank." The girls ran upstairs with their stuff and headed into their rooms. Jim smiled at his mom and just gave her a big hug.

"The girls are upset that we left but they are happy, at least, that they are here, they both said they don't want to go to Liz's. But until the court says they don't have to, at some point today they have to go back." Judi scrunched up her face. Jim knew that she would have to deal with his ex-in-laws, and she had never been a big fan of them.

"Has she reached out or anything?"

Jim just shook his head; he should somehow reach out to her to see what is going on.

"I was thinking that Dad could drop them off, if he is around. I know you are not a fan."

"Oh, I'm sure he would. So, anything else? How are Grace and the boys? Any new developments since Hank talked to them yesterday?"

Jim eyed his mother. She was always so nosey, and he knew if he told her about him and Grace being engaged, she would faint and then spend the whole afternoon shouting it from the rooftops. It might have been total lunacy that he even proposed, let alone that she accepted it this early in their relationship, but he has known her forever, loved her forever, what was he supposed to do, wait? Not when this was meant to be.

"Nope, it was uneventful the rest of the time. Nice and relaxing." A slight blush came across his cheeks as he thought about just how nice and relaxing it had been lying in bed with Grace. Judi saw it and smiled. Jim said "Listen, I am gonna go upstairs and unpack. I'll see if the girls can reach out to Liz to find out when she wants them back today. Dad upstairs?" Judi nodded her head yes as she put on the kettle for tea.

Jim brought his bag up, dropping it in his room, then went to check on the girls. He spent a few minutes convincing them that they needed to see their mom whether they wanted to or not. Finally, Vivian relented and texted Liz to see when she wanted them to be dropped off. Surprisingly, Liz texted that she wasn't feeling well and that it would be best for the girls to stay with their dad until she was better. The three of them just looked at each other, unsure of exactly what was going on, but he knew neither of the girls wanted to actually talk with their mother or see her anyway. Katie went downstairs to let Judi know that they were staying and didn't come back up, probably because Judi had a million questions.

Jim went into his bedroom to ponder exactly what was going on with Liz. She loved the girls, or at least he thought she did. Liz wasn't maternal, but he was sure that she at least loved them and wanted to try to heal those feelings. Especially because of what had happened earlier in the week, wouldn't she want to repair whatever damage she had caused?

Hank had, Hank drove all the way down the shore on a workday to try and talk things out, to apologize. Jim admired that, that Hank had come to realize that his family was so important that he took time out of a busy day to do that. It was possible that she was just taking her time to figure everything out now that she and Hank were not together. She had lost everyone, him, Hank, and now the girls. He hoped that she was reflecting on her bad choices and would learn to make better ones. But something in him knew she probably wouldn't, especially now that he knew why she had started this whole vendetta against Grace. Liz needed professional help and all he could hope for was that her family could see it and get her the help she needed.

After putting the last of his clothes away, he laid down on his bed. He turned and realized that he was not lying in the middle of the bed like he normally did, but on one side, staring at an empty space. Katie appeared in the doorway and looked at him with a smirk. "Missing her already, huh?"

Jim lifted his head off the pillow. "Ha ha, very funny. I can't lay on my bed?"

Katie walked over to the bed and laid down next to him. "You spent the whole week in a bed with Grace next to you, I don't blame you for missing her already. You are both adults, I'm not judging, I'm just saying it's gonna be difficult to get back to being alone every night. Unless..." He made a groan, he didn't like where this was going.

"Unless what?"

"Well, unless you and Grace move in together and get married. Then you won't have to sleep in your bed all alone, cold and helpless." She was mocking him and pushing it. He and Grace had both agreed to wait to say anything about them getting married until after the divorce was finalized. It was best not to say anything, especially since he also had wanted to talk to Ken first. He knew he might say for them to wait, but Grace said that Ken trusted Jim and she didn't think he would have a problem with it. It was the issue of making time for each other. With the book tour just around the corner, he knew she would be gone for weeks, but when they got back that they would sit with Ken to talk about it.

"Alone, cold and helpless, you make me sound like some sad individual. I am quite capable of sleeping in my bed without someone in it. I've done it for the last three years thank you very much." He was pushing her out of his bed. Katie just laughed and got off the bed.

"Okay, well, you let me know just how easy it is for you to fall asleep tonight, and then when you are waking up every hour looking for her to cozy up to. Um hm, you tell me tomorrow how great you sleep tonight." Katie was acting as if she knew, like she knew what it felt like to have a small body curled up in his arms radiating heat, how it felt when Grace would rest her leg over his and wrap her small arm around his midsection while she slept. Shit, she was right, sleeping without Grace next to him was going to be impossible.

But what struck him was that she wasn't just right, she understood how it would affect him. "How would you know about all this?"

Katie stood at his door with a very serious face and said "I read one of Mrs. Cartino's books, Caroline's Lost. It is rather informative and eye opening." Winking at him, she headed to her room.

He sat there shocked. "You are not old enough to read that, Miss." It was the book about him and about their love story.

She called out from her room "Yes I am, and you were an idiot!" That got his attention. Jim got up from his bed and walked into the girls' room.

"What do you mean I was an idiot?" It couldn't be possible that she knew that Grace had written that book with them in mind, could she?

"Dad, the story is about you and Grace, any fool can read that. Well, and Grandma told me about it. The book is really good, it's smart, funny, and spicy. But I'm praying that those scenes are just made up because, gross, Dad, if that really happened."

Jim felt his head exploding. He hadn't read it in twenty-five years so he couldn't remember anything, but did his mom tell her that Grace wrote it or that Janie had? Luckily the book was sitting right on the nightstand next to him. He grabbed the book and opened it. There were certain sections of pages that seemed worn, which he went to. Katie was protesting about him reading it and was trying to grab the book out of his hands. "Hey, I am still reading it."

"Not this second you aren't, and I can't have you reading this if it is as spicy as you say."

Jim knew who the true author of the book was, and he didn't want to give away Grace's secret, she had trusted him with that information, but had his mother told Katie that Grace had written it? Jim stormed down the stairs and took his mother and Vivian by surprise. Katie had followed him and kept trying to get the book back. He held the book over his head and looked at his mother.

"You told her this was about me and Grace?"

"I might have mentioned that Janie wrote it with you guys in mind. They were curious about how you and Grace felt about each other when you were younger, so I just told them to read Janie's book. Oh, come on, it's just a little romance novel, I thought it was perfectly fine to read. Well, okay, maybe not those racy scenes, but girls, that was written by Mrs. Cartino, she is an adult and mature enough to handle the consequence. Don't be doing that kind of stuff till you can handle it."

Jim sighed; they didn't know about Grace. But he did, and now that he knew, he wanted to read these scenes to make sure they were okay to be read by his daughters. Grace was only a year older than Katie when she had written it, how bad could it be? Then he remembered, it could be bad, like *Penthouse Forum* bad. All those things they had done together, all the things they did this week together; he could feel himself blushing and heard the girls starting to giggle.

"You can't have this back until I read this and make sure it is appropriate for you to read."

Had Grace written about their sexual exploits in the book? He was afraid to think about it, and the thought his girls having read it was actually starting to make him a bit queasy.

The chorus of complaints about him taking the book away was left on deaf ears as he went up to his room and went to the pages that seemed a bit worn. He closed his eyes, hoping he would not read what he feared. But there in print was his worst nightmare, things that they had done together. His sexual weaknesses as well as hers. She had documented it all, there was a part of him that felt betrayed; but as he read on the words told him more.

It was about how he made her feel, how she hoped he felt when they were intimate. The words expressing her devotion to his mind and body. He couldn't seem to stop reading, the words leaping off the page as she described his body as well as her own. He could feel her touch on his skin as she described in beautifully agonizing detail how Grace would feel against him. The more he read, the more a heat swirled in his belly, her words turning him on as he read, unable to tear himself away. Putting the book down on his bed, he realized that if he kept going, he would be too far gone and he would need to find a release. Jim needed many things; one thing he needed to do is not let the girls and his mother ever read this ever again, and two, he needed to talk to Grace.

After giving himself a few minutes to calm down, he scooped up the book and charged down the stairs. "I am going out for a few minutes; I'll be back before dinner," Jim called out from the front door as he grabbed his keys and headed out to his car. His mother ran after him.

"Where are you going?"

"I need to talk to Grace." He held the book in his hand.

"Jimmy Wooley, don't you lose that woman again, she is the best thing that ever happened to you!" she yelled as he peeled out of his parking spot and drove to Grace's.

Jim must have looked rather hot under the collar when Grace opened the door. Surprised was etched across her face but a warm smile spread across her lips.

"What are you doing here? Miss me already?" She was acting coy; however, his expression had not changed as he held up the book.

"You and I need to sit down and discuss this." He looked past her and heard voices coming from the kitchen. Calvin came out and smiled.

"Hey Jim, miss Mom already?" Calvin echoed his mother's sentiments. Jim smiled at the teen, trying not to show his irritation at the beautiful but completely insane woman standing in front of him.

"Hey bud, I just needed to talk to your mom." He was trying his best to keep cool. He looked at her. "Are your parents here? We need to chat right now."

"Dad is here," Calvin said and Jim looked at Grace. Remaining calm, Grace gave a loving tap on his shoulder before turning around to call out to Hank.

"Hey Hank, can you watch the boys? I need to run out with Jim real fast, I promised to go help him pick something out for the girls."

It was vague, it was convenient, and it was a total lie. Hank called from the other room that it was no problem and before Grace even had the chance to grab her keys Jim was pulling her out of the house.

He got behind the wheel, steadied his hands, and started the car. Muscle memory taking over with Grace and him in the car alone, he drove and like many times before he pulled in the parking lot behind the library.

"Please tell me you are not here to tell me you are going back to Liz again." Jim looked around and realized where they were. Grace's eyes showed the pain of that night, and it snapped him out of his train of thought.

"I'm so sorry, I didn't even realize, we can go somewhere else, I-" he started; he really hadn't noticed where he was driving. He just knew it needed to be somewhere quiet and someplace that they could talk. "I needed to talk to you." His normally cool demeanor breaking in front of her, there was an odd pain sounding in his voice.

She got out of the car, but not before grabbing the book. He followed suit and walked over to the swings where she had decided to sit.

"You want to talk to me, that is fine, but I will not sit in a car, in this place, because in my mind it will end badly. So if you want to talk, we talk out here. So, what's the matter?"

She had every right to be pissed that he taken her here, but it was their place. Countless hours of making out in either of their cars, hours of talking and laughing. But the last memory they both had was horrible for each of them. This wasn't about that damned night; this was about the book, their book.

"I caught Katie reading your first book." Jim looked at her and she bit her lip. Her and that damned lip.

"Ah. So why are you pissed exactly?" Grace started thumbing through the book, clearly noting that certain pages had been dog-eared. "Wait, this is an old publication, is this your mom's?" She turned to Jim to see him with his head down.

"Alright, listen, yes I am very proud of you for writing this, let me just get that out of the way." He was standing now in front of her, and she looked up at him, letting him continue. "And yes, I understand the story. But I thought your mom wrote this, that the similarities to our relationship were a coincidence." And the intimacy scenes were so incredibly familiar.

"Okay, but you understood when I told you this earlier this week and you were fine, so what's the problem?" She needed him to be more direct.

"The sex in the book, Grace!" Jim yelled a little too loud and she held the book up over her face to cover her smile, only her eyes gave her away. "Don't you laugh at me. You wrote about our sex life."

"Okay, but in fairness, we had only slept together once, and I think I wrote it beautifully." She thumbed through the book to find the scene; she stumbled across an intimate scene that was all foreplay. She started reading it and blushed, biting on her lip. He threw his hands up in the air.

"Grace, I love you, but now when I see this book or read it, I will be thinking of just us. That deep inside if I see my mother or my daughters reading this, they are going to think of me." He was squatting down holding her shoulders as she looked him in the eyes lovingly and smiled at him.

"They don't know it is you!" She shook her head at his frustration.

"Grace, who knows that those sex scenes in the book are actually things we did, I mean besides you and me?" He was hoping the answer was no one; in fact, he was praying to God it was no one.

"Just you and me. I mean, it is possible that Nikki and Kevin might think it is you, but I never confirmed anything. Mom and Dad asked, but I said I got the ideas from stories of friends and pornos. But the truth only lies between us."

She had gotten up from her swing and was standing in front of him. He cupped her beautiful face. *How could he possibly be so upset by this?* he thought. She had chronicled their most intimate moments, as if she had written him a symphony. The way she had written about their experiences made him feel like he was back there in that time. It was her love song to him. Bringing his lips to hers, he closed his eyes and kissed her softly, then taking the book in his hand, he looked at it.

"I cannot let the girls, or my mother, ever read this book again. Are there any other books that I play a role in besides the two that I know of?" Jim was afraid to ask, but figured he should know in advance. She smiled and shook her head no.

"No, you were my first two books only. I did kill you in the second book so I couldn't quite bring you back once I nailed that coffin shut." He looked at her and mouthed the word "Ouch," making her laugh. They started walking back to the car holding hands.

"I still can't believe you killed me off. That is pretty cold, you know." Jim said as a car passed by them, moving her a bit closer to the grass to keep her out of the way of moving vehicles. They stopped to kiss in the middle of the parking lot; luckily no one was coming.

"Yeah, well, you kind of broke me."

She smiled up at him and kissed him again. He took a deep breath. She smelled of vanilla, coffee, and musk; he thought if she is going to be so horribly adorable and wonderful smelling, he had to anticipate that their marriage was going to be him just doing whatever she wanted. He stood there in a complete daze from this creature, his blood pumping so hard in his veins that it was muffling the sounds around him. It muffled the sounds of the kids on the playground, the elderly couple talking on a bench a few feet away, and the car with dark windows aimed right at them.

Jim turned only when he heard the engine of the car coming toward them, and he went to shield Grace, but she had faster instincts and shoved him as hard as she could out of the way. His body landed on his own car and just as he turned around, he saw Grace hit the hood of the car and then watched her tiny form flying through the air from the impact. Everything was happening in slow motion; he watched as the car drove off as fast as it had hit her, and then he watched Grace fall. Her body landed in a crumpled heap in the middle of the roadway with a sickening thud.

Jim ran over to her and was screaming her name. Luckily there were people who had come out of the library at the exact moment and saw what had happened. He knelt on the ground next to her afraid to move her, afraid she was dead.

"Grace, baby please, please open your eyes and look at me." He looked over to the people. "Someone call 911."

Several people came over and someone else was trying to video the car that had hit her. Jim could only hold Grace. Her arm was broken for sure, and possibly even her leg. She had a goose egg and scratches on her face. His vision was starting to blur from the tears in his eyes.

"Please Gracie, open your eyes for me, love, please."

But she didn't move. He knew to check her pulse and luckily the fire station was right across the street, firemen and EMTs were already running over to them with a backboard and equipment. He just held her and rocked back and forth. He had just gotten her back, he couldn't lose her again.

CHAPTER NINETEEN

ospital staff buzzed around them, and Jim had forced himself to remain calm enough to answer whatever questions he could about Grace for the EMTs and hospital staff. He stood there watching them working on Grace, who was still not responding. Jim had called Ken to let them know but he didn't even remember what he had said, their conversation had been a jumble of words because at the time the hospital staff was telling him they were taking her back for scans and x-rays immediately.

He had been forced to sit and let a nurse check on him. One of the EMTs had stuck around and pulled her aside to let her know what had happened. Without saying a word, she silently got to work cleaning him up. His hands still had Grace's blood on them and he thought to himself, if he hadn't taken her to talk, she would be fine, she would be home with her boys. All because of what, a bruised ego, or fear, or pride?

Twenty minutes later, Janie and Ken walked through the ER doors and immediately saw Jim. Janie was looking around to each bed. "Jimmy, where is Gracie?" she asked, tears escaping her eyes as she looked him over. His head down, focused only on his hands, he couldn't get the words out. Luckily, the nurse spoke up.

"Mrs. Nereid is getting some tests done but I'll see if the doctor can come talk to you.," the nurse said, finishing up, and went over to the nurses' station to talk to someone. A petite man walked over to them and introduced himself to keep them up to date with what was going on with Grace.

"Mrs. Nereid is getting a CT now to see the full extent of the damage that she sustained from the impact of the car and then the fall. I did just get the x-rays back, and-" the doctor stopped talking as suddenly there was a code called. He excused himself and went off towards the area that Jim had seen Grace wheeled off to earlier and his heart dropped. Janie buried her head in Ken's chest, and he just embraced his wife.

"I'm so sorry" was all Jim could get out. Janie turned to him and hugged him. "I promised I would protect her, I promised she wouldn't get hurt. I promised-" that was when the tears started again.

He was going to lose her; he closed his eyes, and his mind replayed the vision of her falling. His breathing was coming in short breaths; he felt like all the air was being pushed out of his lungs. Jim needed out, he let go of Janie and ran outside, right past Kevin, Hank, and the boys. He ran past his own parents and daughters and when he finally got outside, he collapsed right to the ground and sobbed. He yelled and cried until he felt a hand on his shoulder to see his dad standing there. Mark helped his son up off the ground and onto a bench.

"I'm going to lose her and it's all my fault again," he sobbed. "Why do I keep fucking this up? Why can't we just have our happy ending?" He was having a hard time breathing and his dad wrapped his arm around his shoulder, trying to comfort him, but nothing seemed to be helping. "What did we do to deserve this? Is it because I asked her to marry me, and the universe doesn't want us together?" He didn't know why he said it, it was like a confession that needed to come out. He looked at his dad, who seemed a bit taken aback.

"Well, I'll be damned. When did that happen?" His tone was steady and calm.

Jim looked at his dad. "Yesterday; and today it's all taken away. All because I took her to that stupid park to talk about the-" He didn't want her secret out.

"The book. Jim, I have ears, you were going on about the damned thing." Jim looked at his dad. "You got all bent out of shape because of the sex scenes that Grace wrote about you two."

Jim wiped away the tears and looked at his dad, confused. How did he know? As if he was reading Jim's mind, he went on. "You know, everyone looks at me like I'm some grease monkey, that I only know about cars, but you know, what I'm really good at is puzzles and mysteries. Grace is a great mystery, but if you read between the lines, she is pretty much an open book."

Mark reached into his shirt pocket and pulled out a pack of cigarettes and lit one for himself, then passed it to Jim. Jim just looked at him confused but took it anyway.

"Have you said anything to Ken or Janie?" Jim asked, passing the cigarette back to his dad. He just shook his head.

"Nah, but I will tell you I read it." Mark looked at his son and watched him blush. "If what she wrote in those scenes is real, well-" Jim wasn't sure what he was going to hear - "good job, son. I don't know what else to say. Women go crazy over those scenes in these books. I would be proud if I were you. Grace wrote it beautifully and if it was as romantic as she wrote it, then I'm very proud that you made her feel as special as you have. As you will continue to in your marriage to each other."

Their marriage to each other. He closed his eyes, she was in there fighting for her life and he was out there crying.

"She's a fighter, Jimmy, you haven't lost her yet. So go in there and fight for her to come back to you."

Jim took the last of the cigarette then crushed it out. His dad was right, she needed to know he wasn't going anywhere. Jim stood up, gave his dad a hug, and marched right back into the hospital. He needed to see Grace. He walked past all of them and went right into the ER to find Janie and Ken standing next to Grace, who had been brought back to the ER. She had been intubated and it was a good thing he hadn't watched that happen. The doctor was letting Janie and Ken know that they were preparing an operating room to try and stop the internal bleeding caused by her broken ribs, but everything around him was almost like a whisper. He leaned down over her and kissed her bruised and bandaged forehead.

"Hey, listen, you promised to marry me next June. I'm not leaving you and you promised not to leave me. I'm holding you to that. I need you to fight and I'm gonna be right here when you wake up," Jim whispered in her ear, hoping that no one else had heard what he had said to her. He held her right hand and just as he was going to walk towards Ken, she squeezed his hand and didn't let go. He bent down and kissed her hand, and she squeezed again, and then suddenly they were wheeling her off. Janie, Ken, and Jim watched together as they took her back and then she was gone from their sight.

𝄢

Joe had seen plenty of women walk into his bar, but never one who looked so beautiful and classy before. For such a warm summer day, she almost looked like she belonged in a spy movie. Her blonde hair pulled back in a bun with light tendrils framing her face, which was almost supermodel-like, with striking features that reminded him of some movie or TV star, except for the bruise that seemed to be fresh on her forehead. He couldn't figure out why someone like her would be in a bar like this at this time of day or how she could have gotten that bruise, but he was going to enjoy the company. "What can I get you, Miss?"

The blonde took off her sunglasses and smiled. "I'm going to assume you don't have any champagne here, I'm in a bit of a celebratory mood."

"Uh, champagne, nah, you are in the wrong neighborhood for that, love. I can make you one of those Cosmos if you want."

She smiled and he felt his heart flutter, someone this beautiful smiling at him was too good to be true. "Cosmos are for little girls, how about a dirty martini?" He nodded; he knew he could make one of those with no problem. Joe got right to work but he really didn't want to rush or the pretty lady would leave.

"So, what are you celebrating? I hope it is something good." He placed three olives in her martini and handed it to her. A lazy smile spread across her gorgeous lips and she took a sip. Tilting her head back, she took a long draft and allowed the martini to slide down her throat, the briny vodka hitting just the right spot.

"A long overdue win." She licked the vodka from the corner of her mouth. Joe watched her tongue and couldn't help but get turned on. He tried to remember he was married.

"You a lawyer? You won a case? We don't normally get a lot of attorneys like you here. Was it a big win?"

"The biggest, and it was delicious." Downing her martini, taking a fifty dollar bill out of her purse and handing it to the stunned man, she said "Thanks for the drink." He rang up her bill for the martini and turned back to give her the change, but she was gone, her car keys left on the bar. He looked in the direction of the bathroom and then to the front door. He hadn't heard either. He figured she would be back since she had left her keys.

A few minutes later the door swung open, but it was a couple of his regulars barking their usual orders telling him to put on the news. Joe turned on the TV and started pouring the beers, all the while news about some hit and run in town, some politicians getting in trouble, and how hot the weather was expected to be over the weekend. He didn't think too much of it, he just kept thinking about that pretty blonde, and wondered what she had won.

Jim sat for a total of five minutes before he was up pacing again; Hank looked back at him.

"She is going to be fine," Hank said, looking at Jim, making him stop in his tracks. "She has to be. I can't be trusted to raise the boys myself, look how I have messed it up already." He laughed, trying to keep things upbeat. "Besides, Grace hasn't organized her own funeral or written her own eulogy yet, so she isn't going to die." Hank smirked and that got Janie to laugh.

"Don't forget her obituary, she will want to write that one too, or what she wants on her tombstone," Ken added as he looked over to Jim, who was still pacing back and forth like a caged animal.

"Oh, God forbid I bury her in something that is too big after she lost all that weight. She will haunt me for the rest of my life and then she would curse me out the moment I got up to heaven, telling God to make me sit in Purgatory for one hundred years because I put her in the wrong outfit." Janie giggled while Ken nodded along. Jim finally stilled; it was all true. Grace would want to control everything, even from her grave.

Another hour went by before the doctor came out. "Mr. Nereid, your wife is stable." Everyone breathed a sigh of relief. "But the next several days are going to be touch and go. We have her in a medically induced coma and are going to be monitoring her the whole time. Once she is able to breathe without the ventilator, we will slowly reverse it." Janie collapsed into her chair and looked up at Ken, who was white as a ghost. Hank ran his hands through his hair, and Jim watched the fear spread across his face. He wasn't the only one afraid to lose Grace. They all were.

"Can I see her?" Jim uttered looking at the doctor. He wanted to see her, he had to. The doctor shook his head.

"Sir, at this point I would advise against you seeing her in this state. We are going to be moving her up to ICU once she is up there, perhaps you can visit her, but at this point, my recommendation is to allow her to rest." Ken just nodded to him, and he took his leave.

Jim collapsed in the chair next to Janie just as George Nicols walked in. Ken walked over to him and had a private conversation. Jim couldn't hear what was being said but he figured it had to do with the accident. He knew George from high school, he had been a defensive lineman on the football team, and he remembered hearing that he had become a cop. Ken nodded yes to George and the two walked over to Jim.

"Hey Jimmy, I'm sorry to hear about Gracie, I'm sure she will be okay, but unfortunately, I'm here on business. I have to get your statement." Jim looked at Grace's parents and husband, not really wanting them to hear the story. He felt like a failure, but he knew that they needed to know what happened.

Jim told them exactly what had happened after their talk. George asked what they had discussed and he just said it was private. Ken nodded his head to George to allow it. Jim went on and replayed the scene. George leaned over and handed Jim a tissue as he was crying again. "Did you see the driver of the car? We have an eyewitness who gave us video of the car, so we know what we are looking for, but they didn't get the driver." Jim hadn't seen the driver; with how fast everything had gone and Grace pushing him out of the way, he never saw them. He just shook his head no.

"Can I just ask a question?" Hank looked at George and then Jim. "How did tiny Grace push you out of the way, I mean she is all of five feet tall, how the hell did she get you out of the way?" Jim had no idea, but George did as he smiled brightly.

"My self-defense class, either that or sheer adrenaline. I had her flipping me over in class. Just because she is tiny..." he said.

"Doesn't mean she isn't mighty," Jim finished and looked up at the ceiling laughing. "Never underestimate Grace." He meant that in more ways than one. She was a marvel.

George took out a business card. "Okay, well, if you can think of anything else that might be important, just let me know." Jim was too tired and emotionally drained to think. His stomach grumbled and he realized he hadn't eaten since breakfast.

Ken walked over to George and started walking him out. Jim watched as them deep in conversation as they walked towards the elevator. Janie looked at Jim and walked up to him. "Sweetie, listen, why don't you go home, wash up, get something to eat, and get some rest." Sighing, he knew she was right, but he didn't want to leave Grace. "You are no good to her if you are a mess, so go home."

Kevin and the boys had just come back, and Janie looked over to Hank. "The same for you, sir. We should all go home, the doctor said there is nothing more we can do." Janie, who was usually so easy-going, was taking charge, and no one was really going to argue with her.

"The second she is in a room," Jim said and Janie just nodded to him that she understood. Jim gave a hug to each of the boys, shook Hank's hand, then reluctantly left with Kevin.

Kevin and Jim just sat in silence as they drove to his parents' house. He rested his head on the window, just watching as the scenery just flew by but his eyes crossed, unable to focus on anything. He wanted to close his eyes, but he was scared to; scared to replay the whole thing all over again. Kevin was looking at him from time to time to make sure he was okay.

"She is going to be okay," Kevin said.

"Yeah" was all he managed until it all burst out. "What was she thinking? Why did she push me out of the way? Out of the two of us I could have handled that impact, I am stronger, I am bigger. It should have been me! That is what everyone is thinking, I should have moved her out of the way, I should have been the one who was hit, not her," Jim yelled looking at Kevin as if he had the answers.

Kevin just kept his eyes on the road and shook his head. "Okay, first no one is thinking that it should have been you, we are all thinking that it should have been neither one of you. Second, you want to know what we are all thinking? WHO would do this? What kind of a nut job would be insane enough to run someone over, Jim?"

There it was the 'ten-thousand-dollar question' and then it hit him. His eyes widened as the idea ran through his head and he looked at Kevin, who had been waiting for Jim to realize.

"No", Jim said. "No" he said it again, trying to convince himself, but Kevin pursed his lips, not wanting to say it out loud either. Jim could feel his heartrate go up immediately and his heart pounded in his chest as if he had just run a marathon.

"She wouldn't. She couldn't. She told the girls she was home sick; she didn't want them to go over there because she didn't want them to get sick. She has been home all day."

"Are you sure? We know it isn't Hank; he was with the boys, you should have seen him when I went over there to tell them, he practically fell on the floor. They may be getting a divorce but at least he is trying to be more caring. I mean, he is still an asshole, but I mean, he was shocked."

Jim didn't know Hank very well, but he was making every attempt to change for the boys, He and Grace may not have had a great marriage, but this was still the mother of his children. And then he thought of the mother of his children.

If they were correct and it had been Liz, then she had motive, means, and opportunity. She had no solid alibi, except the car that hit Grace was not hers. "The car that hit Grace wasn't Liz's. Liz has a white BMW and no tints. This car was black with heavy black tints."

"Haven't you read any of the books that Grace has written? You never use your own vehicle," Kevin said so matter of fact, showing that he wasn't just her brother but a fan. "Listen, between you and me, everything points to Liz. My guess is they just need to find the car she used."

"I need to talk to her," Jim said. He needed to know that it wasn't true.

"Why, so she can finish the job? You go over there and you are as good as dead. Is that what you want?" Kevin was worked up and luckily they were at Jim's parents' house. "You want to know why Grace pushed you, because she knew she could fight anything, but she couldn't imagine losing you. She will fight because that is what she does; but losing you forever would destroy her. So, my suggestion is, let the cops do their job and live to fight another day."

Kevin was many things, the town gossip, a matchmaker, a flirt, but the one thing that Jim wasn't expecting was inspiring. Kevin was also right; they needed to trust that the police would find out who did this, whether it was Liz or someone else, but he prayed it wasn't her. It would crush the girls.

Stumbling into the house, his whole family came running to him. He just said that she is stable but in a coma. He didn't want to talk anymore. Taking his parents' advice, he went right upstairs and got into the shower.

He stood in the shower not moving, he wasn't sure how long he was standing there until his dad knocked on the door to make sure he was okay. Jim just washed himself and dried off. There was an emotional numbness that seemed to go with the ache in his muscles. He looked around the room as he got dressed, noticing a plate of hot food that he assumed his mother had placed there while he was in the shower. He was physically hungry, but the emptiness he felt was making it almost impossible to eat. Vivian and Katie appeared in his doorway, and he turned to look at them.

"Did you girls eat?" Jim still needed to be their dad; he needed to make sure they were okay. But then Vivian started to cry, and Katie followed, both running to him for a hug. He sat there grateful for his girls and their love; he breathed in for the first time to get the smell of the hospital out of his nose. Jim sat there not wanting to move or do anything else, just to hug these two beautiful young women that he got to call his daughters.

"Dad, you have to eat and get some rest," Vivian said, looking at his barely touched plate.

"I'm well aware, that seems to be the general consensus from everyone," Jim said as Katie wiped away her tears and loaded up the fork with food, holding it in front of his mouth waiting for him to take a bite. He looked up at her and opened his mouth so she could feed him. "This is ridiculous. I should be at the hospital with Grace."

"You are not going anywhere until you at least finish this plate of food and talk to us," Katie said, loading up another fork full of food. Jim sighed and took the fork, shoving the food into his mouth. He turned to the plate and started eating it on his own while the girls sat down on the bed. He motioned to them to talk. Katie and Vivian looked at each other.

"Why did you leave before?" Vivian asked. Jim choked on his bite and grabbed the bottle of water that had been brought up with the food. He took a sip and put down the bottle.

"Because I needed to talk to Grace about something."

"What? Was it about the book?" Katie asked. Jim looked at his daughter. Was she as smart as her grandfather and had figured it out? He shoved food in his mouth and mumbled a response that was completely incoherent. "Dad, without food in your mouth, was it about the book?"

How could he answer this without breaking Grace's trust? He couldn't, but the only way to be honest with the girls was to tell them the truth. Jim closed his eyes, took another drink of water, and turned to them.

"You have to swear to me, on my life, that you will never, and I mean never, tell another soul this information." The girls' eyes widened and they just nodded. "I mean it, not even Grandma, especially Grandma." The girls looked at each other and shook their heads.

"I freaked out because Grace is the one who wrote that book. The book is about Grace and I and the things that were in those romantic scenes are things that Grace and I have done in the past. I had read the book years ago, thinking that her mom had written it, so I didn't think anything of it until this past week when she told me. I didn't freak out about it until you mentioned reading it and then I kind of went crazy because when I re-read those scenes-" he paused. "I didn't want you and Grandma reading it, ever. I just freaked out." Both girls just sat there, not sure how to react.

"Okay so, Grace writes romances, but that one is about you and her, and those sex scenes are things you have done with her?" Katie said her face screwed up, completely grossed out. Vivian sat there looking at Katie, knowing that she had read some of it. "Dad, you freak! The stuff in that book, you did that stuff with Grace? Ew dad!"

"Hey, I was a teenager, and I will not be judged for things that Grace and I enjoy doing, alright, and I wasn't the one who wrote it, she did! So don't 'Ew, Dad' me! One day you are gonna have a partner and there are things that you are gonna like doing or having done to you and honestly, I don't want to know about it. But I freaked out because of this exact reason, I didn't want you girls to judge me and my fiancée for our past." The girls had been making faces at each other until they heard the word *fiancée* and then they snapped back to their dad and their faces completely lit up. "Fuuuucck," he said as he dropped his head.

"Did you just say-" Jim slapped his hand over Katie's mouth before she could even finish.

"Don't make a sound, don't say a thing." He looked into Katie's eyes and then to Vivian who was covering her own mouth to keep from screaming. "I did not give her a ring, no one knows, this was supposed to be a secret until after the divorce. Do you both understand me? No one except Grandpa knows. I'm not kidding, not another person is to find out." Katie and Vivian both shook their heads and then jumped on top of Jim, completely thrilled at the idea that Grace and the boys would be part of their family.

"Okay, so you went to talk to her, did you work everything out?" Katie wanted to make sure that her dad and Grace had worked it out.

"Yeah, I told her I couldn't let you and your grandmother ever read that book again. She thought it was pretty funny and was rather pleased with herself, but that is Grace for you." He sighed. "And then the accident happened." The joy of remembering how Grace was dissolved away once he thought about what happened after.

"What happened?" Katie asked. They had heard bits and pieces, but they hadn't heard the whole story.

Jim didn't want to rehash it, but he knew they would be unrelenting. Exhausted, he thought maybe if he laid down, he could tell them. With another bite, he laid down on the bed, and the girl joined him, listening as he told them about the accident. He left out the part that it was possible that their mother might be the one who did it. As they snuggled closer to him, he felt better having them on either side of him' it was almost as if they were containing all his emotions. Maybe Grace had the right idea about snuggle time. It did make him feel so much better, and eventually he closed his eyes and sleep came.

CHAPTER TWENTY

oe was closing up; it had been a long night, and he was glad Gary had come in to help with the evening rush. Gary came back in from taking out the trash.

"Hey Joey, someone left their car here, it's blocking the dumpster. You want me to call the tow company to come get it? Or you want to reschedule the trash pickup?" Gary called from the back door. Joe looked at the key fob for a Chevy that had been left behind by that pretty lady.

"What kind of car is it?"

"Black Chevy, why?" Gary said. Joe dangled the keys.

"I got the keys right here. Some chick left her keys; I was sure she was coming back for it. I'll move it, maybe she'll come back tomorrow," he said, locking the front door and grabbing the keys. Both men finished their night routine and once done, they walked out to the car. Gary was the first to notice the front end had a bit of damage.

"Joey, take a look at this." He pointed out dents to the front of the car. Joe turned on his flashlight on his phone to get a better look. They both moved closer to see that the dents also had some coloring differences. There were some odd reddish-brown streaks on the car that looked as if they might be dried blood. Joe looked at Gary, hoping that he saw what he was seeing.

"Call the cops, Gar, and prepare for a long night." Joe shook his head. "Why do the pretty ones gotta be so damned messy?" As Gary called the police department, Joe called his wife. She wasn't going to like this.

Joe had gone back inside and made a fresh pot of coffee; the least he could do was to have fresh coffee ready for when the cops showed up. Twenty minutes later, Gary came through the back door with two of the police officers. "Hey Joe, haven't seen you since the reunion, good to see ya," George Nicols said, shaking the owner's hand.

"Hey, Georgie Nicols, how the hell are ya? Don't tell me they got you working nights?" Joe was happy to see an old classmate.

"Not this week, but I got a special call just because it was you. I'm gonna have that car towed out of here for ya," George said as Joe handed him a cup of coffee. He took a sip. Joe made awful coffee, but he would drink it considering how late it was.

"Thanks, I appreciate it, otherwise they won't empty the dumpster, and I don't need that." Joe took a sip of the coffee and realized it was awful; this is why he has Gary make it. "So is this about that hit and run I heard about on the news? Some lady got hit, she alright or you can't talk about it?" George looked around, checking to see if anyone was looking, and moved in closer to Joe. Joe loved hearing all the gossip in town and when a cop was willing to offer he was gonna listen, so he moved closer, ready to hear what the deal was.

"I can't tell ya," George said with a smile.

"Aaaahh, you ass. It's about that hit and run, isn't it?" George pretended he didn't know what Joe was talking about. "That car has dried blood on it, you can't tell me that is not what I saw out there. I've had enough bar brawls leaving dried blood on my sidewalks to know what that is."

"Alright, yes. You wouldn't happen to know who the owner is?" Joe shook his head but then pulled out the key.

"Some blonde walked in here earlier today, ordered champagne." George arched his brow, looking at Joe. "I know, not the place, but instead she ordered a dirty martini, downed it and then paid with a 50. When I turned to give her the change she was gone, but she left the keys. Most interesting thing that happened all day." Joe took another sip of the coffee and winced; he really needed to just dump it. George pulled out his phone and pulled up a picture, showing it to Joe. It was a slightly blurry picture but sure enough there she was, not all dark and mysterious, but definitely the beautiful blonde who had walked in earlier today. "Hey, that's her, yeah, she was too cryptic for me. Saying she finally won like a case or something. Why, she looney tunes or some shit like that?"

"No comment. Listen, Mickey's gonna take a formal statement from you and the keys. Also, you won't like this part, I am gonna need that $50 for prints." Joe sighed in disappointment. *Why do the pretty ones gotta be so messy?* he thought again. "I'll have you come down to the station to properly identify her, but the victim's family will appreciate this." George smiled and took another sip, choking on it. "Joey, one last thing, your patrons will appreciate you not making the coffee, this is awful." Joe and George shook hands and then George went outside. He had a warrant to get and some good news to give but Grace's family and Jim deserved some rest.

𝄢

Ken and Janie's phones hadn't stopped ringing all morning long. They had stayed at the hospital until they kicked them out, letting them know that they would inform them when Grace was in a room. That call had come in at 2 a.m., she was in a room and no change. As he had promised, Ken let both Hank and Jim know but told them not to rush up there and to wait until the doctor had called them in the morning.

Then promptly at 6 a.m., Ken got a call from George. He had never felt such relief than to see it was George calling. Janie had been holding onto his arm listening to the call. There was only so much information that George could disclose, but the last thing he said was that it would all be over soon. Ken knew how the system worked, and he just had to trust the system. He thanked George again for all his hard work and asked if there was anything he could do to repay him, to which George replied he'd let him know once everything was over.

They had been getting ready to leave the house when the doctor called at 8 a.m. There had been no changes, she was still intubated and no sign of her fighting to breathe without it. Ken knew there was no time limit on how long they could keep her in a coma, but the standard time frame was 72 hours and then they would wean her off the medication and see how she did on her own. But he knew there were only three things she would fight for, and despite the doctor discouraging him they needed to get those three things there as soon as possible.

Ken hung up with the doctor and had calls he needed to make.

𝄢

Denise and Nikki stood at Grace's front door. "I hate him, you know this." Denise grimaced as Nikki who was holding a bag of food. Nikki plastered a fake smile on her face as they watched through the glass screen door as Hank talked to Calvin, getting him up the stairs.

"Just remember we are doing this for the boys and Grace. It's not for him," Nikki said through her teeth. Hank waved them and they heard mumbling coming from another room, standing there out of breath when he answered the door.

"You come to beat me up or something? Ken was supposed to tell you guys I'm staying here while Grace is in the hospital." He looked distraught. They looked past him and saw the boys had left all their stuff by the front door, nothing had been put away.

"I thought you hired someone to come clean up after you left," Denise said, walking past him as she entered the kitchen. They stood there struck with the realization that things might be worse than they had been led to believe as they saw the total chaos. He sat down to drink the cold cup of coffee he had made three hours earlier.

"I did, this is just from yesterday and this morning," he said after he took another sip and practically gagged. Nikki and Denise just bit their lips and then started laughing out loud.

"Yes, ha ha, serves me right, right? But with Grace in a coma, I have no idea what to do. So, if you came over to make fun of me, go ahead, I deserve it."

He was a mixture of pissed, scared, and smug all at the same time. The coma comment had stopped their laughter. All Kevin had told them was that Grace was in the hospital and not able to talk. They hadn't realized that she was in a coma.

"Hank, we didn't know. We just wanted to drop off some breakfast for the boys and then we were gonna go up and see her. But why didn't Kev tell us she is in a coma?" Nikki looked at Denise, who was checking her texts to see if they had missed something, but they hadn't.

"Probably because of the investigation."

Denise had been trying to help by straightening up the island but the comment about an investigation made her pause. This was bigger than they had been led to believe.

"An investigation? What exactly happened?"

Hank recounted the story and conversations he had had with his in-laws and Jim. They had a bunch of questions, the same ones they all had, who had done this. The women looked back and forth between each other, knowing who they thought it was without saying it. He didn't want to say it because it sounded too far-fetched, but Liz had flipped out when he had broken it off with her. He had done it in the office so that she could not lose her mind in front of everyone.

"I fucked this up, didn't I?" he said. Nikki bit her lip, but Denise didn't.

"Uh, ya think? Have you gotten rid of the psycho?" Denise asked. He nodded his head, hoping that that would end the conversation. "Well okay so you did one thing right. Are you gonna stand in the way of Grace's happiness?"

Denise was gonna hit him with all the hard questions and he deserved it. He shook his head no, because after all he put her through, she deserved someone who would appreciate her and show her.

Hank stood up and went for his phone. He needed to talk to that George guy and tell him what happened, so he called Ken. The whole time Nikki and Denise were still sitting there, Calvin had come down from his shower and started eating as Hank was on the phone with Ken in another room.

"Where did Dad go?" Calvin asked shoving a hash brown in his mouth.

"He is talking to Pappi. Listen, we have to go, but have Dad call us if he needs anything okay," Denise said, giving both boys a hug as they left. Nikki walked out after Denise and as they walked back to Nikki's house, they just kept looking at each other.

"You think she did it, don't you?" Nikki asked Denise.

"Oh yeah! I would say we ride at dawn, but I don't got bail money, you?" Denise was ready to catch a charge if it meant putting that nut job in jail, but then who would be there for Jody.

"No, besides I don't look good in orange and there is no wine in prison either. Let's just let the police handle this one and pray Grace heals quick for the boys' sake." Nikki thought of the condition the house would be in when Grace returned and shivered at the idea of her coming back to it being in shambles.

𝄢

Jim sat at the kitchen table, his whole family surrounding him, but the one person he wanted to be there with was lying in a hospital bed fighting for her life. Ken had called and let him know that he would be coming by to pick him up to go back to the hospital. But the one thing that he had instructed him on was for no one to contact Elizabeth or give her an update on Grace. That was all that he said.

He had a feeling that Ken was doing that for Grace's protection. If Liz believed she had succeeded in killing Grace, then she wouldn't go after her in the hospital. The girls had been told that if their mother contacted them, they were not to answer. The same went for his mother - she was not to talk to anyone at all about Grace or her condition.

When he called George to ask him how things were going, all he said was that he was waiting on the judge to issue a warrant for the person suspected in the accident. That was all he would say, and that was all he needed to hear. Jim remembered George as a stand-up kid in school and he had faith that he wouldn't let Grace's family down. The clock seemed to be moving at a snail's pace as he sat there waiting for Ken to arrive. Unable to stay in one place, he decided to just wait outside, and the girls offered to sit outside with him on the steps. But when he opened the front door, he wasn't expecting who he saw standing there.

"Elizabeth, what are you doing here? You are not allowed to be here. I have a restraining order against you, remember?" Jim said loud enough for the whole block to hear. The girls backed up behind Jim and were clearly scared to see her. Elizabeth just smiled at him as if his words meant nothing.

"Babe, come on, you're just upset my boyfriend got a little carried away the other night. We may have had a few too many drinks. I'm sorry things got out of hand. I just thought instead of this whole "go through a million people" thing, I would come pick up the girls for my week."

He noticed a bruise over her left eyebrow, and he was sure that wasn't there earlier in the week.   Then he remembered that Hank had said they broke up, yet she just had referred to him as her boyfriend. He needed the cops to get here. She looked behind him at the girls. "Hey girls, ready to come home?"

Vivian hid behind Jim, but Katie was braver and stood next to Jim. "We are home." Liz's smile slipped and her gaze grew dark.

"Oh. I see." She turned her attention to Jim. "So you've turned the girls against me, or was it Grace who did that? Your little Gracie. How is she by the way?" Jim moved Katie behind him, and he blocked the doorway completely so she couldn't get in. He needed to act like Grace died, remember she needs to believe she is dead.

"You turned your daughters away from you, not me, not Grace, you. And" he paused for dramatic effect "she was hit yesterday, by a car."

Liz's face had gone from pissed to one of concern. He had to remember she had been in plays too. He remembered the crunching sound of Grace's body hitting the car, seeing her intubated, and his eyes started to tear. He looked at Liz, who was clearly waiting to hear what she had done.

"She died this morning. We were just on our way to her parents' house."

Liz feigned shock. "Oh no, that is terrible, and after you guys were reunited finally after all those years of being apart. Oh Jimmy, I'm so sorry."

A slight smirk on her face gave her true feelings away, but only for a second and then she furrowed her brow to pretend she actually cared. The words were nothing but a filthy lie, and it was eating at him.

"No, you're not." His voice low and cold. "You don't give a shit about me or my feelings or that Grace is dead, do you?"

She straightened her back and looked at him, her eyes completely devoid of feelings.

"You are right, I'm not sorry. And honestly Jimmy, I could give a shit about your feelings, but I am rather delighted she is dead." She smiled as the last word came out of her mouth. Jim realized he was looking into the eyes of insanity.

"Did you do this?" he asked. He couldn't help himself, he needed to hear it from her mouth. She moved closer to him with a Cheshire cat smile across her lips.

"And if I say yes, who is going to believe you? You are just an angry ex-husband whose girlfriend just died who wants to pin a murder on his ex-wife," she said mere inches away from his lips. He stood firm and unyielding.

"Did you kill Grace?" They were nose to nose, her eyes were locked on his trying to read him, but he wasn't wavering. No anger, no hurt, just completely cold. He needed her to say it.

"Kiss me and I'll tell you," she demanded playfully, and he didn't move. He didn't move away or make any movement to encourage it, so she kissed him. She had closed her eyes as she had kissed him and he made no motion to pull back, he wanted his answer. When she finished kissing him, she wiped the red lipstick off his lips.

"Did you hit Grace?" he growled at her, making her aware he wasn't backing down; she got her kiss and now he wanted answers. She rolled her eyes.

"No one will believe you; I was home sick remember." She made a fake coughing sound. "But if it is gonna help you sleep at night, then yes, I hit Grace." She smiled and then unexpectedly Jim smiled right back at her. He looked behind her, and then suddenly she felt metal being strapped against her wrists and as she looked behind her, there stood George Nicols with a smile on his face. Ken stood five feet from there and the look of disgust on his face was enough to know they had heard everything. Her eyes went wide. "No! No! You tricked me! Noooo!" she wailed and thrashed as another officer came over to help George get her into the vehicle as he read her Miranda rights and what she was being arrested for.

Jim just watched as they struggled getting her in. Ken stood by him and knew Jim was a much braver man than any he had ever met. They watched them pull away and finally when they were out of view, Jim turned towards the bushes and threw up his breakfast. Ken patted Jim's back to make sure he was okay.

It had been fortunate that his parents were in the house when they first heard Jim say that Liz was there. Then when Jim had blocked the door, the girls had been smart enough to get into the kitchen with their grandparents who were already on the phone with the police. A wave of relief flooded him as he realized that the girls didn't see what went down, what had been said, and didn't have to see their mother taken away in the police car.

But the one thing he was most relieved about was that Liz would never hurt Grace again. George, his partner, and Ken had all heard the confession, and Ken had been smart enough to video it. The bodycam footage should hold, but he wasn't an attorney or a cop. He was sure that Ken would talk to the prosecutor to make sure that he was aware that she had violated her restraining order not just against Jim but also against Grace and would ask for her to receive no option for bail. He was so furious that he hoped she rotted in jail.

They walked into the kitchen and his girls ran over to him crying. Judi and Mark walked over to Ken giving him a hug and then finally their son. Judi was crying about how brave he was and how lucky he was to be alive. Ken nodded and walked over to Jim. As he wiped away a tear, he embraced the younger man, knowing that he would lay down his life for Grace. He couldn't be prouder of him than at this moment, but there was one more thing he needed Jim to do today.

Jim and Ken stood in the door frame of the ICU room that Grace was in. Her tiny frame engulfed by all the casts that were now on her, all the tubes, wires, and IVs keeping her alive and the monitors keeping her vitals recorded. Jim took the tiniest step forward and he was afraid. Afraid to go near her or even touch her. All the beeping and sounds from the machines affixed to her made him feel like she wasn't really in that bed. Ken walked to the left side of her bed and just looked at her. He felt compelled to brush her hair with his hand.

"Hey kiddo," he choked out. "Um, uh, I brought someone with me and I'm hoping you wouldn't mind opening your eyes for us."

Grace didn't move, the monitors showed no change in her rhythm. He looked at Jim, silently begging him to say something or touch her so she knew he was there. Jim's feet felt heavier than ever as he walked up beside her on her right side and held her hand; her fingers were cold. He remembered just how warm her hand had been in his just a day ago and here now her fingers felt like icicles, so he clasped her hand between his hands to warm them. He bent down and kissed her fingers to try and warm them. "Hey Gracie." He looked at the monitor hoping that just his voice would do it, but no change. Ken looked at him and walked outside the room, closing the door to give Jim privacy.

"Um, do you remember the first time I met you? You were in the lunchroom walking with Nikki and you tripped over that kid's backpack and you started to fall, but I caught you before you hit the floor. You looked up at me and flashed that smile." He smiled and shook his head. "I can't spend the rest of my life without that smile. I have spent so much of my life without you in it that I don't want to wake up tomorrow and you aren't here. I have loved you from the moment we kissed, maybe even when I caught you. A fall for Grace. I want to spend the rest of my days filled with nothing but you and your kisses. So please, for me, for your boys, for my girls who adore you to the moon and back again. Please fight and come back to me."

Jim kissed her hand again and he put his head down next to it on the bed. He prayed, he prayed that she had heard him, he prayed that there would be something, some sign, anything. He lifted his head and saw no change. He kissed her hand again and went to pull away when her hand moved to grasp his hand, and he looked down. Her monitor beeped and he saw her heart rhythm change. His eyes widened as he tried to pull his hand away again only now her grip was stronger. And then it happened, her monitor was showing a change. Ken had been watching from the door and had notified the nurses. Her nurse got up from her chair and came into the room.

Grace was starting to make an odd gagging sound, and the nurse looked at Jim. "I don't know what you said, but whatever it was, keep it up. But you may want to leave for a moment." She walked over to one of the other nurses and they got ready to extubate her. Jim wasn't leaving despite the nurses trying to convince him to. Grace's hand was gripping his hard and he was never letting go. He turned so he didn't watch. The sounds of the procedure were stomach churning but once they were done, he turned. Grace was struggling but breathing on her own. She still hadn't opened her eyes, but she was awake. They got her oxygen and checked all her vitals.

The nurses smiled at Jim; all he had done was tell her the truth. Ken walked in and half hugged Jim as Grace's hand was not leaving his. "I had a feeling Sleeping Beauty over here would only wake for you." Jim wiped away a stray tear and then they heard a gargling laugh. They both looked down. Grace's eyes were open and looking at both of them.

"Very funny," she croaked "I was getting rest," she breathed. "Like you told me to," she finished saying. Her lung capacity was low, but she was awake, breathing, and cracking jokes. Jim lifted up her hand and kissed it again. He had promised her a lifetime of kisses, and by someone who knew how, and then she did the one thing that could knock him off his feet. She smiled.

EPILOGUE

December 25, 2023

The cold temperatures were bothering her leg and arm, a wonderful side effect of the accident. The physical therapist said that it was all completely normal and if she took care of herself, it would eventually subside, but when she got older it could come back. She looked at the young therapist and wanted to smack him. He didn't know that things already hurt, and she wasn't even that old. She would be 46 in four more days, but some days she felt 86.

She sat on the couch covered in a blanket, one of the many she had made while she was cooped up for months recovering, as Jim brought her a cup of hot cocoa as they sat by the tree. He had made a fire in the fireplace so they could enjoy a cozy Christmas evening together. Hank had picked up the boys after breakfast, which had been the agreement, and the girls had gone home after dinner with Jim's parents. Hosting Christmas dinner felt like a bit of normalcy for her; the only thing she was upset about was that her parents hadn't been there.

They were in Arizonia promoting *Breach of Contract*. She had hired an assistant to help her dad with the promotional tour after it was postponed due to her accident. With the hiring of Tara, who was really her assistant, she was able to work on her new book. Grace was using her life events to create a new fantasy romance series. Jim had asked her a bunch of times what it was about, and she just told him that he had to wait like everyone else.

Kevin had brought over his new boyfriend, Jonathan. He was precious. Tall, handsome, and if you asked Kevin, ridiculously out of his league, but they were adorable together. She had seen the rest of the crew at breakfast with the boys. In the chaos of the day, Jim had been a little distracted, a few times even jumpy. She was sure that it was because the girls had been acting especially squirrely lately. Grace figured he was just nervous about their first Christmas together and thought it was adorable how he was doing absolutely everything to make it perfect.

"Mind if I sit with you?" Jim asked. She looked at him, not sure what he meant because he was already sitting next to her.

"Um, aren't you already?" She took a sip of her hot cocoa and put it on the table next to her.

"No, I meant, can I sit behind you? Like we used to sit on the lounge chair of the deck."

He was acting so sheepish, and it was warming her heart. She waved her arm, and he jumped up, moving her so that she was sitting between his legs. Nestling against his chest, he wrapped his left arm around her, and she closed her eyes. This was perfect, she thought, this is where I want to be forever.

He kissed the top of her head, and she hummed. "I love you, you know," he whispered into her hair.

"I might have had an inkling of an idea to that fact, yeah." She kissed the fingers on his left hand. She started with his thumb and was working her way down to his pinky.

"An inkling of an idea, hm. Well, that won't do. How about a confirmation, of my love, would that work?" Jim asked. She stopped kissing his fingers, she had no idea where he was going with this.

"A confirmation, what kind of a confirmation?"

She craned her neck so that she could look at him and when she looked up, he stole a kiss, wrapping both his arms around her. He deepened the kiss, her eyes fluttered closed and relished his heat. His right hand moved to her left, and suddenly she felt him slipping something onto her ring finger. She yanked her head away so quickly that it caused him to laugh, and she looked down to find a beautiful engagement ring there. Her breath stuck in her throat and her vision blurred from newly forming tears.

"You did agree to marry me." He smiled, it had been the one thing that would have made it all perfect that night down the shore, but he hadn't planned anything. "You haven't changed your mind, have you?" He was questioning himself now, knowing they joked about getting married next June all the time. She just kept blinking and shook her head.

"Oh my God, Jim, you are all I ever wanted, everyone will murder me if I change my mind." He looked at her and she screwed up her face. "Too soon?" They avoided the topic of Elizabeth and the trail unless it was absolutely necessary. She slowly and carefully turned herself around. Even though it was months ago, some things still ached, but she was able to sit across his lap and she cupped his face. "You are all I have ever wanted; I can't imagine my life without you." And then she kissed him, and he kissed her right back.

June 2024

"You had to pick the hottest weekend of the year, and I am having a personal summer," Denise said as she tried not to sweat in her dress while she curled Grace's hair. Nikki rolled her eyes at her while looking for Grace's sandals.

"The air conditioning is on and blasting, no one else is complaining. Besides, I don't think George is even going to notice your sweating with how your boobs look in that dress."

Grace was looking at herself in the mirror. She couldn't believe this day had finally come. They had lived a lifetime apart, but now Grace and Jim were about to be married. Katie and Vivian walked into the doorway of the bathroom and looked at Grace as she finished putting on her lipstick and Denise finished off her hair with a comb adorned with shells and flowers. She turned and looked at the girls, who looked upset.

"What are those long faces for? I thought it was all sunshine and rainbows today?" Grace joked and then the girls just looked at each other and Grace's face dropped. "What's wrong, where is your father?" The girls looked at her and Katie held up her hand.

"Okay, Daddy is fine, he is here, he is out on the beach, it's just-" and then there was a rumble of thunder and eyes widened - "That."

Grace shot up from her seat in the bathroom and they all crowded around the deck window and saw a huge storm out on the sea. She watched as people who were hanging out on the beach made their way under the tents they had put on the deck and Jim stood on the beach as the staff moved the arch and chairs under the tent. He looked so handsome in his suit, throwing his hands up to Mike and his younger brother Chris who were telling him to get off the beach and get under the tent.

Her boys walked into the room. "They said they are gonna move the ceremony inside the tent. I'm sorry, Mom, we all know you wanted it on the beach but unless you walk out there now, it's gonna be under the tent," Calvin said to her, a tone of heartbreak in his voice. She looked back out at the storm clouds, and was checking for lightning. No lightning in sight. She turned back to Nikki and Denise with darkened eyes. No storm was going to stop her now.

"Let's go, get that dress on me now! I didn't bust my ass for months in therapy to be married under a damned tent."

She looked at the boys who took their cue and left the room. Luckily, it was a simple gown, nothing too crazy. She knew what she had wanted and luckily, she found a secondhand store that had just the right dress. As they zipped her up, she took one last glance and grabbed her bouquet.

"I've waited long enough, let's go."

Nikki and Denise were yelling at her to walk not run because since the accident everyone was afraid of her falling. Katie and Vivian knocked on her parents' bedroom door and Ken and Janie came running after Grace, who was already down the stairs. Grace was still barefoot and running through the house when she saw Dale talking to a number of other guests.

"Dale, nice to see ya. You ready? Good, let's go." The older man was still bigger than she was and even though she was trying to get him to move he wasn't budging.

"Grace, I'll be out in the tent in a minute." She shook her head as her parents finally made it to her side.

"Grace, slow down what is going on?" Ken asked. Grace pointed out the sliding glass doors and then he saw what had her so worked up, the storm. He looked at Grace and knew why she was rushing.

"Go stand by Jim and when we tell you to, yell."

She looked at him and realized what he meant. She threw her arms around her father's neck, then ran outside. Ken grabbed Dale and the rest of the guests made their way to the tent.

Grace reached the top of the dunes and saw Jim who was still there on the beach with his head down, clearly upset, but then he heard the DJ playing a song and looked up and saw Grace. She locked eyes with him and smiled. This was the moment they had waited years for, no dream or variation could come close, it was *perfect*. Every step on the sand felt more like she was walking on clouds and as she got closer her smile broadened as his jaw just kept dropping while he stared at her.

"Hi," she said. "Feel like getting married?"

"I could be persuaded." Jim smirked as a light mist started.

In the background, from the safety of the tent, all their friends and families stood watching them. Grace and Jim could hear Dale starting the service, but all they really seemed to hear was the ocean and each other breathing. He took the flowers from her hand, tossing them into the sand, and held her hand up, then snaking his arm around her waist started to dance with her.

"Grace, do you take Jim to be your lawfully wedded husband, to have and to hold from this day forward, for better, for worse, for richer, for poorer, in sickness and in health, to love and to cherish, till death do you part?" Dale yelled into the mic, hoping she could hear him.

Grace was wrapped up in Jim's strong arms and staring into his steel gray eyes and lost track of what she was doing. They both had. It wasn't until they heard Dale say her name again that she yelled "I do" and then the rain started to come down a little harder. They looked up to the sky as flashes of lightning lit it up and tiny rumbles of thunder echoed on the ocean.

Ken turned to Dale and shot him a look to speed this up. "Jim, same rules apply, do you want to marry Grace?"

Jim smiled at her and then looked up the beach and yelled as loud as he could "I do!" and everyone laughed and cheered. Without having to be told, he lifted Grace up into his arms and kissed her just as the lightning crashed behind them on the ocean and there was a rumble of thunder as the skies opened above them. He kissed her again and again, because she had to be kissed, a sacrifice he was willing to make for the rest of their lives.

The End

ABOUT THE AUTHOR

G.M. Parrillo is the quintessential Generation X "Jersey Girl." Growing up in the Garden State, it is only natural that G.M. is happiest with dirt under her nails as she digs in her garden with her two boys and dachshund, Pennie, right by her side, or with her toes buried in the sand as she sits on the beach with her husband at the Jersey Shore.

As a child, struggling with a learning disability, her mother encouraged her to become a bookworm and, in doing so, she found herself inspired to write her own stories, but only for her own personal enjoyment, until now.

A Fall for Grace is a love letter to her husband of sixteen years, as their story serves as the sketch for Grace and Jim. This is G.M. Parrillo's first published book. A Fall for Grace is the first book in the Toselle Park series.

The Toselle Park Series:
A Fall for Grace
Bad Decisions
My Person